A COLD KILLING

Also by Anna Smith

The Dead Won't Sleep
To Tell The Truth
Screams in the Dark
Betrayed

A COLD KILLING
ANNA SMITH

Quercus

First published in Great Britain in 2015 by

Quercus Editions Ltd
55 Baker Street
7th Floor, South Block
London W1U 8EW

A CIP catalogue record for this book is available
from the British Library

PB ISBN 978 1 84866 429 6
EBOOK ISBN 978 1 78429 118 1

10 9 8 7 6 5 4 3

Printed and bound in Great Britain by Clays Ltd, Elcograf S.p.A.

Typeset by Jouve (UK), Milton Keynes

For Mary Myles – who fought the good fight.

'To love and win is the best thing, to love
and lose the next best . . .'

William M. Thackeray

PROLOGUE

London, King's Cross, October 1999

Ruby Reilly didn't look up as the waitress slammed the mug of coffee on the table, but she felt like getting up and punching her out. Just because Ruby had suggested she get off her mobile and take her order, the waitress had made sure she waited even longer. She clenched and unclenched her fists, trying to calm herself down. Don't let your short fuse fuck everything up, she checked herself. She was wound up big time. No wonder. She'd never killed before. She wasn't prepared for the range of emotions coursing through her. At first it had been total euphoria as she'd stood watching the house burn down – with that twisted bastard inside. Burnt to a crisp, he'd be. She'd even felt her face smile as she'd calmly walked away, got into her car and sped off into the night, adrenaline pumping her on as she hammered up the motorway and out of the Costa del Sol. Then, there was the dread that she might get caught.

She'd been totally wired since, jumpy as hell, and even quicker to the red-mist rage than normal. But guilt? No chance.

The coldness of the 'murder' – because that's how the cops would view it – wasn't what made her nervous. Fuck that. She wasn't about to start all that muesli-eating analysis shit, because the truth was, she'd waited long enough to do it. Most of her life, in fact. Killing the bastard was the good karma. The bad karma was that they were looking for her, and she'd disappeared off the face of the earth. She knew if they ever tracked her down, she'd attempt to dance her way out of it, say that she knew it was a hit and thought she was next by association, so she did a runner. But she wasn't going to hang around for the old man's heavies to turn up and start strong-arming answers from her. So she'd just kept on running – like she'd done all her life.

She drove for eight hours from the Costa del Sol, stopping only for a pee and petrol, till she reached the French border, where she holed up in a dreary motel for the night. Then she headed north for the Eurostar in Paris, abandoned the car at the hire place and smoked two fags one after the other before boarding as a foot passenger. And here she was, in a busy café round the corner from King's Cross station, in the pissing rain, where every immigrant from Africa to Bombay usually pitched up, dreaming of a better life. Ruby was just hoping she'd come up with a plan for the rest of hers.

But first, she'd go to the care home and tell Judy. She sipped her coffee and smiled at the thought of seeing her sister, at the same time dreading hearing that there had been little progress since she last visited.

'I've done it,' she'd whisper in her ear. 'He's dead, Judy.'

She knew her sister would just sit there, her pale-blue eyes dead, the way they'd been for twenty-five years, her now frail frame motionless, and her skin grey and shadowy like a neglected statue. Catatonic, the specialists had said. Not brain dead in any medical sense – just in another world, and chances are she would never come out of it. She was just thirty-seven. Only Ruby knew their secret. Just the smallest blink of an eye from Judy had been response enough when she murmured to her a few months ago that the time had come. Still trapped inside the childhood trauma that had made her retreat to a silent world, her sister hadn't spoken or moved her head, but she'd squeezed her hand. The memory brought tears to Ruby's eyes, and she quickly brushed them away and sniffed. Man up, she told herself. It's nearly over.

Two tables away, she watched two old guys deep in conversation. They looked quite distinguished, like they were somebody, Ruby thought, or they'd been somebody, long before they were the elegant older men they were now.

She was drawn to their conversation – intrigued at the way the really handsome one kept lowering his voice and leaning across conspiratorially. He was very good looking, his skin scrubbed and fresh, with the weathered tan of someone who spent his weekends on a yacht in a place where the sun was guaranteed. It was him she'd noticed when they first came in, the kind of upper-class confidence about him, he wore a crisp light-blue shirt, and his khaki trousers had a crease you could have shaved with. He was clearly in awe of his friend, like a blushing teenager finally on a date with the sixth-form heart-throb.

The other guy was much cooler, more like a journalist or an explorer than a posh boy. A mop of lush, sandy-coloured, wavy hair, greying at the temples, a cravat and brown corduroy trousers. Ruby could imagine him pontificating at a dinner party, an expert on every subject. But she also noticed how his mouth grew tight as their conversation became more intense. He leaned forward, sat back, sighed and from time to time ran his hands over his face in frustration as he shook his head. Ruby watched, intrigued by his angst.

She'd played games like this all her life, finding a kind of escapism in her vivid imagination, making up scenarios and scripts for complete strangers she encountered on buses and trains. It helped push away the shit that flooded her mind if she didn't keep her head firing all the time.

Now she watched as the sandy-haired guy put his hand in the inside pocket of his quilted jacket and took out a padded envelope, sliding it across the table. She strained her ears, engrossed and thrilled that she could actually hear them.

'They're on to me, Gerard. I know they are,' he whispered, shaking his head, 'I'm not safe any more.' He tapped the envelope. 'But it's all in here. Everything. All the bloody lies, the deceit. Queen and bloody country?' He looked down at the table in disgust and was silent for a moment. 'I'm doing it for Katya . . . Gerard, I never should have involved her. I should have known better.'

Ruby's eyes darted from one to the other, captivated, as the posh man reached across the table and rested a comforting hand on his friend's arm.

'Oh, Tom. I'm so sorry. I do hate to see you like this.' He lowered his voice and put the envelope in his inside pocket. 'It's safe with me. I won't let you down. But you must get away.' He bit the inside of his jaw. 'Where will you go? Do you have a plan?'

Ruby was so fascinated she was almost pulling her chair nearer. She didn't even notice that the four Eastern European men who'd been sitting on the adjacent table, wolfing down bowls of stew had got up and were leaving. She'd been watching them earlier, too, wondering which backwater or bleak town they'd come from, what promises they'd been made in order to up sticks and leave their homeland. They looked like the kind of muscle she'd seen surrounding the various Russian gangsters she'd come across on the Costa del Sol. Guys that would snap your neck with one hand. One of them was a looker, all high cheekbones and big soft lips, and she'd seen him checking

her out when she'd come in, had been aware he was steal-
ing little glances at her. That would be nothing new to
Ruby. She was aware of her beauty and the power she had
over men. Most of them were a walkover, full of shit. But
she could never resist a new challenge. She looked up, but
the hunky one didn't look in her direction as all four of
them walked past her table.

Then, suddenly, it happened. Two rapid gunshots. Not
deafening, and obviously through a silencer, but Ruby
instinctively dived below the table as the third shot was
fired. But not before she caught a fleeting glimpse of the
shocked expression on the old, sandy-haired guy's face
that split second when he became aware, too late, that the
was gun pointed at him. It blew the back of his head open,
an explosion of red against the bright-yellow shiny wall,
and all hell broke loose. From under the table she saw him
slump from his chair and slip down in a heap beside her,
his eyes wide with shock. Then his friend dived across and
knelt down, cradling his blood-soaked head in his hands,
weeping, confused, hysterical. Two women with kids in
pushchairs screamed in horror at the other table, and
people ran from the back of the café to the front and then
to the back, hiding, trying to make for the door, cowering
in corners, some face down on the floor, waiting for the
kind of massacre they'd seen played out on American television. The kitchen staff behind the open counter stood
rooted as though they were watching it unfold on screen,

and the stupid waitress was screeching and wailing as though it was her who'd been shot.

'Get an ambulance! Hurry!' the posh man screamed into the mayhem. 'Oh, Tom! Please! Please stay with me!' he sobbed, grabbing handfuls of paper napkins, trying to stem the well of blood gushing from his friend's mouth.

As she crouched, Ruby's eyes met his and she gave him a genuinely sympathetic look. Poor bastard.

'Did you see them?' he asked, his face contorted in abject misery.

Ruby shook her head slowly. She could hear sirens in the distance. She had to get out of here. Fast. She backed away, got to her feet, her eyes flicking around the room, taking in the chaos. And as she did, she was drawn to a piece of paper with something scribbled in pencil on the table where the assassins had sat. She snatched it like a thief and shoved it in her pocket as she bolted for the door.

CHAPTER ONE

Rosie switched on her mobile at the screech of the aircraft's wheels on the tarmac, and it plinked with a message alert. It was Marion, the editor's secretary. 'Phone Mick as soon as you land,' it read. Christ, Rosie thought. So much for easing yourself back into work. If Mick wanted to talk to her immediately, there must be something big on the go. Her stomach did a little nervous roll, somewhere between excitement and dread. Given that she'd been away for nearly two months, for her own safety, after her last big investigation into Loyalist gangsters, she hoped that it was only a story Mick wanted to talk about.

Heathrow Airport was mobbed, as usual, and Rosie managed to ease her way through the throng at the luggage carousel to get her case. Only then did she press the speed dial to the editor's private line.

'Gilmour! Welcome home! The wanderer has returned.'

'I'm not home yet, Mick. I'm only at Heathrow,' Rosie said, deadpan.

'Well, fatted calves will be butchered in preparation for your return,' McGuire joked. 'How were your travels?'

'Brilliant. I grew a moustache and everything, like a proper nomad.' Rosie was glad to hear his voice. 'But what's going on, Mick? I know you've not been missing me that much that you couldn't wait till I got home before we speak. So what's up?'

'Murder. King's Cross. Scots guy. Older. Retired lecturer at Glasgow Uni.'

'Really?' Rosie's mind was immediately firing off half a dozen scenarios. 'Mugged? Stabbed? What happened? What did he lecture in?'

'Shot.' McGuire said. 'Point-blank range. Looks like an execution. Definitely a hit of some sort. He was some kind of history lecturer. It's not clear yet.'

'Christ! When did it happen?'

'Yesterday afternoon. In the middle of a crowded café in front of women and weans. Some fucker just came up, pointed the gun and blew his brains all over the wall.'

'Bloody hell. What's the word? What do we know?'

'Not much at the moment. His name's Tom Mahoney. He was with a friend – Hawkins. Gerard Hawkins. Another former lecturer at Glasgow. They'd been mates since they were both students a hundred years ago. We still don't know very much, because the cops are saying bugger all. But it seems that there were four men in the café – Eastern Europeans, the word is – and as they got up to leave, one of them pulled a gun and shot our man through the head.'

'So it's not a random nutter then.'

'Nope. Definitely looks like a hit. But the question is why . . . So I want you to take a run over to Scotland Yard and see what the score is. The papers are all over it. Especially the posh papers, because he was a lecturer. If he was just some Romanian fruit-picker coming off the Eurostar looking for a job in London, nobody would give a fuck. But he's a moth-eaten old lecturer, therefore he matters.'

'Fascinating,' Rosie said.

'Aye, that's what his wife said when they told her he was dead.' McGuire gave a little chortle. 'Glad you're still a hard-bitten hack and not just a nomad with a moustache.'

Rosie felt a little twinge of shame that she'd said 'Fascinating' out loud, without even considering the horror for Mahoney's family. She'd gone from nomad to journalist in one nanosecond. She couldn't help who she was.

'Sorry. But you know what I mean. I'm intrigued,' she said.

'Great. Me, too, Gilmour. So take that intrigue of yours across to the cop shop and see what the plods are saying. I'll put you on to Marion. She's got you booked in somewhere for a couple of days, then we'll see what's what. There will be a lot to find out up here as well. I'll email you what we've got.'

'Okay. I've just picked up my bags. I'll jump in a taxi and get to the hotel.'

'Oh, Rosie,' McGuire said, almost as an afterthought. 'And how are you feeling? You know, with everything. How's your arm? Did you have a good rest?'

'Yeah,' Rosie said, not really sure how to answer that one. 'I did. It was great. I'm good to go.' She touched her arm, pushing away the image of the blowtorch. 'I'll bring my photos and maybe we can have a slideshow some afternoon in your office with some popcorn.'

McGuire chuckled. 'Good to have you back, Gilmour.' He hung up.

In the hotel room Rosie sat on the edge of bed and hauled off her suede calf-length boots, tossing them in a corner. Then she unzipped her jeans and eased them over her hips, kicking them off her ankles, and pulled off her T-shirt and bra. The drone of the King's Cross Road traffic below was too far away to disturb her as she lay back on the bed, relishing the tranquility for a few moments before she had to head back into real life.

Scenes of the last few weeks in Sarajevo ran like a movie she was watching herself in. She was either holding court, or listening intently in smoky cafés and bars late into the night with the noisy, good-humoured Bosnians who had taken her to their hearts. And Adrian, laughing and telling stories his friends revelled in hearing, as they all swapped tales of life before the war and where they'd been in recent years as they tried to move on from the hell. She'd seen Adrian relaxed and at home before, when she'd come to Bosnia eighteen months ago and he'd helped her chase down the monsters who were butchering refugees in Glasgow and selling their bones and tissue for money. That was the first time she'd had a different picture of the big, resigned-looking Bosnian who she'd met by chance four years ago. By a twist of fate, he had saved her life not once but twice since, had become her close friend and sometimes minder on big, difficult investigations abroad that required the kind of guts and commitment he brought to the table.

She knew she was playing with fire when she called him last month after they'd returned from Spain following the cocaine-smuggling exposé that almost got both of them killed. She knew in her heart, with the editor sending her away because of the UVF contract on her life, that she should have gone to New York to be with TJ. She should have headed straight into the arms of the man she loved and worked at the relationship that was teetering on the edge. But it had been Adrian she'd phoned. In her head, she'd convinced herself she'd just wanted to run, and she knew she could run safely to Adrian. He would protect her, as he'd done so many times in recent years, without conditions. Or had it been more than that? Her mind drifted and she ran her hand across her breasts and downwards to the softness of her thighs as she drifted into a semi-conscious slumber.

Her laptop bleeped with an email. She sat up, rubbed her face vigorously and opened up her computer. What happened in Bosnia should stay in Bosnia, she told herself. She had work to do.

Rosie had been too late for the Met Police's press briefing, which had taken place earlier in the afternoon at the makeshift incident room they'd set up on the pavement across from the café where Mahoney was murdered. But from what she'd picked up from the Press Association copy on her laptop, she hadn't missed much. She'd also read and re-read the various newspapers that had splashed the story this morning – none of them with any different line than that a former university lecturer had been gunned down in what looked like an execution. The nature of the murder was a big enough line in itself, but there was no detail, and that was the mystery factor. Who shoots an ageing lecturer in broad daylight in a busy café? And why? The story had swirled around in Rosie's head while she showered and got dressed before heading out to meet her old newspaper pal Andy Simpson for dinner. He'd called her mobile after being told by her office in Glasgow she was out of town. She was glad, and would have phoned him anyway, as much to pick his brains as for the company in London. Grizzled old hack that he was, Andy didn't miss

much, and she knew that, when in London, and surrounded by the so-called big hitters and egos, it was good
to have a Scottish ally. Rosie knew Andy would be his usual
wily, charming self, out to prove he was ahead of the pack
but watching her like a hawk in case she stiffed him on the
story. And at the same time she knew there would be a
faint hope on his part that he could get her into bed, now
that she was down in the Big Smoke on what he had made
his own turf after fifteen years as a top front-line hack in
Fleet Street.

Rosie smiled as she clocked him coming into the bar and
striding across the wooden floor. Simpson certainly walked
the walk. A grin spread across his face when he saw her.

'There she is. Scotland's finest.' He pulled Rosie to her
feet. 'Let me get a kiss at you right on the lips.'

He planted a too-lingering kiss and held her tight.

'Steady the buffs.' She pulled away. 'Do you do that to all
the hacks who come from Glasgow?'

Still holding her, Andy scanned her face.

'Only the ones I'm secretly in love with . . . and you know
I've always loved you.' He touched her face. 'You're looking
well . . . Seriously.' He gave her another tight hug then
released her. 'Oh, and I read all about that shit in Spain.
Fuck me! You could have been a dead woman.'

'Aw, don't you start, Andy. Everybody says that. But
believe me, nobody knows it more than me.' She ruffled

his hair, picked up her glass and drained it. 'Come on. It's your round. Tell me what's been happening to you these days. How's life?'

They walked towards the bar.

'I'm good. But listen. About the UVF and the coke story. Fucking hell! Some mad bastard tried to burn your arm off with a blowtorch? Is that true? Christ almighty! Are you all right? Really?'

'Of course I'm all right.' Rosie shrugged, as the image flashed behind her eyes. 'I can't play the piano as well as I used to but, apart from that, it's all good.' She puffed. 'Come on. I can't be arsed talking about that now. It was nearly two months ago. I've been in hiding in Bosnia since then. The UVF put a hit out on me.'

'I heard that, too. You need to watch yourself.' He grinned. 'I mean, a bullet or a stab in the leg doesn't do your reputation at the front line any harm. But you don't want to be getting killed. Because then you'll just be a dead reporter . . .' He leaned into her and whispered. '. . . And we've not even been to bed yet.'

Rosie laughed and shook her head, remembering the drunken clinch with him a few years ago back in the days when she drank a lot more than she did now, and could be reckless with it, too. She knew better now. She paced herself. And she didn't get involved with other reporters. Most of them were a bit mentally deranged, like herself, anyway.

They were good fun, focused on the job, and the job was their lives. But the part that didn't involve work was usually well fucked up. She knew that better than anyone.

They sat back, clinked their gin and tonics, relaxed in each other's company. Rosie was genuinely glad to see him, but she knew Andy would be looking for an equal share of anything she came up with from the Scottish side of the investigation. She'd see what he'd got first, she thought, watching him take out his notebook and flicking through the pages, but she wouldn't be throwing her lot in with him, or any other hack in the press pack who liked to work together to make sure none of them missed out. That wasn't how she operated.

'So what's the rumour mill spewing out on this, Andy? Don't tell me the lecturer was a drug dealer,' Rosie said.

'No. Nothing like that. Strangely enough, there's not been that much speculation at all. We're all over it down here at the moment, but that'll die down if the cops can't keep the interest up. They have to keep giving the hacks something to keep us going. I've told my Met contacts that we need new lines every day to keep it alive.'

'So have they given you any intelligence at all?'

He took a swig of his drink and flipped over a page.

'One line for tomorrow that I've got to myself, but I'll share it with you, for old time's sake,' he winked.

'I'm all ears,' she said, ignoring Andy's game face.

'It's not much really, but just that he had a flat down

here in London, or he had access to a flat. That's all they told me. Didn't say if he owned it or whatever, just that he had been down here for the past three or four days. Looks like he came down quite a bit. I've been round to the place. Neighbours remembered him coming and going over the years. But, typical for London, no bastard knew who he was.'

'Where was the flat?'

'Just off Kensington High Street. Close enough to the posh part but far enough away, if you get my drift.'

'What . . . central London? On a university lecturer's pension?'

Andy shrugged. 'Could have been left to him by a rich relative or something. I'm still checking it out. But there's nothing too mysterious about that. It's not the kind of thing somebody shoots you for.'

'Was he a perv? Maybe using the flat for rent boys?'

'Nothing to indicate that. He was married. Grown-up family. Two sons. One in the USA and the other in Hong Kong . . . And anyway, this was an execution. Professional job. No doubt about it.'

'What about the four guys? The *Sun* story said they were Russians.'

'That might be right, even if it was a flyer by the *Sun*. One of our crime boys got a nod from the cops today that the waitress said she thought they were Russian. And you probably know that Mahoney used to lecture in East European Studies at Glasgow.'

'You think it's connected?'

'Who knows. We don't have enough information on his background yet. That's what's really annoying.'

'Are we likely to get the names of any of the people in the café? Anyone we can get to for a bit of colour? Eyewitness accounts?'

'We're working on it. The café's closed today while Forensics sweep the place. But it's supposed to reopen tomorrow.'

'Great. It'll be good for a colour piece anyway . . . But we really need something more to go on. What about the friend he was with? Apparently, he's an old mate from university. What's his background?'

'Haven't been told much. He lives in Glasgow. But the cops have said he's in a right old state. In shock. I don't think we'd get much change out of him at the moment, and anyway, we don't even know where he is.'

Rosie nodded.

'I'll probably only stay here for a couple of days, then head up the road. We need to dig around on Mahoney's background back home. Maybe someone will come out of the woodwork.'

Rosie was already thinking of her friend Mickey Kavanagh, the private-eye ex-cop with contacts everywhere. If anything was worth hiding, Mickey would dig it out. She'd call him later. But first, she had to charm Andy into staying onside, so her back was covered in London if anything blew up.

'So, Mr Big-time London Hack. Where can an impression-able Glasgow reporter buy you dinner? And, remember, my expenses are only a fraction of yours.'

'Fear not, my lovely. Dinner is on me.' Andy drained his glass and stood up, offering his arm. 'Let's go.'

CHAPTER TWO

Rosie was a little hungover, sitting at a small table in the King's Cross café, as far away as possible from any activity, but close enough to watch. It looked like business as usual – if you didn't know that a man had been shot in the head here less than forty-eight hours ago. Scenes of crime officers had been all over it yesterday, dusting for prints, removing anything that might help identify the killers. But there had been so much mayhem when the shooting started, with frantic customers running around, that much of the crime scene would have been contaminated by the time they got there.

It was almost mid-morning when police allowed the owner, a pot-bellied little Greek man, to reopen, after much huffing and puffing from him that he was losing a fortune. He was clearly aware that the café would be even busier now, with punters eager to see the spot where a man was gunned down. Rosie watched him wringing his hands as he described to reporters what had happened, saying how it was just like the movies, and she could see he was relishing the extra trade that the morbid curiosity factor was bringing in. At least he had had the decency to clean the blood off the walls, Rosie noticed, as she watched him point to the table where Tom Mahoney had sat. Christ! There's money in everything – even cold-blooded murder.

Last night's dinner with Andy had gone on too long. And too much drink had been taken even before they'd gone on to the Soho bar where celebrities and actors hung out. The paparazzi photographers were lurking outside, hoping that some big shot would fall out of the bar drunk, snogging a woman, or man, who wasn't their partner. They were seldom disappointed in this neck of the woods. Andy and Rosie had been engrossed in their one-in-the-morning drunken, intense conversation about life and love and 'where did it all go wrong', with Andy telling her that his latest live-in lover was leaving him. Rosie had jokingly suggested he should try keeping his trousers on when he was out without his girlfriend. He was flirtatious and affectionate with Rosie all evening, both of them knowing they were not going to end up in bed but enjoying the closeness of being a couple of lonely misfits. Now on her second coffee, Rosie called the waitress over and ordered more water. Rehydration Station – too little too late.

Earlier she'd watched as the waitress protested outside as photographers took pictures of the staff arriving at the café. She was pretending to be coy but was obviously relishing her fifteen minutes of fame, as she declared that police had told her not to talk to the media, then seconds later was blabbing to everyone.

'I'm a journalist from Scotland.' Rosie looked up when she came over to her table to take her order. 'From the *Post*.'

The waitress put her hand up as though she were a celebrity.

'I'm not giving interviews.'

Rosie managed to keep her face straight.

Of course . . . I was just thinking . . .' She paused. 'Sorry, I don't know your name?'

'Karen,' the waitress replied.

'Karen. I was just thinking, that with this being such a big story and the interest from the papers and television, that someone like yourself will be crucial to the inquiry. I wondered how that makes you feel.'

'Well,' Karen said, tossing her blonde ponytail and pouting her pale-pink lips. 'I'm doing what I can to help the case. All I can say is what I saw.'

'You were the only waitress here, weren't you?'

'Yeah. The other girl, Jen, was at the dentist. So it was just me . . . I saw it all.'

She batted her eyelashes twice, as if she were waiting for a flashbulb to go off.

'I was wondering,' Rosie said, 'did you actually serve those guys? . . . The four men the police are talking about?'

'I'm not really supposed to say.'

'I understand that. But what you're saying to me right now . . . you know . . . it doesn't have to come from you. I don't have to put it in a quote. You can be anonymous. I'm just trying to gather information, and you are a very important figure in this whole case.' Rosie laid on the flattery thick.

Karen examined her fingernails then rolled her eyes at Rosie.

'Well. As long as you don't say it came from me.'

'Of course not.'

She glimpsed over her shoulder to see if her boss was looking. He wasn't.

'I did serve them,' she said softly. 'They were big, kind of Russian-looking guys. Or Polish. Or something. You never know really. You get all sorts in here, so you do. Locals, office workers . . . and all the passing trade from the street. Loads of people with luggage coming off the Eurostar on their way somewhere, usually going towards Euston Station. You see a lot of foreigners. Loads from Eastern Europe.'

'So it would be nothing untoward to see four big Russian-looking men.'

'Not really. They were just customers to me. They ordered the lamb stew and sat there stuffing it down. They weren't very friendly. Didn't hardly look at me.'

'Where were they sitting?'

Rosie watched as Karen pointed to the spot, two tables away from where Mahoney had sat.

'And who was at the table between them. Anyone?'

'Yeah.' She made an indignant face. 'Some nasty woman. She gave me a hard time for not serving her coffee quick enough. Like, as if I'd nothing better to do. I was rushed off my feet. She was dead edgy.'

'Was she on her own?'

'Yeah.' She paused. 'Actually, she spoke kind of like you. I think she might have been Scottish. Maybe. Yeah. Probably was, come to think of it.'

'What did she look like?'

The waitress shrugged:

'Dark hair, kind of messy. About thirty. Jeans, shabby looking.'

Rosie thought for a moment then asked her to describe what she saw from the second the shooting started. Karen told her she'd just cleared a table at the back of the café and had gone to the counter and put the tray down when she heard the gunshots from behind. She'd turned around in time to see the man slip from his chair and on to the floor beneath the table.

'It was like watching in slow motion. I was totally stunned. Terrified. Blood everywhere. Poor guy. He'd been really nice to me, and his pal was friendly too. He was kneeling on the floor beside him and he was really crying sore, trying to stop the blood. I felt so sorry for him. The girl was there too. The angry one. She was crouched on the floor beside them.'

'The girl? What happened then?'

'I can't remember much. I was screaming and hiding at the side of the counter. I was terrified they were going to shoot more people. I mean, that's what happens in the movies, isn't it? I had my hands over my head, so I only saw the back of the men as they left.' She paused, licked her lips. 'Then she left, too.'

'Who?'

'That girl. The Scottish one.'

'What. She left the café?'

'Yeah. Everyone else was too petrified to move. But she got off her mark.'

'Really. I wonder why?'

'I'm guessing she didn't want to talk to the cops. Maybe she was on the run. Or she was part of it too, maybe, with the men.'

Rosie tried not to smile.

'That's a bit of a vivid imagination you've got there, Karen. Have you told the police all this?'

'Yeah. I did. They said they've interviewed nearly everyone in the café and the ones they haven't got full interviews from yet, they've given their addresses. But they didn't say anything about the girl.'

'So maybe she's got in touch. They're not going to tell you that, are they?'

Karen shrugged.

'She was probably part of it. I told them that.'

'Based on what, though, Karen?' Rosie asked, surprised.

'Just a feeling.'

Rosie nodded. She'd heard more than enough. Whoever the girl was in the café, this daft waitress had condemned her as an accessory to murder. God spare us from amateur sleuths. She drank her coffee and left a fiver tip for Karen.

'See you again, Karen.' She slipped her business card into the top pocket of the waitress's blouse.

Rosie made a cursory trip to the address she had for Mahoney's block of flats but, as she suspected, there was a uniformed Met officer at the entrance, so she couldn't even knock on the neighbours' doors. By early afternoon, she was back in her hotel bedroom, putting her story together for tomorrow's *Post* while trying to negotiate her way through a room-service club sandwich. Why did they do that to a sandwich? Stack it up like a multistorey so that you had to eat it with a knife and fork? By the time she'd given up on it, the plate looked like someone had trampled all over it.

She reread her copy, keeping one eye on Sky News in the corner. They still had Mahoney's murder high up on their news list, but there were no new lines. Her email pinged with copy from Declan, the young reporter back at the *Post*, assigned as her legman on the Scottish end. He'd already been to the Mahoney house, but the wife was saying nothing, was surrounded by friends and old colleagues of her husband, and too upset to speak. Her sons were on their way back from abroad. From Declan's copy, it seemed like Mahoney was hugely respected and revered after a lifetime at Glasgow University. Rosie had written a colour piece on the scene inside the murder café based on what she had from the waitress. But she hadn't decided what to do with Karen's line about the 'Scottish' woman who left the scene before the police arrived. She'd run it past McGuire, let him decide. Her mobile rang.

'Hey, Andy. If you've got a scoop you're not sharing with me, I hope you've got fire insurance – because I'll hunt you down,' Rosie joked.

'Would I ever, sweetheart.' Andy's voice was gravelly from last night's booze and chain-smoking. 'How you doing, darlin'? That was a great night. I was a bit shagged this morning, though – or, in fact, not shagged, if you get my drift.'

Rosie smiled to herself.

'I do. What you up to? I've been round to Mahoney's flat, but a cop's on the door. Couldn't get near enough to doorstep any neighbours.' She decided not to tell him about the supposedly Scottish woman who did a runner from the café, though from the way Karen blabbed to everyone, she wouldn't be surprised if he already knew.

'Not much to go on. I've had a nod that the flat isn't in

Mahoney's name, so I don't know if it's a relative or a friend, or whatever. I'm trying to check it out.'

He told Rosie the name and she wrote it in her notebook.

'Is there nothing from the police at your end to suggest who would want to bump this guy off? What about his mate – Hawkins? Anything from him?'

'Too upset to talk. He's on his way back to Glasgow as we speak.' He paused. 'To be honest, Rosie, this won't run and run here unless it opens up a bit. I've got another story to do – a big drug case finishing today, and I've been doing the background – so I'm heading down to the Old Bailey now. I'll keep an eye on the shooting, and we've got someone else covering for the day, but we've kind of moved on here.'

'How very London,' Rosie said with a hint of sarcasm, though she knew how quickly even major stories slipped down the news agenda back home, if something more tantalizing cropped up. But it was more so in London.

'Yeah,' Andy said. 'You know what it's like. So much going on here. We can't get bogged down on shootings and murder unless they're really big. Happens every day in London.'

'Not to retired university lecturers, Andy. It's obvious someone wanted him dead.'

'Yeah. But I've told my detective contacts that unless they can throw us a bone, the story will be history.'

'Maybe that's what they want,' she said, knowing she had nothing to back it up, apart from her distrust of authority. 'Maybe it will suit them for the story to disappear.'

'Aye, right, Rosie. Conspiracy theories are not fact.'

'But sometimes they turn out to be, if we keep digging.'

'Sure, darlin'. Couldn't agree more. But not for me, not today. What you doing later? Fancy a curry?'

Rosie was already thinking of her next move, and dinner with Andy was nowhere in her plans.

'Don't think so. Not tonight. I might be getting pulled back up the road in the morning. Not much really for me down here. I think Mahoney's background – old students and stuff and former colleagues – might throw a better light on things.'

'Maybe. Listen. You will give me a shout, though, if you get anything . . . you know, mark my card. I don't expect you to share any major exclusive – I know what you're like – but at least mark my card.'

''Course I will,' Rosie said, not convinced that she would.

'I need to go. The judge was already charging the jury, so they might be out by now.'

'OK, Andy. Keep in touch if you get anything.'

Rosie hung up. Her next call was to Mickey Kavanagh, and she gave him the name Andy had given her of the owner of the flat, to see if he could dig anything up.

She ordered more coffee from room service and was about to ring McGuire's office when her mobile rang.

'Mick. I was just about to ring you. How spooky is that?'

'It's nearly two in the afternoon. You should have phoned before this, Gilmour. Have you got anything exciting for me? Anything different from the same old shite that's running on the telly and the wires?'

'Maybe. Let me run this past you.'

Rosie told him the waitress's story about the girl with the Scottish accent.

'How come the cops haven't put that out?'

'Sometimes they don't straight away. They might be working their way through all the punters in the café, and haven't acted on the waitress's statement yet. Or maybe they're keeping it to themselves for now.'

'Why?'

'Don't know, Mick. Who knows the inner workings of Scotland Yard?'

'Well, they're too fucking late. We're using that tomorrow. We have to. It's the only thing that's different. Mystery Scots woman flees bloodbath. Stick a call into the cops and find out if they intend putting it out.' He paused. 'In fact, don't bother. We'll just run it and see what happens.'

'They'll be raging if we do that, especially if they were intending drip-feeding it to the press.'

'Fuck them. They don't run the news agenda – we do. Do it up and bung it over so I can have a look. And plenty of colour in the café. I like blood and screams. I'm funny that way.'

'OK. Sure.'

'Anything else for you down there, apart from enjoying yourself, spending my money?'

'No. Not at the moment.'

'OK. Come back tomorrow then. Give it the morning then get a lunchtime flight. There's more to be done up here.'

'I agree. I'll talk to Marion.'

McGuire hung up.

Andy's suggestion of a curry had put Rosie in the mood, but she didn't want company. Once she had sent her story, she took a stroll around the King's Cross area, along to the station, towards a little corner and a wall a few yards from the entrance. Every time she came to London her feet seemed to make their way to this spot. It was almost a ritual, a kind of reaffirming of who she was, how far she'd come. A lifetime ago, Rosie had pitched up here after she'd had as much as she could take of living with her mother's sister's family and their chaotic existence in the Glasgow tenement. She had just turned sixteen, and all she possessed was twenty quid, a hold-all full of clothes and a head full of dreams. She stood looking down at the spot where she'd woken up shivering after sleeping outside on her first night in London. She recalled the chill, the loneliness, the feeling that she'd been on the run all her life. But nothing had been stronger than the hope that surged through her that drizzly morning. Now Rosie smiled to herself as she gazed around her at the bustle of human traffic around the station, each person with their own story, their own dreams. She had done all right. She'd come a long way. Her mother and father would have been proud. She shook herself out of the moment and walked away.

She found a little Indian restaurant, where she devoured a massive meal, savouring every hot chilli like a true Glaswegian who'd been deprived of their staple diet for weeks. Bosnia had been great for lots of other reasons, but no matter where she travelled to, she missed her curries. She sipped from a bottle of lager and looked out of the window at the steady stream of London traffic, and across the road, at the people with bags and suitcases on wheels heading up towards Euston. She thought of the woman Karen had told her about who had run out of the restaurant. She was intrigued by that. It didn't need to be anything to do with the shooting – the Eurostar probably carried at least half a dozen drug mules or criminals every trip. Perhaps the woman had a bag full of cocaine and couldn't afford to be anywhere near the police. She felt a little guilty that she hadn't passed the line to Andy, and would have to lie to him that it had come to the news desk on wire copy. She knew he wouldn't believe her, but that's how it was. Her mobile rang. It was Mickey Kavanagh.

'Hi Mickey. You were quick.'

'That's what all the birds say.'

'I don't believe that for a minute. An international stud like you?'

'I try,' he said, 'but I just get so excited.'

Rosie heard him chuckle. She was looking forward to having dinner with him. She owed him for his help on her last big story.

'You're going to love this, Rosie. I've checked out the owner of Mahoney's flat.'

'And?'

'It's him.'

'But that's not what I was told. It's a different name.'

'I know. I got one of my mates to run a passport check. The name on the register has a valid UK passport, and guess who's mugshot is on it?'

'You're kidding me.'

'I kid you not. It's Mahoney. He had two passports – well, two that we know of.'

'What the fu—?'

'He's a spook, Rosie.'

'Seriously?'

'Well, I'm still digging. I've got mates looking into it. But I'd put good money on Mahoney having a past that involves more than his Eastern European Studies at Glasgow Uni.'

'My editor's going to love this.' Rosie could imagine McGuire punching the air with excitement.

'Yeah. But you know what that means, Rosie. You'll get bugger all from the cops now on the murder.'

'We're already getting nothing.'

'Not surprised. They'll be playing this close to their chest, but I'll see what I can dig up.'

'Brilliant. Hey, Mickey. Let's have a big dinner. I'm back tomorrow.'

'Sure. I'd love that. I'll keep you posted.'

CHAPTER THREE

Ruby examined her reflection in the full-length mirror of the hotel lift, glancing over her shoulder, satisfied by the way the skin-tight black jeans emphasized her firm bottom. The cream, soft leather vest clung to all the right places, showing her toned, suntanned arms and athletic shoulders to maximum effect. More rock chick than glamorous, and topped off with a luscious mop of shoulder-length jet-black hair, tousled perfectly to give that I'm-fun-and-I'm-carefree look, which was far from the truth of who she really was. But for the next few hours, Ruby just wanted to relax and savour the moment of a job well done. More than a job – an ambition. She'd waited exactly twenty-five years to watch that bastard finally get his day. Revenge was indeed a dish best served ice cold. She pulled down her sunglasses and winked at herself in the mirror as the lift doors opened into the palatial foyer of London's Ritz Hotel. Nobody would ever think of looking for her here. Those halfwits back on the Costa del Sol would still be sifting through the smouldering embers of the house. Fuck them. The jungle drums would be beating all over Glasgow by now, and that definitely niggled, but the bastards would never find her.

She eased herself on to a stool at the bar and ordered a large vodka and tonic, watching the barman as he kept pouring, waiting for her to tell him to stop. She didn't.

'My kind of barman,' Ruby murmured, lowering her dark glasses a fraction so their eyes met.

'My kind of woman,' the barman replied with a hint of an accent.

He had that been-around-the-course glint that said he knew who was up for it and who wasn't from the moment they walked into the bar. She liked that in a man. Straight and to the point. Ruby flashed him a flirty smile. She took a long, lingering drink and watched from behind her sunglasses as he polished tumblers at the far end of the bar, sneaking furtive glances at her. She smiled inwardly. Just for the sheer hell of it, she might even get laid tonight.

The following morning Ruby arrived at Euston just in time to catch the ten o'clock train for Glasgow. She stepped on board and slung her small case in the overhead rack, where she could keep an eye on it, then slumped into a seat, hoping nobody would join her at the other side of the Formica table. She could have gone first class – it was not as if money was a problem. But first class was never all that busy, and she didn't want to risk being in a place where she might be easy to spot. You never knew who was on a train from London. Any of the toe-rag drug runners making a drop or a pick-up for the firm could be sitting on the train; even that far down the food chain they would have heard by now that Rab Jackson had been murdered in Spain. Torched in the famous Costa del Sol villa he'd retired to five years ago. He had left Tony Devlin, the hoodlum who had become like a son to him, to take over the business. Rumours would be flying all over the shop as to who was responsible – there would be claims from rival gangs from Glasgow to Manchester that it was their hit. But alarm bells would have rung at the very top of the organization when they couldn't get hold of Ruby. And once they discovered that her body wasn't in the burnt-out villa along with Rab's, there would be all sorts of serious shit flying around. Because Ruby was the accountant.

She drained the bottle of mineral water she'd brought with her and bought another and a coffee from the trolley as it passed. Gazing out of the window, she sipped from the polystyrene cup as the countryside whizzed past. She sometimes forgot how green it was back home. She'd been away too long, but it had been a means to an end. Call it dedication – more than that: it was a vocation. Everything she'd done in the recent years had been orchestrated so she could finally achieve the retribution her mother and sister deserved – even if it *was* too late for both of them. The landscape of Rosie's childhood sped past her in a flurry of images. Train trips down the Scottish coast to Helensburgh, her mother's adoring face while she and Judy giggled and played games during the journey . . . before it was all snatched so brutally away.

Ruby yawned and sat back, but her mind was too full of business to sleep. Her thoughts wandered back to the previous night at the Ritz, and the barman, who she'd surprised by whispering her room number as she left the bar. Then surprised him even more when she'd kept him up most of the night with her sexual athletics until they'd both collapsed, exhausted. When she'd asked him to leave so she could get a couple of hours' sleep, he didn't look in the least resentful. If that had been a man treating her like that, she'd probably have been upset – though no man she'd slept with had ever asked her to leave the bed.

She carefully took the little red book out of her handbag and ran her forefinger down the various bank account numbers where she'd stashed a fortune away in the past three years, ever since Rab Jackson had been gullible enough to allow her access to his accounts. Fuck him. He was so stinking rich on the misery of others he wouldn't have known exactly how much money he had anyway. That's what made it easier for Ruby. Jackson had been too busy with the sycophant film producers and writers who fussed around him, delighted he'd agreed to let them make a movie of his chequered life, to notice that Ruby was systematically plundering his bank account, siphoning cash to various personal accounts she had set up in different countries. It would take forever to disentangle the complexities of her handiwork on Jackson's investments. But that wouldn't stop them being suspicious. As she closed the diary, a scrap of paper fell out of it onto her lap. She studied the scrawl on the paper, at first wondering what it was, then she remembered picking it up from the table in the café in King's Cross. She strained her eyes to read it, but all she could make out was what looked like the name of a company. J B Solutions. She didn't know why she took it in the first place, but stuffed it back in the notebook and put it away.

As the train disgorged its passengers onto the platform at Glasgow Central Station, Rosie stepped out and melted into the crowd. She'd tied her hair back and pulled on a black baseball cap with the brim pulled low over her eyes, and as she strode through the concourse she didn't linger to look at the throng of people coming and going, living ordinary lives, making their way home from work, heading off for the weekend to be with loved ones. She kept her head down and walked out into the late-afternoon sun and filled her lungs with the fumes of Glasgow traffic. She was home. For the moment. She jumped into a black taxi and closed the door.

'Where to, doll?'

'Bridge of Weir, please.'

She saw the driver eyeing her in his rear-view mirror. It was at least a thirty-quid hire to the affluent country village twelve miles outside of Glasgow. She could see his mind ticking over along with his meter. In her shabby jeans, T-shirt and baseball cap, he'd be hoping she had the money to pay. But without a word, he stuck his car into gear and headed out of Gordon Street and up St Vincent Street, towards the M8 motorway to Renfrewshire.

Ruby stared out of the side window at the sun throwing shadows on the city's magnificent sandstone buildings. Pictures of herself at various stages of growing up flooded through her mind. The carefree Saturday afternoons going to the matinee at the Odeon Cinema with her mother and Judy, then afterwards sitting in George's Square, feasting on fish and chips wrapped in newspaper, until it was time to get the bus back up to the Maryhill tenement where they lived. Happy days – even though she knew that by nine thirty in the evening while she and Judy were in bed, the men would come knocking on their door with plastic carry-out bags of vodka and a few cans of beer. They wouldn't stay long, and then some other man would come, or maybe even two together. Ruby and Judy could hear them laughing, sometimes arguing, then noises they didn't recognize. She'd blackened Billy Millar's two eyes in the school playground one day when he shouted at her that her mother was a whore. He never said it again, but it didn't make it any less true. It was her mammy, and she'd heard her crying in the night too often after the men left for her to feel anger or disgust at what her eight-year-old concept of a whore was.

Ruby swallowed the lump in her throat as the cab pulled out of the city and onto the motorway. Her stomach knotted a little at the thought of seeing Judy again. She'd been coming back as often as she could to see her sister in the home. Three or four times a year, if she could manage it without anyone finding out where she was. As far as most people were aware, Judy was long dead. And Ruby decided she'd keep it that way when she'd found her all those years ago, a half-starved wreck in a locked ward of a Dickensian NHS psychiatric institution. Judy would remain dead so she could work towards the single goal that had driven her since that night all those years ago. She blinked away the picture. At least Judy was in a decent place now, and not in that shithole where they'd left her rotting for years. Ruby's money had made sure she was well cared for, and every time she came over from Europe she'd sit with her, talking to her empty eyes, holding her hand, telling her stories of the two of them as children, hoping to provoke some reaction, evoke some memory. But Judy's fixed gaze never flinched. Nothing. Maybe today it would be different.

*

The nurse on reception looked up and smiled when Ruby came through the swing doors and into the sterile tranquility of the main foyer.

'Hello, Ruby.' She put down a folder and came out from behind the desk. 'How lovely to see you. Are you well?'

'Yeah,' Ruby said from behind dark glasses. 'I'm good.'

She couldn't remember the name of the middle-aged nurse who always greeted her with a caring smile each time she visited. Ruby viewed it with the cynicism with which she had viewed most things as she grew up. You get what you pay for. If it had been the NHS hospital, you'd hardly have got a nod from the staff, they were so hard pressed. Here, amid the oil paintings and leather sofas in the foyer, it was all grace and charm. If you weren't coming in to visit a loved one who was either in a permanent vegetative state or wired to the moon, you'd think you were in a boutique hotel.

'How is she?' Ruby asked, as they walked along the polished corridor to Judy's room.

The nurse turned to Ruby and made a sympathetic face.

'The same, I'm afraid.' She sighed. 'We just have to keep hoping. We should never give up hope.' She paused, turning to Ruby. 'She's up, and we got her dressed. We told her you were coming.'

Ruby nodded as they turned the handle on the door and walked in.

Judy was sitting in a glossy white wicker chair by the

window, a shaft of setting sun catching the paleness of her cheeks.

'Look who's here, Judy. Your wee sister.'

Judy stared straight out of the window, where acres of soft green grass stretched and spread into foothills in the distance. A male nurse pushed a wheelchair carrying an elderly patient down a tiny path towards the lake.

Ruby gave the nurse a nod.

'Thanks. We'll be fine now.'

The nurse backed away, smiling, knowing she'd been dismissed.

Ruby took a deep breath and swallowed back her tears. Every time she came here it was the same. It ripped the heart out of her. Judy was all she had in the world. Even as children they had clung to each other, both somehow aware of the fragility of their lives. Then, after the fire, the terror of that night and the awful brutality, everything died – not just their mother – in the inferno of their home. Judy had retreated into her silent world, and she hadn't spoken a word for years. While Ruby grew up shunted from one children's home to the other, she had believed her sister was dead. The social workers had even told her so. No details. Nothing.

Ruby walked towards Judy and stood in front of her and the window.

'Hey, Judes. How's it going, big sis?'

She bent over and kissed her cheek. She put her arms

around her and held her close, wanting to bury her face in her sister's hair and again feel safe, like they used to when they had curled up in bed like spoons at night.

'Oh, Judy,' Ruby said, fighting back tears. 'I do miss you so much.'

She composed herself and pulled up a chair so that they both sat facing each other. Judy stared past her. Ruby moved around again, so that she was in her line of vision. She knew she could see her. Judy had to know she was there. She had to.

'Guess what, Judy,' Ruby said, pouring them both a glass of fizzy water from the bottle in the ice bucket. 'He's dead.' She smiled broadly. 'I did it.'

She reached out and stroked her sister's hair with one hand, while clutching her soft hand with the other.

'He's gone, Judy. I did what I said I would do. I killed the bastard.' She squeezed Judy's hand and looked into her eyes. 'They say shit doesn't burn, Judy. But it's a lie. Because let me tell you, pal, that piece of shit burned like a fucking stick.'

She smiled, willing Judy to respond – anything. Then, to her astonishment, Judy's empty gaze slowly moved from the window. Her eyes flickered a little, then focused on Ruby, who sat barely breathing, terrified to break the spell. Then Judy's pale eyes glistened with tears, and Ruby watched as they spilled over and down her cheeks. But it wasn't like crying, because Judy's lips had a hint of a smile. Then Ruby felt her sister squeeze her hand tight.

'I know you can hear me, Judy. I know you can.'

Ruby wrapped her arms around her sister, and her own tears fell as she felt Judy's arms slip around her for the first time in twenty-five years.

Ruby lit up a cigarette as she sat in the conservatory of the home's cafeteria. She took a long, satisfying draw, held the smoke in and then let it out slowly, still feeling elated over how Judy had reacted. Somewhere behind those eyes, her sister was there, and her chat afterwards with her specialist was encouraging. It would take time, he said. Time, she told him, was all she had now. But he stressed there were no guarantees.

The couple from the table at the window got up and left, and Ruby squinted at the copy of the *Post* the man had left on the table. She could see a headline on the front page: 'MYSTERY SCOT FLED CAFÉ BLOODBATH.'

She automatically glanced around the empty café before getting up and going across to the table. Beneath the *Post* was a copy of the *Sun*, and another headline jumped out at her: 'RUNAWAY SCOT MAY HOLD KEY TO CAFÉ EXECUTION.'

'Fuck me!' Ruby said quietly, scooping up both newspapers and going back to her table.

Her eyes quickly scanned the front page of the *Post*.

A mystery Scots woman fled the King's Cross café murder scene before police arrived, the Post can exclusively reveal. The woman vanished seconds after the assassins blasted university lecturer Tom Mahoney in the head at point-blank range. Police have confirmed that this woman is the only person in the café unaccounted for. One witness to the execution told the Post, 'The woman had a Scottish accent. She was very edgy, and as soon as it happened and the men left, she left right behind them.'

The witness described the mystery Scot as in her thirties with dark hair and wearing shabby denims. Scotland Yard would not say if she was a suspect, but confirmed they are eager to speak to her as a witness.

'Christ almighty!' Ruby muttered. 'Fucking little bitch of a waitress.'

She quickly scanned the *Sun*'s front-page story: 'Police have not ruled out that a mystery Scot who fled the scene of a horrific execution could be involved.'

Ruby stubbed out her cigarette. 'In the name of Christ! Do they just make this stuff up?'

She folded the newspapers under her arm and left the café to wait outside for her taxi.

CHAPTER FOUR

'Jesus! Look what the wind blew in.' Jean, the big, busty receptionist at the *Post* glanced up and grinned as Rosie came through the revolving doors. 'We heard you were dead.' She put down the phone mid-dial.

'Yeah? I hope you sent flowers.'

'We had a whip-round in the canteen. But in the end we thought you'd appreciate it more if we just got pished with the money. So we did.'

'Class,' Rosie chuckled. 'That gives me a warm glow.'

'So how's it going, sweetcheeks?' She came out from behind her desk and embraced Rosie. 'Where the hell have you been?'

'Great, Jean. I was in hiding. Those bad UVF men put a contract on me, so McGuire sent me away. I was somewhere in Europe, holed up in the hills.' Rosie tapped the side of her nose with her forefinger as she headed for the staircase to the editorial floor. 'That's all you need to know.' At the foot of the stairs, she turned. 'Have I missed any gossip?'

'Nope. Not a sausage, darlin'. Good to have you home.' Jean blew a kiss as Rosie took the stairs to the third floor.

The editorial floor stretched the length of the building and was full of reporters, even though it was lunchtime. Some sat with their feet up, reading newspapers, while others had phones at their ears, taking notes or working at their screens, half-eaten sandwiches and bottles of mineral water at their desks. Nobody went out for lunch any more. Lunch used to be a God-given right for journalists, and often a rite of passage for new starters, who would be taken out by a seasoned hack and brought back mid-afternoon three sheets to the wind, just to see if they could survive. A few years ago the place would have been like the Marie Celeste at this time of the day, as the reporters and feature writers would have been in city restaurants entertaining contacts, as their expenses would reflect, or they'd be in the nearest bar along with a few sub-editors, having a few drinks before the serious work of putting out a newspaper began in the afternoon. It was like one long party, and it wasn't a rarity that a fight broke out on the editorial floor by teatime between two older journalists who'd been drinking on an empty head. Now it was all mineral water and staff chained to desks amid the quiet hum of computers and the television news perpetually playing in the background on three televisions mounted around the news desk. Rosie saw the young reporter Declan look up and quickly get out of her chair.

'Hey, you! What's the score, son? Did you think I was dead as well?' Rosie quipped.

Declan's face reddened.

'Someone was at my desk working when I came in this morning, Rosie, so I just used yours. I didn't know you were coming back up today. You all right?'

'Sure, Dec.' She smiled. 'I'm good. What's happening?' She sat down, took her notebook out of her bag and placed it on the desk. 'I see you were up at the Mahoney house and got no joy. I wouldn't have thought the *Post* would be top of their reading list for breakfast reading in that house.'

'Not exactly.' Declan sat back, flicked through his notebook. 'I saw from your story that the guy who was with Mahoney – Hawkins, Gerard Hawkins – was on his way back from London. I hit his house last night as well, but no answer. So it's a bit of a dead end at the moment.'

Rosie nodded. 'It's early doors yet. We've got to keep plugging away.'

'Yeah,' he said. 'I've also been up to my arse for days now with Rab Jackson getting torched in his villa on the Costa del Sol. Did you hear about it?'

'It happened when I was travelling back to the UK, but I saw your piece yesterday. Couldn't happen to a nicer man.'

'Aye. The cops aren't exactly busting their arses trying to find the murderer, either. Not in Spain, and not here.'

'I'm not surprised. Jackson's just one more scummy bastard off the face of the earth. Cops will be delighted. I mean, even though he was retired, he'd already made his money on the back of other people's misery, and was still raking it in. He should have been dead born.'

Rab Jackson's reign of terror in Glasgow was mostly before Rosie's time, but his reputation had followed him well into his retirement. There were probably more bodies buried beneath the concrete columns of the sixties-built Kingston Bridge over the River Clyde than anybody would ever know – and Jackson was the vicious bastard behind it.

'They were supposed to be making a movie of his life.'

'Yeah, so I heard. Well, at least now it's got a happy ending.'

Rosie's desk phone rang.

'Hey, Rosie. You've to come through. Mick's waiting for you.'

'I'm there in two ticks.' She picked up her notebook and pen, but turned to Declan. 'Listen, Dec. We need to start digging on Mahoney's background. Get into everything in his old life, his studies and lecturing posts at Glasgow Uni. See if we can track down any of his old colleagues – I'm especially interested in the countries he visited. He headed the Eastern European Studies department, so he must have got around. See exactly what area that covers. Can you do that?'

'Sure.' Declan said. 'I'm on it already.'

'Good stuff.'

She headed across the floor towards the editor's office.

Before going in, she stopped at Marion's desk. 'I owe you a curry, Marion,' she said, giving her a thumbs-up. 'Cheers for organizing all my flights and stuff. You're worth your weight in gold.'

'Tell that to the boss man, then.' Marion jerked her head in the direction of McGuire's office.

'I will.' Rosie walked into the office, where the editor was sitting, his eyes fixed on his computer screen.

'You're back, Gilmour. Great to see you,' he said, without looking away from the screen. Then he got up, removed his reading glasses and came out from behind his desk.

'Let's have a hug. So the UVF bastards didn't find you? How you doing?' He put his arms around her and gave her a little squeeze.

'I'm great, Mick,' Rosie returned his hug. 'We live to fight another day.'

'How's your arm?'

'Still a bit painful sometimes, and I've more skin grafts to get organized this month. It's okay, though.'

Rosie tried not to think of the blowtorch burning her arm. She knew she was lucky to be alive, but she didn't want to dwell on what had happened. She crossed the room and planked herself on McGuire's leather sofa, as he sat on the armchair opposite her.

'So,' he began, crossing his legs, examining the

immaculate crease in his trousers then looking at Rosie. 'What's the score on this Mahoney? I want us all over it. Nobody's got anything different so far . . . And, by the way, that was a good shout about the Scots bird doing a runner. I'm intrigued by that, so keep digging. But who would shoot a retired uni lecturer? That's what I really want to know. And why?'

McGuire was easier when he was fired up. It gave Rosie more leeway to do things her own way.

'Wait till you hear this, Mick.' She flicked over the pages of her notebook . 'There's more to Mahoney than we think.'

McGuire's dark eyebrows knitted as he scanned her face for hints while she paused for effect.

'I think he might be a spook,' she said.

'Fuck me! Based on what?'

'Based on a tip-off I got last night from a good contact of mine who's always spot on.'

'And?'

'You see the flat he had in London – where he stayed from time to time?'

McGuire nodded, shifted in his seat.

'Go on? Get to the point, Gilmour.'

'Well, it's registered in another name. So I got my man to check it out, and it's him. Using a false name.'

'Who? Mahoney? You're kidding!'

'Nope. And not just a false name. A false passport.'

'Seriously?'

'Yep. My contact has friends in all sorts of places . . . Don't ask. But he traced the name of the flat owner all the way to the passport office, through his contact there. The owner has a passport with Mahoney's picture but a different name. So Mahoney has two passports – and that's two that we know about. For all we know, there could be another couple with his photograph and a different name. My pal thinks he's spy. Or maybe was a spy at one time.'

McGuire rolled his eyes to the ceiling.

'Is this wishful thinking from your mate, or is there any evidence?'

'You don't get evidence where spies are concerned. That's the whole point. The clue is in the word . . . "spy".'

'Yeah, right.' McGuire let her get away with the sarcasm. 'But there must be something.'

'Nothing solid, but if my friend says the word "spook", that means he's been given a nod. He's not going to draw me pictures. But if he wasn't a spy and was a fraudster, then he would say that.'

'So if he was a spy, it must have been years ago. Why wait till now to bump him off?'

'Who knows? Old scores being settled? We need somebody to take us inside his past life. We need to be looking back a long way – long before he retired. Long before the Berlin Wall came down. See if he was an old red under the bed – touch of the Philby/Burgess and all that.'

'Absolutely.' McGuire nodded. 'We'll get Declan to dig.'

'I've already told him.'

McGuire glanced at her.

'Don't mind me. I'm only the editor.'

Rosie gave him a cheeky look.

'I knew you'd want it done.' She waved her hand dismissively and informed him that Declan was going back through the university staff records, trying to find all the lecturers at the time, as well as the students in his department.

'But we need to get to Gerard Hawkins,' Rosie said. 'He was with him at the time. Dec was there last night and got no answer. Same with the family, as you know.'

McGuire stood up and went back round to his desk. The meeting was over. Rosie got to her feet.

'Right. You take another run at the family and at Hawkins.' He ran a hand through his thick black hair, and looked at her. 'I don't suppose we'll be the only ones on this spy theory?'

'My guy only speaks to me, Mick. But I can't vouch for anyone else. It depends on how keen any of the other papers are to pursue the story. I also need to look at this girl who did a runner from the café. The cops can't find her.'

'She must be a villain if they can't find her! Maybe we'll get lucky.'

'We'll have to get lucky.' Rosie opened the door and left.

CHAPTER FIVE

Ruby had staked out the house, deep in rural Ayrshire, a few times on previous visits back home, so she knew that Malky Cameron's movements were like clockwork. His routine never changed. Every afternoon he headed out of his driveway towards his local golf club. If it was raining, he and his friends didn't play golf but had lunch in the clubhouse and then spent most of the afternoon in the bar. He'd get into his car around seven and would be over the limit for driving, but would take it slowly along the four miles of deserted farm road to his house. He'd drive his gold Daimler straight into the old timber garage, come out, lock the double doors behind him and go through his front door.

Ruby remembered Rab Jackson slagging him off to some old ex-pat cronies one time about how Malky, considering he used to be one of the most feared, sadistic bastards in Glasgow, now took pride in the simplest structures to his day. He'd quit the firm when the time was right for him and come over all respectable, Rab had said, hobnobbing with doctors and lawyers at the local golf club. He lived on his own in a plush, white turreted house set so far back off the road and up a private drive that you'd miss it if you didn't know it was there. Rab said that's how Malky wanted it. He loved the seclusion and seldom had visitors. But every Friday afternoon he drove to all the way to Glasgow and went into one of the saunas, where he enjoyed the services of a hooker for a couple of hours. Ruby had watched him do this over two weeks the previous year when, on a visit home to see Judy, she had driven down towards Elvanfoot and staked out his house. So tonight she knew exactly where to park to lie in wait. She looked at her watch. It was nearly eight, and she'd been here, hiding in this spot not fifty yards away in the undergrowth by the fish pond at the bottom of his garden, for nearly an hour. She had no problem waiting. She'd been waiting twenty-five years for this moment. It didn't take much for her to summon the image that drove her on. It was never far away.

Ruby hadn't seen Malky up close since that night in her home when he and Rab Jackson had raped and beaten her mother until she was lying soaked in blood, her skull crushed. She'd witnessed it all from below her bed, where Judy told her to hide, and she'd lain there eyes wide in terror, too stunned to move. Even when they had dragged

Judy from her bed and slapped the screaming twelve-year-old all the way into the living room, Ruby lay, shivering, her hand stuffed in her mouth to muffle her terrified whimpering. She had been only eight years old. She could hear the screams. Judy's screams. And it brought her from her hiding place to crawl along the floor to where she could peer through the keyhole. Malky was stripping Judy naked and bending her over. Rab was laughing. They both had a wild-eyed, crazy look on their flushed faces, like they were drunk or on drugs, and were shouting at Ruby's mother that she was a 'fucking grass' and this is what they do to grasses. Rab grabbed her mother's hair and forced her to watch Malky. He wasn't spanking Judy – he was doing the sex thing she'd heard older girls talk about in the playground. She heard her sister let out a piercing scream, like she'd been scalded. Then nothing. But for a split second before she passed out, Judy looked towards the keyhole and Ruby instinctively knew she was pleading with her to stay where she was. She stood with her back to the door, her heart pounding in her chest, choking with fear. And then, suddenly, the smell of smoke. She waited, petrified, as it curled through the bottom of the door and up her legs until the room was filled with grey and black choking smoke. When she heard the front door slam, she opened the bedroom door and a huge belch of smoke and flames forced her back. She covered her eyes and pushed her way through, but at first could see nobody. Then she saw the figure of Judy, crawling towards her. Ruby got on her knees and inched closer to her. Then through the fug she saw her mother's leg, and dragged herself to her. She'd never seen a dead body, but she knew from the look in her mother's face, even through the blood and battered flesh, that the eyes staring wildly were dead. She wasn't breathing and her mouth was open in a silent scream. Ruby struggled to her feet, grabbed hold of Judy's hands and dragged her towards the door and down the stone steps, pulling her until they were out of the building. Seconds later, all the other neighbours came rushing out of the tenement and onto the street, staring up at the blazing building as flames licked through the open windows and lit up the night sky. Judy regained consciousness and gripped Ruby's hand tight as she knelt down beside her.

'Ruby . . . Ruby. Don't say a word,' she'd whispered. 'You must never, ever say what happened tonight . . . or they'll come for us.'

Weeping, bewildered, Ruby held her sister's hand until the ambulance came and took them both away. That was the last time she had seen her for eighteen long years. Ruby had passed out in the ambulance and, when she woke up, Judy was gone and she was in some kind of children's home or dormitory, with other children in iron beds next to her. But no Judy. In the months that followed, she wailed every night in the darkness, shouting Judy's name, until the dormitory door was flung open and someone came in and slapped her bare legs until she stopped. And, finally, they'd told her Judy was dead. That she'd gone into some kind of shock, couldn't speak and then lapsed into a coma and died. That was it. Nothing else.

Tonight was about retribution. Justice. Rab Jackson had his last week, and now it was the turn of Malky. Ruby strained her ears and, in the stillness, she could hear by the low murmur of the engine that he was close by. In a couple of minutes the car appeared over the brow of the hill, coming up his sweeping driveway. Ruby crept out from behind the building as she saw him drive straight through the open garage doors. As soon as he was inside, she moved like lightning, quickly closing the doors and clicking the padlock shut. Then she put the iron bar over the handles to make doubly sure. From her rucksack, she took the two beer bottles into which she had placed petrol-soaked rags. She lit them, then picked up a heavy stone, smashed the garage window and dropped them inside, one after the other, onto the floor, which she had sprinkled with petrol earlier. She heard the whoosh of the fire, and it stopped her in her tracks – she'd heard it in her nightmares all her life. She knew Malky would have smelled the petrol the moment he got out of his car and would have assumed he had some kind of leak in the petrol tank. It wouldn't have dawned on him that his number was up until it was too late. That was the beauty of it. She knew it was risky, but she had to stay just a few seconds longer in case he tried to smash another window in desperation. He did, and she watched as he banged it with his fist, smoke swirling behind it and in front of her. But she was just able to see his face. And then, there was the split second where he looked straight at her, and somewhere in the depths of his evil, twisted, murdering mind, perhaps he recalled her face from some distant place in his past. At least, she hoped so. He looked confused, eyes wide as though appealing to her, then suddenly his expression changed. He must have seen Ruby smile as she watched him choking, pleading. She shook her head, hoping that her face was the last thing the bastard would ever see. Then, as the blaze ripped through the garage, Ruby got into her car and pushed her foot to the floor, knowing that any second now, once the tank in the Daimler caught, the whole place would explode. Bits of Malky would be strewn all over his neat, fake, red cobblestone yard. As she drove over the brow of the hill she glimpsed the moment in her rear-view mirror and she savoured it, just as she had when she drove off after torching Rab Jackson in his villa.

The alarm bells would be well and truly ringing now. She had to be ultra careful. She drove onto the M8 and headed for Glasgow, coming off at the exit for the West End, where, unknown to Jackson, Malky or any of the other arseholes who thought they ran the show, Ruby had a tidy little tenement flat where she could be completely anonymous. Job done.

CHAPTER SIX

Rosie remained in her car close to the Mahoney house after the friendly but emphatic knockback on the doorstep. She looked at her watch and decided to give it another ten minutes. The man who had opened the door of the big sandstone villa to her earlier was around her own age, handsome, tall and athletic-looking with lush sandy-coloured hair and a foppish fringe he pushed back to reveal blue eyes that looked red-rimmed from crying. He bore a striking resemblance to a younger snapshot of Mahoney that Declan had dug out of the *Post*'s picture library archives, so Rosie assumed he was one of the sons who'd flown home from abroad. She was genuinely as sorry as she'd said she was to be intruding at this time, and for a moment the man hesitated as though he were going to say something more, but then he told her the family wanted to be left in peace. He understood she had a job to do, but there would be nothing for her here. He was polite, but unambiguous. As she was backing away she caught a glimpse of an older woman crossing the wide hallway, glancing over her son's shoulder, and their eyes met. She must be the wife; her pale face was etched with sorrow. Rosie remembered from the newspaper cuttings that they'd been married for forty-five years.

From where she'd parked she had a decent view of the steps up to Mahoney's three-storey Glasgow West End villa, and her car was hidden behind the huge sycamore trees that lined the tranquil street in this leafy, affluent part of the city. Rosie watched a steady stream of visitors to the house, mostly older couples, some carrying flowers, grim-faced as they climbed the steps towards the massive stained-glass door. She peered over the steering wheel as they went in, then left after a few minutes, tearfully hugging the young man she'd spoken to on the doorstep. She looked at her watch again. It was already seven, and she still had to hit the door of Gerard Hawkins. Time to move on. She was about to start her engine when another car pulled up close to hers and a woman stepped out. She was tall and slim, dressed in that kind of silky, Bohemian get-up circa late seventies or eighties, big flowing blouse and skirt and flat pump shoes. When she had got out of the car, the woman reached back in and picked up a bunch of white carnations from the passenger seat. She seemed hesitant walking towards the Mahoney house, glancing through the big bay windows, and her steps faltered a little as she got closer. Then she stopped altogether, turned on her heels and came back towards her car, bursting into tears as she opened the driver's door. Rosie dropped her sun visor and slid down a little so she could get a better look without being noticed. The woman got back into the car and sat for a few moments, her head bowed. Then she drove off, wiping her face. Rosie followed discreetly out of the West End avenue and down towards Byres Road.

The woman parked her car in a side street and got out, heading towards Ashton Lane. Rosie found a parking space nearby and jumped out of her car, then followed her as she went up the cobblestone alley of Ashton Lane and turned into the Ubiquitous Chip wine bar. Rosie waited until she knew she'd be in the bar on the first floor before she opened the swing door and headed up the steps.

The Chip was bustling with the usual early-evening drinkers. As well as the Glasgow University students who could afford it, the Chip was a trendy haunt for the luvvies who worked at the BBC TV studios nearby and a known watering hole of all the arty folk who liked to be seen or wanted to network. For any other punters, it was a place where you worked on the assumption that most of the people you met there had at least half a brain. On any given Friday night the Chip may have been full of people who were just as blootered as any other punter in the city-centre bars, but in the Chip you met a better class of eejit, or so the story went. It was busy almost every night of the week, and a number of staff from the *Post* lived in the West End and socialized there.

Rosie ordered a glass of red wine and stood at the bar. The woman sat at a table in the corner, dabbing at the smudged make-up around her eyes, then she sat staring bleakly into space. She'd been a looker in her day, but her lined, tanned face showed the effects of too much sun. She lit up a cigarette as she took a long gulp from a large glass of white wine, and Rosie watched, surprised that by the time she had finished her fag she was more than halfway down the glass of wine. Safe to say that, whoever she was, she liked a drink.

The bar was even busier now, so if there was to be a scene, nobody would really notice. Rosie took a sip of her wine, walked towards the empty table next to the woman and sat down. She picked up a newspaper from the table then put it back down.

'Excuse me,' she said quietly. 'Could I possibly have a word?'

The woman gave her a surprised look but didn't answer, just lit up another cigarette, a slight tremor in her hand.

Rosie lowered her voice to a whisper then moved to the chair so she was opposite the woman. The noise level in the bar increased as a crowd of students came bursting in.

She looked at the woman's eyes, dark brown and blood-shot. No easy way to say it, Rosie decided, so just be up front.

'I'm sorry to trouble you, but I couldn't help seeing that you were walking towards the house of Professor Tom Mahoney earlier on.'

The woman screwed her eyes up, puzzled.

'What?'

'I was there, too. I saw you. But I noticed you didn't go in.' She paused as the woman's eyes did a double take around the bar. 'Look' – Rosie drew her chair a little closer – 'my name is Rosie Gilmour. I'm a reporter. From the *Post*.'

The woman glared at her in disbelief.

'For goodness' sake. Are you serious?' Her expression twisted as though there were a bad smell under her nose. She opened her mouth to speak but Rosie interrupted.

'Look, I know . . . I'm really sorry. But I didn't want to bother the family any further. I'm . . . I'm working on an investigation into the murder of Tom Mahoney. It's a terrible tragedy.'

'Did you follow me here?' The woman looked at her, incredulous.

'Yes, I did. I'm sorry.' Rosie plumped for honesty.

'What the fuck? Have you people got no respect?'

Her voice rasped, a mixture of outrage and too many cigarettes, and her dark eyes blazed. Rosie held her stare and didn't speak for four beats. If she was as incensed as she looked, she'd jump up and leave. She didn't.

'Yes, we do.' Rosie leaned forward. 'We do have a lot of

respect. Especially for a man like Tom Mahoney, who was adored by students and colleagues alike, as well as his own family. That's why my newspaper is determined to find out who murdered him and why.' She ran a hand across her face. 'Please forgive me. I know it's a difficult time. But I was in my car close to the Mahoney house and I saw you going to the door with flowers and then changing your mind. So I'm guessing it was too much for you.' The woman shook her head. Tears came to her eyes.

'What the hell do you know?' She sniffed. 'You people don't know anything about Tom Mahoney or anyone else.' She shook her head and swallowed.

'Please,' Rosie said. 'Bear with me. Can I buy you a drink? I only want a little chat about Tom. I'm trying to build up a background of who he was, from his early days . . . The kind of man he was. I know he was a hugely popular figure at the university.'

The woman stared at the table, tears streaming down her cheeks, as though the floodgates had opened. A waitress came past and Rosie touched her companion's arm.

'Have a drink with me. Just one? Off the record, if you want. What's to lose?

'A Chardonnay,' the woman said softly.

'Large one.' Rosie turned to the waitress. 'And another glass of Merlot.' She stretched out a hand. 'Rosie Gilmour.'

'Marianne Brown . . . Mari.'

Rosie shook the damp hand then let the silence hang for a few seconds. She was in.

'Were you a student of Tom's?' she ventured.

Mari nodded, swallowing.

'You're obviously far too young to be a colleague.'

She hoped it didn't sound patronizing, guessing that Mari would be forty-something, but younger looking, with high, fleshy cheekbones and full, soft lips. Rosie was relieved when they curled into a smile.

'I'm not young. Not by a long shot.' She sniffed and puffed out a gust of air. 'I was once, though.' She glanced around the bar, shaking her head wistfully. 'God! The nights we had in this place all those years ago . . . students and lecturers together . . . A different world. All full of dreams and big ideals . . . impossible ideals.' She sighed. 'I've been away so long.'

'You live abroad?'

'Yes. France.'

'You've lived there a long time?'

'Nearly twenty years.'

'What took you over there?' Rosie probed. 'If you don't mind me asking.'

Mari sat back and touched her neck, looking at Rosie then beyond her into the throng of people at the bar.

'I just needed to get away. From here . . . From every-thing . . . Initially I went for a few months, then stayed on.

Ended up teaching English in one of the international schools.'

'I'm wondering why France,' Rosie asked. 'What's a former student of East European Studies doing in France?'

The waitress arrived with the drinks and Mari drained her glass and put it on the tray. She took a sip of the fresh drink, then pulled out a cigarette and offered the packet to Rosie. She took one and lit them both.

'I wanted to put it all behind me.' She inhaled and let out a stream of smoke. 'I had to. I went down south first and did a post-grad in French so I could teach. I just wanted all the Eastern European crap out of my life.'

They fell into silence and, for a moment, Rosie pictured this tired, defeated figure back in her heady, carefree, student days flouncing around the bar.

'I take it you were Tom Mahoney's lover?' Rosie raised her eyebrows, knowing it was a bit of a hand grenade.

For a moment, Mari stared straight ahead, as though the question had triggered a raft of images. Rosie waited. Eventually, Mari turned to her, sniffed and nodded.

'How very astute of you,' she said, with something of a defeated smile. 'That was before . . .'

Rosie raised her eyebrows.

'Before what?'

Silence.

'Before Katya.' She flicked a glance at Rosie then stared into her wine glass.

The tears came again and she let them run down her cheeks.

Mari had been a final-year student of Eastern European Studies at Glasgow University. She almost blushed as she recalled how just about every female student in the faculty was a little bit in love with Tom Mahoney. One or two of the boys were, too, she smiled, as though she were back on the campus in her heyday. Mahoney was in his mid-forties and drop-dead gorgeous: more than that, he was a force of nature, a highly intelligent, passionate lecturer who could take a subject as dull as the Five-year Plans for the economy of the former Soviet Union and bring it to life so that his students hung on his every word, feeling as though they were living through it. He was also relaxed and witty, drinking in West End bars, where he was sought after by students and lecturers alike. Everyone knew he was married, but it was the early seventies and there was a new sense of freedom among the students and women everywhere felt empowered to be able to sleep with whoever they wanted without judgement being passed on them. There were always rumours that Mahoney had bedded a couple of his students, but that didn't stop Mari from falling for him. She'd slept with him on three or four occasions, none of them planned, and no commitment ever made. Sex was what it was, and Mahoney was quite clear about that. Just before their fling, Mahoney had been on a sabbatical, teaching students in East Berlin for a year. When he returned he was bursting with enthusiasm and determined to make the USSR, its history and current situation more understood and accessible to his students. He took eight of them on what he called a field trip to East Berlin.

'It was there,' Mari said, 'that I saw him with Katya. He introduced her to us as a cultural representative of the East Berlin Department of Education. So, you could take it for granted she was a member of Stasi, the secret police. All government officials were part of Stasi,' Mari said, matter-of-factly.

'Can you explain a bit more?' Rosie asked.

'At that time,' Mari said, 'in East Berlin, and in fact all over East Germany, there were about seven Stasi government spies for every single person in the country. Everyone was spying on each other and informing on each other. It was that kind of climate – even in places of work or in apartment blocks, there was always someone informing on their neighbours or workmates. So when this woman Katya was introduced as some kind of educational attaché, we kind of assumed she'd be a spy. The students joked about it during the few days we were there, because she stuck to us like glue.

'But all the time we could see the little looks and secret glances between her and Tom. It was as if they shared something that none of the rest of us did, and we suspected it wasn't just their love of all things in the USSR. We'd be taken to various areas within the education system and the workplace and given demonstrations of how hard the people worked and strived for their country, and Katya was at the forefront of that. But we could see there was more. Or I could. Maybe it's because, by the time of the field trip, I'd been involved with him, so I was perhaps more sensitive. But to me they were lovers, and my heart sank every single day I saw her.'

'But you knew Mahoney was married, surely? Did you really think more would come of the . . . er . . . situation you had with him?' Rosie didn't want to call it a fling, which is clearly what it was – for Mahoney, anyway.

'Of course I knew he was married and we could never be more to each other than lovers. Look . . . I know it sounds stupid and naive, but I thought we had something special.'

Rosie didn't want to say any more and make her feel worse.

Mari went on to tell her that the week passed with dinners, outings and lectures, visits to historical sites. But she'd sensed that the whole city was shrouded in secrecy and suspicion, and everywhere the people had a glum look of resignation. They'd kept on being shown buildings where industrial innovations were apparently taking place, but the truth was they were far behind everyone in the West. Except in gymnastics and some other sports.

Rosie had nodded, as if she knew all this. She didn't want to admit that her knowledge of Eastern Europe didn't go much deeper than what she had seen years ago on the vests of athletes of the GDR (German Democratic Republic) during the Olympics, and it had often been hard to distinguish the men from the women. She recalled shot-putters with arms like hams who walked like John Wayne, and how everyone had looked miserable, even when they won a gold medal.

'So was that only time you went on a field trip like that?'

'Yes. When we got back I was with Tom only one more night, and it was then that I asked him straight out about Katya. He was furious. He told me to mind my own business, that anything he did was nothing to do with me. He became completely indifferent to me after that. But I was in love with him. Long before anything ever happened between us he had made me feel like I was the only woman in the world. I never saw him after we left university, and hadn't heard anything about him in years, because I moved away. But when I read about his murder in the newspaper it took the feet from me. I cried all day. It was like a part of my life – which I realize now was part of me growing up – like part of my life had been ripped away. He was such a big influence in so many people's lives.'

CHAPTER SEVEN

Ruby came off the slip road for Glasgow Airport and drove to the car-rental place, where she dumped the car and quickly dealt with the paperwork. She'd booked it over the phone with a credit card in one of several aliases she'd used in recent years as she travelled the world hiding Rab Jackson's money in offshore accounts from Jersey to the Cayman Islands. She had three different passports for that kind of travel, and two she kept for her own personal use. She couldn't believe how easy it was to defraud her way around banks, hotels and airlines. Money opened every door – especially in banks, where the suits were only vaguely interested in where it came from, as long as you had stacks of it and were lodging it with them. She had safety-deposit boxes in banks from Amsterdam to Paris to Malaga, where she kept wedges of cash in sterling for her own use, just in case the shit ever hit the fan. Which it just had.

She crossed the car park to the taxi rank and headed for the city, asking the driver to drop her in Hyndland Road, close to where her flat was. Ruby had bought the two-bedroom flat in Dudley Drive three years ago, working on the basis that the West End wasn't the kind of place you ran into the lowlifes employed by Jackson's prodigy, Tony Devlin. The foot soldiers lived in the high-rise flats or the run-down council-housing schemes like Drumchapel or Possilpark or Maryhill, where they were handy for their smackhead customers queuing at the door morning, noon and night. Their dens were kitted out with slick TVs, stereos, all mod cons, their wardrobes bulging with designer clothes – all of it blagged from shoplifters and fraudsters. And they lived side by side with decent, ordinary families who busted a gut to try to keep their children out of the clutches of the drug dealers, gangsters and loan sharks who had most of the neighbourhood on the end of a debt that could never be repaid. The lieutenants, slightly higher up the food chain, would be holed up in some of the shiny new city-centre developments, either in the Merchant City or downtown, overlooking the River Clyde, bought by their bosses with laundered drug money and rented to them for next to nothing but on paper for several hundred a month. They were the guys who did anything they were told, organized shootings, beatings or slashings for unpaid drug debts. They'd be used to travel up and down to Manchester, Liverpool or London, making drops or picking up drugs in bulk. The chances of seeing any of this bunch in Dudley Drive, with its neat tenement flats side by side in uniform anonymity was minimal. You seldom saw your neighbours and nobody asked any questions. That was perfect for Ruby.

She walked briskly down the street and into the second-floor flat. It felt good to enter the broad hallway and go into the living room, with its old wooden floors and Rennie Mackintosh replica fireplace, and its big, solid bay window. This was the closest thing she'd ever had to a home since she was a kid. But there were no real signs of herself in it – except for one print of two small sun-burnished children on a beach somewhere in Ireland. She'd bought it years ago because it reminded her of happy days with Judy and her mother. She went into the kitchen and turned on the cold-water tap, let it run for a while, then took a glass out of the cupboard and drank it, enjoying the taste of the pure Scottish water she missed when living abroad. She filled the kettle and switched it on, then went down the hallway and into her bedroom. She sat on the king-size bed and opened the wardrobe doors, running her hand over the half a dozen blouses, tops and jackets on hangers. Seven or eight pairs of shoes. This was just about all she had. A wave of loneliness washed over her. Pick it up, she told herself. No more of that shit. She closed the wardrobe doors.

*

Ruby flopped on to the big sofa with her feet up on the coffee table and opened her laptop. She signed into one of her email addresses and it pinged with two new emails. She knew who it would be even before she opened it, and she cursed herself for ever giving her email to Tony Devlin. He'd have been bombarding her with messages on her regular email address – the one she used for business in Spain and the one most people had for her. But she should have kept her private one to herself. It was careless. She opened the email and read it:

> Ruby – Where the fuck are you? You're not answering your phone, or your normal email. Everyone is looking for you in Spain, but you're obviously not there. Are you? This does not look good. I'm losing patience. I know you're out there, so call me. Don't make me come looking for you. Tony.

It had been sent at eight o'clock this morning, probably not long after Tony got word of Malky Cameron's surprise barbecue. Ruby knew Tony would also have been calling her mobile within hours of her driving away from Rab Jackson's villa, but she'd tossed both her phones into the sea near Marbella before driving north. She hadn't checked her emails – she didn't need to. She knew everyone would be trying to reach her.

She sat back, staring at the high ceiling, suddenly transfixed by a spider spreading its web further across the cornicing so that the whole side of the ceiling would end up as one big web, where it could lie in wait, knowing that once its prey got tangled up, there was no way out. It wasn't much different from the web she'd just cut herself out of. The difference for her was that she'd walked into it six years ago with her eyes wide open, knowing that once she was in, there might be no way out. She pictured Tony's face, fired up with barely contained anger, telling the arse-holes he surrounded himself with that everything was under control now that he was in charge. She knew what a chillingly evil bastard he could be if anyone double-crossed him. She'd seen him shoot one of his men in the chest for trying to pull a stroke with a delivery of coke from London. It was brutal and ruthless, and he'd insisted Ruby remain in the room while he dealt with what he called 'a bit of business' with one of the lads who had fucked up. It was the first time she'd seen anyone executed, and she had to hold on to every scrap of her strength not to faint from the shock as the blood bubbled out of the guy's chest when he shot him. The last thing she could show was weakness. Tony was Jackson's prodigy. When they'd left the office that night he'd taken her to dinner, and he had talked as though nothing had happened. Afterwards they went to his flat, where he made love to her for the first time. That was a shock in itself – the sex had been tender, caring – no sign of the cold-blooded killer he'd been two hours earlier. Ruby had been expecting a hungry, wild encounter, bordering on brutal. And part of her – the dangerous, reckless side she had, which she knew would never allow her to be a normal person – had been looking forward to it. Instead, he'd kissed every part of her, gently asked her permission before he entered her, and afterwards held her for a long time as if she were a baby, while she stroked his back until he fell asleep. A complete psychopath, Ruby had thought as she lay awake, the rest of the night. She realized then her biggest mistake was to have gone anywhere outside of the business relationship she'd had with him. On the occasions they had met over the last three years on the Costa del Sol, she took care of Rab Jackson's money – laundered it through businesses, investments, construction companies, as well as charities in UK and abroad.

Ruby looked up at the ceiling again. The spider had now spread its little empire right across to the other side. Her mind flashed back to the café at King's Cross and the moment the gun was fired at the old guy's head. She could still see his shocked expression as he slipped down the chair and onto the floor. And then the grief, panic and frustration of his friend. She felt sorry for them. Then she remembered the look on the sandy-haired guy's face as he went into his pocket and passed a packet over to his friend. Those bastard Eastern Europeans hoodlums must have shot him for a reason. The newspapers had been full of speculation. But she had that piece of paper, with the name of some company or other on it. She fished it out of her handbag. J B Solutions. She keyed it into her laptop and hit the search key.

Half an hour later Ruby picked up the two newspapers she'd taken from the café in Judy's care home. It had crossed her mind yesterday to make a call to the papers, just throw them a line about the company. But she'd worried they might end up tracking her down. What the fuck did she care anyway? Why bother? She could help the papers, but what would she get in return? She didn't need the money. But maybe she could do something for the first time that wasn't about her. All her grown-up life had been about survival. And once she'd tracked Judy down, she built everything around her sister, squirrelling away enough money to make her life better, dreaming that one day Judy would come back to her. Then, ultimately, her life was about retribution. But that was finished now.

She picked up the *Sun* and flicked through the story, then the *Post*. She found the news-desk phone number at the bottom of the back page and dialled it. She asked for Rosie Gilmour, the name of the journalist under the headline, but when she was put through it was a young man's voice. She told him she needed to talk to Rosie regarding the murder of the university lecturer, and she could hear the voice perk up. Rosie would be in later, he said, but he could take the information. When he seemed reluctant to give out Rosie's mobile number, she told him to forget it and he quickly reeled the number off. Ruby hung up then punched the numbers into her phone, in the impulsive, instinctive way she'd been doing things all her life.

'Hello. Is that Rosie Gilmour?'

'Who's this? Your number didn't come up.'

'Never mind who it is. Am I talking to Rosie Gilmour?'

'Yes, you are. What can I do for you?'

Ruby paused and took a breath. She wanted to ask what the fuck were they playing at, suggesting the woman who left the café was in any way involved with the men who did the shooting. Where was the fucking evidence? She tightened her stomach to restrain herself.

'Hello? You still there?'

'Yeah.' Ruby cleared her throat. 'Well, what you can do for me is stop saying in the paper that the mystery woman who left the café after that shooting at King's Cross may be linked to the murder of that old university guy. Because it's total shite.'

Silence.

'Right. And how do you know this?'

Silence.

'Because it was me.'

Silence.

'You're the woman who was in the café? Seriously?'

'Why? Have you had a lot of women phoning you up and telling you they were in the café?' She knew she sounded sarcastic.

'Actually, no. But are you really that woman?'

'Yeah.'

'Can we meet?'

Silence.

'I've got information you might want. About the men who did it.'

'Listen. Can we meet? I don't like doing things over the phone.'

'J B Solutions,' Ruby said. 'If you're smart, look into them.'

'J B Solutions? I'd really like to talk to you. No names, no pack drill.'

'J B Solutions. Find them. Then maybe we can talk.'

'I'll make sure my newspaper doesn't in any way relate you to the shootings in future articles. You have my word on that. But I'd really like to meet. Can I get your number?'

'No. I'll call you.' Ruby hung up.

CHAPTER EIGHT

It was nearly midday by the time Rosie left the office and made her way up to the West End to doorstep Gerard Hawkins. She'd briefed McGuire about her talk with Mari, and he'd agreed with her that they wouldn't write it as a story but would play their cards close to their chest. It was a fantastic snapshot into Mahoney's life, and right now it was all they had to go on. Declan had dug up only a few old colleagues who'd said nothing other than that Mahoney was a brilliantly committed individual and a gifted teacher who would be sorely missed. Mari's story had revealed a little of who he was, and if Mahoney had been involved with a woman in East Berlin, it opened up all sorts of possibilities.

McGuire was already excited about the murder of Malky Cameron in his garage last night. Declan had been dispatched to Ayrshire, where the police had set up an incident room in the village close to Cameron's home.

Rosie could catch up with that later, but right now her priority was Hawkins, and she steeled herself for a tough doorstep.

Hawkins lived a stone's throw from Glasgow University, where he'd lectured for more than thirty years before retiring. The electoral register had him at his home address for the past twenty-three years. Rosie guessed he didn't want to move too far from where his life was, to stay within sight of the spires and cloisters of the ancient university. The register also said he lived alone, and Declan's background checks hadn't thrown up a wife.

She climbed the steps to his front door, imagining some clichéd crusty old pipe-smoking lecturer in a tweed jacket with elbow patches sipping claret in a dimly lit, book-lined living room. She rang the doorbell and waited. Nothing. She glanced over her shoulder – no sign of other hacks – then she rang again. Still nothing. Automatically, she bent down and looked through the letterbox, hoping some old West End snob didn't call the cops to say she was snooping. But, in this neck of the woods, you'd be more likely to be lynched for being from the tabloids than for breaking and entering. Rosie stood for a few moments then in her peripheral vision she caught sight of a curtain twitching on the bay window of the ground-floor flat. She waited, then heard movement in the hallway. The sound of bolts being clicked and slid back, and a key being turned. The door opened just enough for her to see the face behind the chain.

'Gerard Hawkins?' Rosie put on her most expressive keen but sympathetic face.

She could see blue eyes, greying hair and a fresh face – nothing like she'd imagined. His eyes were a bloodshot and a little puffy.

'Wh– what? Who are you, please?'

'I'm Rosie Gilmour, Mr Hawkins. I'm from the *Post*.'

She heard him take a deep breath.

'I've got nothing to say.'

'But Mr Hawkins . . . I know you were a very close friend of Tom Mahoney all your life. I'm really sorry to intrude, but I'm investigating his murder.'

'The police are investigating Tom's murder. Leave it to them.'

'Are they? Are they really investigating? Are you sure?' Rosie took a bit of a flyer, hoping for a reaction.

Silence.

'Look. What on earth do you expect me to say?' He looked drained. 'Tom was my closest friend. I lov– We were friends for forty years. He was a brilliant individual . . . and now he's been murdered. I'm . . . heartbr– I'm devastated. I knew him all my life . . .'

His voice trailed off. Rosie's stomach tightened. He looked vulnerable, broken. She might get lucky.

'I'm sorry, Mr Hawkins. Really sorry.' Rosie locked her eyes on his for a couple of seconds. 'It's just that . . . well, the police are not saying very much at all. Of course they'll be investigating the murder, but they're putting nothing out to the newspapers and, if I'm honest, that makes us suspicious.'

Silence.

'Suspicious of what?'

'That somehow they are thinking it might go away.' Another flyer.

Hawkins eyes blinked twice, thick, dark eyelashes emphasizing the blue.

'What do you mean by that?'

'I'm not sure. But I don't think they're making this as big an issue as it should be.' She paused, cleared her throat. 'Tom Mahoney was a hugely respected figure within the education system here. He was a known expert in Eastern European Studies, revered all over the UK and abroad. Yet to me, and to my editor, it doesn't look like the police are giving his murder any kind of priority. To tell the truth, I've seen them making more of an attempt to highlight a drug dealer or a routine killing. But this was very different . . . as you know. This . . . this was an execution.'

He gazed at Rosie, his expression somewhere between frustration and grief.

'That's exactly what it was . . . an execution.' His voice was barely audible.

'Can I come in and talk to you, Mr Hawkins?'

He looked through her and didn't speak.

Rosie swallowed. She had one shot left.

'Look, Mr Hawkins. I know about Katya.'

He couldn't have been any more startled if she'd poked him with a cattle prod. He frowned, searching her face. Then he pulled back the chain and opened the door.

'Come in.'

Game on. Rosie hoped the shock didn't register on her face. She'd envisaged three kinds of knockbacks on this doorstep – no answer, the door slammed in her face, or, at best, a single sentence that would perhaps make an inroad for the future. But here she was following Gerard Hawkins into the stained-glass vestibule, where he stood for a couple of seconds, his eyes flicking a glance up and down her before he closed the door behind them. Then he walked along the wooden hallway without uttering a word. Rosie stepped softly behind him, searching for an appropriate opening line. She scanned the array of framed photographs hanging crookedly on the walls – snapshots of his life – and she clocked a black-and-white photograph of two very handsome young men who had to be him and Mahoney a lifetime ago. They looked like matinee idols from some old movie, Hawkins with a cigarette hanging lazily from his lips and a panama hat pushed back on his head. The other young man, the double of Mahoney's son, who she'd encountered on the family doorstep last night, had his arm around the shoulder of his friend. The caption, in pencil behind the glass, read 'East Berlin, 1966'.

'Is this you and Tom?' Rosie asked, as respectfully as she could.

He stopped in his tracks and turned his body to face her, his eyes resting fleetingly on the photograph.

'Yes,' he nodded, his lips twitching as he tried to find a smile.

He looked so distraught it crossed Rosie's mind that they might have been lovers.

Hawkins spoke without turning around.

'I loved Tom. But we weren't lovers,' he said abruptly, as though he'd read her thoughts.

'Oh . . . I wasn't . . .' She knew she sounded flustered. 'I mean, you look like a couple of carefree student mates.'

He stopped at the entrance to the living room and turned to her. This time he did smile, as though he was remembering something.

'It's all right,' he said. 'We were so close at that time that a lot of people used to think we were together.' He gazed in the direction of the window. 'If only . . .' Again, his voice trailed off.

'Oh.' Rosie berated herself for not being able to think of something else to say.

Hawkins motioned her to the sofa, while he stood behind a crimson leather armchair next to the unlit open fire.

'I've just made some tea. Would you like a cup?'

'Yes, please, I would, thanks,' Rosie replied, grateful and

a little surprised he was being this cooperative. 'Black, please, no sugar.'

He disappeared out of the room, and she could hear the clatter of crockery as she gave the place the once-over. It looked like it had been put together by interior designers, all tasteful decor, bright but not over the top, stylish prints and curtains, but it still had a traditional feel to it. It was neat, too neat for a man, but it felt lived in. He returned with two mugs of tea.

'I'm afraid I've got no biscuits,' he said apologetically, handing her a red mug. 'I haven't been able to go anywhere really since I . . . since I came back up from London.'

Rosie gave him a sympathetic nod.

'I've been on a diet for ten years anyway, so you're doing me a favour . . . Ger—' She paused. 'Can I call you Gerard?'

'Of course.' He nodded.

There was a little awkward moment as Rosie wondered if he was going to speak first, and when he didn't she decided to start with a tactful question.

'Gerard, have the police given you any kind of motive for or idea about why Tom was targeted in this way?'

He said nothing, sipped his tea then looked at her.

'They don't have to. And, anyway, I don't think the investigating officers have any idea what is going on.'

Rosie gave him a confused look.

He put his mug down on the table and took a deep breath

then let it out slowly, examining the backs of his hands and picking at his fingernails, his eyes blinking several times as though he were afraid of what he was about to say but was at the same time bursting to say it.

'Tom was assassinated, which we all know, Rosie. But . . . he was executed for a reason.'

He went silent, either for effect, or because he was choosing his words carefully. Rosie waited, but he said nothing.

'You mean, like the Eastern Europeans had been tracking him or something?'

'Who knows for sure? How else would these men know we were in that café at that time? But there is more to it than that.' He sat forward, clasping his hands, and looked Rosie in the eye. 'Look. The only reason I let you in here is because you mentioned you knew about Katya.' His eyes narrowed. 'What exactly do you know? Who have you spoken to?'

'Well . . .' Rosie swallowed, knowing she'd over-egged the pudding with her claim on the doorstep. 'I spoke to a former student. Er . . . I don't want to say who it is, Gerard, as I don't want to betray her trust. But she did talk to me, and it was she who told me about Katya.'

'Mari.' He looked through her.

Rosie didn't answer and tried not to blink.

He half smiled. 'Ah Mari. Poor, beautiful, vivacious Mari. She fell for Tom the way everyone did – including me, if

I'm honest. But then he met Katya and that was that, I'm afraid. Nothing was ever the same again.'

Rosie didn't really know where this was going, but she hoped he hadn't let her into his house so he could talk to her about Mahoney's philandering.

'But who is Katya exactly?' Rosie asked.

Silence. Then Hawkins spoke.

'Therein lies the story, Rosie.'

Rosie waited for him to go on, but he didn't. She felt a little stab of impatience.

'Was Tom Mahoney a spy?'

The question hung in the stillness of the room and Hawkins stared at the floor for so long Rosie glanced down in case there was something there. Then he raised his eyes slowly and looked at her.

'Yes. He was.'

'Really?' Rosie hoped she didn't sound as excited as she was. Silence again. He looked as though he was waiting for her to say more. She ventured, 'I've been given information through a contact in London, suggesting that he was a spy. And that's the truth, Gerard. So . . . so why do you think he was murdered?'

Hawkins sighed, shaking his head, and didn't speak for few seconds.

'Because he was about to blow the whistle. He was about to go to the media over what happened to Katya. About everything. He was going to blow it all sky high.' He picked up his mug and sipped from it. 'The government couldn't risk that.'

A little wave of excitement flipped across Rosie's stomach. She could see this on the front page.

'Are you saying he was assassinated on the orders of the government?'

Even saying it out loud sounded ridiculous.

'Well, we'll never prove that of course.' He raised his eyebrows. 'Or will we? Will you ever prove that?'

'Not unless someone can give me a lot more than a claim that the government murdered him.'

Hawkins stood up and crossed the room. He stared out of the window for a second, his back to Rosie. Then he turned around.

'Minutes before Tom was gunned down in that café he handed me a package across the table. He knew they were on to him – told me himself . . . Those was his exact words: "They're on to me, Gerard" . . . and he knew he would be next.' He shook his head. 'He entrusted the package to me. And I promised I wouldn't let him down.'

'Who was on to him, Gerard? Who was going to get rid of him?'

'MI6, of course. They couldn't risk leaving him as the only loose end. He had too much information.'

'MI6? You're saying they had him killed by these Eastern European guys?'

'Yes . . . Or it was made to look that way. I don't know.'

Rosie struggled for something to say next. She was choking to ask where the package was, but this was going so well – if a little off the wall – she had to be patient.

'Are you going to tell me all about this, Gerard?'

'What will you do with it if I do? Will you and your newspaper publish the story or will they be got at by the powers that be? There are dark forces at work here.'

Christ, Rosie thought. She could hear McGuire asking her was this guy wearing a straitjacket when he told her all this.

'That's not how my newspaper works,' Rosie said, looking him in the eye. 'My editor is very courageous when it comes to stories involving the establishment. We don't bow to people – not government, not cops, not gangsters.' She sat up straight and put her mug on the table. 'If we can get a story that is nailed down and passed by our lawyers, then we will publish. But I need a lot more than just your word and what you've just said. I'll need the information that Tom gave you. I'll need that level of proof.' She took a breath. 'Look, Gerard, I'm not going to mess you around, but I can tell you now that without anything material you have that can help prove this, then Tom's murder will go down as a random shooting by some Eastern European gangsters. End of story. So if we're going to take this forward – and I really want to – then I need your help.'

They sat in silence for what seemed like an age, the ticking clock on the mantelpiece keeping time with Rosie's beating heart. Gerard played with a ring on his finger, twisting and turning it, the light from the window catching the garnet set in gold. Rosie was trying not to take a deep breath, watching and waiting.

Eventually, Gerard spoke.

'Okay. I'll tell you a story . . .'

CHAPTER NINE

'Something is ringing all my bells, Gilmour,' McGuire said as she walked into his office. 'Is there some kind of lone vigilante out there catching up with all the bad bastards? First that old arsehole Rab Jackson in Spain, and now Malky Cameron? Two useless scumbags off the face of the earth in a week. We need to get a real handle on this. The punters love this kind of shit. Declan's down in Ayr for the press conference. I mean, they're both stiffs now, so we can say what the fuck we like about them.'

'I know. The cops are throwing a party. I'm seeing a contact later. He's been moved to the Serious Crime Squad, so that means he gets his finger in all the pies. He might have a bit more intelligence on who bumped them off.'

Rosie sat down on the sofa. 'But first, I've got even better news for you.'

McGuire came out from behind his desk and stood

resting his backside against it, looking down at her. He raised his eyebrows for her to begin.

'I went up to Hawkins' house last night,' Rosie said. 'And much to my amazement, I got in.'

'No way!'

'I did.' She flashed a triumphant smile. 'And it's incredible stuff.'

'Come on then.' He sat opposite her, swung his feet onto the coffee table and clasped his hands behind his head. 'I've got twenty minutes till the conference. Make my day.'

'Okay,' Rosie said. 'I won't go into everything, Mick, because we can talk later and decide how we play this, but his story will blow you away.' She paused for effect. 'Mahoney was a spy for Stasi – you know, the East German secret service?'

'Fuck! Seriously?'

'Yep. But that's not all. He was also spying *on* them – for the Brits.'

'You are *fucking* joking.'

'I'm not.'

'Hawkins knows all this? He has proof?'

'Well, that will be the difficult part. Nobody ever has real proof of these things. Stasi isn't there any more since the Berlin Wall came down, and MI6 are hardly going to admit it.'

McGuire took a deep breath, and Rosie waited while he digested the information. Then he put his hand up.

'First of all, Rosie, what's Hawkins like? Is he a doddery old fucker who would make this up?'

'Not at all. He doesn't seem like a fantasist.' She shrugged. 'But of course you never know. He and Mahoney have been friends since they were students together. Hawkins is gay.'

'Friends? What kind of friends? The kind that play Hide the Sausage when the lights go out?'

'No.' Rosie chortled. 'He loved Mahoney, but I think he established pretty early on that Mahoney liked women. Lots of them, as it's turning out.'

'So what did he tell you?'

Rosie walked McGuire through the full story that she had gleaned from Hawkins during the hour-long chat in his house.

Over a second mug of tea, Hawkins had painted a vivid picture. Back in the sixties, he explained, life at the university campus was a melting pot of idealism and excitement. Young people everywhere seemed to want to be part of some revolution or another. If it wasn't the students rioting in France, it was in London, in Italy, in the US over Vietnam. Tom Mahoney was at the forefront of everything. He'd become the darling of the student union and had particular kudos because his studies took him to Eastern Europe. Many of the lecturers were left wing anyway and relished the upsurge in every area of life. It was a time when people could sense change and power, and the youth were rebelling about everything, from the music they'd been raised on to everything that spelt authority and establishment. Mahoney's studies had taken him to East Berlin for a while, where he spent almost a year, and his thesis was an in-depth study of life there and the Communist ethos in practice. He was drawn to it. After he graduated and began lecturing, he maintained his Soviet connections, at one time going on sabbatical and working at the University of East Berlin. So, Hawkins had said, it was almost a natural process that the Soviets would bring him on board. He was recruited by the Stasi. He had a KGB handler whose name was Katya, and that's where it all went wrong. He fell for her. Rosie had patiently listened to Hawkins's story, resisting the urge to ask him to cut to the chase and tell him how this was all connected to Mahoney's murder.

McGuire interrupted.

'Right. I'm loving this, Rosie. But I don't have time for the full-length version of *Doctor Zhivago*, so what's the bottom line?'

'I was just painting the picture for you,' Rosie said, faking a huff.

'Save it for the colour piece. How did MI6 get involved?'

'That, I don't know for sure. Hawkins isn't sure either, but he suspects Mahoney was a double agent for years. Says he only came out with everything in the last few months to him. Before, he would never tell him anything about his secret life. Mahoney did admit he'd had an affair over there and that there was a woman he'd fallen in love with, but because of his family he had to keep it quiet. Then, of course, the Cold War ends, and there's no need for him to continue spying because Stasi and East Germany are broken up in the new Europe.'

McGuire nodded.

'So,' Rosie continued, 'it was a few years later, after he retired, that he was asked by MI6 to get involved again – this time in the fight against crime. As we both know, the forces from different countries share information on who the major players are. They pull together, all trying to track down drugs, money laundering, organized crime. You know how it was . . . After the fall of the Soviet Union, everyone's suddenly a gangster or some shifty oligarch. Well, apparently, Mahoney was working along with the newly formed united German force which was collaborating with the UK and the rest of Europe in trying to crack open the major crime cartels.'

'So it was the Eastern Europeans who bumped him off?'

'That's the thing. Not sure who it was. That's why Hawkins has all the information. He was handed a package by Mahoney in that café just before Mahoney was executed. He said he hasn't even opened it yet. But Mahoney told him all about it and said it would expose everyone.'

'Christ. Really?'

'Yep. So he says. Mahoney was going to blow the whistle,

because the people they were trying to bring down were involved in the illegal arms trade – selling guns to gangsters and stuff like that. He told me the bones of the story.'

'And?'

'Well, it seems they set up some kind of sting, and the woman, Katya, who he'd brought in to help because of her old East European and Russian connections, got killed. Mahoney was convinced they sacrificed her. The sting didn't entirely fail, as they managed to capture a couple of the bad guys. But the Brits were trying to keep the whole thing quiet, because for years *they'd* actually been dealing with the gunrunners too.'

'What? Dealing with gunrunners? The government?'

'Yes. Let me explain. The same firm that supplied them with weapons was also supplying the gangsters here and abroad. And occasionally the firm would buy guns from Eastern European gangsters. Unbelievable! But that's what he said!'

'Are you seriously telling me that the British government and police force dealt with illegal gunrunners?'

'Yes. And the army. But they didn't know it until it was too late. Hawkins said it was a company down south called J B Solutions. The Home Office and the MoD had been dealing with them for years, unaware of their links to organized crime. J B Solutions had been supplying the British army and police force for years. But it's the very same company the gangsters get their weapons from. Much of the illegal guns and weaponry you get on the streets today originated from this company. Who knows what we'll find once we start digging. I haven't had a chance to look at the cuttings yet.' Rosie paused. 'Oh, and by the way, Mick, I got a call from a woman who said she was the mystery Scot in the King's Cross café when the murder happened. She's raging at our story because she thinks it makes her look as if she's under suspicion. But she said one thing to me – J B Solutions.'

'What? She said that?'

'Yep. Where did that come from?'

'No idea. She said for me to look into them, and that she would call me back. Then she hung up.'

'Christ!'

'I'm sure she'll call back. She must know something.'

'Fuck me! I love the sound of this. All that's missing is 007 and Miss Funnyfanny.' He got to his feet and picked up the schedule for the morning editorial conference from his desk. 'Prove all this, Gilmour. That should be easy for a woman like you.'

They walked towards the door. Rosie loved McGuire's belief in her, even if he was being a bit sarcastic. But she knew she was a long way from proving anything.

'Hawkins said he'll help me. He wants the story out. So I'm hoping he'll come across with the package Mahoney gave him in the café. As for the mystery Scot – we'll just have to hope for the best.'

CHAPTER TEN

Rosie had been tempted to ask the barman at O'Brien's for a large gin and tonic, but thought better of it. The problem with doubles was you drank them just as fast as singles. They had that little extra kick, but if you really felt like knocking back a few, then one double got you in the mood and before you knew it you'd be three doubles down the line and anything could happen after that. Sensibly, she ordered a single, and took as conservative a drink as she could manage.

She turned over all the information Hawkins had given her last night and reflected on her conversation with McGuire. He was hooked into the story, but proving it was another matter. Getting it past the *Post*'s lawyers was sure to be even more tricky. She needed some breaks.

'Here's your fancyman now.' The silver-haired barman cast his eyes beyond her. His strong Donegal accent had become refined over the years, working among the movers and shakers who frequented O'Brien's, so these days his dulcet tones sounded more like those of a friendly radio presenter than a barman.

She didn't need to look over her shoulder for the Strathclyde police detective sergeant, her close friend and trusted contact. They met regularly in O'Brien's, and anyone who saw them together would probably assume they were a couple. The barman knew different – in fact, he knew just about everything that went on at the other side of the bar: who was glad-handing who, and why; what top lawyer was trying to get the drawers off which pretty young trainee; the who's who of the shiny-suited drug dealers – no amount of expensive tailoring could camouflage the knuckle-trailing thugs they were.

'Hello, my little ray of sunshine.' Don put his arms around Rosie and gave her a tight hug. 'You're looking fantastic!' He brushed his hand over her hair and gave her a kiss on the cheek. 'You look as if you've been on holiday – considering you've been getting hunted down by a mob of angry Ulstermen.'

'Nah,' Rosie said. 'I have friends in low places . . . and they spoke to the lads in Belfast with all the clout. The dogs were called off. But it took a bit of time.'

'Good. You need to watch your back, though. There will always be the random nutter who might take a pop at you.'

'Yeah.' Rosie didn't need reminding of that. 'Anyway. Pint?'

'Stella,' Don turned to the barman. 'Tell Stella, I love her,' he crooned.

'So how's life in the Serious Crime Squad, big man? Is it just like on the telly?' Rosie gave him a playful dig in the arm.

'Oh aye. Very glamorous, too. Instead of dragging some wee ned out of his bed at four in the morning in a housing scheme, we get to batter into the bigger fish. It's great. I cannot tell you the joy when you collar some arsehole coke dealer who's living out in Bearsden, and you get to empty his designer furniture onto the front garden while you rummage through his five-bedroom villa. The neighbours love it. It's especially rewarding if you can do it while his wife is getting into the Range Rover to go to the hairdresser.'

'Sounds like my kind of party. You should invite us along to one of your busts. Would be good publicity – cops warning they will hunt the dealers down . . . that kind of line. I could get that in the paper.'

Don looked at her. 'Yeah, well, you'd need to talk to the press office for that.'

Rosie shot him a sarcastic smile.

'You're not going all straight on me now, with the press office phrasebook? "I can confirm there has been an incident," when there's actually a man lying in the street with a knife in his back.'

Don snorted.

'If I was, I wouldn't be here, darlin'. I just have to watch my step a bit, till I get bedded into the squad.'

'Sure,' Rosie said, clinking his glass. 'To the next head of the CID.'

Don's neck went a little red under his collar, and Rosie knew he'd at least entertained the notion that getting to the top of the heap wasn't an impossibility. At forty-one, though, and not yet an inspector, it probably wasn't going to happen.

'So what are you up to?' Don said. 'You were saying you were on another story?'

'Yeah. I arrived back in London just as that Glasgow Uni lecturer got shot in the café at King's Cross, so I stuck around there for a couple of days.' She sipped her drink. 'Are your guys looking at this? Given that it was Eastern Europeans who bumped him off?'

Rosie decided to keep her powder dry. She studied Don's face for a flicker of knowledge. Tom Mahoney's murder was a top-level investigation so she guessed the SCS might have been briefed by the Met. If he knew anything, his face didn't show it.

'Don't think so. It's a Met investigation. Leave it to them. They'll maybe get in touch when they're looking for help. As usual.'

Rosie changed the subject.

'So what do you make of the Malky Cameron murder? Bit of a coincidence with him and his old partner in crime,

Rab Jackson, getting done in the same way within a few days of each other. Old scores?' Don nodded.

'Looks like it. But although they were supposedly retired – Rab was in Spain for years – they were still well enough respected by the arseholes running the show these days. And Rab was still a player. Jackson and Cameron were old school. None of these pricks here would bump them off. We're pretty sure of that.'

'But are the two murders connected?'

'Have to be.'

'Any hints?'

Don took a long drink and offered Rosie a cigarette. She declined, and he lit his, taking a lungful of smoke then blowing it upwards, watching it swirl as though it were a look he'd perfected over the years. It went well with his craggy, slept-in looks and five o'clock shadow.

'Something *has* shown up on our radar actually. I don't know if you know the history of Jackson and Cameron.'

'Bit before my time,' Rosie said. 'But I know they were evil bastards. Pimps, armed robbers and into hard drugs. Back in the early days it was all extortion and protection money from all the places in the city. They controlled everything. Anyone who didn't play ball with them ended up in a shallow grave.'

'That's right. But one of the older guys in the squad was telling us that detectives questioned them about twenty-five years ago over the death of a woman in Glasgow.

A hooker, Jackie Reilly. She worked from her flat up in Maryhill, and she had to pay Jackson and Co. in kind for not forcing her on to the street. They wanted a free shag, they went there. She had two kids. Girls. Then one night she gets burned to death in a fire in the house. The kids were rescued. The wee one, Ruby, managed to pull the big sister out. Amazing story at the time, apparently. You should check back the cuttings'

'I will,' Rosie said. 'Jackie Reilly ... Ruby.' She memorized the names. 'What was the other girl's name?'

'Judy. She was the older one. Thing is, when the cops arrived, no bastard had seen a thing. Usual shite. Everyone looked the other way. But my pal says that the cops found out from a wee snitch that Jackson and Cameron had been up there just before the fire. The word was they started it.'

'Really? Why? Surely she wasn't going to refuse *them* sex?

'No. Wasn't that. Word is that she passed information to the cops on a case they were working on. Think she must have got rumbled by Jackson, so it was payback time. He was that kind of bastard. Didn't matter if it was a woman. You stepped out of line, you were history. Even with two weans.'

'What happened to the girls?'

'Don't know. One of them had been raped. The older one. The injuries showed it. She didn't speak. Couldn't. Just a poor wee lassie. Went into some kind of shock and didn't utter a word to anyone. The wee one got taken into care. So they got split up. My pal said they heard later that the older girl died – Judy. Poor wee bastard. But Jackson and Cameron got away with it. They knew they were safe as long as everyone kept their mouths shut.'

'That's awful. So what do you think?'

Don sniffed and swallowed.

'Don't know really. The only person with a grudge who wasn't a gangster was that wee lassie Ruby. But nobody knew what had become of her for years. Then . . . wait for this . . . around eighteen months ago the Serious Crime Squad was working on a case, and my mate was on it and they stumbled across information that Ruby was working with Jackson.'

'What? Hard to believe, that. I mean, if she witnessed what happened that night – assuming she might have. She'd hardly go and work for the men who did it, would she? Where did that information come from?'

'Yeah, I know what you're saying. That's what we thought: hard to believe. But she was photographed during some undercover surveillance operation in Spain which UK police were working on with the Spanish and Dutch cops. There was nothing to link her involvement, as such, to the case, but one of the snitches tipped the cops that her name was Ruby and she was from Glasgow. They didn't have a surname. There was some kind of search done to trace what became of Ruby Reilly, but it seems she'd disappeared off the radar screen after she dropped out of university.

She'd studied accountancy but didn't graduate. Nobody knows what became of her. Amazing, really, that she amounted to anything if she saw what happened that night to her mother and sister. And the way she was dragged up, her ma a hooker and stuff. Some start in life, eh?'

Rosie nodded, swirling the ice in her almost empty glass, remembering her own early days, the men occasionally coming to her house and the noises she heard at night. She drained her glass.

'One for the road?'

'No thanks,' Rosie said. 'Better not. I've a lot of work to get done tomorrow.'

Her mind turned over the story of the Scottish woman who allegedly did a runner from the King's Cross café.

'Listen, Don, would you be able to get CCTV footage of the street outside the King's Cross café immediately after the shooting? I thought they might have released it by now, as an appeal for any witnesses.'

Don shrugged. 'I think, if they haven't put it out then there's a reason for it. The cops won't throw everything out there all at once. But I'll see if I can get it. Why?'

Rosie finished her drink and put it down on the bar.

'Just thinking. I'm going to sleep on it.' She eased herself off the bar stool.

'You want me to help you sleep? We could spoon.'

Rosie smiled.

'Nah. You'd disturb my train of thought. Come on. I'm

knackered. First couple of days back at work and I feel like I need a holiday.'

Don finished his pint and they walked through the swing doors and out into the street.

Rosie turned to him.

'Would that cop who remembers the Jackie Reilly murder all those years ago talk to me?'

'Why?'

'Just curious.'

'Curious, my arse. Why?'

'Honestly, Don. Just a bit fascinated by what you tell me about the Ruby girl. If I make any progress with my blue-sky thinking, you'll be the first to know. I can promise you that. Could you ask him to talk to me totally off the record?'

'Sure. I'll give you a bell if he's up for it. But he's only got two years till he retires, so he might not want to associate with a hack like you. I'll try.' He kissed her on the cheek and walked away.

Rosie opened the doors to her balcony enough so she could hear the sounds of the city revving itself into a new day. It was only eight in the morning and too chilly to sit outside, but by the look of the sun breaking through the clouds Glasgow was basking in the glory of an unusual Indian summer. She pulled her fold-away director's canvas chair close to the open doors and sat with her feet up on a table, clutching a mug of freshly brewed coffee. The buzz of the Charing Cross traffic was music to her ears. It was good to be home.

In the beginning, when she'd fled to Sarajevo in the wake of the *Post*'s revelations about the UVF coke dealing, McGuire had suggested she sell her flat altogether. It was too risky to stay there, he'd told her, but Rosie had protested – if the scumbags were determined to get her, they'd already know by now where she lived. She couldn't live her life moving house every time she felt under threat. Her entire working life was on the move – if not in the UK, then abroad on some investigation or refugee camp in a far-flung land. She needed somewhere to come home to, not some sterile crash pad, she told McGuire. Her own place, with all her own things, her clutter, was her sanctuary, where she could feel grounded. She hadn't mentioned that now, more than ever, she needed something that was rooted, because at the moment she didn't have TJ on the other end of the phone in his Glasgow flat, or cooking dinner for her or meeting her after work for a drink. Right now, that seemed like a long time ago – but it wasn't. She rested her head back, letting out a long breath as she reflected on her last telephone call to him in New York nearly two months ago. She'd replayed it in her head so many times while she was in Bosnia, hoping it would lessen the impact. But it never did. If ever anybody knew how to fuck up their life, it was her. She re-ran it again:

'What do you mean, you're going to Bosnia, Rosie? Why are you not coming here?'

TJ's tone had been somewhere between bewilderment and hurt. It wasn't an easy question to answer.

'It's just a spur-of-the-moment thing, TJ. Try to understand,' she said. 'I've got to go tomorrow. I need to get out of here.'

'Bullshit, Rosie. You could go to London for a couple of days, hide up in a hotel, then get to New York. Don't insult my intelligence. I can see what's going on here . . . I—'

Rosie interrupted. 'TJ, nothing's going on. What the hell do you mean by that?'

But the truth was she didn't even know herself why she'd phoned Adrian instead of TJ when McGuire had told her she had to leave the country.

'Why did you phone Adrian? Why not me? It's that simple, Rosie.' He sounded hurt now.

'I know . . . I know it sounds simple. But I . . . I . . . didn't want to come to New York. I mean . . . the way you live, the work at the club, the hours you keep. That's not what I want right now. I want to be away somewhere I know I can be safe. My head is all over the place after all that shit in Spain. You know that.'

'You'd be safe here. We could be together every day. Every night . . .' His voice trailed off. 'Christ, Rosie!'

There was a long silence, then TJ spoke.

'Is there something going on with Adrian and you? I know you're close, I know he means a lot to you with everything you've been through. If I'm honest, it's crossed my mind before.'

'What? Jesus, TJ! Nothing's ever happened between me and Adrian. I promise.' Rosie wanted to hit back. 'And anyway, what about the time I called you and Kat was in your apartment over there? You managed not to tell me that.'

'I told you. It wasn't important.'

'What wasn't?' Anger, jealousy and paranoia simmered. She knew she was going too far, but she couldn't stop herself. 'Have you been involved with her?'

'Fuck's sake, Rosie. How many times . . .'

'Just tell me.'

'I told you I won't discuss anything like that with you. It's irrelevant.'

'But you ask me about Adrian?'

'Because you're in the middle of a crisis, with your life at risk, and you're fucking off to see him and not me. That tells me a lot.'

'It tells you nothing – other than the fact that I don't want to be in New York.'

'With me.'

'TJ . . . I can't do this right now.'

There was a long pause, and she could hear him breathing.

'You know what, Rosie. I can't do it either. I . . . I can't do it at all . . . Maybe we should both take the next couple of months to think about things. To be honest, I told you a long time ago you weren't ready. And you know what? You're still not ready. I don't think you'll ever be ready, Rosie . . . As long as there's the job, the people you meet on it . . . All that shit. That's what drives you, and right now I can see it's driving you away from me. Because when *the chips are down it's not me you're coming to. It's some guy you met on the job.'*

'TJ. Listen.'

'No, Rosie. I need to go.'

She could hear the rage and hurt in his voice, and she pictured his grey eyes, the little laughter creases around them, and could see the sadness in his expression. She missed him already. Christ almighty! What was she doing?

'TJ.'

'Go to Bosnia, Rosie. Just go. Let's not say anything right now, or we both might say something we regret.'

And with that, he had hung up.

Rosie finished her coffee and stood up. If she didn't give herself a shake she'd be engulfed with melancholy and guilt all day. She was still trying to make some sense out of the situation in Bosnia with Adrian. She'd get her head around it all eventually, she told herself as she padded along the hall and into the shower.

CHAPTER ELEVEN

More than half of the houses in the street were derelict, with steel front doors and bricked-up windows. 'Fuck the polis' was spray-painted on the grimy rough-cast walls and alongside it a childlike drawing of a man's private parts. Only three or four flats in each block showed any signs of being occupied in the long grey row of drab houses. If hope had ever existed here, it had shrivelled and died among those left behind when the rest had moved on in search of a stab at a decent life. Four children bounced on an abandoned sofa in the front garden of a block of empty flats. They stopped when the car pulled up and eyed it suspiciously.

'Welcome to Blackhill.' Rosie turned to the taxi driver. 'The land opportunity forgot.'

He glanced at her then stared miserably back out of the window. 'You going to be a while up there? If I sit around here too long some of these wee bastards will start noising me up.'

Rosie pulled her handbag onto her shoulder and sighed as she opened the door. It would have been good to have company to go into a building like this, in an area like this, but the driver was right. It wouldn't be long before the kids started to surround the car, poking at the windows, kicking the tyres. If he went inside with her, the wheels would be off his car in ten minutes and there would be a posse waiting to rob them when they came out.

'I'll be as quick as I can. Just drive around the block if you feel a bit conspicuous.'

She could see he was twitching. It was only his second shift with the taxi firm contracted to the newspaper, and he'd been telling her on the way up from the office how he'd taken early retirement from his job as an area manager with a double-glazing firm, hoping to make a few quid driving taxis to pay for his annual golf-club membership. He assumed that working for a newspaper, he might be accompanying photographers and models on a photo shoot somewhere scenic. Maybe Loch Lomond. Nobody told him he'd find himself in a shithole like this, he complained to Rosie, nervously adjusting all his mirrors so he could see in every direction. Poor bloke. He had definitely drawn the short straw on this hire.

Rosie gave the kids a cursory 'How's it going, guys' as she

walked past them up the steps and into the building. It smelled of piss and dampness. A couple of crushed super-lager cans littered the hallway, along with several discarded syringes and a used condom. Whoever Humphrey Boyd was, he certainly hadn't made it as a career criminal.

Don had come back to her quicker than she'd expected, phoning first thing this morning to tell her the name of the snitch who'd tipped off the cops all those years ago about Rab Jackson and Malky Cameron being in Jackie Reilly's house minutes before it went up in smoke. Don's cop colleague didn't want to meet, or say anything other than that he'd been a young detective at the time but he'd heard that the snitch was called Humphrey Boyd, known as Humphy. Humphrey wasn't exactly a name you expected to find in this part of Glasgow's wild north side. Rosie had found a phone number for him, but she hadn't called it, deciding it was better to arrive unannounced. She liked surprising people.

She knocked on the door. Three raps, loud enough to be heard, but not loud enough for whoever was inside to be hiding everything that was stolen in case it was the cops. Nothing. She waited. Then knocked again. This time there was a loud, jungle, screeching sound, like a wild animal.

'What the fu—' Rosie muttered to herself.

She listened again, expecting to hear the noise of a television with the volume up too loud. Nothing. Then suddenly the door chain rattled and a key was turned in the lock.

'Who is it?'

'Er . . . You don't know me. Sorry to disturb you. I'm looking for Boyd? Hum— . . . Humphrey Boyd?' Rosie didn't want to use the nickname yet.

'Aye. That's me. Who are you?'

'My name's Rosie Gilmour. I'm from the *Post*. Can I talk to you a minute?'

To her surprise, the door opened. She did a double take when she saw him. The voice came from somewhere at least two feet below her. The hunchback stood there, looking up, his head crooked to the side. Humphy. Jesus Christ almighty! In Glasgow, a hunched back was not a hump, but a humph. Either Humphy's parents were stark raving mad, horribly cruel, or just had a warped sense of humour to call their hunchback baby Humphrey. You couldn't make this up. She stood staring, speechless.

'Whit is it? You no seen anybody wi a humph before?' He gave her a gap-toothed grin.

'No . . . Er . . . Yes. Sorry. Hum . . . Humphrey . . .' She was flustered.

'Just call me Humphy, darlin'. Everyone else does. We don't do politically correct in Blackhill.'

'Oh, right. Er . . .' Rosie tried to regain her composure. 'Actually, I was expecting somebody much older. Don't know why really.' She lied to cover her awkwardness. 'Can I come in and talk to you?'

'Whit aboot?'

'About Jackie Reilly. Remember her? Years ago she was burned to death in her house? Maryhill?'

Something like rage and hurt flashed across his eyes and his mouth turned down at the edges. He took a deep breath and made a rasping sound at the back of his throat.

''Course I remember. How could any of us forget? Poor Jackie. She was all right, man. And them weans.' He stepped back into the hall, opening the door wide. 'In ye come.'

Rosie followed him along the mosaic-patterned vinyl floor of the hallway. She stopped in her tracks when she heard the loud screeching again.

'It's all right. It's only Cheetah.'

'Cheetah?'

'Aye.'

As he opened the door to the living room, Rosie at his heels, she suddenly felt a little light-headed. Did she just see a chimpanzee jump off the top of the television? Shit! She did. She really did. Because it was now bouncing off the armchair and heading straight for her.

'Holy fuck!' She felt unsteady on her feet. 'It's a monkey! You . . . You've got a monkey in the living room? Jesus, Humphy! What the f—?' She supported herself against the wall.

Humphy grinned as the monkey leapt into his arms.

'She'll no touch you. Don't be scared. She's a wee pet.'

Rosie opened her mouth to speak but nothing came out. She thought she'd seen it all, everywhere, all over the world. But she really was standing here in a derelict building in Blackhill with a chimpanzee in a print frock staring at her as it pulled Humphy's ears and ruffled his hair. She pinched her arm, just to make sure she wasn't in one of her vivid nightmares.

'But . . . Who . . . I mean . . . Why? You can't just keep a monkey in the house, Humphy.'

'She's no mine. She's my mate's,' he said, as though that made it all right. 'I'm looking after her while he's away to Benidorm for a wee holiday. Tam's in the Merchant Navy. He brought the chimp home from somewhere. The Congo, I think.' He hugged the monkey, who hugged him back. 'She's great company. I might keep her longer, once my mate goes back to sea. She's called Cheetah. Like the one in *Tarzan*. Remember?'

Rosie nodded, still taken aback.

'Sit down,' Humphy said. 'Want to hold her? She doesn't bite.'

'No.' Rosie put her hand up quickly as she sat on the sofa. 'She looks fine where he is.' She glanced around, struggling for something to say, as the monkey drew back her lips in a grin, revealing the stained brown teeth of a forty-a-day smoker. 'Er . . . She's a nice monkey . . . I'm . . . I'm just a bit surprised. It's not something you see every day.'

'Aye. Well. I don't get many visitors.' He turned to the monkey. 'Do we, Cheetah?' He stroked the chimp's head.

Rosie caught a hint of sadness somewhere behind his eyes.

'Okay. Anyway, Humphrey . . . I mean Humphy . . .' She couldn't believe she was calling a hunchback Humphy. 'Er . . . about Jackie Reilly.' She pulled her notebook and pen from her bag. 'I'm looking back at the story, and somebody told me that Rab Jackson and Malky Cameron were involved and were questioned by cops at the time.'

'Who told you that?'

'A cop contact. Said they got a tip-off from somebody who informed them those two had been at the house before the fire.'

Humphy gave her a shifty look. He stroked the chimp's arm. 'Aye. I heard that, too.'

Silence.

'What cop were you talking to? Did he say who told him?'

'It was just someone who remembered at the time. I don't think he was the cop who was told. He said it was someone more senior. Didn't really know, though.'

Silence. Humphy stared at the grimy net curtain on the window. Rosie watched him, but kept one eye on the monkey.

'Jackie was all right. She was my neighbour for years up there in Maryhill. We were all close up in the tenements in them days. I mean, I know she was on the game an' that, and I felt for her weans a bit, but she was all right. She was only doing it to survive, same as every other fucker did back then. Same as now. You do what you have to do. I don't blame her.'

'Do you think they were involved in the fire? Jackson and Cameron?'

'Too fucking right they were.'

Silence.

'Humphy. Did you tell the cops? Did you have a contact with the CID you talked to from time to time?'

'That what you've been told?'

'Well. Yes. But obviously I'm not going to tell anyone that. I'm just talking to you privately here. Totally just you and me ... Er ... and Cheetah ... But it's important. It's for a story I'm working on, not just the murder of Jackson and Cameron last week. It's wider than that.'

Humphy's mouth twisted in anger.

'Served the bastards right what happened to them. And good luck to whoever did it and had the sense of justice to do the same to them as they did to Jackie. I was well pleased with that.' He turned to the chimp. 'Weren't we, Cheetah?' The chimp rattled its teeth and somersaulted onto the floor.

Rosie braced herself as it climbed on to the sofa beside her. She put out her hand, praying it wouldn't bite her fingers off.

'She's all right. Just let her play with your hair or something. Don't be nervous.'

'Okay,' Rosie said warily. 'So . . . I'm looking for some more information. I'd like to track down the cop you spoke to.'

The monkey twirled her hair with its fingers.

Humphy sat for a moment then sniffed.

'Ach! He'll be well retired by now. He went on to be a DCI. He was a big mate of mine. I knew that, no matter what, I could always rely on the big man to sort me if I needed anything. Discreetly, like. Nobody ever knew anything about us. But he gave me a few quid down the years for information. It came in handy. There's not a lot of work for hunchbacks, you know – not since that fucking movie.' He chortled.

Rosie couldn't help smiling at Humphy's black humour. There was a little determined glint in his eyes. What a shit start in life, with bullies making his life miserable in a place like this, where a disability, physical or mental, made you a target. If you had the misfortune of being a hunchback with a name like Humphy, you had to develop some kind of thick skin and a barbed sense of humour.

'Would you tell me his name?'

'What you going to do about it if I do?'

'I'd like to talk to him. That's all. Discreetly. Like the way we're talking. Off the record.'

Humphy went silent for a few seconds, staring at the floor. Then he looked at Rosie.

'All right. I think maybe I can trust you. Don't know why really. You've got a kind of honest face. My big polis pal's name was Thompson. Roddy Thompson. Top man. Haven't heard of him in ten years, though. Good bloke . . . for a polis. Don't even know if he's still alive. Lived down Ayrshire somewhere.' His eyes narrowed. 'But this didn't come from me, okay?'

'Of course. That's great, Humphy. Did you ever hear about Jackie's kids? The two girls?' Rosie asked.

'I heard the older one died. She lived for a few months or weeks or something. She'd been raped. They bastards did it. Then she died. Don't know about the wee yin. Wee Ruby. She was a character. She'd have punched any one of the wee boys in the close flat out if they stood on her toes. Tough wee bastard. She was the image of her ma to look at. Pure gorgeous, by the way. But that night when they took her away, the wee thing was greetin' her eyes out. My heart went right out to her.'

'Did you ever hear any more of what happened to her?'

'Nah. Nothing. Maybe she got adopted or something. I hope so. She was a good wee kid.' He got up and went across to the window, gazing disconsolately down at the street. 'Same as a lot of the kids here. They start out the same as the weans from the posh places. Just wee lumps of things, all innocent. Then it's life that fucks them up. It's living in a place like this with guys like Cameron and Jackson all hanging around waiting to pick them up and give them all the stuff that makes them think they'll be like the posh people. They'll have money and motors. But it's all shite. I love wee kids but, it's what they turn into, and it's not their fault.' He went across and lifted the monkey off

Rosie's lap. 'To tell you the truth, that's why I'm better off just with Cheetah here. She's the best wean I've ever had.'

He went back and stared out of the window, lost in some depressing reverie. It didn't get much weirder than this, but he did have a point.

Rosie waited for a minute and, when he didn't speak, she stood up.

'Yeah. I know what you mean. You've been a big help, Humphy. And don't worry. Nobody will ever know. I'll be in touch.' Rosie left her card on the table as she headed out of the living room.

He didn't even turn around.

CHAPTER TWELVE

Just as the taxi dropped Rosie in the car park of the *Post*, her mobile rang. Gerard Hawkins. She got out of the car before she answered it, and headed for the front door. 'Rosie?'

He paused, and Rosie thought she detected an anxious intake of breath.

'Yes, Gerard. How are you? Everything all right?'

'Yes ... Well ... Actually, er ... I'm not quite sure.' He was edgy, and Rosie found herself automatically walking back towards her car. She pressed the key, unlocking it.

'What do you mean? Something wrong?'

'Listen, Rosie. Are you very busy? I'm wondering if you could come up to the flat. You know ... that matter we talked about the other day? I've got something to give you.'

Rosie hoped the little triumphant 'Yesss!' in her head hadn't actually come out of her mouth. He was giving her Mahoney's envelope.

'Of course, Gerard. I'll come straight up now. You okay?'

'Yes. I think so . . . But there's something I want to talk to you about.'

'I'm getting into my car now, Gerard. I'll be there in less than ten minutes. Just relax. Make sure all your doors are locked.'

Rosie sped out of the car park and up towards the West End, swearing at every red traffic light and jumping at least one set as angry motorists honked their horns.

'Gimme a break,' she muttered. 'Shit. Something's wrong. I know it.'

She picked up her phone and was about to dial McGuire when she changed her mind. He'd tell her to hang on until he sent someone with her. Maybe it was just Hawkins getting a little freaked out because of Mahoney. Perhaps the delayed shock from the murder was all beginning to get to him. But her gut instinct told her different. Finally, she was past the university and up the long tree-lined avenue of old sandstone buildings where Hawkins lived. She ditched her car and raced towards the house. On the doorstep she took a deep breath and rang the bell. She didn't even wait until he had time to answer before she bent down and opened the letterbox.

'It's me, Gerard.'

She could see him coming up the hall.

'Hello, Rosie. Thanks for coming so quickly.' He stepped back to let her in.

His face was grey and unshaven and his greying hair unkempt. He pushed it back self-consciously.

'Sorry, I'm a bit of a mess. Didn't sleep a wink last night.'

They walked down the hall and into the kitchen, where he had two mugs sitting on the worktop.

'Coffee?'

'Please,' Rosie answered, relieved that, although he looked rough, he wasn't going to pieces.

'What's happened, Gerard? You sounded worried on the phone.'

'Come,' he said. 'Into the living room.'

He motioned her to sit on the sofa and handed her a mug then set his down on the table. He went across to a small cupboard on the wall, opened it with a key and took out a Jiffy envelope. He turned to Rosie.

'This is it.' He clutched it to his chest. 'It's the package Tom handed to me that morning, just before he was executed.' He swallowed hard and handed it to her.

Rosie could see how choked he was, and she had to put aside her desperation to rip open the envelope and look inside. She placed it on her lap.

'So has something happened? Has there been a problem?'

'I don't know.' He sat down, shaking his head, then leaned forward, his elbows on his knees. 'I just get the feeling I'm being followed or something.'

'Followed? Did you go out?'

'Only for a newspaper and back yesterday evening. Then when I got back to the house I just had the feeling someone had been in here.'

Rosie frowned. 'Has anything been moved? What made you think that?'

'It was as if someone had been in, looking around, but nothing was ransacked or anything. I'm not even certain if there has been anyone here, I've just noticed things – like a small rug in my bedroom has been pulled over and put in a different place. I'm sure I didn't do that. I never move that rug. It's at the other side of the bed and it seldom gets walked on. But last night it had moved, and then I noticed a couple of drawers were open. But nothing was taken, as far as I can see. I want to know why someone would come in the house, and, if they were looking for something, why they didn't pull the place apart. I had the package hidden in a leather bag I keep at the back of my wardrobe with old photographs in it. I only took it out today. It would have been hard to find unless someone knew what they were looking for. I'm glad I hid it now.' He seemed to shiver.

'But would they really be looking for this?' Rosie held up the envelope. 'How would they know it was here in the first place?'

He closed his eyes, pinched the bridge of his nose with his finger and thumb.

'Those men. The killers. I've been thinking back. They were in the café when we came in. I can't remember how many of them. Then, after a few minutes, another bloke came in and joined them. I just happened to notice that, and actually, I forgot even to tell the police. I've been so distraught. But perhaps he was following us, and they were probably watching us from the café. They could have seen the package being handed over.'

'Yes. I suppose so.'

Rosie knew he was right. Perhaps word was only now filtering back to whoever ordered the killing that Mahoney had handed a package over. In the immediate aftermath of the execution the priority would have been to get the assassins away, and they would have gone straight to ground. She decided not to share her thoughts with Hawkins. It would freak him out even more.

'I wanted you to have the material, because I made a promise to Tom that I would get the information out.' His voice dropped to a whisper. 'I promised him. But now I fear they're on to me.'

'What about the police?'

He shook his head.

'I . . . I don't trust them. I can't trust anyone . . . well, apart from you, I hope. I'm not even sure who killed Tom, and that morning in the café he was convinced it was MI6 who were on to him. But I just don't know. I only know that I'm frightened.'

He looked as though his life were falling down around him.

'You need to go away, Gerard. Get out of here and don't tell anyone where you're going. I can organize it for you. Get you on a plane, or get a car to drive you somewhere. Maybe up north, somewhere quiet?'

He nodded.

'Yes, I know. I'm already making plans. I've packed, and I'm leaving first thing tomorrow. Thanks so much for your kind offer, but I'll make my own way – get in my little car and disappear. You're right. Probably up north for a bit, and then maybe take a ferry to the Shetlands or the Orkneys. I spent a lot of time there as a child in summer holidays. I still go on sailing trips there. I can go someplace from that area by ferry if I want to go abroad – the long way.'

He was trying to be pragmatic, but Rosie sensed how acutely alone he was.

'I wish you would let me organize something for you.'

'No. Honestly.' He seemed to shudder as he looked around. 'I don't feel safe. Not even in my own home.'

'Then leave tonight, Gerard. Now. With me.'

He managed a thin smile.

'Thank you, Rosie. You are really very kind. But I'll manage for the night, and I'll be up as soon as it's light and on the road.'

Rosie sighed as she stood up.

'If you're sure. But I really think if you feel worried you should come with me and I'll get you into a hotel for the night.'

'No.' He got to his feet. 'Thanks.'

She didn't want to push him any further. They stood facing each other, Rosie not quite sure what to say to him but suppressing an urge to hug him. She held out the envelope.

'Gerard . . . I want to thank you for this.'

'I haven't looked in it, so I'm not sure what's there. Could be Tom's old shopping list . . . The old bastard did have such a wicked sense of humour.'

He gave a little chuckle, shaking his head as though he'd pricked a memory. Then his face crumpled and he put his hand to his mouth to stifle a sob.

'I'm so sorry,' he said, tears spilling out of his eyes. 'I . . . I miss him so much.'

Instinctively, Rosie took a step forward and put her arms around him, feeling a little awkward to be embracing a relative stranger.

'I know how hard it must be for you,' she said, because she didn't know what else to say. 'But I'm sure Tom would be happy that you have carried out his wishes.'

She eased herself away from him, and he sniffed, regaining some composure.

'You will get better, Gerard. In time,' Rosie said, and she meant it.

He nodded.

'I'm stronger than people think.' He gripped her arm. 'Please, Rosie. Promise me you will not let me down.

Promise me you will tell Tom's story in your newspaper. It's all that matters now.'

Rosie put her hand over his. 'Trust me, Gerard. When I study what is in this envelope, and if it is as incriminating as Tom believes it is, then I will tell his story. Nothing will stop me.'

'Thank you. That's all I can ask.' He led her down the hall.

'Will you phone me when you're somewhere far away from here?'

'Of course. I'll call you by tomorrow afternoon. You'll have read the contents of the envelope by then, I hope.'

'You bet.' Rosie smiled. 'I'll have it read by tomorrow morning – even if it takes me all night.'

He gave her a long hug before he opened the door.

'Good luck, Gerard. Please keep in touch.'

He nodded.

'Go on, Rosie. Tell the story. Don't let Tom's death be for nothing.'

She turned back as she walked down the steps and gave him a mock salute.

The darkness had come down and Rosie subconsciously quickened her step as she walked up the long, deserted avenue towards her car on the corner. A gust of wind whipped up the sycamore leaves piled up beneath the half-naked trees. She thought she heard footsteps behind her and turned around, but there was no one. Christ! She was getting as freaked out as Hawkins. She walked even faster, feeling her heart race, her boots clattering on the pavement the only sound in the street. A front door slammed shut and she jumped. She got to her car, breathing hard, and climbed inside, immediately locking the doors then taking a long breath and letting it out slowly. She started the engine and put the lights on full beam then reversed and pulled out onto the road. Did she see a figure in the shadows on the grass verge in her wing mirror? Calm down, she told herself. It was probably someone taking their dog out. Rosie was glad when she turned onto Woodlands Road, towards the reassuring city-centre evening traffic buzz. She drove towards her flat at St George's Mansions and was about to turn into the car park when she decided to do a quick drive round the block to make sure nobody was following her. She wished she could phone TJ, or Adrian, or Don. Anyone, just to ask them to come and spend some time with her. But there was nobody. She could call Matt, the photographer she mostly worked with on major stories, and ask him for a drink, and he'd be happy to come up. They'd already talked about the story and he was waiting until he was needed for the pictures. She looked across at the envelope on the floor of the car beside her handbag. Come on, Gilmour, she told herself. Get a grip. You've got a whole night's reading to do. She drove quickly around the corner and into the car park then sprinted up to the door and inside, rushing up the steps and inside her flat, quickly sliding across the extra locks and bolts McGuire had insisted were fitted after her last attack. She stood with her back to the door and let out a sigh of relief. The flat was like Fort Knox: double locks on every window and panic alarms in every room. There were also CCTV cameras on the front of the building trained on the car park and street nearby. She was safe. She needed a drink.

Gerard thought he was dreaming when he saw the blurred image before him. It looked like a man – two men even – silently drifting towards him out of the darkness of the doorway into his bedroom. A shaft of moonlight shone through the gap in the curtains, and he could see them now as he began to focus. He opened his mouth to gasp, but a hand was suddenly clamped over it. Someone big and heavy climbed onto the bed and sat on his legs, trapping him where he lay. Then he saw the syringe. He shook his head violently, trying to free himself from the grasp of the big man holding him down, pinning his shoulders back, forcing his face to one side. The room was silent except for Gerard's muffled cries behind the hand pushing on his face. Then he felt the sharp prick of the needle in the side of his neck and he could feel his pulse pumping inside his ears. Somebody was telling him to 'Ssssh'. He thought he heard someone say, 'Just let yourself relax. It's over now.' In his stupor, he thought it sounded like Tom. Because now he could see Tom in the faces of both men, who sat motionless, watching him. He was drifting away. Flickering images of his life ran through his mind. He was young again, with Tom, striding out in the Scottish hills in blazing sunshine; drinking champagne in Venice pavement cafés; walking in the rain-soaked cobbled streets of East Berlin. He could feel a smile spread across his face as he closed his eyes. It was over now.

CHAPTER THIRTEEN

Rosie was groggy from lack of sleep. It had been well past midnight when she'd finally flopped into bed, having spent the evening sifting through the contents of Mahoney's envelope. Some of it was like a handwritten journal, his tiny scrawl difficult to read. She was grateful there was also a typewritten overview, detailing why he was blowing the whistle. It looked like he'd been compiling a dossier in recent weeks or months.

J B Solutions, arms dealers, came up several times. A subsidiary company, Damar Guns, international arms dealers, was also named; they had had their licence revoked. But, Mahoney wrote, they were still dealing. He described how they had recently shipped container-loads of weapons to Nigeria – 'guns and ammunition, enough to equip an army'. He posed the question, 'How the hell did they do it without a licence . . . they didn't. They had a fake one.'

Damar Guns also supplied gangsters and were rotten to the core, he wrote.

Rosie ploughed on to the end, looking for an answer, then she found it. Mahoney had been part of an international criminal investigation looking at fake paperwork for arms being exported abroad, and he was part of a sting set up to trap them.

Other names, highlighted with a pen, meant nothing to her, though Mahoney's notes identified them as key MoD figures – 'spooks', he'd actually written, 'just like me' – and said they'd been in key positions back in the sixties and seventies. She couldn't believe her eyes. There were old black-and-white photographs of men, some of them with women who Mahoney identified as Russian prostitutes. Then one killer paragraph jumped out from his narrative, and Rosie's eyes popped. Alex Goldsmith. Now Sir Alex Goldsmith, Mahoney wrote, the former head of MI6.

She stared at the snapshot of a young Goldsmith sitting on a sofa, smoking a cigarette, with a drink in his hand and a half-naked woman draped over him. She glanced at her watch and was about to phone McGuire to tell him when she decided to leave it till she saw him in the morning. There was also a grainy black-and-white photograph of a beautiful young woman – Katya – with the date – 1968, written in pen on the back. But no image of how she had looked in recent years.

Rosie's head was buzzing when she went to bed and switched off the light. Then she got up, paranoid, and made another check to make sure all the doors in her apartment were securely locked. When she finally did fall asleep, her dreams were of shadowy figures in cold Eastern Bloc apartments and dismal hotels, and a vague nightmare of a woman trying to run away after being shot in the back.

In the morning she stood in a cold shower for as long as she could bear it then downed a quick jag of strong coffee to get her mind firing on all cylinders before heading to the office. It was going to be a long day.

McGuire closed the door and told Marion not to disturb them when Rosie came in clutching the envelope.

'Right. Let's hear it.'

'I'm knackered,' she said, rubbing her eyes. 'I spent half the night reading this and trying to get my head around it, then I couldn't sleep for planning how to write it.'

'Great.' McGuire smiled. 'You can sleep tomorrow.'

Rosie opened the envelope and carefully took out all of the photographs, spreading them on the coffee table in front of them.

McGuire sat down opposite her.

'He gives a kind of narrative confirming everything I've been told – about him being targeted by Stasi when he was over there as a young lecturer,' Rosie began. 'There's detail about the kind of spying he did at that time, and how he worked for both sides. So there's plenty of juice. But the big story is the stuff about J B Solutions. They're the guys who supplied the government and police with guns and ammunition for years, yet at the same time their subsidiary wing, Damar Guns, was also supplying Nigeria in the middle of a war back in 1997. It's all in here. Damar's licence was revoked when the UK government discovered what it was doing. But the company continued to sell arms to Nigeria – enough to equip a whole army, Mahoney says . . . So someone was turning a blind eye.'

'Who? Who was turning a blind eye? Does it say?'

'Well, yes. He's described it. Apparently, the licence and papers were faked up and stamped officially when shown at borders. According to him, since the fall of the Soviet Union, both Damar and J B Solutions have been involved in illegal arms dealing with Russian and Eastern European gangsters.' Rosie pointed to the sheaf of paper. 'It's all in there. That's what the sting was about. They were trying to catch Damar's people setting up a deal selling arms to Russian gangsters based in Spain and the UK. Mahoney explains it all. And also, he's quite frank about his affair with Katya.'

'Fucking magic! But a lot of the stuff on the company will be hard to prove. They'll just say Mahoney was a fantasist who read too many spy novels. The lawyers will have a seizure. But even if we get nothing else to use, we can write about his affair and his claims that he was a spy. That's all good.'

'Well.' Rosie grimaced. 'I feel for his poor wife if we blast his affair all over the front page.'

'Tough. Nobody forced him to get his leg over.'

'Yeah. But he has stipulated in his letter that he would like Katya referred to as his trusted confidante and friend, as well as his KGB handler.'

'Yeah, right.' McGuire snorted. 'She obviously took the handling part quite literally. Is that her?' McGuire pointed to the black-and-white snapshot of the beautiful young woman.

'Yeah. It's from a while ago, though, in his heyday.'

'"Ice-cool Beauty" . . . I can see the headline . . . What's that film called that they're all talking about at the moment? . . . *The Spy Who Shagged Me*?' He laughed.

'Yeah. But wait, Mick. There's another belter in here.' She sifted through the photographs.

They scanned them together. Several were black and white, and from the clothes and hairstyles had clearly been taken back in the sixties and seventies. They were of men and women drinking and partying.

'Who are they? What's the significance? It's years ago.'

'Look closely.' Rosie pointed to one particular picture of a man who looked as though he was in his thirties, with a Russian woman draped around him. It was in a bar some-where. 'Don't you recognize him?'

McGuire shook his head, peering at the picture. 'Alex Goldsmith. Sir Alex Goldsmith now. Former head of MI6,' Rosie said triumphantly.

'Fuck me! You're kidding. I don't believe that.'

Rosie leaned forward, picking the photograph up.

'Look closely. It's about twenty years ago, but there's no mistaking. Plus, Mahoney has written about it. Look.'

She took the note out and showed him the piece in the narrative that referred to the picture. She read it out. Here's what Mahoney says:

> *We were in Berlin . . . It was 1977 . . . Goldsmith and Co. had come over for a few days to do a bit of missionary work . . . On a need-to-know basis. Dinner was preceded by the purest Russian vodka, then afterwards in the bar, it looked like it was all getting a little crazy. I was with Katya, so after a couple drinks we bailed out, taking the opportunity to be alone, and headed for my apartment.*

'Fucking hell!'

'Of course, they'll deny all this on a stack of bibles,' Rosie cautioned. 'Even with the pictures, especially of Goldsmith. They'll say it was all in the line of duty . . . life of a spy and all that . . . They're expected to get involved with girls . . . or at least they do in the movies. But it's still a good tale.'

'Who's the other guy next to him?' McGuire pointed to the photograph. 'And who are these two privileged-looking wankers? Definitely Brits.'

'No idea. It's a long time ago. We'll probably never be able to find out.'

McGuire sat back. He puffed his cheeks and exhaled in little drumbeats, gazing at the ceiling.

'So what do we write tomorrow? I want to get a flavour of this moving – nobody will have a sniff of what we have.'

'We've got so much material here, Mick. We should drop a big hint of what we've got in the paper tomorrow and see what happens. Why don't we leave the Goldsmith angle out for the moment and just write something revealing that Tom Mahoney was a spy for Stasi – *and* a double agent. We can throw in plenty of colour without naming names. Keep our powder dry.'

'That'll put the wind right up the MoD.' McGuire shot Rosie a mischievous grin.

'Of course. But they won't know what we've got. They might even think we've taken a flyer. They won't know we have all this.'

'Right. I like the sound of that. What about this J B Solutions mob?'

'We need to delve further into them. Mahoney's talking about people on the inside being on the take. That can only mean the MoD. He doesn't mention names or give us anything we can prove, but he hints that someone must have been getting paid. Because if Damar Guns had no licence yet continued to supply guns to Africa, then it means someone inside was faking up papers to let them go through. Maybe someone inside Customs, too. It could have been a whole chain of corruption, for all we know. We need to get more on the people behind J B Solutions. I want to get into Thomas Dunn – he's the guy who runs the company.'

McGuire chewed this over for a few seconds.

'Okay. First, let's get a piece written up on Mahoney the spy and fire it over to me. Nothing about the arms dealers yet. Just that Mahoney was a spy for Stasi – explaining all about them, of course – and hinting that we've got more detail, from way back years ago. Say we've got the low-down on major figures within the intelligence service. That'll fuck them up.' He stood up and walked towards the door.

'Okay. First, I'm going to nip up to see Hawkins at his flat. He was a bit nervy last night. I just want to make sure he's all right. He's a good guy.'

Rosie drove up past the university and hit an unexpected backlog of traffic as she reached the quiet avenue where Gerard Hawkins lived. The blue light of a police car flashed on and off, and a smattering of people were gathered on the pavement. Dread throbbed across her gut. She quickly pulled her car over and jumped out, walking hurriedly towards the flat.

'Oh my God!' she said under her breath, picking her way to the front of the crowd.

'What's going on?' Rosie asked a couple of elderly ladies.

'There's been an accident.' One of the women pointed to the ground-floor flat. 'In there.'

'What? What's happened?'

'I think his name is Hawkins. We've lived in the same block for years, but didn't really know him. He was very quiet ... Used to be a lecturer over the road at the uni ... I—'

'What kind of accident,' Rosie interrupted. 'Is he ... ?'

'Yes.' The woman nodded sympathetically. 'I'm afraid he's dead. Police and ambulance ... They're all in there ... I heard it was suicide.'

'No.' Rosie shook her head, backing away. 'No way.'

The women looked confused as she turned away from them and went up the steps to the front door.

'Sorry, madam. Are you a relative?' The uniformed policeman stepped forward, blocking her path.

'No. I'm a friend.'

'Could you hold on a minute, please?'

He spoke into the walkie-talkie on the lapel of his anorak.

'The DI will be here in a moment.'

Rosie felt her chest tighten with emotion. She glanced around at the throng of faces on the pavement. She'd have been lynched if they knew who she was ... A tabloid journalist, the lowest of the low, they'd say, using a poor old man to make a headline. Guilt hung over her like a cloud.

A round-faced woman with curly short hair and wearing a raincoat arrived a minute later and approached Rosie.

'DI Miller.' She raised her eyebrows. 'You are?'

'A friend of Gerard Hawkins. I didn't know him that well, but we had coffee yesterday . . . and also a few days ago.'

'And how was he?' The DI looked Rosie up and down.

'Er . . . Fine . . . He was okay. He was obviously very upset by the murder of his friend Tom Mahoney.'

'And how do you know him?'

Rosie hesitated for two beats, looking back at the DI.

'I'm a journalist. I was working on the murder and we were talking about his friend.'

The DI pursed her lips and glimpsed at the uniformed officer. Rosie squared her shoulders. Just what she needed – a cop who despised journalists, blamed them for everything and did all they could to make sure they got nowhere near the truth. Rosie had stumbled along more than enough of them during her chequered life, but she wasn't about to let this one get in her way.

'What kind of state was he in when you left him?' Her tone was accusatory.

'Put it this way,' Rosie said deadpan, 'he didn't seem to me like a man ready to commit suicide. He was very . . .' She chose her words. '. . . Very determined.'

'Determined about what?'

'Determined to stay strong for his friend.' Rosie's tone was measured. 'He was upset, but he knew Mahoney wouldn't want him to give up, and that he'd want him to get on with his life. They'd been friends since they were students. He wasn't suicidal. Definitely not.'

'Well. Unless you're a qualified shrink, that's not really for you to decide. Who do you work for?'

'The *Post*,' Rosie answered drily.

'What's your name?'

'Rosie Gilmour.'

The DI took a notebook out and wrote it down. In some quarters of Strathclyde's finest the name Rosie Gilmour was loathed – especially among the cops she'd turned over down the years.

'At the moment there isn't a lot to say. There'll be a post-mortem. But it looks like a straightforward suicide.'

'What do you mean? How? Was there a note? Overdose? . . . What method of suicide.'

'As I said, it's early doors.'

'A note?'

'Inquiries are ongoing.' She put her notebook back into her raincoat pocket. 'There was no note. That's all I can say. We're trying to trace his next of kin.'

'I'm not sure he had any. I . . . I honestly don't know.'

Over the DI's shoulder Rosie saw two paramedics come out of the hallway, carefully bearing a stretcher. On it was a black body bag. She moved to the side as they came on to the threshold then watched, swallowing back her tears, as they carried Gerard Hawkins's body down the steps and into the ambulance.

'They'll take him to the mortuary for tests. It's very sad when someone ends up like that,' the DI said matter-of-factly. 'They get so lonely, these old guys, their whole lives about teaching and education, then when it's over there's so little left if they've got no family. I've seen it before, over the years.' She took her notebook out again. 'I'll need a contact number for you, as one of the last people to talk to Mr Hawkins.'

Rosie gave her mobile number and she wrote it down.

'Can you tell me what you were discussing?'

'No,' Rosie said. 'I can't.' She turned to walk away.

'Until this investigation has concluded that the death is not suspicious, police inquiries will be ongoing.'

Rosie kept on walking to her car and didn't look back. She slumped into the driver seat and closed the door, leaning back on the headrest and staring out of the windscreen. They'd got to him. Whoever it was had decided that Hawkins had to be eliminated, the way they had wiped out Tom Mahoney. The claims he'd made in his dossier were now ringing painfully, scarily, true. Rosie spread her hands on the steering wheel and noticed they were trembling. She rolled down the window and gulped a mouthful of air. A shudder ran through her and she quickly started the engine. What if someone saw her come out of Hawkins' flat last night? What if whoever did this was already in his flat when he went out to the shops last night and was lying in wait? She had to call McGuire to tell him, and to make sure the material from the package was locked in his safe. She picked up her mobile as she drove out of the street and was about to dial McGuire's number when it rang. It was Don.

'Hey, Rosie, I've got some interesting news for you.'

'Gerard Hawkins has been found dead in his flat? I know. I just left the place. Christ, Don! What the hell is going on?'

'Haven't a clue, and that's the truth.'

'I've just been given the evil eye by some woman DI who was outside Hawkins' flat.' Rosie described the detective. 'She said they'll want to speak further to me if his death is suspicious.'

'What's her name?'

'DI Miller.'

'Yeah. Nippy sweetie. And I suppose you told her to GTF in your own inimitable way.'

'Kind of. I'm not good at police interviews, as you know. They bring out the worst in me. And, anyway, there's nothing to tell. It looks like suicide, but I'm sure it's not.'

'What do you mean it's not? You and your conspiracy theories.'

'Look, Don. I just know. I can't tell you. And please respect this. But I've been working on something. Hawkins was helping me and now he's dead. It stinks to high heaven.'

'Fuck's sake, Rosie.'

'I can't tell you about it. Read the paper tomorrow. But something's rotten here.'

'You going to upset the cops again? I can tell.'

'Just read the paper. But I'm sure Hawkins has been bumped off – same as Mahoney.'

'Anyway,' Don said, 'that aside. I *was* just about to phone you and give you a heads up on Hawkins' death when I got another call about the King's Cross murder CCTV footage.'

Rosie perked up.

'Yeah?'

'That bird who they say was in the café? Well, she's spotted on CCTV leaving the place immediately afterwards – just as the waitress claimed. Right behind the big Eastern European guys. They're on the CCTV as well. Big lumps of men they are.'

'And?'

'They tracked the CCTV back along King's Cross round to St Pancras Station, and it shows the bird coming off the Eurostar. So whoever she is and whatever she was doing, she came from France on the train.'

Rosie took a second to process the information. Her head was all over the place.

'Fine. But it doesn't take us any further on who she is.'

'Unless, of course, you know what I know.' He was toying with her.

'Come on, Don. Give me a break, man.'

'Listen to this . . . Some eagle-eyed bastard in Scotland Yard has clocked the likeness to the woman who was photographed in that covert op eighteen months ago in Spain that I told you about.'

'What? The one with Rab Jackson?'

'Yep. That's what they think. Looks like the same woman, as I told you. She was never identified officially at the time – only from a snitch that said she was this Ruby bird from Glasgow.'

'You're kidding. Could it be Ruby Reilly? The one you told me about? Could she be involved in the murder with these Eastern Europeans?'

'Who knows? It's just unexplained at the moment as to why she was in the café. And why she left so quickly after the guys. She must have something to hide. She didn't play any role in the shooting and didn't talk to the men who did it. All it does is muddy the waters for the Met, but they're not ruling anything out. She could even be involved.'

'Shit, Don. This story is growing arms *and* legs.'

'Aye. And our boys are beginning to get interested at the Serious Crime Squad, because if it *is* Ruby Reilly then it's a Scottish connection, and we need to find her. So whatever you're digging up, I hope you'll share it with your favourite detective.'

'Sure,' Rosie said, knowing that that depended on what it was.

Don hung up.

CHAPTER FOURTEEN

Rosie tore down the A77 towards Ayrshire, overtaking everything despite the driving rain and creeping late afternoon darkness. Her conversation with Gerard Hawkins played out again and again in her mind, and she could still see his face, a mixture of grief and admiration as he told her the inside story of Mahoney's secret life.

McGuire was completely black and white about it when Rosie phoned to tell him Hawkins was dead. Now the gloves were off. They had to pull out all the stops and get this story in the paper. Whoever had come to kill Hawkins was in search of whatever they suspected he had, and wasn't taking any chances. Rosie also told him about the development from the CCTV cameras and the mystery Scots woman.

Before she left for Ayrshire she'd headed back to the office to rewrite tomorrow's front page, as her initial story had changed because of Hawkins' death.

Now, she kept glancing at her mobile phone on the passenger seat, willing it to ring with the voice of the mystery woman who'd claimed she was in the café in King's Cross. If she was genuine, she was crucial. How the hell could she not be involved in the murder if she was able to give her the name of J B Solutions, the arms dealers? How was it all linked? Why did she do a runner? Rosie's brain ached from going around in circles. She wasn't even sure herself if there was any point in driving to Ayrshire, to the home of the retired Strathclyde detective chief inspector, the cop Humphy Boyd used to pass information to. All she had was gut instinct, based only on Don's phone call and what he'd told her before about the murder of Jackie Reilly.

She took the slip road into the tiny rural village of Kilmaurs, hoping the DCI's home wasn't in one of the outlying areas, mostly farms and deserted roads with little chance of meeting anyone to ask directions. She'd dug his address out of the voters' roll, as it wasn't listed in the phone book. Her first stop, at the newsagent's to fuel up on chocolate and peanuts had been successful – the paperboy delivered to his house, the shopowner told her, and he lived nearby. Rosie got back into her car and drove past the old church as directed and up his long driveway. Most of the lights in the house were off, except for one in what looked like the kitchen at the side. Rosie rang the bell, hoping instinct would kick in to galvanize her frazzled brain. Sometimes, if she was stuck for words, a little panic helped pump the blood to the brain. A light came on in the hall and she braced herself as she heard the door being unlocked. When it opened, a tall, silver-haired man stood before her.

'Roddy Thompson?' Rosie gave him an eager look, as though she'd been trying to track him down for years.

'Who are you?' He raised his eyebrows and looked down at her.

'My name is Rosie Gilmour. I'm from the *Post*.' Rosie took a breath, ready for her pitch, when he interrupted.

'Rosie Gilmour?' He nodded slowly, a wry smile spreading across his youthful face. 'I know that name.' He shoved his hands in his trouser pockets, looking relaxed. 'The Rosie Gilmour who likes giving the cops a good kicking?'

Shit, Rosie thought. She braced herself for an onslaught, but there was a softness about his expression. She tried a half-smile, putting her hands up.

'Only the bad ones, Mr Thompson. I'm on the side of the good guys.' She stood her ground, looking him in the eye. 'Always.'

'So what brings you here?' He looked her up and down. 'I *was* one of the good guys.'

'Jackie Reilly.' Rosie pushed her hair back and wiped a drop of rain from her cheek. 'I'm working on an investigation and your name came up.'

He stood for a long moment, gazing over her shoulder at the rain and the blackness. Then he stepped back.

'Come in out of the rain.' He turned and walked through a small utility room. 'My wife's out at one of her charity meetings,' he said over his shoulder as he pushed open a door into the kitchen.

Rosie went in behind him, her mind firing on all cylinders, not quite believing her luck.

'Where did you get my name?' He crossed the kitchen and clicked on the kettle.

'It just came up, Mr Thompson.'

'Roddy,' he said.

'Your name came up after a bit of digging, Roddy.'

He motioned her to sit down on one of two armchairs at the side of an old fireplace.

'I heard you do a bit of digging. You should watch some of the people you upset, or you could dig your own grave.' He folded his arms, leaning against the worktop.

His tone was friendly and Rosie relaxed a little.

'I have a few police contacts, Roddy, who I value and respect and who help me from time to time. People know the kind of things I dig into, and if sometimes I come up with some dirt on people on high places, then so be it. I don't shy away from that, but that's not why I'm here.'

The silence hung for a moment, then he spoke.

'Jackie Reilly,' he said. 'She wasn't a bad woman, you know. I've known plenty of complete bastards in my day – women who would sell their children for money without turning a hair. But Jackie was all right. She had a good heart.' His eyes rested at the fire flickering in the hearth, then he blinked himself back. 'Coffee?'

'That'd be great.' This was going much better than she'd hoped. 'So, Roddy, can I ask you a little bit about Jackie Reilly and her kids?'

He stood with his back to her as he poured boiling water into two mugs.

'What are you doing about her? Why do you ask?' He turned around. 'Sugar? Milk?'

'Just black is great.' Rosie cleared her throat. 'Actually, I'm working on a story and her name came up. I'm sure you've heard about the murders of Rab Jackson in Spain and his old mate Malky Cameron here. Both burned to death in their homes.'

'Good enough for them.' He handed her a mug and sat down opposite, placing his coffee on the low table. His lips tightened. 'Two bastards who should have been drowned at birth. The stuff they did to people – innocent people, some of them – would make you shudder, Rosie. Someone should have shot the bastards long ago. I'm surprised it's taken so long, to be honest. But I celebrated anyway when I heard – and that's the truth.'

'They murdered Jackie Reilly, didn't they?'

He nodded slowly.

'Aye. They did. Burned her to death in her house. Raped one of her girls. Christ! I can see the faces of those two wee lassies yet.' He shook his head. 'And Jackie. Burned black.

What a fucking thing to do to a woman. Or anybody, for that matter. Everybody and his dog knew it was Jackson and Cameron, but nobody would say a word. That pair of evil bastards had everyone in the scheme terrorized, so we couldn't get anywhere near them. Nothing.'

They sat in silence, Rosie waiting, watching to see if he was going to volunteer anything. But he looked miles away.

'I was told Jackie was killed because she helped police with tip-offs.'

He looked hard at her.

'"Grassing" is the word you're looking for.'

Rosie swallowed and said nothing.

He sighed. 'I don't like to think of her in that way. It was all about survival. Jackie did what she had to do. She took people in.' He flicked a glance at Rosie. 'Men. They paid her. She was on her own – had to keep shoes on the kids' feet and food on the table. They were hard times in Maryhill, Rosie, back in those days. Men like Jackson and Cameron – scum of the earth – they ran everything. People didn't stand a chance, even if they wanted to play by the book.'

'She was taking a real risk talking to the police, though.'

'She was protected,' he said, looking straight at her. 'I protected her.' His voice dropped to a whisper, and he shook his head. 'I was sure I had her protected as tight as a drum.' He ran his hand across his chin. 'It shouldn't have happened.' He looked at Rosie, his eyes full of hurt. 'It's haunted me my whole life. The guilt. I blamed myself. Still do.'

'You never found out how Jackson and Cameron discovered she was talking to the cops?'

He shook his head.

'You were close to her, Roddy?'

He nodded.

'Very close?' Rosie ventured.

He didn't answer.

'Sorry.' Rosie said.

Then he looked through her. 'Too close.' He swallowed. 'It shouldn't have happened, but it did. I knew what she did with men, how she sold herself, but the truth is, I just let it happen. It was like I couldn't stop myself. I was married, two kids, but there was something about Jackie. She was like one of these old screen goddesses. Honest to Christ, Rosie. She should have been out of Maryhill when she was a teenager, before some bastard got her up the duff at fifteen and saddled her with two kids. In another world, with other opportunities, Jackie Reilly could have been anybody. She had a great mind as well. Sharp. A good human being.'

'You fell in love with her.'

'It's a cliché, but I did.'

'Did you ever hear what happened with the girls? I heard one of them – Judy – died and the other one was put in a home. Were you ever in touch with Ruby . . . or ever hear what happened to her?'

He said nothing but the muscles in his jaw tightened. He

ran a hand through his thinning hair and looked back at Rosie.

'Why do you ask? What's it got to do with anything?' He shrugged, staring at the fire. 'She'll be grown up now. She was the living image of her mother. A real beauty. And the same spirit. A cheeky wee bugger, and could fight like a tiger.'

'You never saw her again? Any idea where she is?'

He shook his head.

'Why?'

'Just a crazy notion that occurred to me a few days ago when Jackson got torched in his home on the Costa del Sol and then Cameron's house got burned down. Obviously old scores – somebody with a grudge . . . and balls like coconuts. And none of the cops I spoke to know anybody who'd have the wit or the courage to pull that off.'

He snorted, a smile on his lips.

'Ruby? Is that what you're asking?'

'Just a thought.'

'I can imagine her growing up with a rage burning inside her. That's for sure. She was feisty enough before that night, so Christ knows how she ended up. Tell you what, though, I'd be well tickled if she did kill the bastards. That would be the kind of retribution that should be celebrated big time.' His eyebrows knitted. 'What makes you even think that? You must have a reason?'

'Well, you see . . .' Rosie examined her fingernails then

looked at him. 'I don't know if you know this, but Ruby went on to do all right for herself. She went to university and studied accountancy but dropped out in her last year – just before she graduated, apparently, but she did all right. Makes you wonder how she managed it.'

Roddy's face softened. He looked proud.

'Maybe the kid had a secret benefactor.' He smiled. 'If ever anyone deserved one, it was her.'

'Somebody told me that Ruby came up on the radar as working for Jackson,' Rosie said. 'It came from a good contact.'

Roddy shook his head.

'Hard to imagine that, given what happened to her mum and sister.'

'Have you seen her since she was a kid?'

'No. Never.'

'Did you help her? I mean, were you her secret benefactor?'

He looked at the floor and didn't reply and they sat in heavy silence, but Rosie knew from the look in his eyes not to pursue the question any further. Then he looked straight at her and stood up.

'I think you should go now, Rosie.'

CHAPTER FIFTEEN

Ruby thought long and hard about agreeing to meet Tony. Holed up in her West End flat, she went over the risks of sticking her head above the parapet. Here, she was safe as long as she didn't venture into the city centre or any of the haunts where she might bump into one Tony's sidekicks. She'd always been meticulous about keeping her whereabouts secret, whether it was Spain, Amsterdam, Rome or anywhere else she pitched up for a few weeks to make sure Rab Jackson's money was safely laundered and banked. Ruby had worked hard at cultivating this enigmatic, elusive figure who flitted in and out of the game, only appearing when she was needed to discuss the intricate accounting or to move money around the world. Rab Jackson always knew how to get a hold of her, but nobody else did and, now, he was history. Fuck him. She cursed herself for giving Tony her private email, because he was sending messages every two hours. His last email had sent a shudder of terror right through her.

'I think Judy would want you to get in touch with me, if you get my drift.'

Brief, but toxic. She had no option but to answer the message.

As Ruby walked through the swing doors she spotted Tony lounging on the leather sofa in a secluded alcove at the far end of the bar off Glasgow's Hilton Hotel foyer. Two shaven-headed gorillas sat on armchairs opposite, hanging on his every word. Tony clocked her when she arrived and put his coffee cup on the table as she strode confidently towards him. Attack is the best form of defence, Ruby told herself, but inside, her stomach was like jelly. She'd called the home this morning to inquire after Judy, terrified that something had happened. The sigh of relief she breathed when the nurse said Judy was well and sitting in her room by the window, as usual, had brought tears to her eyes.

'Take a walk, lads.' Tony dismissed his henchmen with a wave of his hand.

They both stood up, brick-shithouse frames bursting out of their shiny suits, and shot Ruby a fleeting glance as they slipped past her.

'Sit down.' Tony patted the sofa beside him.

Ruby stood for a moment, glaring at him, then moved towards one of the armchairs.

'What's the fucking panic, Tony?'

'Where have you been? That's the fucking panic. I've

been phoning you for days. What's the fucking score, Ruby? Don't fanny around with me.'

'Well' – Ruby sat down, crossing her legs, knowing he was watching as her skirt rode up her thighs a little – 'I'm here now. So what's up?'

Tony's eyes darkened and Ruby tried to hold his icy glare.

'Rab's dead, as you know. And now Malky Cameron, too.'

'Yeah. I heard.'

'You were in Spain with Rab before he died.'

'Yeah. And what about it? I'm his accountant.'

'One of the boys said you were at his villa the day before the fire. Having coffee at his poolside.'

'That's right, Sherlock.' Ruby held her nerve.

Tony leaned forward, his eyes narrowing.

'Well, have you any idea what the fuck happened? Someone torched Rab in his house . . . I . . . None of us can work out what the fuck's going on. I mean, how can that just happen?'

'No idea. How would I know?' She gave him an indignant look. 'The Costa del Sol's full of all the shitbags from here to Istanbul, all robbing each other blind. There's no such thing as loyalty. I don't know what strokes Rab may have pulled in his day, or if he's noised somebody up over there. I've only known him since he was more or less retired. I was moving his money around. That's all. Who knows what's going on out there? Not me, that's for sure. I'm seldom there.' Ruby paused, watching the words sink into Tony's head, knowing he'd be clueless as to who would wade in and bump Jackson off. 'You not picking anything up here? Somebody must know something.'

She prayed they didn't. She was doing well with the aggressive front.

'Nope. Fuck all. He was in the house by himself. Spanish cops, of course, don't give a shite about him.' He gave a little shrug, trying to look in control. 'But anyway, Rab's dead and that's it. We just need to deal with it. I'm running things now. That's why you're here.'

Ruby looked at him and said nothing.

'I'm here because you keep emailing me. You said the shit has hit the fan. But what's that got to do with me? I worked for Rab, not you.' She shot him a defiant smile then ran her fingers across the line where her tight blouse showed a hint of cleavage. 'That pleasant little encounter that night in your flat . . . it doesn't mean you own me.'

Tony licked his lips and Ruby could see the lust in his eyes. He was easy.

'We'll talk about that later,' he said. 'But right now I need to know where all the money is.'

Rosie took a long breath and sat back.

'Don't worry about the money, Tony. Surely to Christ you didn't think I'd done a runner with it?' She put on her best would-I-ever face, and leaned across and touched his knee.

'Well' – Tony put his hand on top of hers and kept it on his knee – 'It did cross my mind when I couldn't get hold of you.'

'Don't be stupid.' Ruby massaged his knee a little. She could see that the hard-man bravado was slipping. 'I'm not that daft. Rab's money is all over the place and, by the way, I do know it's not just his money – it's the firm's money. But it's very complicated. It's taken a lot of setting up – accounts and different firms I've created, all over Europe and beyond – to keep the operation looking legit. For that, Rab paid me decent money. I did a good job and all the money is safe. Rab trusted me. So what's the panic?'

The waiter came over and Tony ordered more coffee. Ruby asked for water. 'There's a big problem, Ruby,' Tony said, his voice almost a whisper. 'That's why I needed to get hold of you.'

'What problem?' Ruby's stomach tweaked, not knowing what to expect.

'One of the companies we invest in. Don't know if you know them. They're an export/import company.'

Ruby stifled a laugh.

'Fuck's sake. They're all export/import companies. That's the whole point. How else would you get the coke into the UK?'

'No. Listen. One particular company, they're arms dealers. It's something Rab invested in a few years back. Owned by Tam Dunn. You won't know him. He moved to London years ago and he's connected, big time, to a lot of the villains down south. Rab and him go back to the early days, so he invested with him. Dunn owns this company, J B Solutions, and they're legit – well, on paper anyway. Totally watertight, according to what Rab told me a few months ago. But they have another company, Damar Guns. And they're arms dealers, too, but in a different way. The two companies work hand in hand, but not on paper. Tam runs Damar, too, and he's in with some heavy-duty Russians. There's a load of money – massive amounts – because them fucking Russians buy and sell a lot of gear. You know how it is – they're into everything, spreading themselves all over the shop, and they need to be tooled up big time. They bring guns – and a lot more besides – into the UK through Damar. Sometimes Damar sells guns to them, better than the Russian ones. Plus, the Russians supply birds for the saunas and stuff.'

Ruby kept her face straight but her heart was hammering.

'The names don't ring a bell with me. I set up a good few companies for Rab – everything from property firms to petrol stations . . . Christ . . . even a wooden-pallet company in the Midlands. I moved a lot of his money through them in various places all over the world. But I've never heard of J B Solutions. Or Damar. Never even heard him talking about them. Anyway, what's happened?'

'Well, there was some big international police and intelligence operation to trap the arms dealers while they were in the middle of a deal, but it all got fucked up. Two people got killed. One of Tam's and one of theirs. Over in Berlin. It was a right mess.'

'You mean one of the Glasgow boys got killed?'

'Yeah, but he'd been living down near London for years. He was really working with Tam and for Damar. But it's worse than that. The cops got hold of the guy I sent down from here for a bit of extra muscle. Derek Murdoch – Del. So they'll just pump the wee man for any information then probably fucking shoot him.'

Ruby nodded.

'Presumably, you didn't send some eejit who's going to spill his guts the first time the cops punch his face on a job like that?'

'Who the fuck knows? Once cops at that level grab somebody, they can put the frighteners on them. Threaten their family. Maybe offer the guy money if he puts the finger on anyone. And they know we're not exactly going to report him as a missing person.'

'So who is Del?'

'A wee hard bastard from Possil. He's a sound enough guy but he's not been on a job like this before. He was coming through the ranks and doing well. It was Billy, the guy who got shot, who said he wanted to take him with him. He said he could handle it. And Tam approved it, so I sent him down. He was only there for a bit of muscle during the time they were in Berlin, in case there was any funny business with the Russians. They're serious wankers to work with. You can trust them about as far as you can throw them.'

'So you're sure the cops grabbed him?'

Tony nodded gravely.

'We got word from the Russians. The cunts got away. They shot some bird dead who was with the police. They told us the cops got the wee man.'

Ruby digested this information then folded her arms.

'So, on paper, Del's just another hoodlum caught up in a killing abroad? What do you care, if there's nothing to link you to it? Just keep out of it – that's my advice.'

'But Tam's shitting himself because, four weeks after this happens, there was a hit on some old geezer. The university guy in London. It was all over the papers. Guy got shot in the head in a café in the middle of London. They're saying it was some Russian gangsters who did it.'

Ruby's stomach lurched and she hoped the colour wasn't rising in her face as she pictured the old guy slipping off his chair, his brains all over the wall.

'I vaguely remember the story,' she lied, re-crossing her legs, knowing Tony would focus his mind on them. 'The papers will say anything. And even if it was Russians, what the Christ has that got to do with Tam? Or you?'

'Because the fucking lecturer was in Berlin. He was there. He must have been working with the cops or the secret service or some fucking thing. He must have been part of the operation.'

'I find that hard to believe,' Ruby screwed up her eyes. 'A university lecturer in a shoot-out with Russian mobsters and arms dealers?'

'He was there. Definitely. And now he's dead.'

'How do you know he was there?'

'The Russians told Tam.'

'Christ! So was it them who shot him in the café? Why would they do that?'

Tony shook his head.

'They said they didn't. But as I said, you can't fucking trust these bastards.'

'It said in the papers it was Russian-looking guys who shot him. But why would they?' repeated Rosie.

Tony put his hands up and sighed, frustrated.

'I don't fucking know, Ruby. But something stinks, and we can't trust anyone.' He glanced over his shoulder. 'And since the old guy was shot dead, the cops are all over it and Tam is panicking in case the heat comes all the way through to his company.'

'J B Solutions?'

'Aye. Well, mostly the other one – Damar. But if they look hard enough they might find they're both connected. Damar supplies just about every gangster from Glasgow to London with weapons. And they also ship guns and stuff abroad – Africa – for some crazy fuckin' war out there that's been going on for ever.' He leaned closer to Ruby. 'But fucking Tam hasn't got the right licence for that, and he's shipping container-loads of arms abroad. So now he's shitting himself in case the heat comes to him.'

Rosie gave a soft whistle.

'Big stuff indeed. But surely you and anyone else who deals with Tam on the ground here are far enough away from all that kind of shit if they start investigating?'

'We hope so. But we're thinking that we need to make sure everything's solid – money-wise – and safe. Maybe we should move things around again.'

Ruby thought for a moment.

'It would be risky to start moving a lot of money around. Best to sit tight. Not attract any attention. The companies I've created for Rab are all legit, trading at small profits. There's nothing to connect anyone. I've not even heard of that company you're talking about.'

'You probably haven't. Rab invested a lot of money in Tam when he started out down south. It kept our hand in with the London mob and also the lads up in Manchester and Newcastle. So Tam was useful to Rab and he put some money behind him.'

'Well, I've never heard any of that.'

'It would be before your time.'

'So how did Rab get his kickback? I've moved a lot of money for him over the past three years.'

'Easy. The wads of cash he gave you to set up the companies you created? A lot of that came from Tam. Not all of it, obviously, as a lot was from here and other sources.'

Ruby racked her brain for any memory of Tam Dunn, but she'd never even heard Jackson mention his name.

'Unless Rab's name is anywhere in that company Tam has set up, then it's all okay.'

'That's just the point. He was named as one of the directors a few years ago, when Damar was set up. So if they start looking at the company records, who knows what they might find.'

Ruby nodded.

'I see what you mean. I can't believe Rab was that stupid.' She brushed her hand over Tony's thigh. 'But the money is all safe, the way I've set everything up. Don't worry.'

He reached for her hand and caressed it gently.

'Okay. That's what I wanted to hear.' He glanced around the almost deserted bar and spoke softly. 'But that's not all.'

Ruby wondered what the hell was coming next.

'Listen,' he said. 'You don't need to know the ins and outs of this, but I'm going to invest a whole lot more with Tam. I've already made a promise to him. We shook hands on it the last time he was up.'

'Did Rab know this? That you gave your word?' Ruby asked.

Tony shook his head.

'Look. Rab was old. Past it. He didn't like Tam dealing with the Russians and Albanians. He didn't like the way it was progressing. He was old school. But the old school is dead and buried. Rab was one of the last of the dinosaurs. Down south, you either work with the Russians or you don't work. They need us and we need them. Same goes for Spain. It's big business now. They can get more guns than anyone else and sometimes they want guns that we can supply. Plus, they control a lot of the Eastern European drug markets. We need to work with them.'

'So what are you saying?' Rosie asked. 'You want to invest Rab's money and put your lot in with Tam?'

'It's not all Rab's money,' he said sharply. 'Just remember that. He was getting suitcases full of fucking money driven over to Spain on a regular basis. Where do you think that came from? He was investing *our* money.' He glared at Ruby. '*You* were investing our money.'

Ruby nodded slowly. She knew Tony wouldn't have the first clue how to unravel all the accounts and investments she'd made. But the message was crystal clear. He wanted to get his hands on money – a lot of money. If Rab were here, he'd probably have told him to piss off, but the last thing Ruby needed was Tony or anyone else doing their own version of an audit into Rab's investments. Her own bank accounts, where she'd siphoned off a small fortune from Rab, were safe – as long as nobody had an inkling. But she knew she'd have to give Tony what he wanted. And she would. In good time. Right now she had to provide whatever would make Tony happy.

'Okay,' she said, finishing her drink and tracing her

finger across her bottom lip. 'Don't worry. I'll get things sorted.'

They sat silently for a long moment, then Tony's eyes softened.

'Why did you keep patching my emails and calls, Ruby? I've been phoning you non-stop. I wanted to see you.'

'I lost my mobile. I'm getting a new one. But I'm not in a rush. I'm taking some time out, just travelling a bit. I don't work set hours and I'm not on call, Tony.'

He nodded slowly, stroking her hand, and she felt a little twinge of desire as he ran his fingers along her arm.

'All right. But I wanted to see you anyway.' He touched her hair. 'Listen. I've got a bottle of Moët upstairs in a room. I thought maybe we could have some lunch later and just chill for a while.'

Ruby touched his cheek with the back of her hand and moistened her lips.

As they stood up and walked across to the lift, Ruby could feel her heart quicken and she cursed herself for being so basic. She wanted him. In the lift, Tony pressed the eighth-floor button and as soon as the doors closed he turned to Ruby and kissed her, pulling her towards him, gently squeezing her breast. She slipped her hand down and brushed it across his groin as his tongue probed in her mouth. He was hard already, and he pushed his hand up her thigh and under her skirt, gently massaged her crotch over the silk knickers she'd chosen to wear, knowing how the afternoon would pan out. And, despite herself, despite her rage and anger at this bastard and her confusion of how the fuck she was going to handle everything that was happening around her, Ruby heard herself moan with desire at his touch. Like this, Tony was putty in her hands, and it was the only way she had any control over him, but it also made her a prostitute, just like her mother. She hated herself, because right now his touch and his body hard against her was what she wanted more than anything.

In the bedroom Tony stripped hurriedly, kicking his trousers away as he tugged at Ruby's blouse, pushing her against the door. He didn't speak, but she could hear him breathing hard as he pulled down her pants then lifted her buttocks and pushed himself inside her. Ruby groaned as she wrapped her legs around him while he thrust hard and urgently until she came, quickly, pulling the back of his hair as he kept going until he gasped and she felt the rush of him inside her and his body went limp.

Afterwards they lay on the bed and she watched as Tony drifted off to sleep, studying his handsome, suntanned face, his body hard from working out at the boxing gym, where he spent every afternoon punching the shit out of a heavy bag. He'd had a couple of professional fights and could have made a name for himself in the ring, but for the past four years he had become more and more steeped in the business since Rab Jackson had moved to Spain.

As he woke up, his eyes flickering, Ruby was on her feet and slipping into her skirt.

'Why did you write that about Judy, in the email? What did you mean?' she said coldly.

'It was just to get you to answer. To get a response.'

'Why?'

'I know you have a sister who's got some mental thing wrong with her and that you look after her.'

'How do you know that?'

'Don't ask.'

'What do you know?'

'Nothing. Listen, I'm sorry. It's not important. I don't know why I said it. Come back to bed.' He held his hand out towards her. 'You know you love it.' He pulled the sheet back.

Ruby said nothing as she buttoned her blouse and shoved her feet into her shoes.

Tony sat up on the bed.

'What's the matter? Where are you going? Listen, I'm really sorry. I didn't mean to sound threatening about your sister. I don't know any more about her. I thought she was dead.'

Ruby could feel her throat tighten with emotion. She stood up, looking down at his naked body, his erection already starting to swell. She looked away.

'Listen to me, Tony. And listen good, because I'll never say this to you again.' She paused as he looked up and she stared him in the eye. 'If you ever harm, or do anything, or even plan to harm Judy, I will kill you. Am I clear about that? I will kill you.'

She turned and was about to walk away, her insides shaking with anger and frustration that this fucker thought he had her where he wanted her. And he did – if she was prepared to let him get away with it.

Then Tony spoke, his voice suddenly the voice of the cold, hard bastard she'd heard before.

'You listen to me, Ruby. We need to talk about money and you need to give me the bank accounts and the arrangements. I'm taking things over now.'

'Fine. I'll call you when I can get it all sorted and give you all the numbers.'

'What about us? I mean, this?'

She turned her head quickly.

'This was a shag Tony. There *is* no us.'

She walked out, her hands trembling so much that by the time she got to the lift she could barely push the button.

CHAPTER SIXTEEN

It was pitch black and the rain was falling horizontally as Rosie drove out of Roddy Thompson's driveway and into Kilmaurs' eerily deserted streets. She'd be glad to get back to her flat tonight for a long soak in a hot bath. So many scenarios raced around her mind, and added to them now was the notion that the former DCI had looked after Ruby Reilly financially when she was a forlorn little girl after her mother's murder. Sure, it was possible, if he was riddled with guilt, for him to stick a few quid in a bank account for her to access when she became a teenager. But would a man in his position really do that? She wouldn't tell McGuire about her latest theory just yet. Her gut instinct told her Thompson knew more about Ruby than he was letting on.

Driving out of the village, Rosie was conscious of a car behind her, far too close to her bumper, considering there was only the two of them on the road. Then, she felt herself being shunted forward and she struggled to keep control of the car.

'What the fu—?' She peered in the rear-view mirror to see who the nutter was. 'Bloody joyrider!' she muttered to herself.

Then, she squinted again in the mirror. Shit! The driver was wearing a balaclava. She blinked quickly to make sure, but as she did her car was shunted again. Christ! And now, as she automatically accelerated, she heard the screech of an engine as the car came after her. Blind fear pulsed through her and her head felt foggy and confused. Suddenly, she couldn't even remember the turn-off she'd taken to come into the village earlier. She must have missed it, because now she was on a tight country road with twists and bends leading into pitch blackness. Where was the fucking dual carriageway she'd only come off half an hour ago? She was sure it hadn't taken this long on the back road to reach Kilmaurs, so where the hell was she going now? She put her foot down and hit a bend at over fifty, grabbing the steering wheel tight as the car swerved. Behind her on the brow of the hill she could see the lights of the car hammering on her tail. Wherever she was headed, it was deeper into the country, but she had no option but to keep driving as fast as she could in the hope she would see the lights of a village or a main road. Another stiff bend veered left then swiftly right. She caught a glimpse of a farm-road entrance and thought briefly of turning into it, but there was no sign of life, just the silhouette of a house in the distance with no lights on. She glanced at her mobile on the passenger seat, thinking of dialling 999, but she was too terrified to pick it up as the car gained on her. She put the boot down as the road rose up to a tight hill then dipped down, and as it did, her car nearly took off, suddenly submerged in a flooded road and then aquaplaning out of the blackness at the other side. 'Oh God, please let me get out of this,' she murmured. The car was only a few yards away. Her mobile rang, startling her for second, and she automatically glanced at it. But that was all it took – the car went out of control as she turned and twisted the steering wheel, trying to keep it on the narrow road. Then, as if in slow motion, she was heading for a ditch and an open field. She closed her eyes, bracing herself. This is it, she thought, as the car careered off the road and plunged into the soft earth, coming to an abrupt halt right in front of a huge tree trunk. Another second and it would have been head on. She saw stars as her head banged on the side window on impact, and the airbag nearly knocked her out, but she was conscious enough to recognize that the car had gone past and was now hurtling up the road into the distance. What if it came back? She had to get out of here. No, better to remain inside with the doors locked. But here, she was a sitting target. She was about to open the door when her mobile rang. She answered it.

'Rosie.' A woman's voice.

She struggled for the breath to answer, but nothing came out.

'You there, Rosie Gilmour?'

'Yeah.' She tried to breathe through her nose.

'It's me. The woman from the café.'

'Fuck!'

'What?'

'I . . . I've been in a crash. My car has just been run off the road. Somebody . . . someone behind me.'

Silence.

'Where are you?'

'Don't know. Somewhere off the Kilmaurs road. Some bastard wearing a balaclava tried to do me in.' Rosie paused. She had to pull herself together. 'Listen. Please. Don't hang up.' Her head was thumping. 'I need to meet you.'

'Are you injured?'

'I bumped my head. But I'm okay, I think.'

'Is the person who was chasing you gone?'

'I don't know. I think so. I saw the car speed past me, after he forced me off the road.'

'Is your car moving? I could maybe phone an ambulance or something.'

'I'm in a bloody field. I'm going to phone my office. I'm okay. I'll be back in Glasgow shortly. Can we meet? Tonight?' Rosie couldn't afford to lose her.

Silence. Then she heard the woman take a breath.

'I saw on the news tonight that the friend of that guy who was murdered has been found dead. Hawkins.'

'That's right. Dead in his flat. Are you able to meet me later? I've got some questions.'

Silence.

'I'll call you in an hour.'

She hung up.

'Shit!' Rosie shouted in frustration. 'Shit!' Her hands trembled as she fumbled, trying to search for McGuire's number. He answered immediately.

'Gilmour, where are you?'

'Mick. I've been in a crash. Some bastard ran me off the road.'

'What the fuck? Where are you?'

'Somewhere near Kilmaurs.'

'Kilmaurs? That's fucking Ayrshire. What the Christ are you doing down there?'

'I'll tell you when I get back. Can you get someone down here fast? My car's in a field. It's pissing down. I'm stranded . . . Some bastard in a balaclava was after me.'

'What the fuck are you doing, Rosie? In Ayrshire?'

'I . . . I came to see a retired copper.'

'You didn't tell me.'

'I know. I wanted to see if there was anything to tell, first. But I need to get out of here.'

'Will I get the cops?'

'No! Definitely not! Just get one of the drivers or the boys to come down. I need the car pulled out of the field.'

She gave him rough directions on where she thought she might be and how far she'd come off the road.

'Just sit tight. Someone will be down shortly.'

'Yeah, okay, Mick. I'll sit tight.' Not that she had much option.

Two hours later Rosie was in a little bistro at the far end of Ashton Lane, studying everyone who came in, hoping one of them would be the woman on the phone. She'd called an hour ago and agreed to meet. It had been an edgy conversation, laced with expletives from the woman. What if she turned up, she'd asked, to find that Rosie had brought the cops with her? Rosie had had to convince her that wouldn't happen. It had better not, the woman had said. Whoever this dame was, she sounded like one tough cookie. Rosie would be ready for her.

The place was crowded with the evening mix of students cashing in on the cheap food offers, tourists drawn to the trendy West End, as well as staff and a few well-known faces from the nearby BBC studios. From her table at the terrace doors Rosie could just make out the familiar kitchen window in the nearby tenements behind the high red-brick wall. So many nights she'd spent there with TJ in his flat after dinner, sitting with the large window wide open, the buzz of Ashton Lane drifting up towards them. She thought of all the promises they'd made, declaring how much they needed each other. Her gut ached, she missed him so much at that moment. Yet it had been her who had made it more complicated than it needed to be. The distance between them while he was working in New York had proved to be a bigger problem than they'd both anticipated. But it could have worked. Rosie knew it was down to her, that when it came to the crunch she'd messed up again. She shook herself out of her reverie. She should let it go, she told herself. So why was she still sitting here looking longingly at TJ's kitchen window? What kind of screwed up was that?

Her mind drifted to Adrian and Bosnia, and she scrolled down her contacts list on her mobile and stopped on his name. She'd love to phone him right now and tell him what had happened with the nutcase who ran her off the road. She knew if she asked for his help he'd be over in a heartbeat. But she held back. She hadn't heard from him in over a week, and it niggled – even though she'd convinced herself she wasn't involved with him. Adrian was different. Emails and phone calls weren't his style. But things had changed between them now, because of the reckless moment in Sarajevo when a simple brush of each other's arms on the way back to her hotel room had unleashed a fire. They had fallen into the night together. She sighed, shaking her head. And as she did she saw a striking woman come through the swing doors and stand confidently, scanning the room. This could be her. Rosie made eye contact as the woman looked in her direction, and she strode across to her table.

'Rosie?' Her voice was barely a whisper.

'Yep.' Rosie motioned her to sit down and called a waitress.

'Gin and tonic,' the woman said, giving the waitress a sideways glance.

'Two.' Rosie handed over the empty glass of lime and soda she'd been drinking. She had the feeling this encounter would call for a couple of drinks.

The woman tossed her hair back and took a cigarette out of a packet, offering one to Rosie, who declined. She watched as she lit up. Roddy Thompson wasn't wrong when he said that Ruby was her mother's double and that her mother had looked like screen goddess. She was all razor-sharp cheekbones and piercing blue eyes that darted around the room, part trapped animal, part disdain. Then she looked straight at Rosie as though waiting for her to speak.

'I know who you are.' Rosie held her stare.

It was risky to barge right in, but this blade had an air about her that if you didn't get in first you'd be forever on the back foot.

Silence. She took another drag of her cigarette and blew it upwards out of the side of her mouth.

'Yeah?'

The look was defiant, but Rosie caught just a glint of fear somewhere behind the eyes.

'Ruby . . . You're Ruby Reilly.' Rosie didn't take her eyes off her.

Silence. The mask wasn't exactly slipping, but it had moved a little. She blinked, glanced down at the table.

'Fuck's sake!'

'It's all right,' Rosie said quickly. 'Don't worry. Nobody else knows. Nobody *will* know.'

'How did you find out?'

'I'll tell you later.' Rosie reached across and put her hand out. 'Pleased to meet you, Ruby.'

'Aye.' Ruby shook her hand. A reluctant smile, somewhere between disbelief and defeat, spread across her face. 'Tell me now. How did you know?'

The waitress arrived at Ruby's shoulder and put the drinks down in front of them. She lifted her glass, swirled the ice around and nodded a cheers before taking a huge gulp. Rosie felt like doing the same but kept herself to a sip. She ignored Ruby's question and let the silence last three beats.

'What were you doing in that café in King's Cross that day?'

Ruby glared at Rosie.

'I sure as fuck wasn't there to kill anybody, if that's what you're asking.'

'I'm not. But I'm curious. Well, actually, everyone's curious to know why you bailed out before the cops came.'

Rosie leaned across, her elbows on the table, so their heads were close. 'What were you running from?'

Ruby took another swig of her drink and put the glass down.

'The cops,' she said, deadpan. 'But I'm sure you've worked that out for yourself.' She took another puff of her cigarette. 'But listen to me, Rosie. I've got nothing to do with that fucking shooting, and those big Russian bastards who blew that old guy's brains all over the wall. If you have any suspicions in that direction then say it now and I'm straight out of here. Right fucking now.'

'That's not what I think.'

'Well, your paper, and that other bloody one, the *Sun*, are printing all this shite about the mystery fucking Scots bird who may be involved. I mean, fuck me! That fuckwit waitress giving interviews, just making things up as she goes along. I should have punched her over the table while I was in there at the time. Arrogant wee bitch. I even read somewhere that she said she twigged I was with the guys earlier on . . . that I was giving them a signal. What a load of fucking shite!' She snorted, full, soft lips and a dimple on one cheek as she almost smiled. 'It'd be laughable, if it wasn't so serious.'

Rosie couldn't help smiling. She put her hand up.

'I know, Ruby. That was in the *Daily Star*. We didn't print it, though we had the story from some freelancer. But to be fair, we haven't said anything about your involvement, or even hinted at it.' Rosie paused to make sure Ruby had registered that. 'I don't think that's why you were in the café. But where were you coming from?'

Ruby looked over Rosie's shoulder, her eyes hard as she bit the inside of her jaw. She was edgy, angry and definitely scared. But there was a whiff of danger about her, and she would fight like a man if she had to. Rosie liked that.

'I was on the Eurostar. I came from France. Well, Spain, actually.' She stopped and sat back. 'But before I say any more, what's your angle with me? What do you want from me? Why did you want to meet me?'

'You called me, Ruby. Remember?' Rosie threw it right back at her.

'I know I did.' She fiddled nervously with her cigarette packet, opening and closing it, tapping it on the table. 'Because the more crap that goes into the papers about this mystery fucking Scot who may be at the centre of the murder, the more the cops are going to look for me.' She raised her eyebrows to emphasize her point. 'And that, I don't need. Believe me. I felt sorry for that poor guy lying there that morning, and his pal in a right state. Weeping all over the place. And now he's dead, too. I mean, what the fuck's going on? That's why I phoned you earlier . . . when I saw that in the news. Something's going on.'

Rosie nodded. 'Yeah. You're right. Something *is* going on.' She put a hand up. 'And maybe we can talk about that . . . But tell me this first . . . Where in Spain were you coming from?'

She knew she was pushing her luck. Ruby could blow up and storm out of the bar if she'd something to hide, or if she even suspected that Rosie knew about her history. But there was something about her look, plus the fact that it was Ruby who was the one doing all the phoning. She didn't sense badness in her. Just a wild, primal survival instinct and, somewhere, a vulnerability that she was trying her best to conceal. Rosie was a past master at that.

A blush rose on Ruby's cheekbones. Her lips tightened and she touched her neck, pulling her scarf up a little as though she felt exposed.

'Why are you asking that?'

'Gut instinct.' Rosie took a breath and waited a second. 'Ruby, I know what happened to your mother . . . Jackie. I know what Rab Jackson did to her. And Malky Cameron. I know what they did to your sis—'

'I don't want to talk about that.' Ruby's eyes hardened and she swallowed. 'Don't go there. Right?'

'Okay.' Rosie nodded. 'Were you working in Spain?'

'Look, Rosie, cut the crap. You obviously know more about me than I do, so what's going on?'

'Okay,' Rosie said. 'I have information that you were working with Rab Jackson.'

Silence.

'What information?'

'Well, not working, that's not quite accurate. But you were seen with him. On the Costa del Sol.'

'Who by?'

'Cops.'

'Fuck me, fucking gently!'

'It's okay. You were only seen in his company. It was part of an international covert operation around eighteen months ago, and your face came up in the picture. A snitch ID'd you as Ruby Reilly. But that was all. Nothing else. Then, in King's Cross, when you left the restaurant, you were seen on CCTV.'

'Fuck! So they know who I am?'

'They're not sure. Somebody spotted the CCTV and, when they fed it in, you came up on the earlier operation. They tracked you going onto the Eurostar, but not as Ruby Reilly.'

Ruby tensed up.

'Christ! So tell me one thing. Are they closing in on me? Look. I know you don't owe me anything, but you could tell me that. If you do, you can use my story as "the woman in the café" telling what I saw, but I want to remain anonymous.' Rosie could sense her panic.

'I'm not here to do deals like that. But no. They're not closing in. I don't think you're that important to them, actually. But I'm interested in you.'

'Why?'

'Because I'm also working on the story of the murder of those two vicious bastards Jackson and Cameron.' She paused, studying Ruby for her reaction. 'Only somebody with a thirst for retribution and real balls could do it. I was looking into the story and your name came up.'

'Christ almighty! Now you're saying I'm a killer? Any amount of people could have cause to do them in.'

'Yeah. But they wouldn't. Cops say people would be too scared to touch them. They're still protected by their low-life cronies here and abroad.'

'So you think I did it?' She snorted. 'How many murders do you think I've been involved in? The King's Cross murder, his pal Hawkins, Jackson and Cameron? Hey. How about the Bible fucking John murders? They never got anyone for that.' She shook her head, incredulous.

'Before your time, Bible John,' Rosie joked, hoping to lighten things up. 'Calm down, Ruby. I'm not talking to anyone about you. There are no cops about to march through the door and huckle you. I'm just looking to work on the story of Cameron and Jackson. And anything else you can help with.'

Silence.

'Okay.' Ruby swallowed. 'I do know something about that murder in London. At least I think I do. I've only just found out. That name I gave you when I first called – J B Solutions? That was from a piece of paper I found on the table after the big Russian guys left. I picked it up. Don't ask me why. Curiosity. Instinct. I've been funny that way all my life. But I couldn't believe it when I checked them out. I know who they are. I know them. I know who the owner is.'

Rosie felt a little dam burst in her head. At last. A breakthrough.

'Yeah? Jesus, Ruby! It took you long enough to come out with that.'

'Aye, well, I just wanted to see what you knew.' She leaned forward. 'I don't want to talk about Cameron and Jackson. They're history. End of. So don't go there. Or about my sister. But I can help you with that stuff, about the company.' She lowered her voice to a whisper. 'And other things, too. But I need some guarantees.'

'What guarantees?'

'I'm not working with the cops. I don't trust them.'

'Roddy Thompson.' Rosie threw in the name just to see what happened.

Nothing.

'Who?'

She was either a good liar or had no idea who he was.

'Never mind,' Rosie said. 'Look, I won't be working with cops, but I'd like to nail this J B Solutions company. I have information. You'll see the paper tomorrow. Tom Mahoney was about to blow the whistle on a lot of things. He was a spy.'

'A spy? Christ!'

'And he knew things about J B Solutions and their dealings. They supplied arms to UK cops and to the army.'

'I know. And to half the fucking villains from here to London and Spain.'

'How do you know that?'

'I just do.'

'I need to know how. I mean, how *would* you know that?'

'Because I'm a fucking accountant. All right?'

Rosie looked at her. Ruby Reilly. The frightened little girl she was on a desperate night a lifetime ago is not who she is now. She was a class act.

The second drink arrived and Ruby took a long slug.

'I'll help you, Rosie. Okay? I'll put my trust in you. Because the truth is, I don't have a lot of options in my life right now. But I've been places in my head you won't believe. I'm not normal. I was brought up in a children's home, with all the shite that involves. I've looked after my sister for the last five years while I've moved around the world doing what I do.'

'And what exactly is it that you do?' Rosie asked.

'I'll tell you later. But I had to find a safe place for my sister. Every fucker thinks she's dead, and that's how I wanted it to stay. Except today I found out that's not the case, and it's a problem for me. I have to take action. My sister is my biggest secret – the most important one. I'd have given up years ago if it weren't for her needing me. She's . . . she's the only person in the world who's ever needed me.' Her eyes moistened a little and she blinked twice.

Rosie watched her. The front was beginning to crumble a little. Not a lot, but enough to know that behind the mask was an abandoned, angry, driven child. Rosie knew how that felt.

'I know what you mean,' Rosie said. 'More than you can imagine.'

CHAPTER SEVENTEEN

Driving past her local newsagent's on the way to the office, Rosie spotted the *Post*'s billboard: 'SHOT PROF WAS SOVIET SPY' the headline screamed in bold black letters. The slick marketing boys didn't mess about. The *Post* would be flying off the shelves. She hadn't gone back to the office after yesterday's early-evening drama in Ayrshire, despite McGuire telling her he wanted to see her. Matt had been dispatched, along with the AA, to get her car out of the ditch in Ayrshire and bring her back. To everyone's surprise, the damage was minimal and the car still drivable. Back on the road, she and Matt had stopped at a café, where she'd told him he would be getting pulled into the story in the next day or so, once they had worked out the next move. She gave him only the basics but, as usual, he was choking to get involved.

'Where are you, Rosie? He's looking for you.' It was Marion on the phone.

'In the car park. I'll be there in two minutes.' Rosie was already heading for the revolving doors at the *Post's* entrance.

She stretched her arms above her head, wincing at the pain in her back from the crash.

'Shagger's back?' Jean grinned at reception as she walked in.

'I wish.' Rosie smiled.

Declan glanced up from his screen as she put her bag on the desk opposite his.

'Some splash in the paper today, Rosie.' Then he noticed her limping. 'What's happened to you? Swinging from the chandeliers again?'

'Christ. Everyone's a comedian.' She stretched her neck. 'Bit of a crash last night, early on. Car skidded into a ditch. Yes, I'm glad to be alive. You can quote me on that.' She winked over her shoulder as she walked towards the editor's office.

'Wait till you hear this, Mick,' she said, limping into his office. 'You're going to love it.'

He peered over the top of his reading glasses.

'Don't give me your bullshit, Gilmour. What the fuck?' He took off his glasses, cocked his head to watch her limp. 'And don't try for the sympathy vote. Explain.'

'I will . . . in a minute.' Rosie sat down delicately on the sofa. 'But first . . . I met Ruby Reilly last night.'

His expression changed.

'Seriously?' He sat back, folded his arms. 'She got in touch again?'

'Yep. Just as my car hit the ditch – and I realized I wasn't actually dead . . . my mobile rang and it was her. I met her later in a pub in Ashton Lane. That's why I couldn't come in last night to see you.' She gave a little sarcastic smile. 'I knew you would understand.'

'Aye, fine. But what the fuck were you doing down in Ayrshire? You know I like to be kept informed of where you're going. I can't seem to get that drummed inside that bloody head of yours! I mean, you could have ended up dead in some ditch, and the last place I would have looked for you would be fucking Kilmaurs.'

'I know. Sorry. Won't happen again.'

'Yes it bloody will. I'm going to tag you. I'm telling you, I will.' He gave her a look; part reproach, part affection. 'Right. So where were you?' He took a sip of his coffee. 'Oh. And great stuff this morning, incidentally. None of the other papers was anywhere near us. The bastards just lifted the story once our front page hit the streets . . . But I'm expecting some heat to come our way from the cops or the MoD. Fuck them. Let's see where we go from here first.'

'Okay,' Rosie said. 'I'll explain the Ayrshire run first.'

Rosie told him about the tip from Humphy Boyd, and he shook his head in disbelief as she regaled him with the story of the monkey diving around the living room.

'You're fucking joking! A monkey! Did you have Matt with you for a pic?'

'No. I was on my own. We can't use Humphy anyway. He was just giving us the info. He's got to stay out of it. But his information was solid. So I drove straight down to Ayrshire.'

McGuire listened as she told him of her meeting with the retired DCI Roddy Thompson.

'And it was after I left his house that someone forced me off the road.'

'So who did it? Why would anyone do that, and who knew you were in Ayrshire? I didn't even know, and I'm the fucking editor.'

Rosie shook her head.

'I don't know. That's what worries me. Like you, I'm sure Hawkins was murdered, but there'll be no way of proving it. So maybe whoever did that saw me going into his house a couple of times. That's my thinking and, to tell you the truth, it gives me the bloody creeps.'

McGuire steepled his hands under his chin.

'We're going to have to be ultra-careful here. At least with normal villains you can almost see it coming, but this is different.'

'Yeah. Anyway, never mind. We can't sit here fretting about that. I've got more to tell you.'

Rosie told him about her tip from Don that the woman

in the café had been identified as Ruby Reilly and that she'd been seen with Rab Jackson during a covert police operation eighteen months ago.

'I like the sound of this. So what's this bird like?'

'Striking,' Rosie said. 'Very good-looking. Seems a bit hard at first but a lot of that's just a front, I think. I talked to her for a while last night over a couple of drinks and she basically told me everything. She's all right. She's going to work with us on this.'

'Really?'

'So she says.'

Rosie had been surprised at how much Ruby had been willing to tell her the previous night, and she described to McGuire how Ruby had confirmed what Mahoney had said in his dossier about J B Solutions.

'She said that she's been told that Mahoney was actually there, on that operation. That's the information she gave me.'

'How the hell does she know that?'

'She wouldn't say straight out. The thing is, I hadn't said anything to her about what was inside Mahoney's dossier and yet she was talking about the same stuff. We have to keep her onside. I think she's a way into the heart of this.'

'So why is she suddenly being so cooperative? And who exactly is she in relation to Rab Jackson and that bunch of lowlifes?'

'All she said was that she was an accountant. She said

she'd tell me later what it is she does. Her story goes way back, though, to twenty-five years ago, when her mother, Jackie Reilly, was burned to death. It was Jackson and Cameron who did it.'

'Right. And she goes and works for him? So what exactly does she do as Jackson's accountant?'

'Just moving his money around. Making him legit.'

'So she's just as bad as them. Another fucking gangster.'

'True, I suppose. But she's on our side.'

'Why?'

'She's got this sister. Judy. She was a kid that night when they battered the mother to death. The sister was raped and brutalized by Jackson and Cameron. She's in a nursing home now, apparently in some kind of catatonic stupor. She hasn't spoken since it happened. So Ruby looks after her and she says she needs the money so she can get her the best care.'

'Aw, give me a hanky. I've a tear in my eye here.' He shook his head. 'So what does she want?'

'Initially, it was just to inform us that all this crap in the papers about her being involved in the Mahoney murder was nonsense, that she just happened to be in the wrong place at the wrong time.'

'So why did she get off her mark?'

'She didn't want to be there when the cops arrived.'

'She's on the run?'

'So it would seem. From Spain.'

McGuire sat for a moment, his fingers drumming the desk.

'Wait a minute, Gilmour. She works with Jackson, then fucks off after he dies, comes here, then his cohort Cameron gets torched in his garage. It doesn't take Columbo to work that one out.'

Rosie nodded.

'You think she killed them both.'

It was more of a statement than a question. Rosie suspected she had but she'd pushed that thought to the back of her mind.

McGuire's eyebrows knitted.

'Does she seem capable of that?'

'I don't know. But you know what? I didn't ask. And I won't ask. Because right now she's in a position to help us get an inside track on this story.'

'She may be a killer – twice over. And that's an even bigger story.'

'But she may not be. And that's not the point.'

'Yeah? Tell that to the High Court judge. Of course it's the fucking point.'

'Yes, I know that. But it is not of any interest to us right now. Leave that to the cops. If they can find evidence on her or anyone else, then that's up to them. It's not *our* job. *Our* job is to unravel all the stuff about Mahoney's death. That's our story, and we're already halfway there. Ruby can give us the lowdown on who's who, and she might even be able to get us a proper inroad so we can expose the whole shooting match.'

McGuire sat in silence, his mouth tight.

'What can she give us?'

Rosie told him about the connection again and that Ruby had mentioned Tam Dunn as being the owner of J B Solutions, and his links to Jackson and Tony Devlin.

He nodded.

'And afterwards, if we crack the story? What does she want?'

'I haven't got that far with her. But I know she won't work with the cops, and I know that her only priority is to keep her sister safe and alive. She'd assumed everyone who knew them years ago believed that her sister had died a few months later. She was even told that herself for years afterwards, while she was in and out of care. Then a few years ago she discovered her sister was alive, and it took a long time to track her down. So I'm not sure what she wants. But I think she wants to put these bastards away, and she may be in a position to do just that. She can lead us to them. We can't knock that chance back.'

McGuire took a long breath and let it out slowly.

'Okay. Then we deal with what we've got. We should be looking at these companies.'

'Yes. I want to go down to London with Matt and have a look at J B Solutions. Discreetly.'

'Yeah. Discreetly.' Mick shook his head. 'I've been there

before with your "discreetly", Gilmour. There's usually a body count in the first three days, and you're just lucky that so far you've not been one of the stiffs.' He adjusted his tie. 'I'm wondering about getting the cops involved at this stage. It might make sense to work with them on it. And also, it might keep you a bit safer. I don't think you can go tiptoeing around a major arms dealer. You really could get your head blown off. If these people can blow the head off an old professor in a busy London café, then a journalist poking her nose in is no problem. I have to think about this.'

'I hear what you're saying. But we need to think about an undercover operation—'

McGuire's phone rang, interrupting her, and he answered, looking irritated as he listened. 'Tell them I'll get back to them before the day's out, Marion,' he said, putting the phone down.

'See what I mean?' He spread his hands. 'That's Special Branch already. They want to come and talk to us. Some chappie is on his way up from London.'

Rosie sighed, pushing her hair back.

'It's your call, Mick.'

He nodded sarcastically. 'Thanks for that.'

'You know what I mean. If we work with them, we give up a lot of our own ground.'

'Hmmm. We'll have to see them anyway, see what they've got to say. It'll just antagonize them if we don't. I'll give

Hanlon a ring and we can talk legalities and how we're placed. So don't you dare go anywhere. And that's an order.'

'Yes, sir.' Rosie saluted him as she walked towards the door. 'But I was thinking if we do a bit of undercover on this J B Solutions, maybe I could bring big Adrian into the mix.'

'And do what?'

'Set up a meeting or something. Pose as arms dealers.'

'You don't look like an arms dealer.'

'How do you know what they look like?'

'I don't. But I'm guessing they're not women like you. Do you think you could carry something like that off?'

'Only one way to find out. Can I talk to Adrian?'

'Sound him out, then we can discuss it.'

Rosie stood up.

'Fine. I'm going to work on a follow-up story for tomorrow, and after that I'll have a detailed look at that dossier. I skimmed over a lot last night.'

She headed for the door, but McGuire was already engrossed in his screen, typing with two fingers on his keyboard.

'And get an X-ray on that back,' he said, without looking at her. 'I can't afford to have you packing up on me.'

'Yeah, yeah.' Rosie had no intention of having her back checked out. A hot bath and a couple of painkillers would do the trick.

*

In the office off the editorial floor Rosie sifted through the notes on Mahoney's dossier until she came to the page marked 'J B Solutions', which she had looked at briefly last night. Now she scrutinized it, fascinated. It gave the name of the main players, Damar Guns. There were typewritten notes of payments hidden in bank accounts in Liechtenstein. Mahoney was claiming that fake documents and licences had been granted by the MoD. She sat back, taking a long breath and letting it out slowly. How the hell was she going to get to the bottom of this? Deal with what you've got, McGuire had said. But all they had was information on who the arms dealers were at the centre of this and some of the papers from Mahoney's documents. And that Tam Dunn, the owner of J B Solutions, was involved with Rab Jackson, so whatever else he was he was definitely a thug. But there was only one way to get the proof. She sat back and swung her feet onto the desk, massaging the back of her neck. Whoever Tam Dunn was, he had to be slippery enough to obtain a licence to supply arms, so he would be no pushover. She looked up the company address in Pinner, North London. Then she scrolled down her mobile and dialled Adrian's number.

CHAPTER EIGHTEEN

Rosie was pleased that Ruby had trusted her enough to invite her to meet her sister in the nursing home, but she was also a little nervous, not quite knowing what to expect.

As she drove through the sleepy village of Bridge of Weir, she reflected on what Roddy Thompson had told her of the night Ruby had witnessed her mother being burned to death and her sister raped. How do you survive something like that and go on to function in the world? Rosie knew what it felt like to be alone and abandoned as a little girl, having witnessed her own mother's suicide, and after the agonizing years that followed in the children's homes, waiting, praying her father would come and take her back home. Everything that had happened to her from the moment she'd seen her mother hanging on the end of the rope had made her the person she was. You functioned in the real world as best you could after something like that, but you could never really be the same as everyone else. There was too much damage.

Rosie rang Ruby's mobile as she turned into the tree-lined driveway leading to the Foresthill Nursing Home, which nestled at the edge of a vast pine wood. As instructed, she parked her car and walked down towards the lake. In the mid-afternoon autumn sunshine, she passed a couple pushing an elderly lady in a wheelchair who stared straight into space in her own little world. She nodded sympathetically to them, wondering what it must feel like to watch your mother grow old and disintegrate before your eyes. Maybe she was lucky she'd be spared the trauma of caring for an elderly parent. The scene brought a lump to her throat, but she had to quickly compose herself, because Ruby was waving at her from a bench at the edge of the lake. A woman in a wheelchair was next to her. Rosie took a deep breath and braced herself.

'Good to see you again, Ruby.' Rosie glimpsed at the woman in the wheelchair. Her eyes didn't even register her arrival.

'My sister, Judy,' Ruby said. She crouched down and took her sister's hand. 'Judy . . . I want you to meet . . .' She looked up at Rosie. 'I want you to meet a friend of mine. Her name is Rosie.'

The woman's pale eyes blinked once and Rosie thought her head moved just a fraction in acknowledgement.

But Mahoney has written a lot about the arms dealing an[d]
this company we talked about, J B Solutions, and the gu[y]
who runs it . . . You mentioned him.'

'Tam Dunn,' Ruby interrupted.

'You know him?' Rosie asked, surprised.

'I don't know him, but I know a man who does.'

'Really? That's useful. Who is he?'

'His name is Tony Devlin. He runs the show here for Ra[b]
Jackson. Took over when Rab moved to Spain, and now he'[s]
the man in charge.'

'How well do you know him?'

'Well enough.' Ruby shot Rosie a lazy-eyed glance the[n]
looked away.

Rosie let the silence hang for a moment.

'Does he trust you?'

'Put it this way, I think he's scared not to trust me.'
Ruby's lips curled a little. 'He *needs* to trust me. I'm the only
one who knows where all Rab's money is, which in turn is
his money, and the mob's money, too.'

'Right.' Rosie nodded slowly. This was better than she'd
hoped for. 'Has he talked to you about Tam Dunn?'

'You bet he has. I was with him yesterday, and he's spilling his guts on this whole fucking story. He told me a lot of
stuff, actually – about the shooting of Mahoney . . . how it
was an arms deal that got fucked up. And how one of their
men got killed – Billy. He's from Glasgow but lived down
south for years. And another guy was captured.'

'Rosie's all right,' Ruby said softly to her sister. 'She's on
our side.'

Rosie watched the two of them, pondering what it would
be like to have a sister, even if she didn't speak to you and
her eyes were miles away. You could still hug her, even if
she didn't hug you back. She swallowed.

'I see the resemblance.' It was all she could think of
to say.

Ruby sat on bench and motioned Rosie to sit next to her.

'I wanted to meet you here, away from Glasgow, but also
so you could meet Judy.' She rubbed her hand along her
sister's arm. 'She's . . . well . . . she's everything to me.'

Rosie nodded, glancing at Judy then back to Ruby. 'Is
she . . . I mean, does she . . .' She was suddenly tongue-tied
and awkward. 'What I'm trying to say is, will she get better
in time? Have you seen any improvement over the years?'

'Yeah. Definitely. And the nurses told me that in recent
weeks she's been a little more communicative. Well, when
I say communicative, I mean she's actually acknowledged
their presence and their words when they speak to her.
She's registering things, they think. That's a big improvement. And she can walk a bit more, although she gets tired.
They pumped a lot of drugs into her years ago, because they
didn't know what they were dealing with. For such a long
time she was sedated, because that's what they thought
was best. There's all sorts of damage been done, muscles

wasted and stuff. Things are a little better now, but I'm scared to hope that she will ever really come back to me.'

Rosie wanted to ask if there was brain damage.

'Her brain is functioning,' Ruby said, as though reading her mind. 'They've done tests and there's no brain damage there. But it's the trauma. That, and the fact that for years after it all happened she was left with no proper care.' She leaned over and touched her sister's arm. 'She was shunted from pillar to post, notes getting lost . . . all that kind of shit. Given anti-psychotic drugs when what she needed was a good psychiatrist. They just wrote her off as a hopeless case. At one point they were treating her for schizophrenia. I mean, how the hell does that happen to a kid? There're probably a lot of people like that in institutions who shouldn't really be there.' She gazed out towards the lake. 'But that all changed a few years ago, when I found her. And now, day by day, things are getting better. I feel I can get to her. I hugged her when I got back a couple of weeks ago and whispered to her and – and she actually hugged me back. That's the first time that's happened. So I have to believe that there is hope.'

'What made her improve?' Rosie asked.

Ruby looked at her sister for a long moment but said nothing.

They sat watching a flock of birds swoop across the lake, the peace of the countryside filling the silence. Three people, Rosie thought. Surviving.

'So,' Ruby said, taking a cigarette out of her handbag and lighting up. 'You wanted to talk about your investigation.'

'Yes.' Rosie turned to her. 'I want to ask if you will work with us.'

'Go on.' Ruby blew a trail of smoke and watched it rise and disappear.

'Obviously, what I'm going to tell you now puts me in a lot of danger if it ever gets out, Ruby, so I'm placing a whole lot of trust in you.'

Ruby glared at her.

'Listen, pal. You're here. With my sister. I brought you here. Who's trusting who?'

Rosie nodded.

'Okay. Fair enough. Then here's the situation.' She took a deep breath. 'I have a dossier given to me by Gerard Hawkins – Mahoney's friend – the one you saw that day.'

Ruby raised her eyebrows.

'Really? I did see Mahoney pass something to him in the café.'

'You did? Good. At least that proves Hawkins didn't make it up. Well . . . I think Hawkins was murdered because he was about to make this information public, which is what he told me Mahoney had asked him to do that day.'

'Mahoney did look agitated.'

'The dossier is full of a lot of damning allegations. Some of them we may be able to back up but a lot of them we won't. That will be the editor's call, at the end of the day.

'By who?'

Ruby shrugged.

'By whoever was on the operation. Cops, MI6? Who knows? But the wee guy captured is called Derek . . . Del Boy. He's from Glasgow, but he knows Tam's minder, Billy, who was on the job, so *he* wanted to take him on the job for a bit of muscle. Tony told me Del got sent down in case the Russians were at the capers. Turns out someone else was at the capers. Tony doesn't know how it all went tits up, but he said they lost a lot of money and the Russians were not happy. Tam works with the Russians on a lot of deals. It's how things are these days, apparently. He's pretty big stuff now – Tam Dunn. Left Glasgow years ago and Rab worked with him while he built things up down south. Rab invested in one of his companies.'

'Tony told you all this?'

'Yep.'

'Did he say the name of the company he invested in?'

'Yeah. Damar Guns . . . They're the ones that sell guns to Africa. Dunn has no proper licence. Tony says someone is on the take and issuing fake papers.'

'Christ! That's pretty much what Mahoney's saying.'

'Great. So you know I'm not bullshitting.' Ruby sat back, giving Rosie a sideways glance.

'Never thought you were. But I need to get some inroad into this guy and blow the whole thing.' She paused. 'Would you be willing to help us on that? If we set something up?'

'Like what?'

'I'll tell you more once I work it all out. But we would be undercover.'

'Not me, though.'

'No. But you could maybe help if Tony gives you any information.'

'Sure. If I can.' She looked Rosie in the eye. 'But I want something in return. Are you working with the cops?'

'Not yet. I know they'll want to talk to us after this morning's story in the *Post*. The editor has still got to see them, then we'll decide what to do.'

'I don't want to work with the cops. Because once this is over I'm out of here for a while. Maybe for ever. With Judy.'

They sat quietly.

'But can you do that with her? Is she okay to travel the way she is?'

'Yeah. I'll go to France. I have a place there. I can look after her. I've already looked into it.'

'You have money?'

Ruby looked at her and stubbed out her cigarette on the grass.

'I have money.' Her eyes smiled a little. 'I'm the accountant. I don't have to worry about money.'

The trees rustled as the wind rose. Ruby looked at her watch.

'I'm going to have to take Judy back up. She gets her

dinner at five. We eat together ... I have to help her ... then I'll stay here till she's asleep.'

'Okay.' Rosie stood up. 'But I'll be in touch. And I appreciate your help.' They shook hands. 'I'll give you a call when I know more.'

'Likewise,' Ruby said, getting behind her sister's wheelchair.

Rosie bent down.

'Good to meet you, Judy.'

Judy's blank gaze seemed to veer slowly away from the lake, and she made a slight turn of her head. Her eyes didn't smile or show any emotion, but for a fleeting second they looked straight at Rosie. She was in there. Somewhere.

CHAPTER NINETEEN

McGuire was in rant mode, pacing around his office as Rosie's eyes followed him from the sofa.

He turned to her, rolling up his sleeves. 'I'm not in the mood to take any crap from these guys.'

'Me neither. Did they give any indication on the phone of what's going on?'

'Nope. I only had a brief word with the boss man. Chief Superintendent Boswell-Smith. A pretty fancy name for a plod.'

'Special Branch plod, though, Mick. Some of them are a bit top drawer. If he's that high up the chain, he'll have seen a bit of action in the field.'

'Well, he'll not be throwing his weight around here.' He folded his arms. 'What about Mahoney's dossier? Have you got it all sorted?'

'Yes. All copied twice and hidden away. I took everything

I gave you, just in case they ask you for any paperwork . . . In case they have a search warrant.'

'There was no sign of that from the brief phone call. They said they just want a chat about our front page.'

'Well,' Rosie said, 'I'm deeply suspicious of them anyway. It was probably them who bumped off Hawkins. And I wouldn't be surprised if it was them who ran me off the road in Kilmaurs. I'm not just being paranoid, but there's some dark stuff going on.'

McGuire's phone rang and he picked it up.

'Send them in, Marion.' He turned to Rosie, squaring his shoulders. 'So, here's your chance to ask if they did Hawkins in and made you crash.' He gave her a mischievous grin.

'I might just do that.'

Rosie always felt intimidated when police came marching in on an investigation, because it was never to tell her to keep up the good work. Far from it. In the past when they'd pitched up at the *Post* it had been an attempt to monster her, push her for her information source or make her hand over evidence. It usually ended with a bad-tempered senior cop storming out, threatening repercussions.

A knock on the door, and Marion appeared ahead of two men then backed out. 'Hello, Mr McGuire.' The big man in the blue pinstripe suit stretched out a hand. 'Thanks for agreeing to see us. Chief Superintendent James Boswell-Smith.'

He didn't sound as though he had picked up those clipped tones pounding the beat in London's East End, and he looked more like a politician than a detective.

'Not at all.' McGuire shook his hand. 'Always ready to help out Her Majesty's finest.'

His expression said the opposite.

'And this is Captain Martin Banks.' The superintendent gestured towards his colleague.

'Captain?' McGuire raised his eyebrows. 'Have we sent for the troops already?'

Nobody moved for an awkward moment, then McGuire went on. 'And this is Rosie Gilmour, my Investigations Editor, and all-round top operator.' McGuire had a glint in his eye, and added cheekily, 'She's even been known to noise up the cops from time to time . . . so you'll want to watch her.'

'How are you doing, chaps? Welcome to Glasgow.' Rosie smiled at the big cop as she shook his hand, but her eyes were drawn to the captain.

He was all chisel-jawed and rugged good looks, with close-cropped hair and a broken nose. He looked like the kind of guy you'd want on your side if you had to fight your way out of trouble. His icy blue eyes locked with Rosie's, and she hoped she didn't look as impressed as she felt.

'So' – McGuire motioned them towards his conference table – 'take a seat.' He turned to the captain. 'I'm a little confused here. Are you army?'

The captain opened his mouth to speak, but Boswell-Smith intervened.

'Yes, he is. Captain Banks has been seconded from Hereford to the MoD investigation.' He tugged at the cuffs of his white shirt as he sat down. 'On occasion in the international fight against organized crime, all forces come together. It's not a fact that we shout from the rooftops – but it does happen.'

'I see.' McGuire shot Rosie a look.

Hereford meant the SAS, and if they were bringing *them* in then something serious had gone down. If it came to a fist fight over Mahoney's documents, she wouldn't mind if the captain wrestled her to the ground.

'So, Superintendent' – McGuire took a breath – 'what can we do for you here?'

Boswell-Smith cleared his throat.

'Your story in the newspaper yesterday . . . About Tom Mahoney the university lecturer being a spy.' He clasped his hands on the desk. 'We're very interested in that.'

'Yes.' McGuire nodded. 'So are we . . . and our army of readers.' He waited.

'So . . . er . . . what is that allegation based on?' He looked at Rosie inquisitively. 'I'm aware you'll not want to reveal your sources. But do you have actual evidence to back that up?'

'It came from documented evidence,' Rosie said. 'From information that Tom Mahoney had given in writing.

Before his . . . er . . . murder.' She wanted to say 'execution', but thought better of it.

'You mean a written testament from Tom Mahoney? And do you have that in your possession?'

'No. I don't, actually,' she said quickly. 'It was shown to me by a contact. And I don't have access to that information any more. I took notes from it at the time but I don't have the documents.' She hoped the lie wasn't written on her face. 'And I don't have access to that contact either.'

'So you don't have a contact you can go back to? Even if you want to check your facts again?'

'No.'

'Why?'

'Because he's dead.'

The silence hung over them, and Rosie crossed her legs and sat back, clicking her pen. She was conscious of the captain watching her.

'Can you say who the contact is?'

Rosie caught McGuire's eye, then looked at the cop.

'I don't really think I have to tell you that, Superintendent. I'm sure you already know.'

Again, the silence, Rosie holding her nerve.

McGuire gave an impatient puff.

'Look, chaps. Let's cut to the chase here.' He looked at his watch. 'I've got an editorial conference in fifteen minutes. What exactly do you want from us? Do you want us to help you with your investigation? Because if you do, then we may be in a position to do that, but that will depend on how you want to play this.' He turned to Rosie.

'Rosie. Tell the chief super a bit of what you've been told happened in Berlin.'

Rosie was a little surprised that McGuire was going in boots first.

'Okay.' She sat forward, leaning her elbows on the table. 'I have good, solid information that Mahoney was a spy, or had been many years ago, as our story says. But apparently he was also working for MI6 over the years, and lately was used in the international fight against crime. He was part of an operation – a sting operation – in Berlin, to bust open a crooked illegal arms deal with a UK operator and Russian mobsters.' She paused for effect, feeling confident. 'How am I doing so far, Superintendent?'

He said nothing but Rosie saw the muscle in his jaw tighten. She continued.

'Now, for some reason – I don't know why – the sting went wrong and a Russian woman was caught in the crossfire. Her name was Katya.' She paused again, raising her eyebrows. 'I'm also told that the police – the joint international operation – also took a prisoner. One Derek . . . Del.' Their faces were blank. 'Well. He's gone missing. That much we know. And he was definitely in on that arms deal, working for UK gangsters. So, at the moment, I'm trying to establish more about the man behind the UK arms company. We want to nail him. And obviously we want to find out who killed Mahoney. Was it the Russians, or someone else . . . ?'

'It appears that there was some Russian mafia involvement in the murder of Mahoney,' the cop said.

'Yeah,' Rosie said flatly, shooting him a sarcastic look. 'It would *appear* that way. But I'm not sure that's the case. Anyway. We're going to expose this arms dealer. I'm sure you know who we're talking about?' Rosie flicked over a page in her notebook, glancing at notes more for effect than necessity. 'Because the operation that the police were involved in to nail this guy went – for want of a better expression – belly up, if my information is accurate.'

The cop said nothing. They sat in tense silence.

McGuire cleared his throat.

'Well, if that's all, gentlemen, I must be getting on. I'm not sure we were of any help to you. But . . .'

'Hold on.' The chief Superintendent put a hand up. 'We may be able to assist you – perhaps we can help each other on this. I will have to consult with my department and the various bodies involved. This a very high-level inquiry.'

'Yes. I'm sure.' McGuire rolled his eyes. 'Well, once the left hand reveals to the right hand what's going on, you chaps know where we are.' He looked at Rosie. 'Oh, and I think my Investigations Editor has something else to ask you. Rosie? Tell the chief super how you were forced off the road the other night.'

'Yes. That's correct,' Rosie said. 'I'd been meeting a contact down in Ayrshire, and when I was driving home I was run off the road by another car. A bit of a close shave, actually. Very strange. I don't suppose you can shed any intelligence on that?'

'No. Absolutely no idea. I'm not even sure why you're asking.' The chief superintendent shook his head, looking straight at her.

'Yeah. Thought not.' Rosie gave him a sarcastic look.

'Did you report it to Strathclyde Police?' The cop bristled.

'No. I didn't think there was much point.'

The two men stood up. Boswell-Smith stretched out his hand to McGuire.

'I hope we'll be seeing you again, sir.' He nodded to Rosie, shaking hands. 'And you, Rosie. Thanks for your information.' His mouth was tight.

Rosie said nothing and shook both their hands.

When the door was closed, McGuire turned to Rosie as he walked across to his desk.

'What the fuck was all that about?'

'Fishing expedition,' Rosie replied. 'They're trying to find out what we've got.'

'They must be rattled to come all the way up from London. And what's with the SAS guy? What's that all about? At least they didn't get all heavy-handed and ask me to turn out my drawers. They'd have been told to GTF if they had.'

'I'm guessing the SAS man was, as the big man said, there as part of the international fight against crime. They do work together on certain things, but I've never heard of SAS involvement.' She paused. 'They might be working on the basis that we have Mahoney's dossier. Because if what Hawkins told me is true, then Mahoney had already threatened to expose them. Maybe he even told them he had a dossier that could blow them all out of the water. And that's why they got rid of him.'

'We've no evidence whatsoever that they killed Mahoney – or Hawkins. Do bear that in mind, Gilmour.'

'I know. But they'll be shitting themselves in high places if they believe Mahoney has got some kind of dossier exposing the dodgy arms company, and drawing attention to the fact that people who work for the government are turning a blind eye so it can get a fake licence. Can you imagine the blood on the walls if that gets out?'

'But it's not going to get out, because we don't have proof.'

'Not yet. I'm working on it.' Rosie felt a little impatient. 'But we're obviously on the right track, Mick, or they wouldn't have sent someone scurrying up to Glasgow.'

'So you'll have to watch your step.' He turned to his computer. 'Oh, and by the way, I noticed James Bond giving you the eye.'

'You don't need to look so surprised,' she said over her shoulder as she headed for the door.

CHAPTER TWENTY

Rosie walked up from her flat to St Vincent Street to meet Adrian. She wasn't quite sure what to expect. She'd toyed with the idea of inviting him to stay at her flat for the duration of the job, but she didn't want awkward questions from McGuire or Matt. She needn't have worried. He declined the offer of a hotel, saying he was staying with Bosnian friends he hadn't seen since he left Glasgow a couple of years ago. Decision made. Rosie's paranoia kicked in. Had he gone cold after their encounter in Sarajevo, which, on reflection, probably shouldn't have happened? Jesus! She was behaving like a teenager on a first date.

She saw him through the window as she approached the bistro. He was sitting in an alcove, his arm resting on the cushioned wall seating, gazing into the middle distance. He looked cool and relaxed, but knowing Adrian, that was only half the story.

He stood up when she opened the door and stepped

inside. It was always hard to tell what was going on behind his flat, naturally gloomy expression, but his eyes softened and she knew it was as close to delighted as Adrian got.

'Rosie.' Towering above her, he tilted his head to the side and reached out both hands.

'Adrian.' Rosie automatically slipped into his arms.

They hugged for a long moment, and she could feel him squeeze her tight against his body. Then he pulled back and his eyes searched her face.

'Rosie. My friend.'

Then he kissed her. A soft, glad-to-see-you kiss on the lips, pulling back after a second as though not sure. Then they kissed again, this time longer, and Rosie felt his hand grip her hair as she kissed him back. She could feel his heartbeat. They eased apart, and Adrian gazed down at her. Now he did smile.

'It's good to see you.' He brushed the back of his fingers across her cheek.

'You, too.' Rosie put her hand over his. 'Come on. Let's sit down. People are staring at us.'

The waiter showed them to a table in the corner and Rosie ordered a gin and tonic and Adrian a beer. Rosie also asked for a bottle of house red, too, as she knew she would need a few drinks to get through this. For a long moment they just sat looking at each other.

Rosie reached her hand across the table so that their fingers were almost touching. She wasn't quite sure what to say. What she really wanted to ask was how he felt. They'd ended her sixweek trip to Sarajevo with an explosion of sweltering passion for the final three nights, but they'd barely spoken about it while it was happening and it was clear they weren't an item, which suited them both. But what were they?

'Adrian . . . I . . . Er . . . How are things with you? . . . Is everything okay? I'm so glad you're here. This will be a big job, if a bit dodgy.' She felt awkward, conscious of Adrian studying her.

'Yes . . . I am also glad.' He ran a hand over his face and sat back as the waiter arrived and put his beer on the table. Adrian raised his glass towards her. 'Thank you for asking me. I have done already some work on this.' He shrugged. 'But we can talk about that in a minute.'

He took a long drink of his beer and brought his cigarettes out of his top pocket. Rosie watched as he lit up, sucking in the smoke and letting it out slowly. She wasn't comfortable with lingering silences. She wished she could be in control here, be her usual strident self. But here she was, sitting, waiting to be addressed by a man she had developed feelings for, even though right now she wasn't sure how deep those feelings were. It wasn't supposed to be like this.

'Rosie. I wanted to ask you. Are you . . . I mean . . . Are you okay with what happened between us in Sarajevo?' His hooded eyes locked on hers. 'I thought maybe you would feel that . . . well, maybe that it should not have happened . . . You know . . . between friends. To be lovers like that.'

Rosie swallowed, partly taken aback by his frankness and partly glad it was out in the open.

'And you, Adrian? Are you okay? She threw the question back at him.

He shrugged. 'Of course. I was very happy.' He placed his hand on top of hers. 'I like being with you very much. I enjoy it . . . But then you . . . and I think maybe you don't want any more . . . and I worry we have ruined the friendship.'

Rosie gulped a mouthful of gin and tonic and put her glass down.

'No . . . I mean yes . . . I'm . . . I'm okay with everything. No regrets, if that's what you're asking. But if I'm really honest, I'm not great with relationships and I'm still not really sure where I'm going with anything in my life.' Christ! She was close to babbling.

Adrian put his hand up.

'Of course. I understand this. We are friends first. Always. That is what I mean. I . . . I don't want to make a plan.'

'Good,' Rosie said, glad the air had been cleared. She hoped her face didn't show the little stab of upset she felt that he seemed to be playing down their encounter. 'Then let's just not worry about it. Take things as they come.' She picked up the menu. 'Let's eat. I'm starved.'

*

After dinner they sat drinking wine and Adrian listened as Rosie went over the full story. She'd briefed him on the phone while he was still in Bosnia, but face to face it was easier to fill him in on the latest developments. He explained that he'd set up a bogus security company in Sarajevo, as Rosie had instructed, with a fake address, and he'd already emailed J B Solutions in London requesting a meeting. His cover story was that he supplied bodyguards and minders to various figures in the Balkans, and that his company was expanding at a swift rate and required more weaponry, which he preferred to source from outside of his own country. Mickey Kavanagh had told Rosie that was how a lot of dodgy arms deals were done.

Adrian reached into the zipped pocket of his green safari shirt and pulled out a piece of paper.

'I have this.' He handed it across the table. 'It came this morning before I left my house. He has taken the bait.'

Rosie's eyes widened as she read the email and saw the name at the bottom. Thomas J. Dunn, Managing Director. The email thanked 'Sef' – the name of the bogus company Adrian had set up – and said Mr Dunn would be happy to talk about assisting a growing enterprise such as theirs, and would be delighted to meet their representative when he was in the UK in the near future. It was well written and professional, so, regardless of what else Tam Dunn did, he was also smart and literate enough to pass himself off as a pro.

'Brilliant!' Rosie said. 'He writes like he knows the game. Anyone reading this who didn't know Dunn would think he was a legit businessman supplying legit companies – not the gunrunning, toerag gangster he really is.' She scanned it again. 'This is a great start.' Rosie checked her watch and signalled the waiter for the bill. She felt a twinge of desire as Adrian sat back, stretching out his long legs in jeans and scuffed cowboy boots. For a moment she considered being reckless and inviting him back, but she thought better of it. He was here to work. They had an important job to do. And anyhow, perhaps he was no longer interested. She knocked back the remains of her wine.

'We best get moving.' Rosie stuffed the receipt for the bill into her bag. 'We've got a lot of planning to do. I think you should email our man back and say you can see him the day after tomorrow. That gives us time to get organized.'

Adrian nodded. He stood up and pushed his cigarette packet into his breast pocket.

'I will walk you to your flat.'

They strolled to Rosie's flat like two old friends, chatting about Sarajevo and the people Rosie had met during the weeks she'd just spent there. Adrian looked relaxed, giving her all the news of his mother, and that his sister was now pregnant, bringing great excitement to everyone in their village. But she detected a sadness in his eyes as he talked about how wonderful it was to have a little baby. It must bring back the agony of losing his own child, Rosie thought, ripped from its mother's womb during the Bosnian War. As they got up the steps, Adrian was still at her side, and for a moment they stood on the stair as Rosie pushed the key in the door.

'I make sure you are inside your house,' he said. 'To be safe.'

'It's fine,' she said, stepping into the hallway. 'My flat is like a fortress these days. I can't allow myself to be spooked out, Adrian. I've put a lot of that crap behind me now. I'll be okay from here. Honest.'

He nodded. 'If you are sure.'

They stood looking at each other, the air crackling with tension.

'So,' he said. 'Thanks for dinner. I will see you tomorrow?'

'Yes. Before twelve. We'll talk. If you send the email early in the morning, we'll start making plans.'

He stepped forward and touched her hair, then bent to kiss her, and Rosie wrapped her arms around him. He kissed her again, and she tasted the tip of his tongue as she kissed him back. Then he stopped.

'Sorry.' He released her. 'I forget we are working.' He let out a breath.

'Yes.' Rosie composed herself, feeling the taste of him on her lips. 'Let's . . . er . . . leave this for the moment. We'd better get some sleep.'

His eyes fixed her for a few seconds, then he took a step back. She resisted the urge to throw caution to the wind.

CHAPTER TWENTY-ONE

From the private room of the rooftop restaurant Ruby could see the lights twinkling across the city and all along the banks of the Clyde. Tony Devlin had opened Santino's last year in a blaze of tabloid publicity. It was the place to be seen in, frequented by footballers, gangsters and minor celebrities – and anyone who could afford its exorbitant prices. Tony was obsessed by Hollywood gangster films and had adorned the restaurant with tacky Mafia movie memorabilia, from Al Capone to *The Godfather*. He'd even named the place after the James Caan character of Santino 'Sonny' Corleone from the blockbuster films. He'd watch them again and again, copying Sonny's walk and demean- our. Tony really was *that* unhinged. He'd invested a lot of money in the restaurant, poached a top chef from one of the most established restaurants in Glasgow, boasting that he'd made him an offer he couldn't refuse. People snig- gered behind his back – but never to his face. His palatial office was on the top floor, off the private room, where he sometimes entertained other hoodlums, bent lawyers or cops he wanted to impress but who didn't want to be seen by other diners.

Ruby wished to Christ the night would hurry up and be over, because this Tam Dunn character that Tony had brought along for dinner gave her the creeps. When they'd been introduced when she arrived a couple of hours earlier, he'd given Tony a dig in the ribs, declaring he was horny as fuck and that he shouldn't present a beautiful bird to him if he wasn't allowed to shag her. Charming. Tony had joked that Ruby was out of bounds, but a couple of girls would be along later once they finished their shift at the sauna. And so they were.

Tony racked up a few lines of coke on the table and everyone hoovered it up – except Ruby. She never touched it, she told them, deadpan. They'd looked at her as though there was something wrong with her mind, and as the coke kicked in the party – Tam Dunn style – got started. The half-naked Eastern European girls spoke little English and apparently worked as hookers in one of Tony's two saunas in the city. The blonde girl, with the Marilyn Monroe hairstyle and stunning looks who'd been snogging Dunn, was now rubbing his crotch in full view of everyone. But it was Ruby, in her crimson figure-hugging dress that the lecherous bastard was looking at as the bulge swelled in his trousers.

'Hey Ruby, darlin',' Dunn said, his eyes heavy as the girl pleasured him. 'I'm sure Tony wouldn't object to a wee threesome. I mean, we're all friends here.'

'No way, big man,' Tony chuckled, picking up his ringing mobile from the table to answer a call.

Dunn kept his eyes on Ruby as the girl unzipped his trousers and bent over to take him in her mouth. Ruby glared right back at him, her eyes full of contempt for this piece of shit as he closed his eyes, grabbing the girl by the hair and pushing her head further down on him as he let out little gasps. A flush of anger rose in Ruby's chest as a vivid image came to her of a little girl being raped by two men – a lifetime ago. She stood up and mouthed to Tony, who was still on the phone, that she was going to the loo.

She walked through the glass doors onto the roof terrace. She lit a cigarette and stood gazing across the Glasgow rooftops, black and shiny in the steady drizzle, and reflected on the conversation around the table earlier, before the evening had descended into the orgy it was becoming.

Tam Dunn was everything Tony had told her he was, only more so. He'd regaled them with stories of growing up in Glasgow's East End and rising through the ranks when Rab Jackson was one of the biggest players in the city, and he reeled off a few names who had crossed them, saying they were buried beneath the foundations of the famous Kingston Bridge. The difference between Rab and Big Jake Cox, he said, was that Rab knew when it was time to pull back, look at the long game, and reinvest sensibly. That was what Rab was all about. He was the first of the hard men to plough the money into property, to take it offshore and put it in banks across Europe. Rab had properties and apartments across the Spanish resorts, and also in Amsterdam and Liverpool's docklands. The money was being expertly cleaned, and Rab was out of the picture, living the good life in Spain.

Not any more he isn't, thought Ruby, as she played along, nodding at all the right moments, as if she were impressed. Tam was surprised that Rab hadn't told him about Ruby, but said now that he'd met her he could see why the old bastard didn't want to share her with anyone else. Ruby swiftly pointed out that she'd been Rab's accountant and nothing else, that she only visited when she had to. She was her own woman, she'd said, clocking Tony watching her and hoping she hadn't gone over the score. She'd been keeping everything on an even keel with Tony, especially now that she'd agreed to help this reporter. She liked Rosie Gilmour, and had a bit of respect for the way she was committed to her job. But for Ruby the most important thing was the future. She was getting out of this altogether. If things worked out, and if this Rosie had a proper plan, then all of these bastards would get their day. She was looking forward to that, big time.

Tam Dunn was puffed up with his own importance, bragging about the arms dealing and that he had people in high places in his pocket. Ruby had listened hard as he talked of a fake arms-dealing licence. He ranted about some recent big deal that went tits up in Berlin, saying there must have been a grass. They'd been dealing with the Russians for years, but suddenly there were cops everywhere and one of their own boys got done over. As well as that, Derek 'Del Boy' had been captured by them. They might never see him again. If he opened his trap to them, Dunn spat, he'll be better off dead anyway.

He also bragged about a new potential customer who'd contacted him and that, if it worked out, they'd be breaking into the Balkans, and that could bring in megabucks in the future. Tony piped up that he wasn't quite sure where the Balkans was, and Dunn had called him a thick bastard and told him to get a fucking atlas. The Balkans was big business, Dunn said, and to get a foothold in that region would open up all sorts of opportunities. But they'd have to cut the Russians in, because they also supplied him with some of the most popular guns, which would end up on the streets of the UK. But apart from that, the Russians had a lot of the Balkan region sewn up. It was all about scratching each other's backs – you worked together because you had to.

Ruby flicked her cigarette end into the distance and headed back to the restaurant. She wouldn't be staying long. She'd already made her mind up to tell Tony she had a splitting headache and would go home early. Tam Dunn's exploits with the blonde bird had dulled her appetite for sex tonight.

When she opened the door to the room, Ruby stopped, her mouth dropping open. There was blood everywhere. Dunn was stamping viciously on the bloodied head of the blonde girl, who was lying lifeless on the floor. His sweating face was contorted with rage, his eyes crazed as Ruby heard the sickening sound of his boot tearing open the girl's cheeks and her teeth bursting out of her blood-soaked face. The other hooker cowered in a corner, shivering and sobbing.

'Fuck's sake!' Ruby shouted. Her hands went to her mouth and she steadied herself against the wall. 'What the fuck ...? Oh Jesus Christ almighty! Stop! ... You're killing her!'

Tony suddenly arrived at her back and burst past her, stopping in his tracks as he took in the scene.

'Aw, for fuck's sake, Tam!' He was across the room in a second. 'Fuck me, man! Stop! Enough! Enough, for fuck's sake!' He dived across to his desk and pressed a red button on the phone. 'Davey, get up here now. Bring Pete with you. Hurry.'

Ruby's legs turned jelly as Dunn suddenly stopped kicking and stood over the girl's body, his eyes wild, saliva dripping off his chin.

'Wee cunt!' He gave her one last kick then turned to Tony. 'Wee slag gave me a lot of shit. Making a cunt of me. Fucker.'

'What happened, for Christ's sake?' Tony knelt down beside the girl.

He lifted her hand, but it fell limp on to the floor.

'Is him, Tony,' the other hooker sobbed in broken English, pointing to Dunn, 'He couldn't . . . fuck . . . and Lujca made a joke . . . and he goes like fucking crazy. He starts punching her face, and then kickng her.' She wept. 'Oh God . . . I think he's killed her. She is my friend.' She rocked back and forwards, her arms wrapped around her knees.

The door burst open and two burly minders in dinner suits came in. They turned to Tony in disbelief.

'Fuck me, man!' one of them said as he rushed across to the girl. He put his hand to her neck for a second then looked up at Tony. 'She's dead, boss.'

'Aw, fuck me, man!' Tony shouted. 'Fuck me, Tam! What the fuck, man! Look what you've done! Christ all-fucking-mighty!'

Dunn suddenly looked shaken, as though he'd come back to the real world. Ruby stood, her hand still at her mouth, as he stared down at the girl.

'It just . . . It just got out of hand, man . . . I fucking cracked up . . . She was making me look like a cunt, slagging me for losing my hard-on. I just lost the place. Sorry, mate.' He looked down at his light-grey trousers, splashed with the girl's blood. 'Look at the state of my fucking trousers.'

Tony was still kneeling on the floor, shaking his head.

'What a fucking mess.' His voice was barely audible. He stood up and turned to the two bouncers. 'Right, boys, listen. You need to deal with this. Just get rid of her.'

Ruby looked down at the girl's Marilyn Monroe hair, now matted with blood. Her face was battered to a pulp, her skinny white arms so translucent you could see her veins. At some stage she had left home in whatever country she came from in search of a better life, Ruby thought. But the dreams got lost along the way, in saunas and massage parlours or any of the other shitty dens that had become a way of life for girls like her.

'Wait a minute.' Ruby couldn't help herself. 'Just get rid of her? Fuck's sake, Tony! She's a wee girl – she's just been kicked to death by that fucker!' She looked at Dunn. 'What kind of fucking animal does that?'

'Shut the fuck up, Ruby! Keep out of it! Right?' Tony's eyes blazed as he jabbed a finger to her. 'Just keep the fuck out of it! It's nothing to do with you. Shit happens! You never saw this. Remember that . . . Unless you've got some kind of fucking Plan B for the rest of your life.'

Ruby glared from one to the other, then to the minders, and finally looked at the girl on the ground and her friend weeping in the corner.

Her chest felt tight as she fought back tears of rage.

'Who is she?' She looked at the friend.

'She's nobody,' Tony barked. 'Illegal fucking immigrant.

From East Europe somewhere. Junkie. If it hadn't happened now it was going to happen sometime. Just forget about it.'

Tony went across to the other girl and pulled her to her feet. She cowered, covering her face with her hands, waiting for the blows to rain on her.

'It's all right. I'm not going to hurt you.' He made her face him. 'Listen. You keep your mouth shut about this, and I'll look after you. All right? You'll be well looked after.' The girl nodded, shaking. He went into his pocket and took out a fat wedge of twenty-quid notes. 'Take this tonight and come to the sauna tomorrow and we'll sort you out with a place to stay. And a new job.' He touched her face. 'All right, darling? This . . .' He looked down at the girl. '. . . This was just a wee mistake. Shouldn't have happened. But you'll be all right. Now on you go. The boys will get you a lift to your flat.'

She took the money in her trembling hands and nodded, her face gaunt and sweating, tears spilling out of her big blue eyes.

Ruby stood, swallowing back tears.

'I'm going home, Tony. I've had enough. My head's splitting. I need my bed.' Ruby tried to sound as matter of fact as she could.

Tony came over to her. 'Okay, sweetheart. I'll talk to you in the morning. Sorry you had to see this.'

Ruby said nothing, pulled away when he tried to kiss her.

As the girl walked towards the door, Tony turned to one of the guys, lowered his voice and spoke behind her back.

'You need to take care of her, lads. Know what I mean?'

The men nodded.

Ruby waited till they were out of the room then gave Tam Dunn one last look and left. She felt vomit rising in her throat but managed to hold on until she had raced to the toilet at the top of the stairs. Then she threw her guts up.

Back at her flat, Ruby poured herself a stiff gin and sat down, her hands still trembling as she lit a cigarette. She knocked back half her drink and slumped on the sofa. She felt so utterly alone. She had the same sick feeling in the pit of her stomach that she remembered from all those years ago when they had taken her away the night of the fire, after she saw her mother's charred face and her sister raped by those beasts. And later, when they held her in the children's home and they put her to bed, Ruby had lain staring at the ceiling, the acrid smell of smoke still in her hair, unable to cry until eventually her chest burst and she wept and sobbed so hard they had to come in and sit with her until she fell asleep, exhausted. She was alone then, and the same feeling of desolation now overwhelmed her. The tears came and she wiped them away. She needed to be strong. Then they came again, and she couldn't stop weeping, her sobs crashing the stillness. After a few minutes she composed herself and sniffed, blowing her nose and trying to think straight. She picked up her mobile.

'Rosie?' She sniffed. 'Sorry it's so late.'

'No problem. That's okay, Ruby. What's wrong?'

'I need to see you.'

'Now? What's happened? Is there some kind of trouble? Are you crying? You sound upset.'

Ruby was so choked she couldn't answer when Rosie asked again if she was okay.

'I'll come now. Where are you?'

'No,' Ruby said through tears. 'Tomorrow. First thing. I'll call you.'

'You sure? I can come now. You sound terrible.'

'I have to go. Tomorrow morning, Rosie. I'll phone.'

She hung up, wiped her eyes and finished her drink.

CHAPTER TWENTY-TWO

Rosie was ten minutes early, but Ruby was already inside the café waiting for her. From her distraught phone call last night she knew something bad had happened, but she hadn't wanted to push Ruby. Afterwards, Rosie had been awake half the night, fretting over what the problem could be, worried something had happened to Judy. Her gut niggled with guilt that she'd placed Ruby in danger by getting her to agree to give her an inside track on the investigation.

'You all right?' Rosie slid into the booth and sat opposite Ruby. 'I was worried about you.'

Ruby shook her head, dark shadows beneath puffy eyes.

'Oh, God.' She wiped her nose with the back of her hand as her eyes filled with tears. 'Look at the state of me ... Give me a minute.'

Rosie waved the waitress over and ordered a skinny latté, and Ruby nodded for the same. Then Rosie watched as Ruby tried to compose herself.

'Listen, Rosie. Something bad happened last night. Something really fucked up.'

'What? To you?'

Ruby shook her head.

'No.' She took a cigarette out and lit up. 'No. Not me. That bastard Tam Dunn. I met him last night . . . I was with Tony. We were invited for dinner at Santino's – it's Tony's restaurant. We were in a private room off Tony's office, having dinner.'

Rosie nodded.

Ruby pressed her fingers to her mouth.

'Oh Christ! That bastard killed a girl there last night. Kicked her to death. A hooker. Just a wee lassie.'

'Jesus!' Rosie whispered. 'Who? Tony? Tam Dunn? Who kicked the girl to death?'

'Tam Dunn. I can't believe it. I can't fucking believe it happened. Right in front of my eyes. The poor girl's face was kicked to a pulp.' She broke down.

'Jesus almighty, Ruby.' Rosie reached across and touched her wrist. 'Listen. Take a minute. This is awful . . .'

The waitress returned, interrupting the moment, and glanced at Ruby crying into a tissue. She put the coffees down and turned on her heel. She would have gossip for the woman behind the counter who stood watching the scene unfold. Rosie's journalist instinct was desperate to push for more details, but she held back.

'Sorry about the state I'm in,' Ruby said. 'I don't do

falling to pieces, and I won't. I won't go to pieces. Ever. But this . . . this just got to me. I can't get the picture of the girl out of my head.'

'What happened?'

She listened as Ruby described what happened.

'It's hard for me to even say it. I still can't believe I saw it. The girl was on the floor and there was blood everywhere. Tam Dunn was booting her face in.' She winced, closing her eyes. 'Fuck. I can still hear the sound of the boot hitting the flesh and the noise it made. Blood and bone everywhere, his boots just bouncing off her face. The wee lassie's head was being kicked like a football, and then he stamped on her. Dunn was like a fucking madman. He *is* a madman. A total fucking psycho.'

'Jesus,' was all Rosie could say. 'Where was Tony? Did he just stand by and watch this?'

'No.' Ruby shook her head and swallowed. 'I went out of the room to go to the loo, because I couldn't stand watching the girl and Tam. She was a hooker. They were going to have sex right in front of me, so I went onto the balcony and had a fag. Tony must have gone out after that. I'm not sure. Then I walked in and saw what was happening, and then a second later he came in behind me. He was raging, really shocked. I know he's a nutter, too, because I've seen him do bad things, but even he was stunned by this. I mean, Rosie, you'd need to have seen this. It was unbelievable. That poor wee girl.'

'Who is she? A hooker, you said?'

'Yeah. Eastern European. Illegal. Working in the sauna. That's what Tony says. He just got a couple of the bouncers up from the door and told them to deal with it. But there was this other wee kid in the corner – her friend. Another Eastern European . . . she was sobbing and terrified. Tony gave her money and told the boys to take her home. He said he would look after her if she kept her mouth shut.'

'My God! What did you do? You must have been terrified yourself.'

'I was. Dunn looked completely mental. He was slavering at the mouth and his eyes were crazy. He was all coked up. Seems there was something about him not being able to get it up with the girl, and he suddenly went berserk. I screamed at him to stop when I came in, and I was giving pelters to Tony, because he was just treating the whole thing like someone had spilled a fucking drink on the carpet. I was told to shut the fuck up. I couldn't say anything.' Her eyes filled up. 'Couldn't do a bloody thing. I felt completely useless.' Her voice cracked with emotion.

'What about the other girl?'

'Don't know. I had to rush to the toilet and throw up. The bouncers were taking her home.'

Rosie puffed.

'They'll have bumped her off, Ruby. She saw too much.'

'I know.'

They sat in silence, Rosie trying to work out what to do.

If she went to the cops it would blow their investigation. But how could she go to the police anyway? What with? There would be evidence all over the private room, but she couldn't tell the police without putting Ruby up as a witness.

After a while Ruby spoke.

'You know what happened to my mother, don't you? And Judy?' She sighed, gazing beyond Rosie. 'I think that's why I'm in this state. I've seen it before. The night they set fire to our house, Rab Jackson and that bastard Malky – they battered my mammy and raped my sister. They dragged Judy out of the room from below the bed where we were hiding. And they raped her. I saw it through the keyhole in the door. Terrified. But I couldn't do anything to save her. Same as last night.' She put her face in her hands. 'Oh, I'm sorry . . . I'm telling you all this about myself when a wee girl is dead . . . But the truth is, I've never really got over what happened to my ma and Judy.' She sniffed. 'I never speak about it, but it's always there. It's been what my whole life is about. That's why I'm the way I am. That's why I ended up working for Rab Jackson.'

She paused, and they looked each other in the eye but said nothing. It didn't need saying, and it didn't need asking. Right now, Rosie didn't want to know. She reached across and touched Ruby's arm.

'I'm so sorry that happened to you, Ruby. Christ! It must have been so hard for you.'

Ruby nodded.

'Thanks.'

'So what do we do now?' Rosie asked.

'Well, I can't go to the cops. That's for sure.'

'But we can't just let him get away with it. He's killed a young girl, and the other one is probably history by now. We *have* to tell the cops. You *have* to go the cops, Ruby. That's my gut instinct.'

'No way. No way can I do that. I can't afford to have them digging around my life. I can't. We have to find another way.'

Rosie puffed again.

'I know what you mean. Look. You know we're working on the story of Dunn being involved in the illegal arms dealing. I'm heading to London today with the guys who are working with me on the story. If we can get him done on this, then he'll be jailed. But the bastard should swing for what he did to that girl.'

'I just don't know what to do.' Ruby looked at her watch. 'I have to get moving, Rosie. I'm going down to see Judy, and I've got to go in case she's expecting me. I think she is. At least, I have to believe that.'

'It's okay. But you need to keep in touch. You must be careful. Call me later.'

Ruby stood up.

'I will. But I can't go to police. Not right now. I've got too much at stake.'

CHAPTER TWENTY-THREE

'Hey, Rosie. You just about ready to roll? I'm all packed up.' Matt closed the boot of the sleek black Audi in the car park of the *Post*. 'We're travelling in style in this baby, since I'm supposed to be the chauffeur.'

'Yeah,' Rosie said. 'But first I've got a quick meeting with McGuire. Urgent stuff. Why don't you pick up Adrian and have a coffee and we'll meet back here at midday?'

He looked at her. 'Everything all right?'

'Yeah. Great. I'll text when I'm ready.'

'Fine. I'm choking to get stuck into this. I've got all the surveillance gear, and we'll have a dry run before we use it tomorrow.'

'Fine. We'll do it in the hotel tonight.'

She headed towards the revolving doors.

'What's happening, Gilmour? I had to cancel a meeting upstairs for this. Don't tell me you're in the shit. My ulcer's been giving me gip this morning.' McGuire was on his feet as Rosie came into his office.

'No. Nothing like that. We're all ready to drive south. But I need to talk to you. Something happened last night, Mick. Bad. I've just had a meeting with Ruby. She's in a right state.'

'Well, don't keep me hanging about.'

Rosie took a deep breath.

'Okay. Subbed down, it's this: Ruby was at Santino's last night having dinner in a private room with Tony Devlin and Tam Dunn. And Dunn kicked a young prostitute to death. Right in front of her.'

McGuire looked at her as though she was mad.

'Shit! You're not joking?''

Rosie shook her head.

'Nope. Straight up. A young Eastern European girl. Brought into the dinner party with her pal for a bit of rumpy, and the next thing is Dunn goes apeshit over something – apparently, he couldn't get it up. Then he batters the girl to death.'

'Who's telling you this? Ruby?'

'Yes. She was there. She'd gone out to the balcony and came back to find the girl on the floor with Dunn kicking seven shades of shit out of her. Blood everywhere.'

'In the name of Christ! What did Ruby do? Get the cops?'

'Are you kidding? What do you think, Mick? She's been hiding from the cops for weeks. She *can't* call the cops.'

'She has to.'

'She won't.'

He bit the inside of his jaw.

'Right, give me chapter and verse of what she told you.'

Rosie described the scene as Ruby told it. He listened, shaking his head in disbelief and disgust.

'What a fucking animal! I take it you believe her?'

'Absolutely. She wouldn't make that up.'

'Then we need to take it somewhere. This changes things. We can't be in possession of information like this – about a murder – and not tell the police. We just can't. You know that, Rosie.'

'I hear what you're saying, and I agree. But what do we tell them? The first thing they're going to ask is who told us. We can't say Ruby told us. Then it could get crazy. We've been down this road before.'

'But not like this. Not with murder.'

'It may be two murders,' Rosie said. 'The other girl who was with her. Tony told the bouncers to take her home. But I'd be surprised if she's still alive. She saw too much.'

'Christ! Right, let's think about this. How could we tell this to the police without getting ourselves in all sorts of shit? We could just say it was an anonymous tip. They could go to Tony's place and have a look. There must be blood everywhere . . .'

'It doesn't matter what we tell them, Mick, it could still

come back to us. And there's no way I'm handing Ruby over to them.'

'I know. I wouldn't expect you to.' He shook his head then glanced at the clock on the wall. 'Look. I've got a conference. We'll talk about this later. But we have to do something.'

'I'm going down to London – remember? To see Tam Dunn with Adrian. He's posing as an arms customer from Bosnia looking to buy from J B Solutions, and I'm his personal assistant in the UK.'

'Okay. I forgot about that for a minute.'

'I think I should still go.'

McGuire thought for a couple of seconds.

'Yes. We have to get Dunn on the arms deals. But this is a lot bigger. And if it was dangerous before, then it's a lot worse now. This bastard sounds like he could flip at any time.'

'I've got Adrian with me, and we've got a good plan.'

'What if you get rumbled?'

'Let's not even think about that. We'll be careful.'

'Okay. Well, you'll want to be in and out as fast as you can.'

'Sure.' Rosie headed for the door.

'But we need to do something about that poor girl who got murdered. And soon.'

'I'm going to talk to somebody. A contact. See where I can go with it. I'll let you know later.'

'You'd better let me know. Every move, Rosie.' He reached into his drawer and took a card of tablets out, popping one into his mouth. 'Now look what you've done.'

In Matt's hotel room, Rosie and Adrian watched as Matt put the recording and filming equipment together. The camera was tiny, but they had used it before when filming inside the UVF secret headquarters in Glasgow. The wire was standard. He fitted both to Adrian and they did a test. It worked.

Over dinner Rosie told them of Ruby's account of the murder. Matt sat stunned, but Adrian's eyes just looked dark, as though he was already thinking ahead.

'So.' Rosie looked at Adrian. 'This is the kind of psycho we're dealing with. I feel like we're going into the lion's den.'

'He is not a lion,' Adrian said. 'He is a coward. He's nothing.'

After Matt went to bed, Rosie and Adrian sat drinking the last of the wine.

'I'm worried about tomorrow, Adrian, and I don't mind admitting it.'

He shrugged.

'Is normal to be nervous.'

'You? How do you feel?'

He sighed, ran a hand through his hair.

'I am all right. Not nervous. Not worried. But I am always thinking of the things that can happen, maybe if he has a few people around. He is a bad piece of work. So we must be careful.'

Rosie wanted to ask if Adrian would be carrying a gun, but she decided it would be better not to know.

'I think we should get some sleep. It's getting late.' Rosie stood up.

Their rooms were on different floors, and they stood in awkward silence in the lift. When it pinged for the third floor, Rosie turned to him.

'Goodnight, Adrian.'

He bent over and kissed her on the lips, taking her face in his hands.

'Goodnight, Rosie. And don't worry for tomorrow. It will be fine. Trust me.'

CHAPTER TWENTY-FOUR

Rosie was wrecked from lack of sleep. She'd spent most of the night drifting from one fevered nightmare to another. Vivid images of Marilyn Monroe's face, bloodied and battered, merged with horrific pictures of a little girl being raped and a house on fire, with the mother reaching through the flames for her children. And suddenly, she was the girl trying to save the woman from the blaze and the arms stretching out to her were her own mother's, her face smiling from her lipsticked mouth. She woke up, moaning, her eyes wet with tears.

'You're a bit quiet, Rosie.' Matt glanced from the corner of his eye as he drove the car towards North London. 'You all right?'

'Yeah,' Rosie said. 'Fine. Had a bloody sleepless night. All that shit I was telling you about the girl being kicked to death became one epic nightmare. But I've had two stiff coffees, so I'm starting to function. We must be nearly at this place by now.' She checked her notebook again for the address.

They drove up the long, winding hill towards Pinner, a picture-postcard English town with massive mock-Tudor black-and-white houses and red-bricked villas standing in manicured lawns at the end of leafy driveways. Everything screamed of affluence, privilege and order.

'Some place, this,' Matt said. 'Look at these houses. I wonder what they do with the poor people. They must hide them away.'

'I think I saw a sign on the way in: "No Poor People Here,"' Rosie said as they drove through, past the old-fashioned shopfronts and little pavement cafés. 'They call the roads "boulevards" down here. Kind of like Possil Boulevard back home – well, without the junkies and jakeys. In fact . . . nothing like Possil! It must be quite interesting to be brought up in a place like this, so far removed from how people live in the most deprived areas of the UK. If this is all you know, and your friends have grown up the same way, I suppose you'd probably think everyone lives like this.'

'Aye,' Matt said. 'But I wouldn't trade my shitty childhood, punching my way out of primary school in Drumchapel, for any of this splendour.'

Rosie chortled.

'Oh yeah. Me neither. You can't beat a single-end

tenement flat and a shared lavvy for giving you a sense of self-worth.'

Rosie pulled down the visor and looked in the mirror, wondering what was going through Adrian's mind as he gazed absently out of the side window.

'Here's the industrial estate,' Rosie said. 'Turn in here, Matt.'

They stopped at the billboard at the entrance and scanned down the list of companies.

'There it is. J B Solutions,' Matt said. 'Game on.'

'So, Matt,' Rosie said, 'when we get there, don't forget to get out and open the doors for us. You're the chauffeur. Don't look in anyone's direction.'

'Don't worry, pal. I'm all over this.'

The estate was mostly made up of small businesses and units – printing works, tyre suppliers, computing and office supply companies, plus a couple of larger places that looked like warehouses for some of the bigger department stores. Delivery lorries and vans passed them as Matt drove around the maze of roads until they saw the sign. J B Solutions sat at the corner of the estate, next to a haulage company with a few massive trucks in its car park. There was nothing beyond the two buildings but open fields and woodland.

'It looks closed up,' Matt said as he got nearer the buildings. 'Look. Gates are padlocked.'

Rosie rolled down the window and sucked in a mouthful

of air. Her stomach tightened as they got near the high perimeter fence, which was topped off with razor wire. Two cars – a blue Mercedes and a black Range Rover – were in the car park close to the main door, and she spotted at least two CCTV cameras. She was about to ask Adrian to ring the number he'd been given on the email when the main door opened and two burly men came out and strode towards them.

'Christ! I hope I don't have to fight them big bastards,' Matt said. 'Remember. I'm just the driver. Any rough stuff and I'm out of here.' He winked at Rosie.

'If there's any rough stuff in a place that sells guns, it'll be a short fight.' Rosie replied as the men opened the padlocked gate and one of them slipped outside.

'Ready, guys?' Rosie reached inside her blouse and switched on the hidden tape recorder then eased the switch on the hidden camera on the button of her jacket.

'Will I get out?' Matt said as the man approached.

'No. Sit tight. Open your window.'

Matt eased down the window as the man drew near.

'Hello.' Rosie leaned across, smiling up at him. 'Mr Kovac for Mr Dunn. He has an appointment.' She gestured to the back seat. 'I'm his assistant when he's in the UK. Mr Dunn is expecting us.'

Rosie's English accent was perfect. The big man eyed all three of them and for a second said nothing. Rosie could feel her heartbeat. The big man took out a walkie-talkie.

'Boss, a Mr Kovac and er . . . some bird, I mean woman.' He spoke in a broad Cockney accent.

The device crackled, then a voice came back.

'Bring them in, Dave.'

He took a step back and beckoned them towards the gate.

'You should be on the stage,' Matt quipped to Rosie as they drove through the tall steel gates.

'Shut up. I'm concentrating,' Rosie said in her English accent, her face straight. 'You ready, Adrian?'

'Of course,' he murmured.

Matt got out and went around to open Rosie's door, then the back door for Adrian. Rosie's stomach jolted as the men pushed the gate closed and padlocked it. They walked behind them to the main entrance, where one of the men pushed a button and the big security door opened.

Inside, the hallway was dimly lit with grey bare walls and no proper reception area. The men led them down a corridor to a black door at the end and knocked on it softly.

'Come in.'

Rosie glanced at Adrian, who was staring straight ahead. She took a deep breath and cleared her throat.

As they came through the doorway a tall man in a dark pinstripe suit who was seated behind his desk stood up and gave them a practised, painted smile, showing off his bleached teeth. He ran a hand over his mop of lush, greying hair. He looked somewhere between a slick City trader and a dodgy car dealer. Rosie immediately clocked the fresh grazes on his knuckles, and a chill ran through her. They'd come to the right place, and she wished she could turn on her heels and go. She blinked away an image of him punching the face of the defenceless young hooker.

'How's it going, folks? Thanks for coming.'

He stepped from behind his desk. Controlled, charming, flashing the teeth again. A wolf that could tear you to pieces. Rosie swallowed, holding her nerve.

'Mr Dunn.' She stretched out her hand. 'Melissa Parker . . . I believe Mr Kovac told you that I'm his assistant when he travels in the UK.'

'Yes, he did. Pleased to meet you, Melissa.'

'And this is Mr Kovac.' Rosie gestured a hand towards Adrian.

'How you doing, Mr Kovac? Thanks for getting in touch, and for coming all the way over from Sarajevo.' He glanced at Rosie. 'Actually, I would have made the trip over to Sarajevo, no problem. I've always been interested to see how things have panned out since all that terrible carry-on during the war.'

Adrian nodded. 'Is much better now, Mr Dunn. Is a very beautiful city these days. Many people from all over Europe now visit.' He paused. 'But I had some business already in the London, so it suit me better to come here.'

'Excellent,' Dunn said, turning to Rosie. 'And I'm curious

as to why you have an assistant here. It's not as if you need a translator. Your English seems very good.'

'Not perfect. But is improving.' Adrian glanced at Rosie. 'Melissa works in my company in Sarajevo. As I told you in the email, it is growing all the time. Is a new world now in Bosnia, and many, many opportunities. Melissa is involved in – how you say? – in the public relations.'

Rosie smiled.

'I'm kind of a personal assistant, but I'm also involved in creating a good image for the company,' she enthused, beginning to believe it herself. 'The security and body-guards industry is also growing, especially in the Balkan region and beyond. So I'm helping to promote it.'

'So, you based in Sarajevo?' Dunn asked.

'A lot of the time, yes.' Rosie winged it. She had expected to be questioned closely. So far, so good. 'But if there is a new client to see for business, I usually accompany Mr Kovac.'

'Good.' Dunn gestured them towards two chairs. 'Take a seat. Please. And we can get down to business.' He went back behind his desk and sat down, pushing back on the leather office chair.

Rosie and Adrian watched as Dunn looked at the back of his raw knuckles. He flexed his hand as though he'd seen them looking at it, and grinned.

'I do a bit of boxing training at the gym,' he said, patting his firm stomach. 'Keeps me in shape. But I got a bit carried away punching the heavy bag the other day.'

Rosie said nothing.

'So.' He turned to Adrian. 'Talking business, Mr Kovac. What are we looking at here, in terms of hardware?' He paused. 'I'll show you some of what we've got in a few minutes. But what exactly are you looking for?'

Adrian took a deep breath and exhaled slowly, clasping his hands together, looking at the blank wall above Dunn.

'Well, I am thinking. We will be requiring say, thirty to forty handguns. Probably Glock, as they are very reliable. I also like the Smith & Wesson, so maybe we would look at six or seven of them. Are you able to do that? And ammunition, of course. And silencers – for all of them.'

Dunn looked serious as he took notes on a pad on his desk.

'Sure. That wouldn't be a problem. If you wanted as many as forty Glocks, then we may have to wait a couple of weeks. But Smith & Wessons we have plenty of, so no problem there.'

'Good. And rifles. I think ten. With range and eyesights. I like to use in the field . . . Can you get them? . . . Give me a price?'

Dunn nodded, licking his lips.

'No problem.'

'And how is delivery? You can deliver them to us in Sarajevo? Things are very different now with border controls, but of course, if you have all the licence and papers for exporting, then is no problem.'

Dunn's lips tightened a little.

'Delivery is good. You can trust me on that.' He leaned forward. 'I don't know how much you know about J B Solutions, but we've been around a long time. We've sold weapons all over the shop. Europe, Africa. You leave all the delivery and papers up to me. If we make a deal, then we decide where and when, and that's all you have to worry about. I'll get the stuff to you.' He paused, looking from Rosie to Adrian. 'But I'll be very frank with you. It's upfront money, Mr Kovac. You need to pay 75 per cent up front when you place the order. That's the deal.'

Adrian's face showed nothing and there was a stony silence.

'Is a lot of money. When we don't see the guns till they come to Sarajevo. A lot of money.'

'That's how we do business here.' He sighed. 'There are some countries – and I'll tell you this in confidence – there are some places we've made deals with and sent the arms and didn't get the full amount of money – nothing like it. We took a hit. We've taken a hit in Africa, for example, with another small firm I operate. We lost our licence in that debacle, and it was basically because they fucked up . . .' He turned to Rosie . . . 'if you'll pardon my French. And these African countries . . . you can't trust any of them because they're all bloody corrupt. They assured us they were organizing stuff at their end, but the money never materialized. We don't risk that any more. We can't deal with that. So that's how it is now. But don't worry, we will deliver. We are the experts.'

Adrian nodded.

'Okay. I think that sound good to me. Is possible, maybe we can do business.'

'Great.' Dunn stood up. 'We can sort the details later if we come to a deal. I'm sure I can offer you better rates than anyone else. Come on, I'll show you some of the stock we have.'

He led them along a corridor and into a side room, then through to another corridor with a steel door at the end. It opened into warehouse piled high with metal boxes marked 'Ammo', and gun and rifle boxes. He turned to them, again with the killer smile.

'This is our warehouse. As you can see, we have to keep it all top secret. Actually, that's why we don't advertise or anything any more. Our success is through word of mouth. I take it that's how you heard about us.'

Adrian made a non-committal face. Dunn eyed him approvingly.

'That's good. It's important to keep things tight. We get all sorts of shit from the powers that be trying to put guys like me out of business. Sometimes we have to bend the rules a bit. But you don't look like a man who worries about that kind of stuff.'

Adrian half smiled.

'I am from Sarajevo. When you live through the Bosnian War, you are used to bending the rules.'

'That's what I like to hear. I hope we can do business together. What's your first name?'

'Danko,' Adrian replied.

'Thomas. But people know me as Tam. Self-made. Built myself up from the streets of Glasgow when things were hard, I'll tell you. Guys like me in Glasgow at that time could have flourished anywhere – Sarajevo, Belfast, Africa. If you're prepared to take risks, you win. But you have to know who you're dealing with. It's all about trust. I hope we can trust each other, because if we can then a lot of things could open up for us in your neck of the woods. For both us.' he winked. 'If you get my drift.'

Adrian nodded.

Rosie watched as Dunn took Adrian across to a long bench, where there were already four metal boxes, the lids loose on top of them. Dunn removed the lid from one and pulled out a gleaming handgun, then another, smaller one. He handed them to Adrian, who weighed them and worked at the trigger and safety catch, loaded the clip as quick as lightning. Rosie tried not to look surprised. He said nothing, just nodded approvingly at Dunn. Then he went to another box, and then another, then to the rifles. He examined some of them closely, glancing at Dunn, who was scrutinizing him. The only thing Rosie knew about guns was the business end of them, having had one or two pressed to her head. She stood back as Adrian went through his cache, examining bullets, ammunition and silencers.

'You have some good material here. I think we can do business. We can talk again soon about financial arrangements once you work out a price.'

'Good man.' Dunn shook Adrian's hand vigorously. 'Look, are you in town for the night? If you fancy dinner I'd be delighted to take both of you to a great little place where you get the best steaks this side of London.'

Adrian glanced at Rosie, who blinked what she hoped was a yes. There wasn't much option. Dinner with this scumbucket was the last thing on her agenda – they already had great material, as long as the secret camera and recording devices had worked – but you never knew what he'd blab about once he had a few drinks.

'That seems perfect . . . Tam.' Adrian said.

CHAPTER TWENTY-FIVE

They were already two bottles of red wine down by the time they'd finished their main course, and Dunn ordered another. Rosie nursed her half-full glass, careful not to drink much, terrified she'd lapse into her normal voice. But she was impressed at how Adrian had matched Dunn drink for drink, including the large whisky they'd had before dinner, and still looked sober. Dunn was flushed and talking continuously, becoming more and more animated as the night wore on. The fact that he kept nipping out to the toilet confirmed Rosie's suspicion that he was coked out of his nut. Everything was going perfectly, as long as Dunn didn't flip. Rosie would be glad when this night was over. It was just a question of getting through the next hour.

'So you have a lot of connections in the Balkan region? You must have a good reputation in the security industry,' Dunn asked.

'Yes,' Adrian nodded. 'My staff are well trained. Most of them are former comrades and fought together in the war. They know what they are doing. Our reputation, it is growing – that is for sure.'

'Clients expect quality,' Rosie chimed in. 'Sef is a respected company, and it constantly delivers. Put it this way, we've never lost a client we were protecting.' Rosie flashed Adrian a knowing smile. 'And with some of the clients we've protected, that is a surprise.'

'I'm sure you see all kinds of people,' Dunn agreed.

'Well, the ethos of the company is that we will protect whoever asks to be protected. We don't judge people for what they do as a business, if you know what I mean.' Rosie hoped to draw him out.

'You can't survive as a security and bodyguard firm any other way.' Dunn spread his hands and shrugged. 'If, let's say, your client was shifting thirty kilos of coke or heroin across Europe in lorries and they needed protecting, then, of course, you'd have to make a judgement call. If you said no to that, then you're in the wrong business.' He paused, eyeing one of them then the other. 'That's just my opinion.'

'As Melissa says, we don't make judgements.' Adrian was deadpan.

'That's good. Believe me, you'll become a bigger player by treating everything as business. Nothing is ever personal. Everything is done for one reason – to make money and to keep the firm alive. That's my philosophy.' He

Rosie. 'You can send the help back to the hotel. You won't be short of action, big man.'

Adrian smiled at him, and for a moment Rosie thought he was going to go.

'Next time,' he said. 'Not tonight. We can celebrate once you tell me you have weapons ready and when is the delivery, and, of course, when we pay the first part of the money.'

'Yeah. Right. Good idea. We need to work out how to do that. Probably best if I drive somewhere, say Belgium or Amsterdam, and bring the cash back that way. It's a lot of money, so I don't want to leave it to anyone else. I can get a couple of the lads to drive me there, and we can meet.'

'Perfect.' Adrian said. 'Maybe we will take you to some nightclubs in Amsterdam.'

'You won't be taking me to any I haven't already been to. That much I can guarantee.'

'Or if you prefer,' Adrian said, 'I can come back here. Or anywhere in the UK – in Scotland if you like. You are Scottish?'

'I am. But Amsterdam is better for nightlife. I was in Glasgow the other night and the place is crap, no good clubs. Just crap. I left all that behind years ago and only go now for a bit of business.'

He stretched out his hand with the grazed knuckles and Rosie felt sick as she had to shake it.

*

sniffed and touched his nose. 'And let me tell you one thing . . . there isn't anyone out there who won't take a bung. And I know that for a fact. Everyone will take a backhander.' He lowered his voice. 'Listen. Between us, I have people in my pocket, on my payroll, that go all the way to Whitehall – the MoD. They're *greedy* bastards, mind you. But they'll turn a blind eye, do any fucking thing, as long as you stick the money in their offshore accounts.'

Rosie shook her head in mock disbelief, glancing at Adrian.

'It's incredible, isn't it?' she said. 'You know what they say – the people in power are bigger gangsters than anyone. The MPs, the civil servants. It's one rule for them and another for the rest of us.'

'I agree.' Adrian gave a measured nod. 'If we'd waited for the politicians to make life better for us then we would all have starved to death in Bosnia during and after the war. We have had to go out and fight for our living.'

'Exactly,' Dunn agreed. 'In fact, I'll let you into a secret, now that I know we're on the same wavelength. J B Solutions is operating and making more money now than ever – and we've not been short of problems.'

Rosie and Adrian nodded and said nothing.

'We had some hassle with the Home Office after our sister company sold a container-load of weaponry to Nigeria. Some big bastard dictator over there wanted them to shore up his regime in the civil war. Me? I don't judge, as I told you. A deal is a deal. But we didn't have the proper paperwork at the time . . . well . . . put it this way . . . I didn't put all the facts down on the paperwork we had. I took a chance and shipped it. But it got rumbled and that was it. Big problem with the licence after that, and we were nearly out of business. You have to laugh at the government really. They don't give a fuck what regimes they bankroll quietly, who *they* sell arms to, and who is killing who with the guns *they* sold to these dodgy tyrants. They just don't want us to get a slice of the action.'

'So what did you do?' Rosie asked. 'I mean, how did you survive?'

Dunn grinned.

'By paying the fuckers to turn a blind eye.'

'You mean the Customs and Borders people?'

'Yeah. Them too. But also we have someone inside the MoD, some mid-ranking civil servant who does the paperwork. He's in our pocket – took a bit of organizing and plenty of dosh, but he's in, because he couldn't resist the money.'

'And you can ship arms without any problems?'

'Well, as you saw today, they're all boxed up, so when we sell a lot, they go in a lorry from our haulage firm next door – you may have noticed it when you came in.' He grinned. 'They're not delivering to supermarkets, I can tell you that. So, the guns and hardware go in among a whole load of other things we ship abroad. Mostly car

components, steel, metal and rods for the construction trade – that kind of thing. It's all very well camouflaged, so that unless they take the whole container apart, nobody knows a thing. They accept what is on the paperwork. When we have a shipment going out, I make a call to my man, and off it goes. Simple as that. I know it sounds unbelievable, but that's how it happens. That's how the world goes round, not by hard graft. Fuck that for a living. There's money in everything except hard work. It's dog eat dog.'

Adrian nodded and raised his glass in a toast.

'To good business,' he said. 'Without frontiers.'

'Well put, big man. Our game. Our rules.' Dunn knocked back his drink.

Rosie checked her watch again. It was almost midnight. The restaurant was empty apart from one table, and the waiters were hovering near the bar, looking bored.

'We should be getting back.' Rosie looked at Adrian. 'We're flying in the morning, so we have an early drive to Heathrow.'

Dunn waved the waiter over and Rosie watched as he paid the bill, pulling a wad of notes out of his inside jacket pocket. The tip must have been at least fifty quid. He stood up, turning to Adrian.

'I was going to take you to a club if you fancied it. I have a little share in a place where they have a proper VIP room with no riff-raff and plenty of birds. It's only twenty minutes away.' He gave Adrian a playful dig, gesturing to

Matt was asleep in the driver's seat when they got back to the car. Rosie knocked the window.

'Try to keep up, for Christ's sake,' she grinned when his eyes snapped open. 'You're supposed to be a chauffeur. Not kipping at every turn.'

'Christ! It took you long enough. What were you doing? Lap dancing at his table?'

'Thankfully, it didn't come to that.' Rosie got into the passenger seat.

'How did it go?' Matt rubbed his face with both hands to wake himself up.

Rosie swivelled her body around to face Adrian.

'Couldn't have been much better, could it, Adrian?'

He let out a long breath from pursed lips.

'Was good. I think he believed us. He is a piece of shit. I wanted to punch his face all over the table.'

'You did brilliant. You should get an Oscar for that performance.'

'By the way,' Adrian said, 'when I examined the guns earlier, I can see that some of them have been converted from replica guns so they can fire live bullets. It happens. Mostly they are used by crime gangs. There is a market for them. It is only a matter of making some changes, such as the barrel. I didn't want to mention it to Dunn, but I think he is aware that I noticed that. He thinks I am a criminal, which is good.'

'Yeah. While you two are congratulating each other . . . what about me?' Matt said. 'I've been sitting out here all night. All I got was a takeaway pizza and a bottle of Irn-Bru.'

'What have I told you about eating in the car, driver.' Rosie gave him a playful punch on the shoulder. 'Any more of that and I'm going to have to let you go.'

'Aye, right. Where to, madam?'

'The hotel, and if you don't give me any more backchat I'll buy you a drink in the bar.'

'You're all heart,' Matt said, driving out of the restaurant car park and onto the main road.

CHAPTER TWENTY-SIX

Ruby could see the difference in Judy, even if it didn't look like much to anyone else. Small things like the slightest movement in her facial expression were treasured, because every tiny flicker meant she was responding. In the very beginning, after Ruby had found her sister in the locked ward of a grim psychiatric hospital, there had been nothing behind her dead eyes. Even when Ruby was telling stories of them growing up, talking to her as though everything was perfectly normal, Judy's gaze had been locked straight ahead, stuck in whatever world she was trapped in. But now, when Ruby spoke to her, enthusing about everything, even if it was just the ice cream they were eating or the coffee they drank, she sometimes caught a glimmer that Judy was listening, that things were registering. Now and again, she even turned her head and looked straight at her. Today had been like that, and Ruby was elated, the happiest she'd been since she came back.

She'd collected Judy from the home mid-morning, and with the help of one of the nurses had carefully strapped her into the passenger seat of the hired car. Then she drove down the coast to Ayr, where they'd gone on day trips on the train from Glasgow with their mother during summer holidays. Ruby was hoping it would trigger a response – anything at all.

They sat on a wooden bench on the promenade, watching the waves, choppy in the autumn winds. A kid ran up and down the beach, flying a kite, and Ruby saw her sister's eyes following the path of the bright blue-and-gold bird shape as it danced and dived under a cloudless sky. It was still sunny and surprisingly warm for the time of the year, and the promenade was busy with families, kids playing on skateboards and bicycles, joggers. She was conscious of people staring at her sister as they passed, because of the way she sat leaning against her as though she couldn't sit up by herself. Ruby linked her arm in hers, talked to her, telling her everything they used to do here and how the town had changed so much in recent years. She reminded her of the fairground, of the candyfloss, of the time they won a coconut, which they brought home and smashed against the cooker, drinking the milk and pretending they liked the taste. Ruby could see the pitying little glances from people as she talked but got little response from her sister, who stared blankly out to sea. But she didn't need their pity. She knew different. She was happy, because once or twice the corners of Judy's lips turned upwards in a smile. This was progress.

Ruby lit a cigarette, her mind drifting back to the other night with that evil bastard Tam Dunn. She couldn't get the image of the battered girl out of her head, or the thought of what must have happened to her friend. She wished she could tell Rosie to bring in the police. In the last few sleepless nights it had crossed her mind to put her hands up, tell everything. But she couldn't. She was in so deep with all the work she'd done with Jackson, hiding his money all over the place. If she went to jail, what would become of Judy?

She hadn't answered any of Tony's emails, and he knew she didn't have a mobile phone, as she'd stressed she was taking time out and didn't want to be contacted. He'd emailed her again this morning, demanding to know where she was, telling her he needed to see her, that he was as angry as her about what had happened in the restaurant. He wanted to take her to dinner again, just the two of them. But also, he needed to talk business. There were things happening and he needed to free up some money, so they wanted things sorted out pronto. She couldn't just disappear, he told her. Ever.

Ruby had blanked his emails. Fuck him. She would answer him when she was ready – once she'd spoken to the various banks and other places holding investment accounts which she'd set up and had to decipher. She needed to spend a whole day at her flat to work it all out.

She stood up, took Judy by both hands and gently eased her to her feet.

'Come on, Judy. Let's have some lunch.'

She linked her sister's arm through hers and walked slowly, aware that Judy's steps were faltering and unsure.

They ate in a café a couple of streets off the seafront, where the smells took Ruby back to her childhood. She cut up a piece of fried fish for Judy, coaxing her to hold the spoon, putting it into her hand. But when she didn't move a muscle to do it, she fed her.

'Where are you, Judy?' She pushed her sister's fringe back. 'Where are you in there? I want you back, Judy. I need you. You are coming back. I know you are.'

When they finished eating, they went out to the patio in the back, deserted apart from one old man reading the newspaper. Ruby drank tea and helped Judy with some lemonade, which she sipped through a straw. They sat for almost half an hour, Ruby telling stories about friends they had from primary school. Eventually, she got up and went inside to pay the bill, leaving Judy sitting on the bench.

At the counter, she waited impatiently until the couple in front of her had paid, slowly counting out their money in coins. Then, as she was about to pay, a shout came from the kitchen and the girl excused herself. Ruby shook her head impatiently. She could see the girl talking to her boss in the kitchen and arguing over something. After what seemed like minutes, she came back and Ruby glared at her and paid without leaving a tip. She went back along the corridor and into the garden.

She opened the door and stepped outside. The place was deserted, the picnic benches and tables empty. Nobody. Judy was gone.

'Oh Christ!' Ruby looked around her, bewildered. 'Oh Christ, no, Judy! Oh, please no!'

She turned fast, stumbling as she sprinted back into the café, along the corridor, then ran back out again, confused, lost in her panic. She dashed to the open patio gate and outside. Nothing. The pavement was quiet, but the road was busy with traffic heading out of town. Ruby ran along the street, then crossed on to the seafront and scanned the promenade. The sea suddenly looked angry and threatening, and a chill ran through her.

'Oh, God. No. Please . . .' Ruby ran twenty yards and grabbed a woman who was feeding the pigeons. 'Have you seen a woman? I mean . . . a woman walking up along here by herself?'

The woman looked at her puzzled.

'Whit? Are you lost, hen?'

'No . . . No . . . I've lost my . . . Oh God!' Ruby turned away, ran back to the other end of the street, gasping for breath as shouted.

'Judy! . . . Judy! . . .' Her voice trailed off as tears came to her eyes.

Her head began to swim amid the din of the traffic, the

bustle of people coming and going, lorries, day-trippers, buses making their way home. She felt faint, and she could hear the thud of her heart as she turned and sprinted back towards the café and burst in the door. The woman behind the counter gave her a surly look.

'The . . . the girl . . . The woman I was with . . . My . . . My sister. Has she come back in?'

She knew it was a pointless question. Judy could walk, but her steps were always hesitant. She wouldn't have gone anywhere by herself.

The woman shook her head slowly.

Ruby went back out and stood on the street again, her eyes everywhere. Nothing. She felt her legs buckle, and she steadied herself on a lamp post.

'Tony . . . You fucking evil bastard! I'll kill you for this.'

She ran to her car and opened the door, getting into the driver's seat, trying to catch her breath as she exploded in sobs.

Matt had made good time, so they stopped for a coffee at the service station on the M74, just over the border after Carlisle.

They sat in the conservatory, going over all the material they had, delighted they had come out of it unscathed. McGuire would be happy. Now all Rosie had to do was sit down with him and work out how they'd write the story.

Rosie's mobile rang, and she answered it.

'Rosie . . . Rosie . . .'

The voice was breathless, desperate, and Rosie's heart skipped.

'Ruby? What's up?'

'She's . . . Judy . . . She's . . . Oh my God . . .'

Rosie stood up and walked away from the table.

'What? What's wrong? Is Judy sick? Just calm down.'

'They . . . They took her. Judy's been kidnapped.'

'Oh my God! Kid— . . . Kidnapped? Who by? Listen, Ruby. Just calm down a bit. Take a deep breath. Where are you?'

Ruby heard the sobbing. Matt and Adrian looked anxiously at her.

'Ayr. I'm in Ayr. We came down for the day. Oh Rosie! What am I going to do? She's gone!'

'What happened? Just take your time. Tell me what happened. It'll be okay.'

'No, it won't! Rosie. No, it won't! They've taken her.'

'What happened?' Rosie asked again.

'I . . . I drove her down here for lunch . . . I went inside to pay the bill, and Judy was in the patio garden at the back . . . and . . . Oh God! . . . When I came out she was gone.'

Rosie didn't know what to say. From what Ruby had told her, Judy walked with difficulty.

'Christ! . . . Listen. We're on our way back from London. We're over the border now. We'll come and get you.'

'It's Tony who's done it! I know it's that bastard. He's

been emailing me all the time since the other night, but I didn't get back to him. He wants all the business wrapped up. But I just ignored his emails. He's done this because he knows that's where he'll hit me hardest. The bastard! I'll fucking kill him.'

'Okay, just sit tight till we get there.' She turned to Matt. 'We need to do a detour to Ayr. How long till we get there?'

'Forty-five, fifty minutes. Not long.'

'We'll be there in an hour. Just try to stay calm. Don't do anything. Don't phone Tony.'

'I can't even go to the cops. What am I going to do?'

'We'll be there soon. If Tony's got her, he'll get in touch with you. Can you go to a hotel or somewhere and get on the Internet, check your emails?'

'I'll try.'

'Right. We'll phone you when we're nearly there. It'll be okay, Ruby. We'll get her back.'

As Ruby hung up, Rosie could hear her weeping.

'What's happened?' Matt said.

'Ruby's sister, Judy. She's been kidnapped.'

'Oh fuck!'

'Ruby's hysterical. And she can't even go to the cops. We need to get to Ayr fast and then work out what we do.' Rosie puffed. 'This is as bad as it gets. Knowing what they did the other night . . . These scumbags will stop at nothing.'

CHAPTER TWENTY-SEVEN

As they pulled into the car park in Ayr, Rosie spotted Ruby getting out of her car.

'Wait here, guys.' She leaned in the window to Matt and Adrian. 'I'll see how she is first.'

Ruby's face was grey, her eyes smeared from crying. Rosie was taken aback when she crumbled and collapsed into her arms, sobbing. It was as though the floodgates had opened and all the years of punching above her weight, fighting everyone she came across, had suddenly dissolved in tears and she was a helpless child again.

'Ruby. Listen. It'll be okay,' Rosie said, not really believing it herself. 'They wouldn't dare do something to harm Judy. I mean, she's a patient in a nursing home. They can't just kidnap someone like that and make them disappear.' Rosie gave her a reassuring pat on the back and eased herself away. 'You'll see. Now, you need to calm down now and think straight. Did you get a look at your emails?'

Ruby nodded, sniffing. She went into her jacket pocket and pulled out a sheet of paper, handing it over. Rosie read the printed email, and her blood ran cold.

I told you not to fuck around with me, Ruby. Maybe now you'll lis-
ten. I'm running the fuckin show here − not you. By the way, a
couple of the boys think your sister's not a bad looking bird. You
wouldn't want to leave her with them too long . . .

Rosie tried to keep calm.

'What a bastard!' She folded the paper and put it in her pocket.

'I told you. He's a complete cunt. I'll kill him! No matter what happens − no matter what − he's a dead man. I'll kill him myself.'

The resolve in her eyes made Rosie shudder. It confirmed her niggling belief that the murders of Rab Jackson and Malky Cameron were about old scores being settled − but not by gangsters, which was the story the police were leaking to the press. This was a woman whose whole life had been built on retribution. Whatever happened to Judy, Tony was underestimating her if he thought he could get away with this.

'Listen, Ruby. We need to do something here. But you need to think this through.'

'I have.' Ruby tried to light a cigarette with trembling fingers. She took a long draw, looked out at the sea and sniffed. 'I can't call the police. It's just not possible. There's too much shit. But I'm going to have to call the nursing home very shortly and tell them I'm keeping Judy with me tonight. They'll be okay about it, but if I just don't turn up they'll call me and then they'll call the cops if I don't have a convincing story.' She pulled her collar up against the rising wind. 'I'll just say it's part of Judy's progress . . . that I'll be taking her to my place in Glasgow for a couple of days and I'll get in touch if there's any immediate problem.'

'Can you just do that?' Rosie asked. 'Is she not on medication? Do you not have to sign something?'

'She's not really on any medication. As long as she's eating normally and stuff. And I don't have to sign any papers unless she's being discharged. I'll tell them I'll bring her back in a couple of days. I'm her guardian and have power of attorney. I sorted that a couple of years ago.' Ruby paused, looking at Rosie. 'I have to call them first. Then I need to work out how I'm going to meet Tony. I haven't thought that far yet.'

'You think he'll just hand her over if you agree to meet him and turn up?'

Ruby nodded.

'I hope so. But I know that he'll not let me out of his sight until I give him everything I've got.' She looked at the ground. 'Then I'll be next for the chop.'

'What do you mean?'

Ruby took a breath, ran a hand over her mouth.

'Look, Rosie. I told you I was Rab Jackson's accountant. I have his money in bank accounts all over Europe, and in businesses I set up for him. It's all very complicated, and it's a lot of money. But it's me who did all that with the mob's money. Now he's dead and that's the real reason Tony's been courting me for the past couple of weeks. He's trying to do it in a nice way, but I know, sooner or later, if I don't come across with all the accounts, then he'll get nasty.' She shook her head. 'I didn't even fucking know that he knew about Judy until the other day. That took the feet from me. He'd been emailing me since I left Spain, every email getting angrier the more I ignored the bastard. And then he mentioned Judy. That's the only reason I went to see him last week, and have been playing along. That's why I was brought along to meet that fucker Tam Dunn the other night. He's got a lot of money tied up with Rab – which I didn't know about. It was Tony trying to let him know that everything was under control.'

'But what were you going to do with all Rab's money and assets? Were you going to give them over?'

'Yeah, of course. But when I'm ready. When I'm out of here with Judy once and for all. I was getting things sorted, planning for us to go away, because if I give him everything now, he will get me killed.' Her eyes filled up and she blinked back tears. 'Today with Judy is the best day I've had. She is getting more and more responsive all the time.

And I think she's nearly ready for me to take her away. I was going to give everything over to Tony, leave all the details somewhere in an envelope, and go to France. But first I have to speak to the various banks and investment funds, because I am the only signatory on the accounts now that Jackson's dead. Tony knows that, and that's why he's so angry. He's feeling he's losing his grip and the only way he can hurt me is through Judy.' She threw her cigarette end away and looked at Rosie. 'But I'll tell you one thing. He has made the biggest mistake of his life, Rosie. Because the moment he made the decision to take my sister, he signed his own death warrant. Trust me on that.'

Rosie didn't answer. She didn't really want to hear that, because now she was going to have to call McGuire and try to explain this whole mess, then make a decision on how to handle it. But however this played out, there was no guarantee that Judy would be returned to Ruby alive. In fact, given how easily they disposed of people, they'd probably kill her as a message to Ruby that she'd stepped over the line.

They stood for a long moment, listening to the plaintive sound of gulls wailing as the rain began to fall from the slate-grey sky.

'Okay,' Rosie said. 'Here's what I think. Let's go back to my car, and you can phone Tony. Just be calm, talk to him and arrange to meet him.'

Ruby looked at her, biting her bottom lip.

Rosie explained. 'And, Ruby . . . You're going to have to trust me.' She put her hands up. 'I know you're not used to trusting people, but this time I think you should. I'm going to phone my editor.'

'What? A fucking story?'

'No. No story. Let me explain. We have connections with certain people, and maybe, well, maybe we can involve them.'

'What people? What connections?' Ruby looked confused.

'I can't say. Just trust me. You don't need to know at the moment. Please. We don't have a lot of options and I'm not even sure if this will work, but I don't want you just going in to see Tony without any kind of back-up, because you might not come back out again. You and Judy.'

Ruby looked at her and swallowed, shaking her head, her mouth tight with emotion, and they stood in silence.

'Come on,' Rosie took her arm. 'Let's go.'

Matt and Adrian got out of the car as they approached. Ruby stood back, a little unsure.

'These are colleagues of mine,' Rosie said. 'It's cool. We're already working on the Tam Dunn story. That's where we were last night . . . down south . . . and we've got him bang to rights on a lot of stuff, so you can trust these guys implicitly.'

She introduced Adrian and Matt. Ruby acknowledged them with a nod but said nothing.

'Can I have your mobile, Adrian?' Rosie asked.

He handed it over, and she turned to Ruby.

'This is a pay-as-you-go, it's set up to withhold the number, and there's no way of tracking it. So if you phone Tony on this he'll not know where you are. Tell him you borrowed the mobile.' She paused. 'But you need to keep calm, or he'll turn the screw. Just be matter of fact. Tell him you're angry, because you were working on the accounts and were going to email him very soon. Say you're furious at what he's done but you're prepared to put it behind you as long as you can see Judy right now.'

Ruby took the phone and looked in her own mobile for Tony's number.

'He doesn't think I have a phone,' she explained, as she punched the number into Adrian's mobile.

They watched and waited. When he finally answered, they listened while Ruby gave quite a convincing performance, keeping reasonably calm, just enough edge to her voice.

'Look. I know you were impatient, Tony. I absolutely understand that,' Ruby said. 'But you went right over the score. I told you before that Judy has nothing to do with anyone. She is not well, Tony. She's a poor soul.' Her voice wavered a little and Rosie reached over and squeezed her arm, gesturing with her hands to tell Ruby to stay in control.

Ruby appeared to be listening to whatever Tony was saying.

'But I want to see her now. Today. Tonight.'

Ruby pulled the phone from her ear and threw her eyes up to the sky, frustrated, then put the phone back to her ear.

'Why not today? What do you mean, you're too busy? Tony . . . You've got my sister. She's due back. What am I going to tell the home?'

Ruby put her hand over the phone and mouthed 'Fuck you.'

They watched as she listened again.

'Okay. Tomorrow. But there's no guarantee I will have everything sorted with the accounts. I have to talk to all the banks and sort the accounts all over the place. That's going to take me the best part of the day and night and it's already four o'clock. I've already got some things organized, but there's a lot to do. But you've wasted an afternoon because you couldn't wait. This is *your* fault.'

Ruby listened again.

'Tony? Tony? Are you there?'

She looked at Rosie.

'Fuck! Bastard's hung up.' She stamped her feet and turned away. 'Fucking arsehole!'

Matt grimaced at Rosie as Adrian looked from one to the other and made a sympathetic face.

'He is a nasty piece of work, this Tony. Like the people who took my sister. They are scum,' Adrian said.

Rosie remembered the time she'd spent with Adrian last year in Spain as he rescued his sister from people traffickers and knew just how deeply he'd be empathizing with Ruby.

'So what did he say?' She walked Ruby, who had turned away from them, crying, and put her hand on her arm.

'He says he's too busy today. It has to be tomorrow. After-noon. Bastard was laughing.' She shook her head. 'How do I know Judy's even still alive?' She put her hands on her head. 'I don't even know if he's killed her. Oh fuck!'

'Don't even think that way.' She took her mobile out of her bag. 'I need to talk to the editor.'

Ruby said nothing.

Rosie walked a few yards away from everyone and stood facing the sea, breathing in a lungful of the salty air as she dialled McGuire's direct line.

'Gilmour. I'm up to my arse.'

'Mick. There's a problem.'

'What?'

'They've kidnapped Ruby's sister. That Tony bastard.'

'Oh fuck! Where are you?'

'In Ayr. I was on my way up when I got the call from Ruby, so I came straight here with Matt and Adrian. She's in a real state.' Rosie took a breath. 'We need to do some-thing. Not the cops.'

'What the fuck are we going to do if we don't get the cops?'

'I'm heading back up the road now. I have an idea.'

'Tell me now.'

'I'll tell you when I see you.'

Rosie hung up.

CHAPTER TWENTY-EIGHT

Rosie watched McGuire pace up and down his office like a trapped animal. For the past hour, they'd gone over their options. There was no happy ending for anyone. If they called in the police, Ruby would be in the spotlight, under scrutiny, and they'd want to know exactly what her role and relationship was with Tony Devlin. McGuire was uncomfortable enough that they were harbouring someone who had laundered drug money for the kind of pond life they investigated and exposed in his newspaper. But the fact that she'd also witnessed the murder of a prostitute was pushing him close to the edge. If this girl's body turned up any time soon, they were sitting on information that could nail the killer. And if the cops found that out, there would be more than Ruby going to jail, he warned. He listened to Rosie's idea as she walked him through the possible consequences. They were far from happy. But their only option was to make the call.

Twenty minutes later McGuire's phone rang and he answered it.

'Send them in, Marion.' He clasped his hands behind his head and looked down at Rosie.

'Right, Gilmour. Let's see if these guys have got any balls.'

The door opened and the editor stepped forward, offering his hand.

'Thanks for coming at such short notice, gentlemen.' He cleared his throat. 'But this is important.'

If Chief Superintendent Boswell-Smith was irritated at being summoned by a newspaper editor, he hid it well. His body language was more relaxed than at the last meeting, where he'd bristled and seemed on the defensive.

'Not at all, sir.' He shoved his hands in his trouser pockets and squared his big shoulders. 'We never close.' He glanced from Rosie to McGuire. 'And I'm sure two very busy people like yourselves wouldn't be asking us to come down here at this time of night – as you're no doubt putting your newspaper to bed – unless it was crucial business . . . So here we are.'

McGuire crossed the room to his conference table and pulled out chairs, gesturing them to sit down.

The editor sat at the head of the table, with Boswell-Smith on his left and the captain next to him. Rosie was opposite them, her eyes resting on the captain in his darkblue suit and pink shirt. He could have stepped out of the pages of a glossy magazine. McGuire sat with his elbows on the table and his hands steepled under his chin.

'Okay, chaps.' His eyes narrowed a little. 'I want to ask first of all if we can speak off the record to you, around this table. As you see, we've no lawyer present. I didn't ask him to join us, because I want to have a frank discussion with you.' McGuire paused, looking at them for approval. 'About the matter we discussed the other day. There's been a development, and we want to draw your attention to it.' He glanced from the superintendent to the captain. 'But . . . Well. We're also looking for your help.'

He waited for a response. Nothing for at least four beats, as Boswell-Smith held eye contact with him. He was good at this. Rosie was barely breathing. The clock on the wall said seven fifteen. Ruby would be frantic downstairs in the office canteen, where she'd left Matt and Adrian looking after her.

The superintendent linked his fingers together on the table, studied the palms of his hands as though measuring his response, then looked up.

'It depends on what you have to tell us, Mr McGuire. And what kind of impact it has on this investigation.' He sat back, crossing his legs, confident, in control. 'Tell you what. Why don't we do it this way: you tell us what has prompted you to call us back here so . . . so quickly . . . because if we're being frank, I didn't expect to hear from you again after our meeting the other day. I got the impression that you don't have a lot of time for the establishment, if I may say so, sir.'

McGuire gave him an earnest look.

'I'm a newspaper editor, Superintendent. My job is to question and probe everything that comes across my desk – especially the establishment.'

The superintendent nodded, stroking his chin.

'Fair enough. Good answer.' He sat forward, gazed admiringly up at the pictures of historic *Post* front pages on the walls. 'You know, I did consider becoming a journalist myself, back in the day. My father was editor of the local rag in our town and it was expected I'd follow in his footsteps – so, growing up, I did get a bit of a feel for the old newspaper business. There was something exciting about it. A real buzz.' He gave Rosie what she took as a friendly nod. 'But I opted for the police. I'd encountered a few detectives in my time at functions with my father, and I liked the cut of their jib. What I found was that these guys impressed me more than a reporter standing outside the court in the rain waiting to interview some waste of space who'd just been freed on a murder charge. In the end, I opted to be a copper – call it an idealist mission to do something to sort the bad guys out,' He put a hand up. 'But believe me, I do have respect for what you chaps do, and the lengths you go to tell a story. Having said that, we live in a country where the law is the law, and I firmly believe we must uphold that.'

Rosie made eyes at McGuire. She didn't want to hear Boswell-Smith's life story. She shifted in her seat, then the words were out before she could stop herself.

'I agree with you. But not everyone in the establishment upholds the law.' Rosie flicked a glance at the captain, thinking that the SAS seemed to make their own rules. 'I think we all know what I mean here.' She took a breath. 'There are . . . well, always have been, people in positions of power and influence who will bend and use the law to suit themselves, for their own gain. Those are the kind of wrongs we try to expose. And without being too dramatic, that's what drives us as journalists . . .' She looked at McGuire, who nodded that he trusted her to go on. 'So, what the editor is saying here is that we have information that will assist your investigation into the murder of Tom Mahoney. But, much more than that − we have information that will lead you to nailing the gangsters behind it. All of them. We're prepared to help you with that. But . . . And here's the catch . . . We also need your help. And what I really need to be clear about here, to be completely blunt, is that what I've just admitted in terms of us having information . . . I will robustly deny on a stack of bibles if you ever take what I've said and use it against me, if this meeting should go, how can I put . . . tits up.'

The captain bit the inside of his jaw trying to stop himself from smiling as he looked from the corner of his eye to the cop.

Boswell-Smith examined his big hands again and looked from McGuire to Rosie.

He nodded slowly.

'Okay. Understood. Off the record . . . So . . .' He took a long breath and let it out like a sigh. 'Can we stop fucking around, and can you tell us why you brought us here?'

Rosie relaxed a little, hoping she could trust them.

'You take it from here, Rosie,' McGuire said.

'Okay.' Rosie pulled her chair closer to the table. 'We've been working with a contact on the investigation into Mahoney's murder, and it's opened up a few different lines – unexpected lines – for us. But the problem is that our contact – a woman who is in a position to take us inside this story – is now under threat from the men behind the murder . . . the same gang you were trying to trap in Berlin when the sting operation failed.' She waited to make sure they were with her. 'We asked you to come here because our contact's sister has been kidnapped by these people. The sister is ill, a mental-trauma thing, and she's not responsive, hasn't spoken for twenty-five years and needs a lot of care and attention. She was taken yesterday when my contact took her out for the afternoon from the nursing home where she lives. My source had stepped inside to pay the bill in the restaurant where they'd had lunch, and when she came back out her sister was gone. Certain people have contacted her and told her they have her sister.'

'Why would they take her?'

Rosie glanced at McGuire.

'Well, that's where it gets a little difficult. My contact has connections with them. She has assisted them in business.'

'In the drug and murder business?' Boswell-Smith's eyebrows went up a fraction.

'Not quite. She's not involved like that – I mean, in the drugs or in murder. But she is involved financially. Taking care of some of the money for them.'

'Laundering it?'

'Well . . .'

'Laundering it,' the superintendent confirmed. 'So why have they taken the girl? She must have crossed them in some way – this contact of yours who launders their money . . .' His voice was deadpan. 'Has she bumped them for money?'

'It's a bit complicated. But she has some information she has to pass to them regarding money and bank details, and she hasn't done it yet. She was supposed to do it earlier, and they got impatient.'

'Who got impatient? Give me names.'

Rosie glanced at McGuire, who nodded for her to go ahead.

'Tony Devlin, a Glasgow hood . . . His associate down south is Tam Dunn, of J B Solutions. A bad lot, as you know. They had investments tied up together. And Rab Jackson, the man murdered in Costa del Sol recently, was part of that.'

The superintendent said nothing for a few seconds while he processed the information.

'So what has this kidnapping to do with Mahoney's murder?'

'They were the gang who were buying the arms. Dunn is J B Solutions. But you must know that. It was his guys who were doing the deal with Russians.'

He said nothing, appearing to gaze out of the window in some momentary reverie, then spoke without looking at anyone.

'So tell me this. Where are you on the Mahoney investigation for your newspaper? The last time I was here, you told me that the information and documents you'd been given access to were no longer accessible. Is that still true?' He gave Rosie a look; he was toying with her.

Rosie said nothing. McGuire folded his arms.

'Okay,' the superintendent continued. 'What I'm hearing here, and correct me if I'm wrong, is that you have some bird who launders gangsters' money, and her sister has been snatched. You don't report that crime to Strathclyde Police. You don't call the police because you're protecting her. Which, of course, is breaking the law. Am I right so far?'

Rosie's stomach tightened.

'And you want us to swing into action like the cavalry

and rescue her – in, presumably, an SAS-style operation worthy of a tabloid front page.' He almost smirked at the captain, who remained poker-faced.

That was exactly what Rosie wanted them to do, but when he put it like that in his clipped tones it sounded ridiculous.

'You watch a lot of movies, do you, Rosie?' The superintendent smiled.

Rosie felt her face burn. He was making an arse of them. She looked down at the table.

'Now . . . tell me this, Rosie. I'll ask this question again. As a matter of interest, are these documents, which you couldn't give me access to the other day, still not available? Or have they now suddenly become available? And what incriminating stuff do they contain involving government departments?'

He gave her a don't-piss-me-around look.

Rosie could either lie or take a chance. She swallowed hard.

'We have information that someone inside the MoD was assisting this gang with export licences, enabling J B Solutions to continue selling arms abroad after their licence had been revoked over the sale of arms to Nigeria.' She looked him in the eye. 'But I'm sure you already know that.'

His face was blank.

'So why haven't you printed that?' He turned to McGuire.

'We're not there with it yet,' McGuire replied, straight-faced. 'We haven't quite tied down all the ends. We're still investigating. But to be honest, the main thrust of our story has shifted slightly. We've been digging around on Tam Dunn and J B Solutions and we now have incriminating evidence against them. Our *own* evidence. So we have two stories, so to speak, both connected, in that they involve what happened to Tom Mahoney. But also they are stand-alone stories.'

Another stony silence. After what seemed like an age, the superintendent spoke.

'Right. I'm not a newspaper man, but right now you have one story. The story of J B Solutions' involvement in arms dealing and how you as a newspaper can nail them down, help put them behind bars. Okay? Let's say you have that. Are you still planning to use the MoD and the corruption line? By that, I mean, do you plan to use the MoD line as a big factor in your exposé?'

'We're not quite there with it,' Rosie said, glancing uneasily at McGuire.

'So ditch it.' The superintendent's mouth turned down.

'What?' Rosie glared at McGuire.

'You heard me. Ditch it.'

'Ditch it?'

'Yes. Dump the MoD line, give me the documents that I *know* you have . . . and forget that side of the story. Then we simply forget we ever met.'

Rosie looked at McGuire, then at the superintendent.

'Are you serious?'

'Listen, dear . . . I'm so serious I came all the way up here on the instructions of Whitehall to get this documentation that we *know* Tom Mahoney had, and I now *know* you now have, but failed to turn over to me when I asked about it. But that's my problem. Well . . . it *was* my problem until you and your editor suddenly need my help to get the sister of your money-laundering contact back from the kidnappers. I'm sure you get my drift.' He paused, sniffed. 'So this is fairly straightforward, as far as I'm concerned.' He turned to McGuire. 'You dump your MoD scandal story, and we'll get your sick girl back to her sister. And we'll all live happily ever after.' He looked at his watch.

'Now . . . if I were you, I'd make my decision quickly, for two reasons. One . . . this girl is being held by the kind of evil bastards we've been dealing with, and if she's not released soon, she'll be dead – if she's not already dead. Two, if you're *not* going to do it *my* way, then the good captain and myself have a table booked for dinner at eight, and he's paying . . . So make your mind up.' He folded his arms.

Rosie was seething. Boswell-Smith had just steamrollered over them. This wasn't about truth or police work, it was about defending the establishment at all costs. That's why he'd been sent from London to find out about their investigation. His demand was about selling out everything she, McGuire and the paper had always fought for – their right to unmask the liars and the cheats and the crooks, whether they were in housing schemes, banks or government departments. They were almost there on a massive story that might even spark resignations at Cabinet level. They couldn't just let that go. How could they? She thought of Ruby, the shitty start she'd had in life, not unlike her own, and so many of the souls she'd encountered over the years, from Glasgow to Kosovo, who had to scrap and fight for everything they had. Judy was all Ruby had. Her eyes met McGuire's and he looked away. He had already made his decision.

The superintendent looked at his watch again and fiddled with his gold cufflinks. McGuire put his pen down on the table and stood up.

'We have a deal, Superintendent.' He looked at the captain. 'Now, let's get that poor girl out.'

Rosie felt her shoulders sink, a wave of disappointment and anger hitting her like a punch in the gut. Tom Mahoney had been murdered because he was about to expose corruption and greed at the heart of the MoD. More than that, he died because he was able to reveal how someone, with the stroke of a pen, could allow a lowlife like Tam Dunn and his outfit to sell guns and ammunition that could kill and maim innocent people in Nigeria who were already disenfranchised, who had already lost hope. And the profits that these gangsters here made were ploughed into their stinking drug empires in the housing schemes, in towns and cities where heroin helped blot out their shitty existence for too many people. Everything that underpinned Rosie as a journalist was enshrined in the determination of her newspaper to expose this kind of greed and corruption. Now that very principle was being trampled upon in front of her eyes in the editor's office. If she couldn't unmask these kinds of people, there was no point in getting out of bed in the morning. But she knew that by handing over her dossier she might save one life – Judy's. There *was* no choice.

CHAPTER TWENTY-NINE

Don was already at the bar when Rosie walked through the swing doors into O'Brien's. He eased himself off the bar stool as she made her way through the usual throng of early-evening, well-heeled punters, either in for a drink on the way home from work or getting tanked up to go out on the town. A noisy bunch of designer-smart, twenty-something blokes in party mode were knocking back champagne. Rosie picked her way through them towards the bar, conscious of them eyeing her up. One of them stood in front of her, blocking her path, then moved to block her again, a big, daft grin on his face as she attempted to squeeze past him. It might have been amusing for a nanosecond the first time, Rosie thought, as she forced a smile, but she was not in the mood for it when he did it the second time. She made a give-me-a-break-guys face at him and he moved to the side. Whatever he'd said as she slid past him sent the rest of them into guffaws of laughter.

'Just what I need' – Rosie leaned in to give Don a kiss on the cheek – 'a bunch of bloody hooray Henrys.'

'Stag party,' Don said, nodding to the barman. 'Obviously a rich one. They're on their third bottle of Dom Perignon and they've only been in an hour.'

'They must be cops,' Rosie joked as she climbed onto a stool.

'Yeah, right.' Don replied. 'Gin and tonic?'

'You bet. I need at least one.'

He offered her a cigarette and she put it to her lips as he flicked the lighter. Watching Ruby chain-smoke for the past two hours had put her in the notion for a fag. She inhaled deeply, enjoying the buzz of her first cigarette in a few days, then swallowed a mouthful of her drink, feeling better already.

'That's more like it.' Don scanned her face. 'You sounded a bit wired on the phone.'

Rosie puffed out smoke. 'I passed wired about two o'clock today.' She screwed up her face as the stag party erupted into more raucous laughter. 'Christ! They're a noisy bunch of twats. I can't hear myself think.'

'They'll be going shortly.' Don looked over her shoulder. 'I see one of them asking for the bill.'

'Good.'

'So what's the story, pal?' Don ran a hand over his chin and loosened his tie.

'I've got something for you. Big time, Don . . . But

whatever I say in the next few minutes goes absolutely nowhere until I give you the nod. Understood?'

Don's craggy features barely moved a muscle.

'Sure. Goes without saying.'

Rosie took a moment to decide where to start. She'd spent all morning in the West End at Ruby's flat, ploughing through a pile of paperwork she'd printed off earlier at the *Post*. Ruby had taken a bit of convincing last night that the only way to get Judy back was to work with Boswell-Smith and the captain. Even though she wouldn't have to meet them in person, Ruby was still suspicious she was being led into a trap. But she'd made up her mind to go along with it after she'd phoned Tony again to arrange to hand over all the bank details and documents. He kept changing the goalposts. He'd said flatly that *he* would decide when he had time – probably in a couple of days. He told her to be ready. Then hung up. Ruby was inconsolable when she'd come off the phone, weeping that Judy was probably already dead and that Tony was just being an evil bastard. She vowed again to kill him with her bare hands. Rosie had to convince her that she was the only one who could crucify Tony and his mob by turning him in, along with all the bank details. She knew where all the bodies were buried – in financial terms. She could ruin all of them. Not only that, she had witnessed Dunn kick a girl to death. Eventually, fired up, Ruby agreed. And to Rosie's astonishment, she even decided she would make a statement about the murder of the prostitute, as long as she could be assured that she'd never have to appear in court. But she would only make the statement once she was safely out of the country – hopefully, with Judy. If it worked, it would be a major coup for the cops, bagging all the main players – and Rosie would have a massive exclusive for the *Post*. But they were a long way from that. McGuire remained sceptical, but when she'd told him she had the bank accounts and paperwork in her hands, he was in. All she had to do now was test the water with Don and get reassurances. She knew the pitfalls of passing information to the police, especially the statement about the prostitute's murder and not bringing in the eyewitness. She'd cross that bridge when she came to it.

'Okay.' Rosie swivelled around in the stool so that she was facing Don. She leaned closer, lowering her voice. 'Listen. If the information I have is accurate, I can deliver Tony Devlin . . . and no doubt a few of his cohorts . . . including all their dirty money and assets. Everything. Straight into your hot little hands.'

Don stopped in mid-draw, his mouth dropping open a little.

'Have you been at the drink?'

'I'm serious, Don. And I mean bank accounts, statements, company names, directors, details on how and where they laundered their money. Everything. I can give you all that stuff, then it's up to you to move on it and start breaking down a few doors, pulling in the bodies.'

Don pushed his hand through his greying hair, his eyes narrowing.

'How? I mean how the fuck can you get your hands on that? We have teams of people from the Serious Crime Squad to the Fraud Squad trying to track that kind of shit all the time, but everything is so well hidden these days.'

'I know. But Devlin, as you know, has companies all over the place. All sorts of businesses, from property to petrol stations. The money moves around them all, getting cleaner the more it's laundered. Then most of it goes abroad.'

'So how can you get this information? '

'Put it this way' – Rosie looked at him, then away – 'I have access to the person who set up the companies, the bank accounts . . . the whole shooting match. Even going back as far as Rab Jackson's day.'

'You're kidding.'

'Nope.'

'So this person is either terminally ill, or they're about to be.'

'No. Just very angry. It's all about retribution.'

They sat for a long moment, Rosie watching Don gnaw the inside of his jaw, his brain ticking over. He signalled to the barman for two more drinks.

'Retribution?' he said. 'There are a lot of poor bastards buried in the foundations of the Kingston Bridge who thought they could dish out retribution to Rab Jackson and his mob.'

'This is different. This is here and now. I'm talking bank accounts that can show money moving all over the place. I'm not an expert on that kind of shit, and frankly, balance sheets make my eyes glaze over, but I have access to the actual person who has legitimized all the business.'

He looked at her, incredulous.

'Would they meet us? Totally off the record? Guarantees up front they'd be protected?'

Rosie shook her head.

'Not a chance in hell. No way.'

'Why?'

'Don't ask, Don.'

'It's obviously someone on the inside then?'

Rosie said nothing, stared through him.

'Fuck me, Rosie!' Don shook his head, a smile almost coming to his lips. 'This could make a huge impact, pull the rug from these bastards, if we could get our hands on that kind of paperwork.' He grinned. 'I think I'm getting a hard-on.'

'I thought it was just the way you were sitting,' Rosie snorted. 'But seriously. There's more . . .' She pushed her hair back, fiddling with her earring. 'My contact witnessed the murder of a young prostitute. Eastern European.'

Don screwed up his eyes.

'We don't have a prostitute murder.'

'Yes, you do. You just don't know about it yet.'

'Fucking hell! When?'

Rosie hesitated.

'Recently.'

'How recent? A month, a week, a year?'

'Very recent.'

'So why no body?'

'My contact said it was disposed of . . . And there was another girl who also witnessed it. A hooker – also Eastern European. Don't know where she is, but I'd be surprised if she's not dead too.'

'Shit, Rosie. You need to give me more.'

'I can't. I'm not in a position to. Not right now.'

'So what does this contact want from us?'

'Nothing. The contact will disappear, no questions asked. You will get a full statement on the murder but they will absolutely not testify in court. So be clear about that.' She paused. 'Let me put it this way, the murder is so recent and so bloody, Forensics will find enough DNA once you get the location.'

Don was silent for a few moments, as though he was trying to work out all the rivalry between Rab Jackson and any of his cohorts over the years.

'I can see you're trying to figure who the traitor is.' Rosie looked at her watch and pulled her bag onto her shoulder.

'I am. I'm all over the place here.' He puffed. 'When can we get this stuff?'

'Soon. In a few days. But you can't mention it right now. Not to anyone. Just be ready, because we'll be doing something about it in the *Post* before we hand over the full dossier. And when the time comes you can tell your bosses not to even think about kicking the editor's door in and demanding to know who the contact is, because that's not going to happen. Understood?'

Don nodded.

'It'll have to be discussed at the top level.'

'I don't give a toss if you consult Christ himself. The deal is totally anonymous, or forget it. No names, no pack drill. It's not up for discussion. And forget even trying to track down the contact, because whatever else they may be – they are not stupid.'

Don drained his glass.

'Okay. Deal. I'll wait for your call.' He eyed her curiously. 'Oh, by the way, how're things going with the Mahoney murder? I liked your piece about him being a spy and all that. Good read.'

'It's ticking along,' Rosie lied, keeping her face straight. She finished her drink. 'I'd better head home. I've got a busy day tomorrow.'

Don got off the stool.

'Me, too. But I'll be up all night now trying to figure out who the "Deep Throat" contact is. You drive me nuts, Gilmour.'

They walked out of the swing doors and into the evening drizzle.

'You'll not be saying that when you're the head honcho

in the CID . . . By the way, I hope we can continue to have our wee drinks if you do ever get to the top of the heap.'

Don leaned down and kissed her cheek.

'Any time, darlin'. I miss you when I don't see you . . . . You stayed in Bosnia too long.'

'Yeah,' Rosie said, glancing beyond him into the rain. 'You're probably right, there, pal. Too bloody long.'

She waved down a black cab and headed off.

As the taxi pulled into her car park Rosie thought she saw a figure on the steps of the entrance to the flats. She rubbed the steamed-up side window with the back of her hand and peered through the rain. Ever since the death threats last year she'd been twitchy whenever she came home in the dark. She peered again and breathed a sigh of relief. It was Adrian. She paid the driver and got out, a little puzzled, as it was unlike Adrian to turn up at her home unannounced. But she was glad to see him.

He stepped out of the doorway, soaked to the skin, rain running down his face and into the upturned collar of his light bomber jacket.

'Sorry to come here like this, Rosie. I was calling you, but no answer.'

'Really?' Rosie pulled her mobile out of her jacket and noticed a missed call on the screen. 'It must have been the noise in the pub. Sorry, Adrian. Don't worry. What's the matter?'

'I saw the girl . . . The prostitute . . .'

Rosie gave him a bewildered look as she fished her keys out of her bag and pushed them into the lock.

'What prostitute?'

'The other girl, who was with the one who was killed by Tam Dunn'

Rosie's eyes widened. 'You saw her? How?'

'I am walking in the city today and I am thinking if she is alive she must be somewhere. I was curious. I have talk to some of my friends from Bosnia and from Poland here – people I knew when I lived here – and one girl tells me that two girls she knows was working with her in one of the factories, packing vegetables. But she said they are also working in nights . . . with an escort agency. She says they haven't been seen for four days. She gave me the names and where they live.'

'You're kidding! You went looking for her?' Rosie opened the door. 'Come on in. It's cold. You're soaked through.'

She was surprised he'd gone without consulting her. If it had been anyone else working on a story with her, they would have got a sharp rebuke, but she knew Adrian would have been discreet. If the girl was out there, he'd find her. In fact, given his background, he'd probably have a better chance of making a connection with the girl than with her.

As they climbed the stairs to her flat Adrian grabbed hold of Rosie's arm.

'Are you angry with me, Rosie? For going to find the girl

'Rosie's all right,' Ruby said softly to her sister. 'She's on our side.'

Rosie watched the two of them, pondering what it would be like to have a sister, even if she didn't speak to you and her eyes were miles away. You could still hug her, even if she didn't hug you back. She swallowed.

'I see the resemblance.' It was all she could think of to say.

Ruby sat on bench and motioned Rosie to sit next to her.

'I wanted to meet you here, away from Glasgow, but also so you could meet Judy.' She rubbed her hand along her sister's arm. 'She's . . . well . . . she's everything to me.'

Rosie nodded, glancing at Judy then back to Ruby. 'Is she . . . I mean, does she . . .' She was suddenly tongue-tied and awkward. 'What I'm trying to say is, will she get better in time? Have you seen any improvement over the years?'

'Yeah. Definitely. And the nurses told me that in recent weeks she's been a little more communicative. Well, when I say communicative, I mean she's actually acknowledged their presence and their words when they speak to her. She's registering things, they think. That's a big improvement. And she can walk a bit more, although she gets tired. They pumped a lot of drugs into her years ago, because they didn't know what they were dealing with. For such a long time she was sedated, because that's what they thought was best. There's all sorts of damage been done, muscles wasted and stuff. Things are a little better now, but I'm scared to hope that she will ever really come back to me.'

Rosie wanted to ask if there was brain damage.

'Her brain is functioning,' Ruby said, as though reading her mind. 'They've done tests and there's no brain damage there. But it's the trauma. That, and the fact that for years after it all happened she was left with no proper care.' She leaned over and touched her sister's arm. 'She was shunted from pillar to post, notes getting lost . . . all that kind of shit. Given anti-psychotic drugs when what she needed was a good psychiatrist. They just wrote her off as a hopeless case. At one point they were treating her for schizophrenia. I mean, how the hell does that happen to a kid? There're probably a lot of people like that in institutions who shouldn't really be there.' She gazed out towards the lake. 'But that all changed a few years ago, when I found her. And now, day by day, things are getting better. I feel I can get to her. I hugged her when I got back a couple of weeks ago and whispered to her and – and she actually hugged me back. That's the first time that's happened. So I have to believe that there is hope.'

'What made her improve?' Rosie asked.

Ruby looked at her sister for a long moment but said nothing.

They sat watching a flock of birds swoop across the lake, the peace of the countryside filling the silence. Three people, Rosie thought. Surviving.

'So,' Ruby said, taking a cigarette out of her handbag and lighting up. 'You wanted to talk about your investigation.'

'Yes.' Rosie turned to her. 'I want to ask if you will work with us.'

'Go on.' Ruby blew a trail of smoke and watched it rise and disappear.

'Obviously, what I'm going to tell you now puts me in a lot of danger if it ever gets out, Ruby, so I'm placing a whole lot of trust in you.'

Ruby glared at her.

'Listen, pal. You're here. With my sister. I brought you here. Who's trusting who?'

Rosie nodded.

'Okay. Fair enough. Then here's the situation.' She took a deep breath. 'I have a dossier given to me by Gerard Hawkins – Mahoney's friend – the one you saw that day.'

Ruby raised her eyebrows.

'Really? I did see Mahoney pass something to him in the café.'

'You did? Good. At least that proves Hawkins didn't make it up. Well . . . I think Hawkins was murdered because he was about to make this information public, which is what he told me Mahoney had asked him to do that day.'

'Mahoney did look agitated.'

'The dossier is full of a lot of damning allegations. Some of them we may be able to back up but a lot of them we won't. That will be the editor's call, at the end of the day.

But Mahoney has written a lot about the arms dealing and this company we talked about, J B Solutions, and the guy who runs it . . . You mentioned him.'

'Tam Dunn,' Ruby interrupted.

'You know him?' Rosie asked, surprised.

'I don't know him, but I know a man who does.'

'Really? That's useful. Who is he?'

'His name is Tony Devlin. He runs the show here for Rab Jackson. Took over when Rab moved to Spain, and now he's the man in charge.'

'How well do you know him?'

'Well enough.' Ruby shot Rosie a lazy-eyed glance then looked away.

Rosie let the silence hang for a moment.

'Does he trust you?'

'Put it this way, I think he's scared not to trust me.' Ruby's lips curled a little. 'He *needs* to trust me. I'm the only one who knows where all Rab's money is, which in turn is his money, and the mob's money, too.'

'Right.' Rosie nodded slowly. This was better than she'd hoped for. 'Has he talked to you about Tam Dunn?'

'You bet he has. I was with him yesterday, and he's spilling his guts on this whole fucking story. He told me a lot of stuff, actually – about the shooting of Mahoney . . . how it was an arms deal that got fucked up. And how one of their men got killed – Billy. He's from Glasgow but lived down south for years. And another guy was captured.'

sniffed and touched his nose. 'And let me tell you one thing . . . there isn't anyone out there who won't take a bung. And I know that for a fact. Everyone will take a back-hander.' He lowered his voice. 'Listen. Between us, I have people in my pocket, on my payroll, that go all the way to Whitehall – the MoD. They're *greedy* bastards, mind you. But they'll turn a blind eye, do any fucking thing, as long as you stick the money in their offshore accounts.'

Rosie shook her head in mock disbelief, glancing at Adrian.

'It's incredible, isn't it?' she said. 'You know what they say – the people in power are bigger gangsters than any-one. The MPs, the civil servants. It's one rule for them and another for the rest of us.'

'I agree.' Adrian gave a measured nod. 'If we'd waited for the politicians to make life better for us then we would all have starved to death in Bosnia during and after the war. We have had to go out and fight for our living.'

'Exactly,' Dunn agreed. 'In fact, I'll let you into a secret, now that I know we're on the same wavelength. J B Solu-tions is operating and making more money now than ever – and we've not been short of problems.'

Rosie and Adrian nodded and said nothing.

'We had some hassle with the Home Office after our sis-ter company sold a container-load of weaponry to Nigeria. Some big bastard dictator over there wanted them to shore up his regime in the civil war. Me? I don't judge, as I told

you. A deal is a deal. But we didn't have the proper paperwork at the time . . . well . . . put it this way . . . I didn't put
all the facts down on the paperwork we had. I took a chance
and shipped it. But it got rumbled and that was it. Big
problem with the licence after that, and we were nearly
out of business. You have to laugh at the government really.
They don't give a fuck what regimes they bankroll quietly,
who *they* sell arms to, and who is killing who with the guns
they sold to these dodgy tyrants. They just don't want us to
get a slice of the action.'

'So what did you do?' Rosie asked. 'I mean, how did you
survive?'

Dunn grinned.

'By paying the fuckers to turn a blind eye.'

'You mean the Customs and Borders people?'

'Yeah. Them too. But also we have someone inside the
MoD, some mid-ranking civil servant who does the paperwork. He's in our pocket – took a bit of organizing and
plenty of dosh, but he's in, because he couldn't resist the
money.'

'And you can ship arms without any problems?'

'Well, as you saw today, they're all boxed up, so when we
sell a lot, they go in a lorry from our haulage firm next
door – you may have noticed it when you came in.' He
grinned. 'They're not delivering to supermarkets, I can
tell you that. So, the guns and hardware go in among a
whole load of other things we ship abroad. Mostly car

components, steel, metal and rods for the construction trade – that kind of thing. It's all very well camouflaged, so that unless they take the whole container apart, nobody knows a thing. They accept what is on the paperwork. When we have a shipment going out, I make a call to my man, and off it goes. Simple as that. I know it sounds unbelievable, but that's how it happens. That's how the world goes round, not by hard graft. Fuck that for a living. There's money in everything except hard work. It's dog eat dog.'

Adrian nodded and raised his glass in a toast.

'To good business,' he said. 'Without frontiers.'

'Well put, big man. Our game. Our rules.' Dunn knocked back his drink.

Rosie checked her watch again. It was almost midnight. The restaurant was empty apart from one table, and the waiters were hovering near the bar, looking bored.

'We should be getting back.' Rosie looked at Adrian. 'We're flying in the morning, so we have an early drive to Heathrow.'

Dunn waved the waiter over and Rosie watched as he paid the bill, pulling a wad of notes out of his inside jacket pocket. The tip must have been at least fifty quid. He stood up, turning to Adrian.

'I was going to take you to a club if you fancied it. I have a little share in a place where they have a proper VIP room with no riff-raff and plenty of birds. It's only twenty minutes away.' He gave Adrian a playful dig, gesturing to

Rosie. 'You can send the help back to the hotel. You won't be short of action, big man.'

Adrian smiled at him, and for a moment Rosie thought he was going to go.

'Next time,' he said. 'Not tonight. We can celebrate once you tell me you have weapons ready and when is the delivery, and, of course, when we pay the first part of the money.'

'Yeah. Right. Good idea. We need to work out how to do that. Probably best if I drive somewhere, say Belgium or Amsterdam, and bring the cash back that way. It's a lot of money, so I don't want to leave it to anyone else. I can get a couple of the lads to drive me there, and we can meet.'

'Perfect.' Adrian said. 'Maybe we will take you to some nightclubs in Amsterdam.'

'You won't be taking me to any I haven't already been to. That much I can guarantee.'

'Or if you prefer,' Adrian said, 'I can come back here. Or anywhere in the UK – in Scotland if you like. You are Scottish?'

'I am. But Amsterdam is better for nightlife. I was in Glasgow the other night and the place is crap, no good clubs. Just crap. I left all that behind years ago and only go now for a bit of business.'

He stretched out his hand with the grazed knuckles and Rosie felt sick as she had to shake it.

without asking? I did try to call you, and I thought it best to make a look for her soon instead of leaving it too long. I hope is okay?'

She turned to face him, and for a moment they stood in silence, the rain on his face glistening in the glow from the hall light. Their breath steamed in the cold and she fought to control the rush of desire.

'No, I'm not angry.' She heard her voice, weak.

'Good. I have a lot to tell you.'

Rosie turned away from him and put the key in the lock, pushing open the door. As they stepped into the hallway, she automatically put her hand on the wall to switch on the light, but Adrian slipped his hand over hers. For a moment they stood in the darkness, Rosie's throat so tight she couldn't trust herself to speak. He moved closer so her back was to the wall, and she could feel her heart pounding as he leaned down and kissed her face, the chill of his wet cheek against hers. Her body shuddered as she felt him against her, and she could hear Adrian's breath quicken as he ran his hands gently across her breasts. He pushed her hair back as he took her face in his hands, and they kissed with the same hunger as they'd done when they found each other that sultry night in Sarajevo.

CHAPTER THIRTY

Rosie lay awake, watching the darkness give way to a pale-grey sky. Then she slipped out of bed and pulled on her bathrobe, standing for a moment to gaze at Adrian sleeping peacefully, his muscular chest rising and falling with each soft breath. The cold light of day brought with it a stab of apprehension. She had no idea where she was going with this relationship – in truth, it wasn't even a relationship. She could have stopped Adrian at any time last night or before, and he was the kind of man who would have understood and moved on. But Rosie couldn't stop *herself*. An image flashed into her mind of them last night in the throes of passion. She shook her head. The rights or wrongs of it would have to wait.

She padded quietly around the flat, brewing up coffee, preparing her breakfast of Greek yoghurt and blueberries, then switched on Sky News and kept the volume down low as she sat on the sofa, thinking over what Adrian had said about the girl.

Her name was Olenca. She was Polish. She and her friend Lujca had been here for over a year working, as many of the Eastern European immigrants did, in the vegetable-packing factories on the outskirts of the city. Adrian described how he'd waited until she came out of her flat at the address he'd been given, then followed her into the café downstairs, where he sat at the next table. He'd started a conversation and they chatted about living in Glasgow and the things they missed about back home. That was all. She'd spoken about working in the vegetable factory and also with the escort agency. He didn't broach the subject, but at one point she'd told him her best friend, another girl, had gone, and that was when she suddenly burst into tears. When he asked her what had happened, had she gone back to Poland, she'd nodded her head. But Adrian said she looked like she was hiding something. He didn't want to ask any more. He couldn't be one hundred per cent sure, but there was too much of a coincidence for it not to be the girl. Rosie was grateful, but the girl wasn't today's priority. She picked up her mobile phone from the coffee table and was about to phone Ruby when it rang.

'I was just thinking of calling you,' Rosie said. 'Are you okay?'

Rosie heard her puffing.

'Yeah . . . I mean . . . Well, as okay as I can be . . . Rosie, I just had an email from that fucker. He wants me to meet him today. This afternoon.'

'Really?'

'Yeah. I've been awake since five this morning, watching my laptop, waiting for a message. Twisted bastard.'

'So what did he say?'

'I'm to meet him, bring along all the paperwork, the contacts I've talked to at the banks, all the letters with me signing over the accounts. I spent most of yesterday talking to the people I deal with at the banks. A few of them are abroad. There were also investment fund managers I had to talk to, to tell them I was taking another job.'

'Did that all go well?'

'Yeah. Only this shit to get through now.' She paused, and Rosie could hear the tension in her voice. 'I'm a nervous wreck. What if I go and Judy's not there? What if they've killed her? I can't stop thinking about that.'

'Don't, Ruby. You can't think that way today. You need to be totally focused on this. What's the plan?'

'No plan yet. I'm to meet him in Glasgow. He said to be ready and waiting for his call, that he'd email me in an hour or so with the location and time.'

'Okay. I'm going to get hold of these guys – the big cop from London and that SAS guy. We need to work things out.'

'Rosie, them guys scare me and I haven't even met them.

What if they go swinging in there like the cavalry and it all goes wrong?'

'That's not going to happen. This is what they do,' Rosie said, more in hope than real belief. 'Look, I don't even know myself what these guys will do or how they'll go about it. But we have to trust that they know what they're doing. Don't worry. I'll talk to them, then be down to see you soon.'

'Okay. Thanks.'

The line went dead.

Rosie watched through her windscreen in the car park of the Grosvenor Hotel in the West End as Superintendent Boswell-Smith and the captain came through the revolving doors and out into the rain. She flashed her lights and they acknowledged her with a nod. They walked over to a black Range Rover and the captain waved at her to join them.

'Morning, Rosie.' Boswell-Smith turned his body around as she climbed into the back seat of their car.

'Chaps.' Rosie nodded to both of them.

'So' – the Superintendent adjusted his tie – 'looks like this nasty bastard, Devlin, means business, eh?'

The captain pulled the sun visor down and his blue eyes met Rosie's in the mirror.

'Yep,' Rosie replied.

An unexpected wave of anxiety swept over her and she suddenly felt claustrophobic. Christ! This was no time to get wobbly. Get a grip, she told herself, trying to pull in a controlled breath through her nose. She opened the window a little, feeling the blast of damp air.

'You all right?' The superintendent searched her face.

'Yeah.' Rosie managed a deep breath, exhaled slowly. 'Well . . . if I'm honest, I'm a bit edgy about all of this.' She felt mortified admitting weakness in this kind of company.

Boswell-Smith glanced at the captain then at Rosie.

'That's good. Nerves are normal before going into any operation. Especially something like this.' He clasped his hands together. 'But then again, from what we've heard about you, you're no stranger to the hazards of investigative journalism.'

The superintendent's expression softened, and in the mirror Rosie saw the lines around the captain's mouth crinkle a little and the corners of his lips nearly curl to a smile.

'You didn't expect us check up on you?' the captain said.

Rosie smiled back, feeling a little more relaxed.

'Oh, right. I forgot. You guys are in the spooks game.'

The superintendent and the captain didn't answer, but the iciness was gone.

'Okay, Rosie,' Boswell-Smith said, 'we've got a bit of a game plan here, so let's go through it while we wait for this contact of yours to come back with some firm arrangements for the meet. You all right with that?'

She nodded.

'Excellent,' he said. 'I think it would be a good idea if you and this contact of yours could find a way so that the two of you both go to meet this character.'

Rosie felt her stomach flip. She hadn't expected this.

'Go together? Why? I mean, how are we going to do that?

'Well, your contact could say you're a friend, or someone she knows in the city that she can trust. Tell them she's in a bit of a state about losing her sister and needed a bit of moral support. She's in a tight corner and all that.'

'But she doesn't even live here . . . She's . . . er . . . she's hardly ever here. Lives abroad.'

'Yes,' the superintendent replied. 'But you could be a friend who she's turned to in her hour of need, as it were. Someone she knew a while ago.'

'Maybe,' Rosie said through gritted teeth. 'I suppose so. I . . . I mean, would they not be suspicious?'

'Perhaps. But it's a reasonable scenario for them to believe. Girl here in trouble, nobody to turn to, confides in old friend for help and support . . . that kind of thing. You with me?'

'Yeah,' Rosie agreed, but she could see the danger signs screaming all over this. McGuire would never wear it, for a start. 'But obviously, er . . . even if my contact agreed and this Tony character agreed, I still have to run it past my editor. I'm not sure he'd want me to do that.'

The two glanced at each other.

'You won't have anything to worry about, Rosie,' the

captain said. 'We'll have your back. You will never be out of contact with us.' He turned away, clicked open an aluminium case on his lap. 'We'll get you all wired up. You don't have to worry.'

Rosie glimpsed inside the case, all tightly-packed little compartments and what looked surveillance hardware far superior to anything she'd used undercover before. The captain dug into one of the sponge-lined compartments and plucked a tiny disc no bigger than a wristwatch battery.

'You see this?' He held it between his thumb and forefinger. 'This is a tracking device. If where you meet is away from our view, which I'm sure it will be at some stage, we can pinpoint where you are when we have to come looking for you. If you go into a car and are driven elsewhere, then we can track you all the way. It's brilliant. Never fails. You won't disappear.'

'Okay. But why do you need me there at all?' Rosie swallowed. Nobody spoke for a moment and she felt the heat rising in her face. 'Look, guys, it's not that my bottle is crashing or anything like that. But if you've researched me, then you'll know I've been in a few shit storms of late. So if I'm sounding a bit apprehensive ... no, actually sounding scared, then it's because I am. And that's the honest truth ... I ...'

The superintendent put his hand up to interrupt.

'Rosie. Listen to me.' He looked her in the eye. 'If you weren't shitting yourself when we asked you to go into

what will be a dangerous situation then we wouldn't consider even asking you. Of course you're scared.' He glanced
at the captain, who stared out of the window. 'Everyone
gets scared. Don't worry about that. But we'll look after
you. Your contact won't meet us, so we can't get her wired
up. And if something happens, then we have no control
because we don't know where she is. If you can get her to
see us, then we'll wire her up instead.'

Rosie shook her head.

'That's not going to happen. She won't see you. But I
understand what you mean. Actually, I hadn't considered
the finer points. I was thinking . . . well, I don't really know
what I was thinking . . . but I imagined that . . . maybe this
would be done in an open place. I don't think my contact
will agree to go anywhere with this character and his
henchmen because there is a very real possibility that once
she gives him what he wants he'll just bump her off . . .'
Rosie looked from one to the other.

'Of course. But she may not have an option,' the superintendent said. 'And if we're being honest, it's a very real
possibility that there will be some danger for both of you,
if he agrees to let her bring you.' He paused. 'Incidentally, I
think he won't allow you to go with her to the meeting,
but if he does, that tells us he's a lot thicker than we anticipated. And that's a good thing, from our point of view.'

Rosie nodded, not quite knowing what to do. The captain turned around again and half smiled.

'Don't worry, we'll make sure nothing happens to you.'
He spoke as though this was routine for him.

'Famous last words.' Rosie gave a nervous smile.

She sat back and folded her arms, staring out of the side
window, and seeing Matt's car at the far end of the car
park, where she'd left him and Adrian. Images flashed
through her mind of being thrown into the back seat of a
car when she'd been kidnapped in Belgrade, of kicking the
door open and running for her life through the streets.
Then her fingers automatically went to the arm that sometimes still ached from the blowtorch on the rooftop in
Seville. She closed her eyes to blink away the flashback of
being held over the edge of the building. During the two
months she had spent in Bosnia to recover from that
ordeal, Rosie had been filled with dark moments when she
felt that the Seville trauma had really pushed her over the
line. She couldn't go on living like this, on the edge all the
time. She'd used up most of her nine lives. She should walk
away while she still could. She took a deep breath and let it
out slowly, clenching her fists so they wouldn't notice her
trembling hands.

'Okay,' she said. 'Let's do it.'

CHAPTER THIRTY-ONE

Rosie drove across Jamaica Bridge, her guts churning with nerves. From the corner of her eye she saw Ruby wringing her hands as if gripping them tight would stop them trembling. Her striking features seemed to have faded into a ghostly paleness and her expression was drawn from lack of sleep. Seeing her like this, with all her defences down and jangling with nerves, made Rosie even more edgy.

'I'm so fucking wrecked,' Ruby sniffed and swallowed. 'Is it okay if I smoke?'

'Sure. You need to try to take things a minute at a time right now, Ruby. You're tired, and I can sense your panic from here. Try not to look any further than getting through the next five minutes. That's how you deal with panic. Try taking controlled, deep breaths and letting them out slowly.'

'What, are you a yoga teacher now?' Ruby snorted, and a kind of nervous chuckle came out.

Rosie smiled. The tough nut was still in there.

'Seriously, though, I've been there with panic. It takes over. You feel like you can't see any way out, and that makes the panic worse. Trust me. I sometimes feel it now and again.'

Ruby opened the window a little and blew out a trail of smoke.

'I wouldn't have had you down as a bottle merchant.'

'It's not about bottle. It's about shit that happens – one thing after another – and sometimes gets too much. There's no shame in admitting that sometimes you can't cope. You just . . . well . . . find someone to lean on and admit that you're not Superwoman.'

'Aye. Well, I've never had anyone to lean on.' Ruby gazed out of the window disconsolately. 'Not really. In the children's homes, the staff weren't big on hugs. More likely to try to get into your pants if you showed weakness. And that wasn't just the men.'

'Believe me,' Rosie said, 'that I do know.'

'How come?'

'I was in care. From when I was nine.'

'What happened? Is it all right to ask?'

'Yeah. My father went AWOL on the boats – he was a merchant seaman. My mum died, broken-hearted.' An image flashed up and Rosie swallowed. 'Suicide. She hanged herself.'

'Fuck me!'

'Yeah. Was rough. I found her when I came home from school, hanging from the staircase.'

'Christ almighty! I'm sorry.'

Rosie nodded, the memory still catching her chest after all these years. She tightened her mouth and kept her eyes on the road as she turned off the bridge.

'I was in one home,' Rosie went on, 'then I ran away. I'll tell you about it sometime – when this shit is all over. Anyway, I ended up living with one of my aunties – my mum's sister and her family. They were a bit mental. But by that time I already knew quite a bit about survival. Eventually, when I was sixteen, I upped sticks and ran away again. To London. Lived on the edge for a while. Not long, but at the time it seemed long.' Rosie shook her head, recalling the lonely days and nights, the drifting in and out of menial jobs until she got her first break. 'It's a story for another day.'

Ruby sighed and said nothing. Rosie went on.

'Obviously, I've never witnessed anything like you did that night with your mother and sister, but you know something? There are so many people out there carrying a load of shit on their backs, and somehow we all just have to find a way through.' She paused. 'Look how far *you've* come.'

'Yeah. But I'm a headcase, though.' Ruby said, matter-of-factly.

Rosie half smiled.

'Well. Nothing like a fucked-up childhood to prepare you for growing up in the big bad world. You'll be fine – once you get all this crap out of the way.'

Rosie drove on, and in the silence she could hear Ruby trying to take a long, slow breath.

When Ruby had phoned her earlier to say that Tony had agreed to let her bring an old friend, Rosie had to pretend she was glad. There was no backing out of it now. She should try a few deep breaths herself. She automatically called McGuire to brief him on the plan – but decided not to mention that she was going in with Ruby. She knew he'd hit the roof and instruct her to leave it to the professionals. She'd given Boswell-Smith and the captain the low-down on the location of the meet, and they wired her up with the tracking device and camera. What if they frisk me, Rosie had asked, as she'd pulled up her shirt to let the captain fit the wire around her body. They won't, the superintendent had insisted. How do you know? she'd asked, perplexed. Because he's fundamentally a thicko, he'd replied, with such conviction that she'd had to believe him. She hoped Boswell-Smith had got this far up the chain by doing more than just talking the talk.

'Just hold your nerve and leave the rest to us,' were his parting words. 'It's best you don't know the plan.'

She'd agreed, tight-lipped as she left, praying that they actually *had* a plan. Whatever. It was too late now, because the old grey sandstone warehouse they were headed for in Kinning Park on the edge of the River Clyde was up ahead.

'This has to be the place,' Rosie said.

'Jesus!' Ruby murmured.

'It'll be fine,' Rosie heard herself saying, as though she believed it.

She slowed down along the broad, deserted street. The whole area had once been the lifeblood of the ship-building industry, when Scotland was turning out battleships and cruise liners on a yearly basis. Along the banks of the Clyde were the ancillary yards of chandlers, workshops and supplies. Now it was all back-street car repairs and Asian cash-and-carry warehouses. It was a creepy, desolate enough place at any time of the day, Rosie had always thought, never mind at a time like this. She glanced around to see if she could see any cars. Nothing. Matt and Adrian knew where she was, and she knew they'd be somewhere close. Boswell-Smith and the captain were nowhere to be seen. She drove up to the entrance, where a BMW with blacked-out windows was the only car parked outside. Two men emerged from it as Rosie pulled in.

'I'll get out,' Ruby said. 'I recognize these guys. They were with Tony last week when I met him. Fucking apes.'

'Are you okay?' Rosie squeezed her arm. 'Are you ready for this?'

'Nope. But I don't exactly have a choice.' Her eyes took in

the deserted street and the fading late-afternoon light. 'Are your guys somewhere out here?'

'I'm sure they are.'

Rosie tried to sound reassuring as Ruby pushed open the door and stepped outside. Her mouth was dry as a stick and she swigged from a bottle of mineral water, watching as Ruby seemed to pull herself up tall and walk with something bordering on a strut towards the two big oafs with the shaven heads and shiny suits.

'Wait there,' the guy with a neck like a tree trunk snapped at her.

Rosie opened the window a little and saw him stab a beefy finger into his phone. He mumbled something into it as his mate stood, arms folded, giving Ruby a long, lustful look. The guy talking on the phone flicked his narrow eyes at Rosie.

'Tell your mate to get out the car.'

Ruby turned around and beckoned her. Rosie slipped her hand inside her blouse and switched on the tape and the tracking device. She prayed that a signal was going off somewhere. Her mobile was on silent. A few seconds later it vibrated twice – the sign they'd agreed with her earlier. At least they knew where she was.

She got out of the car and walked across to the two men, her legs a little shaky. She acknowledged them with a nod, and both of them looked at each other slyly as they gave her the once-over, the way a hungry beast would eye a piece of juicy meat. They looked like an experiment between the DNA of an ugly human and a silverback gorilla. She looked away, her eyes taking in the flocks of starlings making stunning patterns against the grey sky as they soared and dived towards Jamaica Bridge, as people headed home to the security of their normal lives. They followed the boss silverback towards the entrance of the office block, where he pushed a button on an intercom and the door clicked open. He jerked his head to Rosie and Ruby to go in ahead of them. They went inside and stood in the dark hallway, which was damp and eerily silent.

The boss man went ahead, towards a winding stone staircase, as his mate hung back, then jabbed a finger roughly into Rosie's shoulder, grunting for them to move forward. She exchanged a fleeting glance with Ruby as they walked along the short corridor and followed him up the stairway. Rosie could feel sweat on the back of her neck, but at least they hadn't frisked her. Well, not yet. At the top of the stairs there was a long, narrow corridor and off it were rooms that may have been offices at one time but now had no doors. From brief glimpses inside, Rosie could see they were completely empty, with old telephone wires hanging out of the damp walls. Large wooden windows were smeared with years of grime. Outside, the sky was growing black and she could make out the Kingston Bridge over the M8 in the distance. The last room facing them at the end of the corridor had a closed door marked 'Manager'. Silverback knocked on the door and a rough voice shouted, 'Come in.' He pushed open the door and they followed, Ruby first.

The man behind the desk sat back in a grey padded chair that looked out of place in the derelict surroundings. He glanced up, fixing his gaze on Ruby and holding it for a long moment, as though everyone else in the room were invisible. This was obviously Tony Devlin. He didn't speak, and Rosie ran her eye over him. He was handsome and fit-looking all right, suited and booted in black pinstripes. But despite his clothes he was the kind of scumbag Rosie could spot straight away as the thug in any roomful of businessmen. He had pond life stamped all over his Costa del Sol tan. Guys like him, who got rich from punting smack and coke in the city slums, could dress in the best handmade suits and shoes but they would still be the dregs of the earth. Rosie felt a rising disgust that this piece of shit had taken the only person that Ruby had in the world . . . because he could. Bastards like him should be taken out and shot. She swallowed her hatred and stood in the tense silence.

'Ruby.' He sat back and swung his feet onto the desk, then he shot her a smug look. 'Took you long enough.' His voice was dripping in sarcasm.

'I'm here now, Tony.'

Ruby's tone belied the nervous wreck that had been in the car not ten minutes ago. She folded her arms in defiance. Rosie wasn't sure if this was a good tactic.

'Listen. What the fuck, Tony? I ca— . . . I can't believe what you did. Where is she? Where's Judy?'

Tony stared at her and said nothing.

'Why did you take her like that? What did you think I was going to do? Run off with the fucking money? Christ, Tony!' Ruby shook her head, her tone softening a little. 'I've been frantic. Totally freaking out, man.' She paused, shifted on her feet. 'So where is she? I want to see her.'

'Where's the stuff?'

Ruby held up her bag.

'In here, for God's sake. Everything. I was two days speaking to all the relevant people in banks and investment companies. These things take time. A lot of them were abroad. I told you that. Why did you do this?' Her voice quivered a little, and she swallowed.

'You disappeared off the fucking radar, that's why,' Tony snapped. 'And by the way, I don't like people threatening me. Especially a fucking bird. So you want to watch that mouth of yours.'

Silence.

'I'm sorry about that, Tony. I was a bit upset that day in the hotel. Look, Judy is all I've got. It's been a hard road for us, and I felt threatened. Okay? Right. I was out of order, and I'm sorry. So where is she? Is she here?'

'Aye. In a minute. Gimme the stuff.'

'I need to explain it all to you. Not here. Another time. But I've written a lot of details down, so you should be able to follow what's what. It's a bit complicated.'

'Gimme it.' He shoved a hand out.

Ruby brought out the folder from her bag and handed it to him. He opened it up and sat for a few moments, leafing through it. Rosie was praying it made sense to him. Then he put it to the side and looked up.

'Who's your pal?' He nodded in Rosie's direction but kept his eyes on Ruby.

'Linda.' Ruby looked at Rosie. 'We went to school together. She's the only one I've ever kept in touch with from here. But I hardly ever see her.'

'So what makes you think you can trust somebody you went to school with? Most of my schoolmates are in jail or dead. I wouldn't tell them the fucking time of day.'

'Tony, you can trust her. Believe me. She doesn't know anything. All I'm doing is coming in here to give you the documents, then taking Judy back to the home . . . Anything else, we can talk about later.' She gave him a lingering look, moistening her lips. 'That's if you still want to.' Her voice lowered.

He didn't reply, but his eyes took in Ruby's long legs in her short black skirt. His mobile rang and he swung his feet back down from the desk as he answered it.

'Sure. I'll send somebody down to let you in.' He signalled to one of the henchmen, who nodded and left.

'So is Judy all right? She's been here for nearly two days. I need to see her, Tony. Come on. Stop fucking around.'

He turned back to the folder.

'Right. I hear you. Give me a minute. There's a couple of things I want to talk to you about.'

The bastard's stalling, Rosie thought, and she exchanged an uneasy glance with Ruby. She could hear footsteps along the corridor getting closer. Then the door opened. And in walked Tam Dunn.

Rosie's eyes met his, and their mouths dropped open. She felt the colour drain from her face.

'What the fuck, Tony?' He pointed to Rosie. 'What's she doing here?'

'Eh?' Tony looked startled.

'This bird.'

'It's Ruby's pal. From school. Linda.'

'What? Linda? No it's fucking not. Hold the fucking fort here. What the fuck is going on?' He stood in front of Rosie. 'You' – he stabbed a finger in her face – 'are in deep fucking shit, Linda. Or Melissa. Or whoever the fuck you are.' He turned to Tony, glowering. 'Are you totally fucking clueless or what?' he bellowed.

Tony stood up, his face crimson.

'Wha–? . . . I . . . What do you mean, Tam?'

'Jesus fucking wept!' Dunn shouted.

He slapped Rosie so hard that she reeled backwards, barely able to keep her feet. For a few seconds she heard their voices in the distance and thought she was going to pass out. Christ almighty! This was really happening.

CHAPTER THIRTY-TWO

Rosie tasted blood when she came to, and as she eased her head from her chest she looked up just in time to see the bucket of cold water being thrown at her. Dazed, she automatically tried to put her hands up to defend herself. Where were her hands? It took a split second to realize that they were tied behind her back. She gasped as the icy water hit her face, then her eyes scanned the room. No Ruby. Just her. And Tam Dunn. Then it all came back flooding back to her.

Dunn had been like a crazed animal when he had realized what was going on. Or at least what he thought was going on. He was screaming to Tony that he'd been shafted by this Melissa cunt and some Bosnian fucker who'd come down to J B Solutions to buy weapons. Who the fuck were they? he'd screamed at Tony, who stood dumbfounded, looking from Ruby to Tony to Rosie.

'Who the fuck are you?' he screamed at Rosie as he hit her again, dragging her by the hair and pushing her up against the wall.

Rosie was utterly helpless. She hadn't even considered a scenario like this. The last thing she had expected was Tam fucking Dunn to come walking into the place. She wasn't even thinking straight enough to give him any kind of answer. Whatever she would tell Dunn now, he wouldn't believe her and he would beat the shit out of her. But if she told him she was a reporter he would kill her. Even her fuddled brain told her that.

'I . . . I'm Ruby's friend,' she croaked, knowing she was digging an even bigger hole.

'So what the fuck were you doing talking to me in an English accent, trying to buy weapons? Conning the fuck out of me.'

He'd turned on Ruby.

'And you? Fuck you.'

He slapped Ruby hard, bringing blood to her lips. She didn't lift her hand to wipe it but stood glaring at him. Then he turned to Tony.

'And you've obviously been fucking this bitch so much that all your brains have gone to your dick. She's done you up like a fucking kipper, you bastard moron.' He threw his hands in the air, frustrated. 'I knew there was something dodgy about her when you brought her for dinner that night. So I asked a couple of the boys over in Spain about this Ruby bitch. They said she was around that night Rab got torched.'

'I know that, Tam,' Tony said sheepishly. 'I've asked as well. But there's nothing to link her.'

'And who the fuck are you? A polis? Of course there's something in it. And did it not occur to you that it was a bit of a coincidence when wee Malky got torched in his house?'

'Look, wait a minute,' Ruby protested.

'Shut . . . the fuck . . . up!' There was a spray of spittle from his mouth as Dunn slapped Ruby again with the back of his hand. She staggered back.' He turned to Tony. 'And by the way, dickshit, she saw everything that night in the restaurant, with that wee tart. Fuck me!' He glowered at Tony. 'You need to deal with this. Right. Fucking. Now! Today!'

Tony shifted on his feet and said nothing.

'Do you hear me? Because if you don't, then every cunt from London to Glasgow will have your balls on a plate.'

'I hear you.' Tony looked at the floor.

Dunn turned to Rosie again. He signalled to one of the silverbacks.

'Get her next door. Out of here. I'll get the fucking truth out of her if I've to punch it out of her face.'

She didn't even see the punch coming, but the force of it knocked her clean out.

Rosie was soaked and shivering. She could feel her lip puffing up and her cheek swelling. She gagged at the taste of blood as she swallowed it. There was no noise coming from the room next door.

'So who the fuck are you?' Dunn stood over her. 'You're going to tell me eventually – you know that, don't you? Because let me tell you something, sunshine, whatever reason you were down at my place, pulling the wool over my eyes with your big-time arms dealer from Bosnia, I fell for it. And that's made me really, really angry. So you're dead anyway. History. Whoever you are. The only choice you get to make now is how you die.' He pulled out a revolver from his jacket pocket and pointed it at her. 'It can be quick, a single shot to the head. Or I shoot you in the legs and leave you to bleed to death here. Your choice. It's no problem for me.' He placed the gun on a table against the wall. 'And by the way, your old school pal Ruby. She'll be fucking dead meat an' all. And her zombie sister.'

Rosie looked up at him and closed her eyes as the tears stung. She gritted her teeth and tried to hold them back but they were spilling out of her eyes and now rolling down her cheeks. Had it really come to this? In some shit-hole with a psycho holding a gun to her head? He and people like him who took what they wanted and murdered their way through life so they could be top of the heap of shit they lorded over. But she had no answers left. Because nobody was coming to help this time. For all she knew, Boswell-Smith and the captain could have been bumped off by now, and Adrian, too. She still had the tracking device behind her collar but she had no way of knowing if it was working – and even if it did, how the hell were they going to get in here?

Dunn left the room and slammed the door, leaving Rosie alone. She tugged at the rope tying her hands, stretching and pulling at it with her fingers, but there were no loose ends. She tried to pull herself together, but the thought that Ruby was somewhere in this building waiting to die along with her sister brought the tears again. Ruby had got involved in this because she'd asked her. She hadn't had to do it. Whatever Ruby was, whatever she'd done or however she'd lived her life, she'd done it to survive. And she had been planning to get out. She could probably have been gone by now if she hadn't agreed to help Rosie with her investigation.

Suddenly the door opened and one of the silverbacks came in, dragging Ruby by the hair. Her face was bruised and battered, her eyes puffy and black. He shoved her roughly onto a chair and tied her hands behind her back. Rosie caught her eye and saw the defeated, broken look of a frightened little girl. But Rosie was relieved to see her. At least she was still alive.

Tony stood watching both of them, saying nothing. All his wind and swagger had evaporated, humiliated in the company of Dunn, who was now calling all the shots.

Dunn walked across and leaned over Ruby and into her face.

'So you killed Rab Jackson, didn't you?'

Ruby shook her head.

'And Malky? You set fire to the poor cunt's garage, leaving him to burn to death, didn't you?'

Ruby shook her head again and looked at the floor.

'Look at me, bitch.' He yanked her head up by the hair.

Ruby winced with the pain and looked at him.

'Just so we're clear here, I was telling your mate from school,' Dunn said sarcastically, 'you fuckers are history. Finished. It's nothing personal. I don't hate you or anything, and I know Tony likes a shag at you, and I'm always okay with that kind of thing. So it's not personal. But you've tried to shaft me. Not just me, but the whole team here from Glasgow to London. What the fuck made you think you could do that?' He went across to Tony and took the folder from him, leafing through it. 'You see this shite? That's all it is. How do I know if any of the stuff in here is true, or just something you've made up to keep us happy while you fuck off somewhere?'

'It's not. The information is solid. I don't want your money.'

'Shut the fuck up. I'm talking. Do you think I'm going to believe a word that comes out of your mouth now after what you've done? You brought this bird into your life – for whatever reason, I don't know. And suddenly she's down at my place conning me with some business deal. That's bad enough in itself. But then she suddenly pitches up here with you? I mean, what's the fucking score? It would be funny if it wasn't so serious. So. You don't have a choice any more.' He paused, a smirk spreading across his face. 'Well. You have one choice actually.'

He nodded to one of the silverbacks, who turned and left the room. Rosie and Ruby glanced at each other again. Seconds later, the door was pushed open and he walked back in, supporting an unsteady Judy, who tottered through the doorway.

'Judy! Oh Judy!' Ruby shouted, tears coming to her eyes as she tried to move in the chair.

Judy gazed in her direction and then blankly out of the window.

'Judy. It's okay. Don't worry. It's all right. I'm going to . . .' she sobbed. 'I'm going to look after you, just like I promised.'

The silverback pushed Judy onto a chair by the wall, and she sat staring at the floor.

Rosie swallowed her tears, watching helplessly as Ruby dissolved into sobs. Dunn went across to Judy. He put the gun down on the table and grabbed hold of her hair with both hands. Her face tightened with shock and pain. He shook her head wildly.

'See your sister there, Judy? She's a fucking liar. Don't believe her. She's always been a liar.'

Judy's eyes flickered towards Ruby, and Rosie thought she saw a flash of recognition. Dunn let her go, then crossed the room and stood in front of Ruby.

'So,' he said calmly, 'here's the deal. You have one choice. Not about your life, but about the life of that fucking zombie over there. Before you die, you can tell us what's going on here and if all that shit in the folder about the bank details is genuine. Because there's a lot of our money tied up in there, so if it's not genuine then we can't get it after you're dead. Here's what's going to happen. You tell us what's going on with you and your school pal, and we take Judy back to the home unharmed. We'll drop her off, and you'll make the phone call to them telling them she's outside, that you couldn't cope with her and you won't be back to see her again. You do that before we kill you, and we'll take her back – if you tell us right now what exactly is going on. Now, if we find that the bank details are wrong in the next couple of days, she's dead meat. We'll go to that home and we will kill her.' He gave her a menacing look. 'And by the way, you were in the restaurant the other night, so you know I've got no problem doing somebody in.' A sick smile crept over his face.

Ruby's whole body trembled and her head rocked from side to side in despair.

'Tell me, bitch!' Dunn slapped her hard. He grabbed her hair, almost pulling her out of the chair, then punched her again and again in the face in a frenzy. 'Tell me!' he screeched. 'Tell me!'

From the corner of her eye Rosie saw Judy's face crumple in horror and her lips move. Then it happened so quickly that for a split second Rosie thought she was imagining it. Did Judy just move her hand from her lap and pick up the gun on the table? Judy opened her mouth in a silent scream, then suddenly let out a tormented, piercing squeal.

'No! No! Stop!' Judy wailed.

Everyone in the room turned, startled. But it was too late. Judy had already fired the gun. Bang. A shot whizzed past Dunn and smashed a window behind him. Before he had a chance to dive or move towards her, she fired again, this time hitting him. He staggered backwards towards the window.

'Fuck! Get the fucking gun!'

But Judy was now randomly firing around the room as everyone dived for cover. Then she turned and fired again at Dunn as he collapsed to the floor. Another shot hit his body, then Rosie turned away as another opened up his gut and he lay motionless.

'Judy! Judy! Oh, Judy!' Ruby screamed and sobbed. 'Oh my God!'

Nobody moved. Then suddenly the door burst open. Two men in masks charged in and Rosie's heart sank. Tony must have had a panic button somewhere on his desk. This was it. She braced herself. One of the men quickly moved around behind the desk to where Tony and the silverback lay on the floor.

'Move a fucking muscle and you're dead.'

Rosie's mouth dropped open as she recognized the abrupt tones of the captain.

The other gunman came towards her and pulled up his balaclava. Superintendent Boswell-Smith grinned broadly.

'The cavalry has arrived, ma'am.'

'Christ almighty! You cut that a bit neat, did you not?' Rosie managed a smile through swollen lips, grimacing at the pain, but relief flooding through her.

The captain slapped handcuffs on Tony and the silver-back, then went across to Dunn. He pushed at his body with his foot.

'Might not need cuffs for this one, guv,' he said.

'Get an ambulance,' the superintendent said. 'I want this bastard alive.' His eyes scanned Rosie's face. 'You all right, Rosie? Give or take a few bruises?'

She sniffed, trying very hard not to cry.

'I'm okay. Can you untie me, please?'

He placed his gun back in his shoulder holster and untied Rosie. She stood up but felt her legs go weak. The superintendent held on to her.

'Easy there,' he said. 'It's the shock.'

Rosie looked across at Ruby, who was sobbing, tears of relief streaming down her cheeks.

As soon as the captain untied Ruby, she leapt out of her chair and across the room, throwing her arms around

Judy, both of them sobbing. 'I take it this is the lady you didn't want us to meet?' Boswell-Smith said as he watched them.

Rosie nodded, unable to speak.

He glanced around the room.

'Right. Let's get this show on the road,' he said. 'Since I'm not officially here, Rosie, I can't call in the plods. So do you have a plan?'

'Yes. I can call a contact. I've made an arrangement. But they can only come after Ruby and Judy are out of here.'

'Fair enough. We'll wait until they're in the building, then we'll disappear.' He paused. 'And we'll talk later, regarding our own arrangement.'

'Sure,' Rosie said, knowing he was referring to the dossier. Losing the story was a small price to pay.

She pulled out her mobile, but there was no signal.

'I'll need to step out to get a connection.'

In the corridor she breathed in the musty, damp air as though it were elixir to her lungs. She could feel tears coming to her eyes, and she bit her lip to keep them back as she walked into one of the empty rooms to get a better signal. She stood at the window, gazing at the inky blackness of the River Clyde and out across at the lights of the city, wiping away tears of relief. Then she thought she saw a passing shadow on the window. But it was too late. The click of the gun came just as she felt the cold metal on her neck.

'Don't say a fucking word or your brains will be all over the window.'

An arm went around her neck and she was dragged backwards towards the door, struggling to keep her feet. As the other silverback kicked open the door, Rosie saw the colour drain from the faces of the supintendent and the captain. He pulled her in, his arm locked around her neck. The gun was now pressed so hard against her temple she could feel it grazing her skin.

'Okay. Here's the drill.' He was breathing hard. 'You cunts are going to give me your guns and take the cuffs off the boys.' He pointed to Ruby. 'Then we're going to walk out of here, with this bird and her mental sister.' He jerked his head towards Dunn, a pool of blood spreading across his shirt. 'We'll just leave that fucker on the floor. He's an arsehole anyway.' He motioned to Tony and the other silverback who were lying on their stomachs on the floor. 'Handcuffs off! Now!'

Nobody moved. His eyes darted around the room.

'Listen. This is only going to go one way. We're leaving here – whether you're all fucking dead or alive. But we're leaving. I'll shoot every one of you and then we'll walk out. Now get the fucking cuffs off.'

The superintendent glanced at Rosie, his eyes blazing.

'You won't get away with this. That much I can promise you.'

'Fucking move, ya posh cunt, or I'll shoot you.'

The superintendent blinked towards the captain, whose face was ashen. He crossed the room to Tony and knelt on the ground, fiddling with the keys in his hand.

Rosie could hardly breathe as the gunman pulled his arm tighter and shoved the gun against her head. She looked down at Ruby, who was sitting with her arms wrapped around Judy, and at the superintendent, whose face was blank. It was then that she heard the click.

'Drop the gun or I shoot you.'

It was Adrian.

'You shoot me and the bird gets it.'

'Drop the gun. Now. Or you die.'

Silence. Rosie's heart was beating so fast she could hear it in her ears. Then, suddenly, the grip eased around her neck and she heard the clatter of a gun dropping to the floor as he released her. She opened her mouth to speak as she looked at Adrian and was about to rush towards him when he shook his head and put his finger to his lips.

The superintendent glanced at her, confused.

'You two know each other?'

'He's nobody,' Rosie said. 'Like you. He wasn't here.' She took a deep breath and puffed out, rubbing her neck, her fingers touching blood on the side of her head from the gun. 'Okay. Now I'll phone the cops.' She moved across to Adrian and squeezed his arm, then leaned in and whispered, 'You saved my life. Again.'

His expression didn't change. He put the gun in his

waistband and didn't even exchange a glance with the superintendent or the captain.

Rosie whispered, 'I need you to take Ruby and Judy out of here. Now. Can you do that? Is Matt nearby?'

Adrian nodded.

Rosie went across to Ruby, and she stood up. They hugged for a long time, then Ruby pulled Judy to her feet and Rosie hugged her, too, feeling the frailness of her body and her arms around her.

'Welcome back, Judy,' she said.

CHAPTER THIRTY-THREE

'What the Christ's going on down there, Gilmour? I've phoned you five times already.'

In the pub toilet Rosie pressed a paper towel soaked in cold water to her swollen lip, holding her mobile a couple of inches away from her ear. McGuire was ranting. She winced in the mirror at the angry bruise beginning to show around her eye and on her cheekbone. When she'd left the warehouse she'd nipped into a bar in Kinning Park that she knew was so rough that nobody would flinch if a woman walked in with a sore face.

'I know, Mick. But I couldn't take the call.' She dabbed at her mouth.

'Why?'

Rosie said nothing, not quite knowing where to begin.

'What the fuck happened?' McGuire barked.

'I . . . er . . . My phone . . . I've got a few missed calls, actually. But Ruby and Judy are out safe. Everything went with the plan . . . Well. Give or take a couple of unexpected events.'

'Gilmour, I can smell the bullshit through the phone. Don't fuck about. You were in there, weren't you?'

'Umm . . . Well . . . Wait and I'll tell you what happened.'

'You went in there, despite my express instruction not to. Tell me you were in there.'

Rosie splashed water on her face and spat out blood into the sink, running the cold tap and watching almost absent-mindedly as it swirled and washed down the plughole.

'Yes.'

'Fucking hell! What part of a straightforward order is it that you can't seem to comprefuckinghend? I told you not to go. To leave it to the professionals. I take it they showed up?'

'Of course. Just in the nick of time. Look . . . I hear what you're saying. I'll explain everything.'

'I want you in here, now.'

'Well . . .'

'Now, Gilmour!'

'Listen, Mick. There's a situation that's developed. Let me explain. Just give me a minute. You know the prostitute who got kicked to death by that bastard Dunn?'

'Yeah. What about her?'

'I have a chance to talk to the witness – the other girl. I get the feeling she's not going to last much longer, because

Tony Devlin already said to Dunn that she's been dealt with. And you know what that means. I was there and I heard him say it. But she's the only witness to the murder – well, apart from Ruby. If all else fails here in the broader investigation we're doing, then this girl can put these bastards in jail.'

There was a long silence and Rosie checked that none of her teeth was slack from Dunn's heavy blows.

'Where is she?'

'She lives in the city centre. I know where she goes, and Adrian has already spoken to her, but not about this. We're sure it's her, so I think I should go and talk to her . . . sound her out. If I can get her to talk, she's a crucial witness.'

Eventually, McGuire answered.

'Right. Okay. Do that. So what happened inside the warehouse?'

'There was a big problem.'

'What problem?'

'Tam Dunn turned up.'

'Oh fuck! He turned up and you were in there?'

'Yeah. I don't know who was more shocked.' Rosie laughed nervously. 'No. Correction. I was definitely more shocked. A phrase like shitting your pants would be appropriate.'

'Jesus! So what happened?'

'Well. To put it mildly, Mick, it went a bit downhill from

then. But hey, I'm here talking to you, so I got away with it,'
Rosie said it with bravado, but when she held a hand out in
front of her it was still trembling.

'Christ, Rosie! This has to stop. Okay. Go and see the girl,
then phone me. Have you talked to the police yet?'

'Yeah. I phoned my contact. They've got all the documents Ruby had prepared. All the bank accounts, company
records. Everything. That stuff could nail them by itself.
But if we can deliver the witness to the murder, then they
won't see fresh air for a very long time. And we get a belter
of an exclusive.'

'Great. That's all very well, but I'm not happy with you.'
He paused. 'Listen. I'm almost reluctant to ask, but is there
a body count in that warehouse?'

'Not quite. But Dunn got shot.'

'Shot?'

'Look, I'll explain everything when I see you. I need to go,
Mick.'

She hung up, and as she did Adrian's name came up on
the screen as her phone rang.

'The girl is here,' he said. 'I'm in the café. She just came
in and smiled at me, so I'm going to have a coffee with her.'

'I'll be there in five minutes.'

Rosie gingerly patted a little moisturizer around her
eyes and cheeks. Pale-blue eyes, a little bloodshot, looked
back from the mirror.

'So, what now, Rosie?' she murmured, letting out a long, relieved breath and shaking her head. She'd be glad when this day was over.

The café was one of these trendy city-centre places with a few sofas. It was nearly seven in the evening by the time Rosie got there, so there weren't many other customers dotted around the place. Adrian's back was to Rosie as she walked in, and the blonde girl next to him glanced up at her but didn't pay much attention She walked up to the bar so Adrian could see her and then approached the table.

'Olenca' – Adrian gestured towards Rosie – 'this is a friend of mine. Do you mind if she joins us?'

The girl seemed a little bewildered, her blue eyes darting from one to the other.

'Sure.'

She shrugged and shifted on the sofa, her long, slender legs stuffed into leather knee-length boots. Adrian handed his packet of cigarettes round and they all lit up as the coffees arrived.

Rosie inhaled deeply, enjoying the nicotine kick, and nodded to Adrian to begin.

'Olenca.' Adrian's rich Slavic tones were soft and consoling. 'I want to explain something to you. My friend here is a journalist. A reporter. From the newspaper. You know the *Post*?'

Olenca nodded but looked a little uneasy.

'I see it sometimes. It helps with my reading in English.'

'She wants to talk to you about your friend Lucja.'

Olenca's expression froze.

'Lucja is not here.' She shifted on the sofa, away from Rosie, her body suddenly rigid, her eyes fixed on the floor.

'I know you're afraid,' Rosie said. 'Olenca, please, look at me. I want to tell you something. I know what happened to your friend.'

Olenca looked up, her face reddening, her mouth tight as she flicked a glance from Rosie to Adrian.

'My friend is gone away. Back to Poland. What is this? What is going on here? I not understand.'

'Please, Olenca.' Rosie spoke gently. 'I know that you saw what happened to Lucja. In the restaurant that night. That she was murdered. I know someone who was also there. Another girl, who I know you saw. You remember her?'

Olenca shook her head slowly.

'I . . . I don't want this . . . Please. I don't know what you say.'

'Olenca. You are in danger because of what you saw. I know that Tony said you'd be looked after, but that's not true. Please believe me. Your life is in danger.'

Olenca looked at Adrian. Betrayal was written in her eyes, which were now filling with tears.

'Why you do this? Why you do this to me? Who are you? I am frighten now.' She shook her head.

'I know you are afraid, Olenca,' Adrian said, 'But my friend here, she speaks the truth. You are in danger. Because the night in that place you saw what the man did to your friend. You saw him kill her.'

Olenca bit her lip and her face crumpled.

'Please. I must go. I'm frighten.'

She moved her feet as if to rise and Adrian reached over and held her arm gently, whispering, 'Olenca, please. Sit down. Rosie can help you. You must hear what she has to say. You are not safe here. Trust me. I know you are afraid and you are far from home. I am the same one time some years ago in this city. I wouldn't do anything to hurt you. Believe me. I promise. You must hear what Rosie has to say.'

Olenca looked from one to the other again, her eyes a mixture of fear, hurt and desperation. They sat in silence for a long moment then she sniffed and nodded, swallowing hard. Rosie moved a little closer to her.

'Olenca, I am a journalist with the *Post*, as Adrian has explained. The two of us have been friends for years. Close friends. He knows you can trust me.' She paused as the girl nervously wrung her hands. 'I'm working on an investigation. The men you know and sometimes deal with here in the city . . . Tony Devlin . . . They are bad people. Drug dealers. Gangsters. Murderers.'

'I know.' Olenca voice was almost inaudible. 'I know what they are.' She lifted her coffee cup with trembling hands.

'I'm investigating them, and the other people who are

involved with them. One of the men is Tam Dunn. He is the guy who beat your friend to death that night. The other lady, the one who was there, is also now working with me. She's told me what happened – that you were taken away by Tony's men that night. They gave you money.'

Olenca immediately dissolved in tears, her face in her hands.

'You think I take money and forget my friend is murdered? No. I never do that,' she sobbed, wiping her cheeks with the palms of her hand.

'No, no, I'm not saying that. Not at all. I'm saying that they gave you money and told you they would look after you. But, the truth is, Olenca, they are planning to kill you. I don't know what happened that night after you were taken away with one of Tony's bodyguards, but they were supposed to get rid of you.'

She nodded vigorously.

'I know.'

'So what happened?'

Olenca sniffed and swallowed.

'David – the bouncer – he took me in his car. I ask him please to let me go, that I would never in my life tell what I saw. He took me to the river and he was going to throw me in. I beg him again, and say please I will do anything for him to save me, to not kill me. I tell him, please just let me go and I will never tell anyone.'

Rosie looked at Adrian.

'And he just let you go like that?'

Silence.

'I . . . I gave him sex that night.' She looked at the table, embarrassed, shaking her head. 'I gave him sex to save my life and my friend is lying dead. What kind of woman does that? You think I don't know what that makes me?' She broke down again.

'Olenca, nobody is blaming you for anything.' Rosie squeezed her arm. 'You were frightened and in shock because of what you saw happen to Lujca. You did what anyone would do to survive. Please don't think anyone is going to blame or judge you. But you cannot live like this, frightened all the time. Have you see this man again? This David?'

'Yes. Sometimes. He calls me and comes to my flat for sex. He doesn't pay. Not like the escort agency.' She glanced at Rosie. 'You know Lujca and me work at the agency, and sometimes the sauna?'

'Yes. I knew that.'

'Dave comes to me for sex. He says it is our secret and that he can choose any day whether I live or die. He says I have no choice.' She burst into tears again. 'I just want go home to my family. This is not good country for me any more. Every day I'm scared. Dave said to me that he can get good money for me, if he sells me. And he told me I may be going to London because some friend of his offers him good money for me. But I not want to be sold like slave – that happen to many other women from my country. I had normal job. Now this. I am frightened every morning I wake up it is my last day.' She bent forward, hugging her knees, her head dropping to her chest.

They sat listening to her sobbing for a few moments.

'You have to go to the police, Olenca. They will protect you,' Rosie said.

'No. Police not protect women like me. I am prostitute.'

'Yes. They will protect you. They'll get you back home. But your witness account of what happened that night will get these men a very long time in jail, and they won't hurt or damage any more girls like you. But you must go to the police now, because you don't have much time if what you are telling us about this David character is the truth.'

'It is the truth. I not lie.'

'Then you don't have much time.' Rosie lowered her voice to a whisper. 'I can tell you now that Tony is in custody already with the police. So is Tam Dunn.'

Lucja looked up, surprised. She stopped crying.

'You are telling me the truth?'

'Yes. Absolutely. I can bring someone in here in the next five minutes who can prove that.'

'How you know this?

'Because I was there when it happened. They did something bad to the other girl who was there that night. They kidnapped her sister, who is ill, and they tried to kill us all. Me, too.' Rosie pointed to her bruised face. 'Where do you think I got this? It only happened an hour ago, and that's why we had to get to you quickly. Because now that they have been arrested, anything could happen.'

Olenca lifted the cup but her hands trembled so much she put it back down again. She turned to Adrian.

'I am so frightened. I am only twenty-two. I want to have a job, a husband, a family. I don't want to die. I don't want to go into court where everyone can see me. I want to go home.'

'It might not come to court, Olenca,' Rosie said. 'From what I hear happened that night at the restaurant, there will be so much blood and forensic evidence there that Dunn may even plead guilty once his back is to the wall. But that is for later. Right now, you have to make a decision. I'm pleading with you to trust me. Because I want these people in jail as much as you do. People like them destroy the lives of innocent people like your friend and you, people who only wanted a better life. It's not fair what they do. It's too late for Lujca, but you can help yourself, and you can help others like you, by going to the police. Trust me. You have to.'

Rosie could feel the catch in her throat, looking at this young girl, her life ruined no matter what happened now. Even if she could get back home, she'd be forever haunted by what she saw in the room that night, and the guilt that she had survived while her friend was battered to death. They sat for a long time in tense silence. Then, eventually, Olenca looked up at Rosie, her eyes full of tears.

'Okay. I will tell what I saw.'

CHAPTER THIRTY-FOUR

'Listen to this, Mick.' Rosie produced the tape recorder from her pocket as she walked into McGuire's office the following morning. If she could get him to listen to Olenca's account of Tam Dunn's brutal murder of her friend, it would distract him from the bollocking she was expecting.

McGuire looked up from his screen, his eyes widening when he saw Rosie's bruised face. He took off his reading glasses and tossed them onto his desk.

'I knew you'd have a sore face. Christ almighty, Rosie! I fucking knew.'

'It's okay. I'm fine.' She planked the tape on his desk and switched it on. 'This is much more important. Just take a minute to listen to the tape, then I'll explain everything.'

Rosie turned up the volume before he had a chance to say anything else, and sat on the sofa opposite his desk. McGuire screwed up his face as Olenca's voice came on, straining to make out what she was saying through her heavy Polish accent.

'You'll get used to it, if you listen closely. Honest,' Rosie insisted.

They both listened. Olenca's voice broke with emotion as her graphic account of what happened in the restaurant that night filled the room. Rosie hadn't made a big issue of convincing Olenca that she needed to tape the conversation, and she knew she was playing on the girl's lack of knowledge of how these things worked. But to get her on tape with this kind of narrative was as explosive as it gets. It was even more valuable as Rosie had it before Olenca was handed over to the police. Olenca named the escort agency she worked for, and how many times in the past she'd been to Tony Devlin's restaurant and entertained his friends in the private room.

McGuire's face was impassive as Olenca described the sex scene with Dunn, how at first her friend and her were both kissing and fondling him, and then how he wanted to have sex with Lujca. He'd taken a lot of cocaine and alcohol, she said, and he wasn't able to get a proper erection. Lujca had laughed at him. It was only one time she laughed, Olenca said, but Dunn exploded. He began slapping her, and then punched her hard on the face two or three times and she fell on the floor. Then he started kicking her. Olenca was in tears as she described how there was a lot of blood, and that she saw one of Lujca's teeth come out and fall on the floor. She stepped in and pleaded with him to stop, that

Lujca was sorry, that they were both very sorry. But he turned on Olenca and kicked her in the stomach and told her not to move. At one point Lujca had tried to crawl away, but Dunn had grabbed her by the hair and started kicking her head as if it was a football. Olenca said she was on her knees in the corner, sobbing, terrified, believing she was next. She could see that Lujca was by now unconscious, and every time he kicked her head, it just flopped, as if she was a rag doll. Then the door opened, and a woman who had been having dinner with them came in. She was screaming at Dunn, but he wouldn't listen and was shouting back at her. And then Tony came in, and he was very angry. He and Dunn were shouting at each other. There was blood all over the carpet and some on the desk and the walls. Dunn said it was all Tony's fault. Then two men came in and Tony told them to deal with it. One of them took Lujca away. For a few seconds there was only the sound of Olenca crying on the tape. Then she seemed to compose herself and went on to describe what she'd also told Rosie about the bouncer, David, and his plans to sell her to a friend in London.

McGuire shook his head slowly when the tape clicked to the end and didn't speak for a moment.

'Jesus Christ! Poor kid.' He picked up the tape and let out a long breath, puffing his cheeks. 'But that is dynamite, Gilmour. Good job. Unbelievable stuff. And the detail – Christ! I take it you've got a picture of her?'

'Yeah. And she gave us one of Lujca – before you ask.'

'Well done. I want these bastards strung up. Big time.'

Rosie didn't answer. A sudden wave of depression swept over her.

'What's the matter with you?' McGuire said. 'You did well.'

Rosie sighed.

'Yeah. But I feel for the girl, that's all. She's just a kid. Twenty-two.'

'Yes. I know what you mean. But save your emotions for the piece you're going to write when that bastard Dunn gets jailed. There's no way he'll go to trial with this. What do your cop pals think?'

'My detective friend called a little while ago. He said they've already told Tony Devlin that he's looking at life in jail, that he's as guilty as Dunn because it was he who disposed of the body. He's down at Stewart Street cop shop right now, sticking Dunn right in. Telling them everything to try to save his own skin. So much for honour among thieves.'

'Scumbags, one and all. Well, they'll be in jail soon. But we need to think about how we can write a story. Has anybody been charged yet?'

'Not yet. But if Don's saying that Tony's grassing up Dunn, then there'll be charges very soon. They've got Forensics people all over the restaurant and the private room.'

'Okay. I think we should write a form of words that we

can run past the lawyer. No other papers will know any-thing about this – or the girl that's been kidnapped. So we're bang in front. I think we have to just blast as much as we can get away with before the lawyers and the Crown Office come on and tell us we can't write anything.'

'I agree. I'll go and make a start.' Rosie got up.

McGuire looked at her.

'And you haven't told me what happened. How the hell did you end up going in there?' Rosie shrugged.

'It seemed like a good idea at the time.'

'So was it Dunn who gave you the sore face?'

'Yeah. He's a right bastard, Mick. Real psycho.'

'When did the cavalry arrive?'

'Just as he was about to kill us.'

'Who shot him?'

'Believe it or not, it was Judy.'

'Judy? I thought she was completely in another world.'

'So did everyone. But something must have flipped, because we were all sitting there terrified as Dunn was going mental. Then I looked out of the corner of my eye and suddenly I saw her pick up the gun he'd put on the table. She started screaming. Then firing randomly. Any one of us could have caught a bullet. But she got lucky. Shot Dunn. Then shot him twice more.'

'Give that girl a fucking coconut.'

Rosie laughed as she went on to describe how Boswell-Smith and the captain had burst in wearing balaclavas.

'Then I stepped out to get a better connection on my mobile to call the cops. And all of a sudden one of the big gorillas – I'd forgotten about him – got a hold of me outside and it all went pear-shaped.

'What happened then?'

'Adrian. That's what happened.'

'Did he kill anyone?' McGuire rolled his eyes.

'No. Not yet.' Rosie said, knowing by the look on Adrian's face as Olenca had spoken last night that he had some retribution of his own in mind.

'So what about this Ruby character?'

'Haven't spoken to her since last night. She's planning to do a runner. Any time in the next few days.'

'And what about Boswell-Smith and James Bond. Where are they?'

'I'd say they got very pissed last night. I've to see them today. Lunchtime.'

'To hand over the dossier.'

Rosie sighed.

'Afraid so. I know we made an agreement. But it doesn't feel right. We're suppressing a story that we know is true, and there are people at the top of the heap who know what happened to Mahoney, and to Hawkins. I feel sorry for Hawkins especially. He wasn't even a spy. He was just a nice old guy. It's not fair. And now we can't even bloody write about it.'

'I know, Gilmour. But we both know that Judy's life was

at stake. Things are more important than this shit that we get out of bed for every day.' He lifted the dummy of tomorrow's paper and dropped it back on the desk.

'Yeah. It doesn't make it right, though.' Rosie picked up the tape from his desk and went towards the door.

Rosie pulled on her jacket and headed out of the office after taking a call from Ruby asking to meet her at her flat.

'I don't know who looks worse.' Ruby touched the bruise on her cheek as she stepped back in the hall to let Rosie over the doorstep.

They stood, looking at each other.

'I know,' Rosie said, shaking her head. 'Jesus! I'm too old for all this.'

She automatically glanced down the hallway, wondering if Judy was in the living room, surprised at how excited she was at the prospect of seeing her.

'How is she?' she whispered.

A smile spread across Ruby's face, and she bit back a tear.

'Amazing. I still can't believe it. She's asleep now. She didn't sleep much last night, kept waking up and crying a lot. Actually, I'm a bit scared now that she's asleep that she'll wake up and whatever happened inside her head yesterday will be gone and she'll be back to the silence again.'

'No. Don't think that way,' Rosie said, as they walked towards the kitchen. 'It's incredible, though, what happened, isn't it?'

Ruby shook her head, smiling.

'Coffee? It's too early to drink – though I could do with one.'

'Me, too,' Rosie said. 'But coffee would be great.'

A while later, they clinked coffee mugs and stood in the kitchen.

'So has she said anything else at all?' Rosie asked.

'Not much. I think we've got a long way to go. I've been talking to her and telling her things, and I'm getting some responses now, more than ever before. She's said a few words. Says she's scared, mostly. But happy. She nodded and smiled when I asked, "Are you happy, Judy?", and when I asked her did she want to come away with me so we can be together, she gave a big smile. I never saw that before.' Ruby's eyes filled up. 'I can't believe it, Rosie. I've got my sister back.'

'So what are your plans?'

'I want to leave tomorrow and get the ferry to France. I'll go to my house in the village and then get to a doctor and the specialists I've already consulted with, and see where we go from here. As I've said, they filled her full of so many pills down the years without really addressing the situation that I'm not sure how much of her I will get back. But it's a start. I'm looking forward to going away. I'm not even going back to the home to get Judy's things. All that's in the past now. I'll fax them tomorrow and say she's staying with me.'

'You're going to drive all the way to Dover then to the middle of France yourself?'

'No choice. It's a long trip and Ruby needs a bit of help and care.'

'It's a lot to take on.'

'I know. But I've no option. I've got nobody.'

For two pins, Rosie would have volunteered, but she knew she couldn't.

'I'd love to help you, but I'm up to my eyes with this story now, it's moving so fast.'

'No, no. I wasn't expecting you to. You've done enough. Really.'

They stood for a moment in silence, then a thought came to Rosie.

'Ruby. Remember I asked you about Roddy Thompson? You said you didn't know him?'

Ruby gave a confused look.

'I vaguely remember you mentioning a name. But I don't think I do know him.'

'Can I ask you something? Just curious. How did you finance your way through university?'

Ruby folded her arms and leaned back on the worktop.

'You really want to know? The truth is I've no idea. I was told by my social worker that when I turned eighteen, I had access to a trust fund that had been set up for me. Christ knows where it came from, because my ma had nothing, and I was raised in children's homes. But when I was seventeen I got a letter sent to the home telling me to go to a solicitor, and there they told me there was a trust fund. For my university education. The lawyer said I had a benefactor who wanted to remain anonymous. No idea who it was and, honestly, I was always waiting for some pervert to come out of nowhere, but they never did. I just took the money and ran. Went to uni for a couple of years. I got part-time jobs, too, but the money helped a lot. I wouldn't have been able to go to uni without it.'

'I think I know who it is.'

'You're kidding. How would you know something like that?'

'During part of my investigation I came across a retired detective. He was very close to your mum. I mean, *very* close. She gave him tips about things.'

'My mum grassed to the cops?' Ruby looked aghast.

'Well, I think it was one particular thing – what got her killed. Rab Jackson.'

Ruby said nothing.

'So who is this cop, this retired guy?'

'I think you should meet him. I know he'd want to see you. I can call him, and perhaps he can even help you get away.'

'I can't imagine why he'd want to do that.'

'I think he was in love with your mother. He was already married.'

Ruby said nothing, shook her head.

'How would you feel if I got in touch with him? He remembers you and Judy as little girls. I mean, you're leaving anyway, and I think he would be a good connection. Why not? You have nothing to lose. He's out of the force for five years now, but from what I hear he was a good cop. I think he was your secret benefactor, but he didn't admit it. I think you should meet him.'

Ruby shrugged and sighed.

'Sure. What harm can it do?'

Rosie looked for Roddy Thompson's number and rang it.

CHAPTER THIRTY-FIVE

Rosie glanced at the envelope on the passenger seat as she drove to the Grosvenor Hotel and her heart sank. The dossier that Hawkins had died for was now about to be handed over to Boswell-Smith to be buried or destroyed. Sure, she was doing it for all the right reasons, and she also knew there was no other way. But it still felt as if something precious was being ripped from her. As she turned into the car park she spotted the captain loading up two small cases into the boot of a Range Rover, then get into the driver's seat. Boswell-Smith emerged from the hotel and pulled up the collar of his raincoat as he crossed the car park. When he noticed Rosie he beckoned her to park next to them.

'Morning, Rosie,' he said as she got out of her car with the dossier under her arm. 'How's the face?' He grimaced. 'Looks a bit sore.'

'Yeah. It is. But I'll live.'

'Climb in the back.' He opened the door and closed it after her, then went round to the passenger seat.

'So how's your story going?' He turned around. 'You must have some good material now, after all that chaos yesterday?'

'Yeah.' Rosie knew she sounded downbeat. 'A few questions have been asked by the police as to what we were doing there – but I'm hoping we got away with it. Dunn is in hospital under guard. I was hoping he'd bled to death, the bastard. They had to remove his spleen and a good bit of his stomach. So he hasn't actually been charged yet – well, not with the murder of the prostitute. But he'll get done for that no problem, because the girl's friend is going to testify. She saw it all. Plus, so-called hardman Devlin is singing like a canary to keep himself from being an accessory to murder. So it's all good stuff.'

'Great.'

'Yeah.'

There was an awkward silence, then Rosie held out the dossier.

'So.' She glanced at the captain, who was watching her through the rear-view mirror. 'Here are the incriminating documents . . . Tom Mahoney's inside story of everything that happened. The names in the frame. All the people who were part of the corruption.' She handed it to Boswell-Smith and they made fleeting eye contact.

'Thank you.'

He opened it up and took out the bundle of papers, firstly turning over the black-and-white pictures and examining the captions, then reading briefly over the first page of Mahoney's notes. Rosie shifted about in the back, opened the window, feeling the damp air and soft rain cooling her face. Eventually he put the papers back into the envelope and sat silently staring through the windscreen for a few moments. Rosie wondered if she should just go. Then he turned his body around so he was facing her.

'Okay, Rosie, thanks for being as good as your word. Much appreciated.'

She nodded.

'Yeah, sure.' Her hand went to the door handle. She just wanted to get out.

'Right,' Boswell-Smith said, 'here's the deal.'

Surprised, Rosie turned to face him. He tossed the envelope on the back seat beside her.

'This conversation never happened. You understand what I'm saying?'

Rosie glanced at the document for a second before the penny dropped, then she nodded slowly, her eyes automatically going to the captain, who looked through her.

Boswell-Smith straightened his tie.

'Here's how this is going to play out. We drive back to London and, by teatime, all going well, I'll meet with my boss at Whitehall and tell him the following . . .' He paused, sniffed. 'My journey north was largely a waste of time. No dossier. No information. No buried stories. They weren't there – or if they were, then I couldn't find them.'

Rosie swallowed, afraid to speak as he went on.

'I'll tell them the whole thing was fucked up by whoever went in and did Hawkins over in his flat that night.'

Rosie looked at him, not sure how to react.

'No,' he said. 'It wasn't us, if that's what you're thinking. But someone was sent there, and fucked up. That's how we ended up on the scene.'

'What do you mean, fucked up?' Rosie asked tentatively, terrified to say the wrong thing in case he took the envelope back.

'Just that,' he said. 'Don't ask me the finer details, because I don't know, but I can tell you that someone in the shady-bastard-department that is MI6 thought it would be a good idea to come up and eliminate Hawkins, as he was the only one they believed had the dossier. They saw you going into his flat and coming out at some stage, and at that point they thought perhaps you had it. Hence the reason you were run off the road that night.'

'Jesus,' Rosie said. 'They tried to kill me?'

'Well, I'm not sure really. But they wanted to stop you doing what you were doing. Frighten you. Without really knowing what the hell you *were* doing. It was ham-fisted, to put it mildly. Christ! Spies can be bloody thick at times. It's not like the movies, you know.'

'So who was this? Who tried to run me off the road?'

'Don't know. Someone from the other side.'

'What other side?' Rosie was bamboozled.

'Well, it wasn't one of ours, put it that way. It was some-one from the Russian intelligence service, I think. Someone looking at the investigation into the gunrunning and organized crime. They sent one of their men to mop up the mess after the failed operation in Berlin and the murder of Mahoney. But they didn't do it very well. All they did was bump that poor old bastard Hawkins off, and still come away empty-handed.'

Rosie shook her head, confused.

'I'm not sure I really understand it.'

'No. Me neither. But that's how these guys work. Anyway, bottom line is they had wind that the newspaper might have the dossier. So they sent me up to try first of all to establish if you had it and, secondly, to get it from you . . . by whatever means it took.'

'What do you mean, by whatever means?'

Silence. Then Rosie felt her mouth drop open in disbelief.

'Hang on a minute! Jesus Christ! Don't tell me it was you who kidnapped Judy?' She shook her head. 'You have to be joking. Christ almighty! Why?'

Silence. The captain opened his window and let out a little steam that was rising on the windscreen.

'Leverage,' Boswell-Smith said. 'We needed leverage. We couldn't *demand* the dossier from you – that's if we even established that you had it – because we couldn't actually be seen to be involved in anything at all, or even to acknowledge that there was a dossier. Best-case scenario for us was just to return with the document and no questions asked. But you and your editor wouldn't give us it.'

'So you kidnapped Judy and handed her over to Devlin? I mean . . . you can't be working with him? Surely not!'

'No. But one of his minions is working for us now – Del Boy, I believe he was called.'

'Wee Derek. The one who got captured during the Berlin shoot-out?'

'That's the one.'

'But how?'

'People do all sorts of shit when their life is at stake, Rosie. Especially if you throw in a few quid and a new identity and a new life far enough away from here. Del Boy is all set up.'

Rosie shook her head, incredulous.

'But how the hell did he know about Ruby and her sister?'

'He was in Ruby's company about eighteen months ago – in a photograph we had of her with that plonker Jackson during an earlier surveillance job. Then, we had CCTV pictures of her coming off the Eurostar when we were trying to trace the mystery women who left the café. Del Boy was also in the earlier photograph and now we had him in our hot little hands. We established, or at least had good enough suspicions that it was the same woman who came off the Eurostar as the woman in the picture with Jackson eighteen months ago.'

'So why connect her to Devlin and all this stuff?'

'Del was able to tell us that she is the accountant for Jackson and his mob, moving his money around the world. And he told us that she was also involved with Devlin. So it was a question of bringing them together. By the time we put the screws on Del, he would have done anything to save his skinny little neck. He got in touch with Devlin to tell him he'd managed to give the cops the slip and was on his way back from Europe – all bullshit, of course. He knew that Devlin was desperate to get Ruby to move on the money – and that she was stalling – and he needed to get control back. So Del told him that the only way to get to her was to take the sister – that was sure to bring her running.'

'So where did I fit in?'

'Well, you were the one with the dossier. You were seen with Ruby in the bar that night and a couple of other times.'

'You've been watching me?'

'Well, the good captain here has. I don't do that kind of stuff any more. Too old for stake-outs. But yes, you were being watched.'

'So are you seriously saying that when you came to our office that day at the *Post* you knew that we had the dossier and you had to find a way to get it because you knew we wouldn't give you it? So *you* arranged for Judy to be kidnapped? How?'

'Del Boy told Devlin that was the best way to get to Ruby. So we kept track of her, then when the time was right got the word to Devlin of where she was. He did the rest.'

'Christ.' Rosie could hardly take it in.

'But how did you know I'd be with Ruby when she went to meet Tony?'

'Well, we did advise you that you should be . . . or don't you remember?'

Rosie recalled the conversation they'd had when they'd promised her she'd be safe if she went in with Ruby. She shook her head.

'But you couldn't have known that Tam Dunn was going to turn up and how it all went after that. You couldn't have known that, surely?'

'No. We didn't know that. It did get a little messier than we'd expected. We'd hoped you would be grateful enough that Judy was safe to give us the documents. Then, when Dunn came in, it got more difficult.'

'Jesus! All to get this dossier.' Rosie shook her head.

He raised his eyebrows, glancing at the envelope.

'The dossier, which, of course, you don't have.'

'Yes. Of course.' She almost smiled. 'The dossier I don't have.' She folded her arms and looked him in the eye.

'But, Superintendent, we nearly got killed in that bloody

place the other day. Dunn was ready to kill us all. Why in the name of Christ did you not come a few minutes earlier, before he beat the shit out of us?'

'Well, I'm sorry about that, Rosie, but these things happen. We had a bit of a logistic problem getting discreet access to where you were inside the building. Yours wasn't the only bottom that was twitching. It was a pretty close shave that we got there at all – I'll tell you that.'

'Yeah. I'll bloody say it was.' Rosie shook her head. She glanced at the envelope beside her.

'But why? I mean, why give it back? After everything?'

'Give what back?' He said, deadpan.

Silence. Boswell-Smith examined the back of his hands.

'You know something, Rosie . . . I reckon I've had a few good breaks in my life. My old dad was a newspaper editor, and he'd come from Fleet Street back in the tough old days. He left the front line for family life and took the editorship of that paper down in Eastbourne. But he never lost his sense of determination or justice. He was working for a paper where the main stories of the week were reports about coffee mornings, tourism and parish councils, but now and again his young reporters smashed a few stories, and one or two of them went on to better things. So, put it this way, maybe it's the frustrated journalist in me . . . Maybe I did it as a nod to his integrity, or maybe I'm just too old for all this crap and it's time I retired to pruning my roses in the home counties. But the truth is, once I met you and that mad bastard of an editor, McGuire, it restored my faith a little. I took a view of this entire caper and thought, Fuck it, I'm going to do something else for a change – rattle a few cages that need to be rattled.'

'Jesus! I can't believe this.' Rosie picked up the envelope and held it close to her. 'Now I'm not even sure if, when I walk out of here, if I'm going to get arrested or shot. There's so much underhand shit going on. I don't know whose side anyone's on any more.'

'You know what, Rosie? Neither do I. And that's maybe the real reason I'm doing this. Because the bastards at Customs, and the civil servant who was working with Dunn, turning a blind eye and faking licences – they should be in jail too. They collaborated with a firm which brings guns in for gangsters, as well as exporting them to places where they are used to kill innocent people. These bastards are part of the establishment, and they're supposed to be on our side . . . But they're not. Especially the high-ranking civil servant who was smoothing the way. It's all about money and how much he can stick away in his offshore account while he's pretending to be one of us, and getting away with it. And when the powers that be found out about it, they were prepared to cover that up. Well, that's not on in my book.'

Rosie pushed her luck a bit further.

'Do you know who he is?'

His lips curled to a smile.

'I thought that might be your next question.' He put his hand into the inside pocket of his jacket, took out a piece of paper and handed it to Rosie.

She read the name, afraid even to say it aloud. Written down was his full name, his extension at work, his home address in central London and his home telephone number.

'I can hardly believe this is happening. I honestly don't know what to say.'

'Believe it.' He winked, then nodded at the captain, who started the engine.

'Off you go now. I'll be looking out for your story when the shitty house of cards starts to collapse.'

'I'm speechless. But thanks . . . I suppose that's the only thing I can say.'

'Don't thank me. This never happened. Good luck, Rosie.'

As she opened the door, the captain turned and smiled at her.

'See you around. All the best, Rosie Gilmour.'

'Thanks.' She closed the door, got out and into her car and watched as they drove out of the car park and onto Great Western Road. Almost dizzy, she rang McGuire.

'Mick, you'll never guess what's just happened.'

CHAPTER THIRTY-SIX

Rosie read over her story one last time, making the final changes as she prepared to send it over to McGuire's private email. She'd listened to Olenca's tape-recorded account of the murder so many times it was sure to bring another dimension to her already frazzled nightmares. But she ran the tape once more as she sat back in her chair, gazing out through the window of her flat across the city as a watery October sun slipped behind the office blocks. Olenca's soft tones in fractured English somehow made the picture more graphic each time she listened to it. The images brought back dark memories of the voice of Emir, the Kosovan refugee, and Rosie was transported to the café in Central Station that day when he'd come to her, a ghostly, terrified figure, beaten and bruised. He had fled his captors in Glasgow only to be murdered while he was being protected by the police. And her mind drifted to the hospital bedside where she'd held his hand and told him not to be afraid as he slipped away. Her shrink had told her over many sessions that Emir's death wasn't her fault, that she had to rationalize it and put it somewhere in her head where she could manage it. Even the Bosnians she'd spoken to recently in Sarajevo had talked about their own guilt because of everything they'd been through. Everyone in Bosnia carried guilt, not for what they did but for surviving when so many had perished. They'd found a way to rebuild their lives, and so must she, they told her. She'd be helping Emir by exposing the people who'd murdered his best friend and were killing refugees and selling their body tissue. She knew Emir hadn't died because of her, but the guilt still hung like a shadow over her life. Of course, she had to function, and she could keep the darkness at bay, but now and again it would sweep over her like this. She closed her eyes and massaged her head, trying to push the thoughts away. Her mobile rang and shuddered on the coffee table.

'Adrian,' Rosie said, 'you outside? I'll be down in five minutes.'

She attached the story to an email and pinged it across to McGuire, with a brief line saying she was off to pick up Olenca at her flat and take her to the police HQ, where Don and his bosses would take over. The detectives were booked on a flight out of Glasgow to Amsterdam that night and would be in Warsaw by the morning.

'How are you, Adrian?'

He had his back to her, leaning on her car smoking, staring into space, but turned when he heard her voice. There was a little awkward moment when she wasn't sure if he was going to greet her with a hug or if they were back to simply working together. She watched him come towards her, then he tossed the cigarette away and stepped forward to embrace her, tracing his fingers gently across the bruise on her cheek.

'Is still painful?'

It was, but Rosie shook her head. She hugged him tight and felt a mixture of desire and safety against the warmth of his body. But more poignant than anything was the heaviness that the job was almost over and that he would soon be going away.

'You okay?' Adrian studied her face as though he sensed something was wrong.

'Yes.' Rosie let out a sigh. 'I was just thinking about Emir while I was writing my story. Listening to Olenca's voice brought back thoughts of him and everything that happened . . . I know it's not good to dwell on things too much.'

Adrian nodded and eased her out of his arms, taking her by the shoulders.

'Rosie, we cannot change the past. But if we don't live our own lives now we are not true to the people who cannot be with us. People like Emir . . . and . . .' His voice trailed off.

He didn't need to say it, but Rosie could see that the image of his wife was in his head. It always would be.

'Let's get moving,' she said. 'Olenca will be waiting.' She pressed her key and the locks on her car doors clunked open.

They drove down towards the Merchant City, Adrian staring through the windscreen. The silence in the car was broken only by the low chatter on the radio and the din of the late-afternoon traffic. Rosie managed to find a parking space close to the block of flats where Olenca lived in Ingram Street. They both got out and Adrian managed to get to the security door just as someone was coming out.

'We'd better ring the bell.' Rosie scanned the security buzzers and rang the one for the top flat. 'In case she's in the shower or something.'

No answer. She looked at Adrian, who shrugged. They waited and then Rosie rang again. This time they could hear the intercom crackling.

'Hello?' It sounded like Olenca.

'Olenca? It's Rosie. I'm downstairs.'

Two beats, then Olenca spoke.

'Er . . . Could you come up, please? I . . . I have some heavy luggage.' The security door clicked but Adrian had already pushed the door wide.

'Sure. Be there in two ticks.'

They climbed the three flights of stairs, Rosie a little out of breath from trying to keep pace with Adrian, who took the stairs two at a time, defying all the rules about smoking and impaired lung function. At the top of the stairs the door was open. Rosie glanced at Adrian, then a voice came from down the hall.

'Come in, Rosie.'

They stepped inside and through the short, bright hall with its cream walls, their footsteps clacking on the fake wooden floor.

'In here.' Olenca's voice came from the living room.

Rosie glanced at Adrian, and she thought she detected a flicker of alarm flash across his eyes as they stepped towards the doorway. But it was too late.

'Get fucking in.'

The big guy was built like a tank and had a gun pointed at the side of Olenca's head, which was wedged in the crook of one of his beefy arms. Both her eyes were black and puffy. Rosie's stomach dropped to the floor. She risked a glance at Adrian. His face wasashen and his expression blank as he fixed his eyes on the guy.

'And don't you even think about moving a muscle, you big prick,' the guy spat at Adrian.

'I'm so sorry, Rosie.' Olenca's voice was a whimper. Tears and mascara smeared her face.

'Fucking shut it, ya wee slut.'

Rosie opened her mouth to speak, but nothing came out. She tried to swallow, but her mouth was dry as a stick. She took a short breath.

'Listen,' she managed to say, 'whoever you are. This is just stupid. Really stupid. The cops will be here shortly.

They know we're here,' Rosie lied, conscious of her voice shaking.

'Fuck off and shut up.'

Rosie stood her ground.

'I'm telling you. They're coming up in about ten minutes, and you're in big trouble, pal. So why don't you just do the sensible thing and walk out of here now. Nobody knows who you are or where to find you. Nobody will come looking for you.'

'Shut the fuck up, I said.' His voice rose an octave and his eyes were crazed.

He pushed the gun into Olenca's head and tightened his grip on her neck. She struggled for breath and scraped at his arms. He loosened his grip a little and she gasped a lungful of air.

'Who the fuck do you think you are anyway?' the fat guy said. 'Well, I know *who* you are – you're that reporter bird. But what are you trying to do? I heard about that shite the other day that got Dunn and Tony locked up. And I'll tell you this. I don't give a fuck about them. They can rot in jail for all I care. But this is *my* money.' Olenca squeaked in agony as he grabbed her hair and yanked her head back. '*My* fucking money. She's *my* property. I was supposed to do the bitch in that night, but I kept her, because I'm fucking pissed off with doing Tony's dirty work. I'm my own man now, and this wee slut's going to make me a right few quid.

I've made a deal to sell her. Right? Then I walk in here and find she's packing up to leave.'

'Listen,' Rosie pleaded. 'It doesn't have to be like this.'

'Naw, you're right. It doesn't have to be like this. I can pump a bullet into you and big Lurch there and walk right out of here with this bitch under my arm, and nobody will even know where to find the pair of you.' He grinned from wild, coked-up eyes. 'Aye. She told me all about you. She was fucking stupid enough to think that you were going to get her out of this and away back home to the shithole she came from. *You* – selling her a fucking fairy story about the cops protecting her. What a load of fanny. Because the cops don't give a fuck about anybody – especially people like her.' His eyes flicked around the room. 'You think they're coming here to save her? Are they fuck! They don't give a shit.'

'They do. Please. Listen to me. Just let her go and you can walk right out of here.'

'Fuck off!' he bellowed.

Then, the gunshot. Rosie jumped as the bullet went through the floor inches from her foot. Christ! This nutcase really was going to kill them. He had a mad smirk on his face as he fired again, this time past her. She heard glass smash behind her and something slip off the wall onto the floor. Then another shot rang out, and the fat guy stared at them, stunned. Blood gushed from the side of his head and for a second he stood wavering on his feet. Then another shot, and he went down like a sack of potatoes. Rosie turned to Adrian and saw the gun, no bigger than the palm of his large hand. Olenca passed out on the floor.

'Jesus, Adrian. How the fu—?'

'Hurry. We must get out of here. Get some water on her. Hurry. The neighbours will call police. They will have heard the gunfire.'

The fat guy lay on the ground as Rosie went to the kitchen and returned with mug of water and a cold cloth. She cradled Olenca in her arms and patted her face with the damp cloth. She sparked back to life, her face red and swollen.

'It's okay, Olenca. You're safe. We're getting you out of here. But we must be quick. Can you stand up?'

The fat guy shuddered on the ground, a pool of blood forming around his head and spreading across his shirt. But his eyes were wide open, and his face was contorted in anger and shock. Rosie got Olenca to her feet as Adrian went across to him.

'Go,' he said to Rosie.

She looked at him.

'But?'

'Go. I'll be there in a moment.'

She supported Olenca and walked her to the door. She looked over her shoulder and saw Adrian going through the guy's pockets, taking anything he could, including his mobile. Rosie helped Olenca along the hall and out of the front door. At the top of the stairs she heard a muffled shot. She exchanged a glance with Olenca, and said nothing. When they got to the second floor a man came running towards them, taking the stairs two at a time, and he brushed past them, almost knocking them over. Olenca gripped the bannister and Rosie gently pulled her fingers away and slowly they made their way down the stairs. As they got to the ground floor they heard a scuffle above and a sharp groan. They looked up in time to see the man who had pushed past them now flying through the air. He hit the stone floor with a sickening thud.

'Don't look!' Rosie said.

She pushed Olenca ahead of her towards the front door. Then Rosie looked over her shoulder and saw the mangled figure splattered on the floor, his skull cracked in half and the contents of his head like a thick, blood-soaked sponge seeping on to the tiles. By the time she had got Olenca into her car and the engine running, the front door opened and Adrian casually appeared from the building as though he were going out for a stroll. He got into the passenger seat and closed the door.

Rosie drove towards Pitt Street police HQ in traumatized silence.

'I get out here, please, Rosie. It's for the best.' Adrian said as they stopped on the corner of Blythswood Street. He turned, fixing Rosie with his soft grey eyes. 'I call you later.'

He opened the door, stepped out and lit a cigarette. Then he walked away and didn't look back.

CHAPTER THIRTY-SEVEN

'We need to get Hanlon in here to work out what we tell the cops, Gilmour. Because a couple of plods are on their way down from Pitt Street and they'll want answers pronto. I mean, this is fucking crazy. Not one but two dead bodies. What is it with this big Bosnian guy? Every time you're with him there are stiffs all over the place.'

'Mick, it was us or them. It's that simple. If it weren't for Adrian, I'd be dead, and so would Olenca. That's a fact.'

'Yeah, but fuck me, Rosie! You could just have given the cops the girl's address and told them to go and get her.'

'I know, but I wanted to take her myself. It was me who got her to agree to cooperate with the cops. And thank God I did go to the flat, because I'm not sure the police would have handled it the way Adrian did. They might have screwed the whole thing up, and Olenca would have been killed. It was the right thing to do. I don't care what you say.' Rosie's voice shook with emotion. She'd been on the verge of tears since she handed Olenca over to the cops.

When Rosie had met Don and his DCI boss in the side room at police headquarters in Pitt St, Olenca was so upset they had to bring in a nurse to calm her down before they were able to speak to her. Rosie stepped outside with Don and the DCI. Don had told her his boss was old school and didn't always play by the rules when he wanted to nail a villain. So she'd decided to put her cards on the table, stressing it was off the record. There were two bodies, she said, one in Olenca's flat with gunshot wounds and the other at the bottom of the stairwell. They had to get someone down there quickly. The DCI had looked at her, incredulous, as Don nodded to him that she would be telling the truth. His face reddened as he paced up and down the corridor, his voice an exasperated whisper.

'You can't just bump people off in Glasgow city centre and walk away,' the DCI said.

Rosie had been tempted to reply that it hadn't stopped a succession of hoodlums getting away with it over the years.

'We need a statement from you, Rosie,' he insisted.

'I have to speak to the *Post*'s lawyers first,' Rosie replied.

'So who shot this guy?' Don asked.

'I can't tell you that. It would compromise my contact.'

'He's fucking killed two people,' the DCI rasped. 'Christ almighty!'

'It was them or us. I'll testify in court to that. But I'll never reveal the name of my contact.'

The DCI shook his head, defeated.

'Fair enough. I see where you're coming from. But you'd better see your lawyer sharpish, because someone higher up than me will want to talk to you very, very soon.' He paused. 'Listen. I appreciate what you've done here.' He gestured towards Don. 'He's told me the risks you take. But there'll be problems with this. And I can't do anything about it. Go and see your lawyer.'

Rosie had then driven down to the office, explaining to McGuire that nothing had gone according to plan at Olenca's flat. She could hear him almost hyperventilating as she spoke.

Tommy Hanlon, the *Post*'s lawyer and the youngest QC in the country, came breezing into McGuire's office, still wearing his court attire, stiff white shirt and bow-tie under a black jacket. And a wide, playful grin on his face.

'Fuckity fuck, Gilmour! You don't mess about, do you?' he chuckled as he slapped a file on McGuire's conference table. 'I've been in court all day, then I've just had to cut short a briefing with one of my biggest clients to come down here and wipe the blood off the fucking walls!' He kissed Rosie theatrically on both cheeks. 'Right. Let's hear it.' He plonked himself on the sofa next to her.

Rosie explained what had happened when they went to Olenca's flat.

'And where's this big bloke? Adrian?'

She shrugged.

'I don't know where he is now. But I'd be surprised if he's anywhere around here.'

'The cops are going to want to know who he is . . . Everything about him. Do you know him well?'

'I do. But I'm not about to tell the cops. No chance.'

Hanlon looked at the editor, who gave a defeated shrug then turned to Rosie.

'We'll just have to see how it pans out with the plods. But there are two stiffs lying in the city centre, and you and the Polish girl are key to this investigation. That's the tack they'll take.'

'They're not murders, though. The guy was going to kill all of us. He had a gun pointed at us, for Christ's sake. And by the way, Olenca doesn't know how to get in touch with Adrian either. She'll have told the police this was the first time she saw him. But it's not a murder. It was self-defence.'

'Yes, I know. But since this isn't actually the movies, or downtown Beirut, the authorities here like to be able to put things in boxes. They call them trials, Rosie.'

'Listen. I've just handed a girl to the cops who can bring down some of the biggest criminals in Glasgow and beyond for arms dealing and for murder. What more do they want?'

'I know. And that's how we'll need to play it.' He sat back with his hands behind his head. 'I'm not that worried about it – depending on who comes in here. And I think you'll have been forgiven for turning over the police chief a couple of years ago, once they realized the kind of bastard he was. I don't think there will be a bad feeling about you as such. But they will need to mop this up. They can't just have dead bodies and pretend it didn't happen.'

'I can talk about that. I can back up what Olenca will say, what the guy was trying to do – sell her for money. I'm happy to do that.'

'And about the shooting?'

'Well, I can say the truth of what happened. But not give the name.'

'And what about the guy on the stairwell?'

'I don't know. Maybe he slipped.'

'Aye, right.' Hanlon shrugged. 'Fine. If you get away with that. You might. We need to speak to some people.' He looked at McGuire. 'How's your clout with the chief constable these days?'

'Let me make a call.' McGuire went behind his desk and dialled.

Rosie sat in the canteen on the ground floor drinking coffee with Hanlon while McGuire talked to the chief constable on the phone in his office.

Hanlon took notes as they discussed how best to handle

the cops when they arrived, and he made it clear to her what would happen if she refused to give up the name of the shooter in the flat. She explained to him that no matter what happened she could never give Adrian up, and she recounted how Adrian had been there for her for the first time nearly two years ago when one of big Jake Cox's thugs had come to murder her. It was the first time she'd admitted to the lawyer that it was Adrian who had saved her life that night. Hanlon told her their best hope was that McGuire could pull a few strings, given how the *Post* had more or less solved their crime for them – and not for the first time.

Rosie's mobile rang, and she saw it was Mickey Kavanagh.

'I need to take this call.' Answering, she said, 'Hey, Mickey. What's happening? I've been meaning to call you, but the last couple of days have been mental.'

'So I hear,' Mickey said.

'Really? You don't miss much. What do you hear?' He couldn't possibly know about the last hour's events in the flat.

'I heard about that stooshie in the warehouse with that prick Dunn and Co. What a result that was, getting them wrapped up like that. But by all accounts you nearly got done in. Did you get hurt?'

'I got a few slaps,' Rosie said. 'But my face is still as lovely as ever.'

'I'm sure it is, sweetheart, but listen, I've got a name

for you. In London. The heart of the corruption. Fuck me. It's a middle-management guy in Customs, but it's been covered up by the top brass.'

'Do you mean the fake licence and the arms dealing?'

'Yep. Apparently the guy was on the take big time, taking bribes to issue a fake licence. Once you've got the paperwork with the official stamp on it, nobody really questions it hard at the border.'

'And they've traced who the guy is?'

'Yep.'

'Is he arrested yet? Are they going to do him?'

'I'd say they'll do him, but he's not arrested yet.'

'What do you mean?'

'Well, the spooks will probably take care of it. I mean, nobody wants to see a guy at the heart of the system being in court for faking an arms-dealing licence. That just doesn't sound good at PM's Question Time or in the papers. They'd get hung out to dry.'

'But we have a story to that effect.'

'But you haven't got a story you can prove, Rosie – well, not yet, as far as I know.'

'No. We don't, Mickey. But if I can get to the guy, then maybe I can prove it. We can just go down there and monster the bastard.'

'That might work – he might just burst if you tell him you know everything.'

'I'm up for that. What's his name?'

'Terence Rygate. He's the civil servant. Here's his address. He's actually been earmarked for better things. There was talk of moving him to the Foreign Office.'

'Not any more, I take it.' Rosie was delighted that it was the same name Boswell-Smith had given her.

'No. But the chain of corruption money goes higher up.'

'How high up?'

'All I've been told is that a big name was a director in the company – or used to be.'

'Christ, Mickey. You don't half love this drip-feed shit. Who is it? Give me a name before I burst.'

'Thomas Elridge.'

'The deputy finance minister? You're kidding!'

'That's what I said when I heard it.'

'Jesus!'

'I said that too.'

'Why would he get involved in that?'

'Don't know. Maybe the company seemed legit in the beginning. Who knows?'

'So does he know he's been rumbled? Will he have heard about Dunn's arrest?'

'Apparently he hasn't been around for a couple of days.'

'I need to speak to the editor about this. I want off the leash and down to London pronto.'

'Well, if it were me, I'd get moving fast, Rosie. Because

this shit will be cleaned up very quickly. Know what I mean? They will want to make this disappear.'

'Not if I can get there first.'

'I'll call you if I get any more. But be careful. You owe me a big dinner.'

He hung up.

CHAPTER THIRTY-EIGHT

Rosie looked out of her hotel bedroom window onto Kensington Gardens in all its autumn glory, wishing she could go for a relaxing stroll through London's pleasant streets. One of these days.

She reflected on the meeting earlier with the Serious Crime Squad detective superintendent in McGuire's office – Hanlon on hand in case things got rough. The big cop was reasonable but kept pressing her for Adrian's name. She didn't know his real name, she lied, or even where he was. He changed his contact numbers all the time. The cop made a face that said he knew she was lying through her back teeth. If she said that in the witness box, he told her, it could get her a three stretch in Cornton Vale for perjury. He told her not to leave town, that she could be facing charges. Rosie promptly ignored his command and breathed a sigh of relief when the plane took off from Glasgow Airport to London.

McGuire's brief was simple. Find Terence Rygate, get his

picture and a reaction. Tell him he's nicked, that it's not up for discussion. Then bail out.

Kavanagh had told her that Terence Rygate was single, a fitness fanatic and gay. He drank in a popular gay bar close to his flat most evenings. Rosie was hoping they could melt into the background when they went there, but homophobic Matt was already uncomfortable.

There was a knock on her hotel bedroom door and when she opened it, Matt stood there smiling in faded jeans, a T-shirt and a leather bomber jacket.

'You're looking well,' Rosie said. 'I was a bit worried you'd turn up like one of the Village People.'

'I thought about it, but where was I going to get an Indian headdress at this time of the day? Do I look gay, though?'

'I don't know. It's hard to tell. There's no such thing as looking gay. Don't be daft.'

'Yeah, but do I look like I'm up for anything. I mean, I don't want to have to fight anyone off.'

'Stop being homophobic. Just act normal, because if you look all freaked out every time somebody gives you a second look you'll blow our cover.'

'As long as it's the only thing I blow.' Matt grinned.

'C'mon. Let's do this.'

After dinner in the hotel restaurant, where they downed a bottle of red wine between them, they headed in a taxi to the bar.

Inside, the place was jumping, every table packed, and at least three deep at the bar, cheering on a drag artist who was strutting across the stage in fishnet stockings and a leather dress . . . with an Adam's apple the size of a golf ball. There were a few women in the bar, too, and Rosie assumed it was a mixed bag of people, not exclusively gay. They sat in a corner watching the bar and hoping for the best.

'I'll have a pint of lager,' Matt said to the waiter.

Rosie noticed that Matt's voice had dropped an octave, and that he avoided the waiter's eyes.

'Lighten up, you, for God's sake.' Rosie dug him with her elbow. 'You don't have to go all macho. Nobody's going to pay the least bit of attention to you. Just keep your mind on your work and don't worry about who's looking at you.'

'I'm fine,' Matt said. 'I'm cool. Honest. Just that there's a guy at the bar and he's been staring at me for ages. Should I smile back?'

'Maybe best not to. There's a lot of activity goes on in the toilets at these places and often it's agreed with just a nod and a smile.'

'Fuck me!'

'I wouldn't say that too loudly either.' Rosie chuckled.

They sipped their drinks and relaxed.

'So, is big Adrian gone?'

'For the moment, yes.' Rosie had told him earlier about the scene in the flat with Olenca. 'I've left a couple of messages on his mobile, but no answer. He'll be all right though. He'll call when he can. Unless he's already gone back to Sarajevo.'

Rosie said it as though it didn't matter, but it niggled that he hadn't got in touch. Of course, she understood why he had to make himself scarce, and knew she was being irrational. But because things had moved on between them, it clouded her judgement. She chastised herself for getting involved in the first place. It felt like a mistake, and it probably was. But she couldn't help wanting to see him again.

'Shit!' Matt said.

'What, you getting eyed up again?'

'No.' He leaned forward. 'Don't look now, but our man has just walked in.'

'Really? Where?'

'At the bar, four down and close to the stage. He's ordering a drink now.'

Rosie strained her eyes to see the figure Matt was describing. He did look like the image Kavanagh had sent her this afternoon. But it was hard to tell from this distance.

'I'm going up to the bar to get a drink.' Rosie got to her feet. 'I'll stand next to him and see if I can strike up a conversation.'

'He'll not be in here to meet a woman.'

'I know. But it's quite a relaxed atmosphere. People are

just at the bar having a chat and a night out. Maybe it's not exclusively a gay bar.'

Rosie went up to the bar and squeezed in through the throng so that she was next to Rygate. She heard him talking to the barman. He ordered a large vodka and tonic.

'There you go, Terence? How's it going, mate?'

Game on. Rosie ordered herself a gin and tonic and another beer for Matt. She glanced at Rygate and smiled.

'Good crowd in tonight.'

'Yeah,' he said, sipping his drink and looking away. 'Always.'

She didn't pursue it, but she was certain it was him. The barman handed over her change, and as she was putting it in her purse she heard the voice over her shoulder.

'Terence, darling, how the hell are you?'

He turned and embraced the man who'd come up behind him.

It had to be Rygate. But she needed to be a hundred per cent certain. They'd have to hang around until he was going home, then follow him.

They watched the bar for nearly an hour as Rygate chatted animatedly to other punters, then he went to the toilet. After a few minutes he came back out, drank up and left. They followed and watched him get into a taxi, then followed him in another cab. Matt had already reccied the street, so he was pleased they were going in the right direction. Rosie asked the driver to let them out a few yards before the block of flats where Rygate lived, and they stood in a doorway while the other taxi drew up and he got out. He walked towards the flats.

'It's him,' Rosie said. 'That's all we need to know. We'll hit him in the morning as he's coming out for work.'

'Don't you want to do something now so we've got it in the bag?'

'No. He won't open the door at this time of night unless he knows who it is. He'll probably have a security chain and won't even open enough for you to get a snap. Let's leave it till the morning so we can get him out in the open.'

The following morning Rosie and Matt were outside the flats first thing, both of them a little hungover and regretting staying up in the hotel bar for too long. The main door of the flats had been opening all morning, with people going to work, but no Rygate. Then suddenly the door opened and he appeared.

'I'll go over first and make the approach. You just keep snapping,' she said to Matt.

She crossed the road and went up to him.

'Terence Rygate?'

There was a flash of recognition in his face, as though he were trying to work out where he'd seen her.

'Sorry?'

'Terence,' Rosie said, 'I spoke to you last night at the bar. Terence Rygate?'

'Yes. But . . . what do you want?' He looked puzzled.

'My name is Rosie Gilmour, Mr Rygate. I'm a reporter from the *Post* newspaper in Scotland. I want to ask you about J B Solutions.'

She waited while his face changed colour.

'What? Excuse me.'

He stepped out to pass her. Rosie blocked his path. He stopped, irritated, trying to pass her again, but she blocked him.

'J B Solutions, Mr Rygate. They're part of Damar Guns, international arms dealers. The people who were banned by the government but were able to continue dealing because they were given a fake licence to trade arms, granted by your department? By *you*, in fact? And you were, in turn, paid by Mr Thomas Dunn, the boss of J B Solutions?'

'Look here.' He glanced around him furtively. 'Whoever you are, you're quite obviously deranged. And, to be honest, I'm a bit troubled that you stalked me from last night. So please get out of my way or I will call the police right now.'

Rosie flashed her press card.

'There's my ID. I'm here for your reaction and comments to the story we are about to publish.'

'What the hell are you talking about? I'm going to call the police.' He took his mobile from his pocket.

'So call them.' Rosie stood back. 'But you won't. Because you're up to your eyes in this. And now that Tam Dunn is in police custody, he's singing like a canary, about everything he did . . . all about the money he squirrelled into your bank accounts offshore. It's all there. We have it all, Terence . . . documents, the lot . . . so . . . this is not up for discussion.'

By now Matt was at her side, snapping away. Rygate stood and for a moment his eyes were filling with tears, his face crimson. He shook his head, backing away, then turned, put the key in his lock and scurried back inside.

'Did you get plenty of pictures?' Rosie asked Matt.

'More than enough. Great stuff. Looks like he shat himself.'

'Just a bit. He tried a bit of bluster, but it's him all right, and he's guilty as hell. Stuff him.'

'So what now?'

'I think we should GTF before anyone turns up.'

As Rosie said it, they both turned, startled by the sound of tyres screeching. For a moment it didn't register. There was a black Jaguar speeding up the tight side street towards them. Then they realized it wasn't stopping.

'Shit! What the fuck?' Matt's eyes widened in disbelief. 'It's coming for us.'

'Oh, Christ, Matt. Run.'

'Run? We can't outrun a Jag.'

The car sped towards them, its main beam full on. Rosie glanced around for somewhere to jump into – a doorway or alley. But there was nothing. She spotted two huge industrial wheelie bins and a skip outside a building.

'Quick. The bins, Matt.'

They both sprinted, the car on their heels. Rosie dived behind the bin, but not before she saw Matt getting clipped and hurled across the bonnet and onto the road. The Jag stopped for a second, then the wheels screeched as it sped off.

'Matt! Christ! Matt!' Rosie jumped out from behind the bins and dashed where he lay on the road. She bent down. He looked up, groggy, blood coming from a graze to his head.

'Fuck me!' Matt said. 'What the fuck was that all about?' He moved, groaning and grimacing. 'Quick, help me up. We need to get the hell out of here. Is my camera all right?'

Rosie picked it up. There was a crack on the lens.

'Don't worry. We'll check it later. They might come back. Hurry, Matt! Take my arm.' Rosie crouched down and helped him to his feet. 'Can you walk?'

'Yeah, I think so. But my leg's jumping with pain. Shit.' He limped.

'Let's just get to the end of the street and we'll get a cab.'

They walked as fast as they could, blood dripping from Matt's head.

'Is that okay?'

'Yeah. Flesh wound.' He wiped it with his sleeve. 'I hope it leaves a scar, though, so I can brag about it.'

Rosie smiled.

'You're nuts.'

'I must be – working with you.'

Rosie spotted a taxi and waved it down.

She helped Matt into the back seat.

'What's going on? I don't want no trouble,' The driver said.

'It's okay,' Rosie said. 'He just slipped off the kerb. Can you take us to the Tara Hotel in Kensington.'

The driver pushed his car into gear and drove off, keeping a suspicious eye on his rear-view mirror.

CHAPTER THIRTY-NINE

Rosie sat in front of her computer screen, re-reading and tweaking the main piece for tomorrow's splash and spread. It was written as carefully as possible, given that they were hanging a Ministry of Defence official out to dry, as well as suggesting that a government minister was, at the very least, reckless, for not researching the company where he'd once been a non-executive director. At an earlier meeting in McGuire's office with Hanlon and the boss of the legal firm playing devil's advocate, they'd pointed out that the minister's links to the company had been a number of years ago. They suggested the story wouldn't lose impact by dropping the minister and Rygate out of it. They already had a fantastic exposé of J B Solutions' illegal gunrunning and the fact that an investigation was going on at government level. They didn't need to name names. But if we do that, Rosie had protested to them, then we leave it open for somebody else to dig deeper. Then they would get the claim of unmasking Rygate and the minister. We have to name names, she told them. Her mobile rang. It was Adrian, and her stomach did a little unexpected leap.

'Rosie, I'm sorry I couldn't answer your calls.'

'It's okay,' Rosie said, even though deep down she didn't mean it.

'Look, I have to go. It's not safe for me here. Can you meet me?'

'Yes. When are you going?'

'Now. Well. In a couple of hours. I have to.'

Rosie looked at the time on her computer screen. She knew that as soon as she sent her piece she'd have to be available for queries from the lawyer as well as the editor and subs. It was going to be a long night. She checked all the various parts of the stories once more, then sent it to McGuire.

'Where are you?'

'At Central Station. I'm taking the train to London, then to France and will drive from there.'

'I'll be there in ten minutes.'

Rosie grabbed her bag and jacket and called McGuire as she was getting out of the lift to the car park, telling him she had to go out for half an hour, but the copy was on his desk.

In Central Station Adrian stood at the coffee bar smoking a cigarette and drinking from a paper cup. He raised his chin a little when he saw her walking across the busy concourse, then put his cup down and came to greet Rosie, flinging his arms around her. He kissed her on the lips, fleeting at first, then a little longer.

'Sorry, Rosie. It was not safe for me to be around the city. I think people will be looking for me.'

'No change there, then.' Rosie hugged him again, then stood back.

She was suddenly stuck for words. They'd come a long way since their first encounter in a café years ago. She swallowed, wondering if the reality was that she might never see him again, or if she did, how different things would be. They couldn't keep this kind of relationship up, because it had moved on from what it had been, yet she wasn't sure there was anything they could really build on.

'I kind of don't know what to say to you, Adrian,' she said. 'I'll miss you . . . I . . . I . . .' What she wanted to say was that she had feelings for him but didn't know what to say or do about them in case he didn't feel the same way. The words wouldn't come. She felt disarmed and stood looking into his eyes.

Adrian nodded.

'I'll miss you, too,' he replied.

There was an awkward silence, and Rosie looked at the ground. Suddenly, to her surprise, she was choked.

'Sometimes I wish it could be more than this,' she ventured, her eyes flicking at Adrian and then away. 'What I'm trying to say, Adrian, though I'm not saying it very well, is that I've so loved being with you these past couple of weeks, that I wish . . . I mean, I know it's impossible because of how we live . . . But I wish we could . . . well . . . be more like that.'

Adrian gently touched her face and half smiled.

'Is the same for me.' He took a deep breath and let it out slowly. 'But . . . is not easy . . . And I think . . . is hard for a woman like you to stop your life and be with somebody. I can see that, Rosie. I . . . I respect you for that. Is very important. You . . . you are very important to me. But also . . . I'm not good at these things . . . I don't know sometimes where my head is . . . so much of me is in my past.' He looked into her eyes. 'I want . . . Maybe we can see each other again . . . Like in Sarajevo. I see you then and you are different, away from all this . . . I think you were happy there. No?'

'Yes, I was, Adrian. Really happy. But I know myself. And after a while I'd be wanting this again.' She gestured with her hands. 'All this crazy shit I do.'

'That is good. It is you. I like that. You are my friend and I love you . . . all of the things I see about you.'

Rosie swallowed. He had mentioned the 'love' word. Not commitment and love like TJ, just the love of a friend. Yet they'd been more than that. She couldn't quite get her head around it. But she had a feeling this wasn't over.

She looked at her watch.

'I need to get back, Adrian. The editor is waiting for me. We have a big hit in the paper tomorrow, so I have to see it through tonight.'

Adrian stepped forward and took her in his arms. He kissed her on the lips for a long time and she could feel him holding her tight against his body. Then he released her.

'I must go. I will call you tomorrow,' Rosie said, her eyes searching his face.

He nodded. Kissed her one more time, ran his hand through her hair.

'Goodbye, Rosie. I will see you. Be careful.' His lips brushed her cheek again, then he turned and left. She watched him as he made his way across the concourse to the platform for the London train, hoping he would look back, because if he did maybe it would mean something more, that he wanted more, that he felt deeply. She willed him to look back. But he didn't.

Her mobile rang and she pulled it out of her jacket pocket. It was McGuire.

'Where are you, Rosie?'

'On my way back.'

'Hurry up.'

'You've to go straight through,' the night news editor said, peering over his pince-nez reading glasses as Rosie stepped on to the almost deserted editorial floor.

The day-shift reporters had all gone home and there

were only a couple of night-shifters working quietly at their desk. Rosie glanced at the back bench, where the editors were working on their screens, and she squinted to see if she could catch a glimpse of anything that looked like her story. There was nothing. On screen was a picture of some bimbo model and a kiss-and-tell football story. They must be saving her story for the final edition, which they often did with a major exclusive. That way it outwits the opposition, who aren't able to steal it from the front page and claim it as their own in the morning. The door was open in McGuire's office and she went straight in.

Hanlon was sitting at the conference table, and next to him was the boss of the legal firm. Fair enough, she thought. It was a big story; it needed a lot of attention. But there were glum faces all round, particularly from McGuire.

'Sit down, Rosie.'

'You're all right,' she said, glancing around at everyone. 'Is there a problem? Copy okay?'

'Copy's great, Gilmour.'

'So what's happening?'

'We've had a call from Westminster. About the government minister.'

Rosie's stomach sank a little. She knew what was coming. She looked at the managing editor, who was sitting next to the *Post*'s managing director.

'And?'

'Sit down,' McGuire said again, this time a little more sternly.

Rosie sat next to Hanlon and he gave her a troubled look. She'd been here before.

'But first of all I've got something to tell you. That Rygate – the guy you fronted up in London. The corrupt civil servant who faked the licence?'

'Yeah?'

'He's been found dead in his flat.'

'Jesus. When?'

'This afternoon.'

'I only saw him this morning.'

'Well. Might have been not long after that.'

'What happened. Suicide?'

'Christ knows. Trussed up like a turkey and zipped into a hold-all.'

'Christ almighty! What . . . like Harry Houdini?' Rosie almost smiled.

'Well, not quite. Harry Houdini always managed to get out. This guy didn't.'

'Well he certainly didn't zip himself inside a fucking hold-all, Mick. I mean, who the Christ does that?'

'Well, the cops are saying it might be one of these sexual asphyxiation things. A fetish.'

'A fetish? Where you zip yourself into a hold-all and there's nobody around to get you back out? Absolute crap.

First, you couldn't actually zip yourself into the hold-all, not completely anyway, and secondly, you just wouldn't even if you could – no matter how perverse your sexual fantasies were. But hey, it makes for a right good front page.' She glanced around the room. 'The spooks have bumped this guy off. No *doubt* about it. This story gets better every minute.'

'It does. And you need to get it done pronto.' He paused. 'But that's not all.' McGuire fiddled with his tie then looked at Hanlon.

'This stuff about the minister and his involvement. It was years ago, Rosie, and though we've nailed it down, he's apparently claiming that the company at the time of his involvement was completely unblemished. It was totally legit. We had a call from Westminster an hour ago.'

This time Rosie did laugh.

'Now there's a surprise. Well, I hope you've told them to take a flying fuck to themselves.'

Silence.

'Mick. You have, haven't you?'

The managing editor piped in.

'It's not as simple as that, Rosie.'

'Yes it is,' Rosie snapped back.

'It's not,' the managing director said.

Rosie looked from Hanlon to the MD and then to McGuire.

'Mick, it is as simple as that. And I'll tell you why. It's okay with Westminster and the cops and the Special Branch if we're exposing the gangsters and helping stick the guys behind this in jail. In fact, the cops have even turned a blind eye to bodies lying all over Glasgow so they can nail these bastards. But when it comes to the shady bastard at the top, they think that's going a bit too far. Come on! For Christ's sake, guys! This is staring you in the bloody face. We have to be able to link the minister. He's part of the story. Can't you see that the government wants to cover up the shit trail because it leads right to them? They're sacrificing everyone to save their own skin. Tom Mahoney . . . Gerard Hawkins – murdered in his bed. Now Harry Houdini in a fucking hold-all? But when it gets too close to them *we* have to back off? Tell them to fuck right off, Mick. You have to.'

'They've issued a warrant for your arrest, Rosie,' the managing editor said. 'For withholding evidence about the deaths in the Polish girl's apartment. And for not naming your contact.'

'They can piss off with that,' Rosie blazed. 'When did the bastards do that?'

'Around the same time I got the phone call from Westminster,' Mick said, disconsolate.

Rosie stood up.

'Shit! And we're all just going to wet our pants because of that? Are you kidding me?'

'They'll arrest you, Rosie, and you'll go to jail. If you lie in court you'll commit perjury,' the MD said.

'It won't come to that.'

'How do you know?' asked the managing editor.

'Well, if it does, we'll cross that bridge when it comes.' She looked at the editor, whose face was flushed. 'Mick, we need to tell this story. *All* of it. And then we worry about what happens. That's what we do. Christ, guys!' She turned to the others. 'That's why we're here at this time of night working, that's why we take the risks. If we don't fight back now we can shut up shop and forget it. We can't bow down. If we let them get away with this, next thing is we'll end up running every bloody story past them for their approval. Christ, guys!'

Silence. Rosie looked at all of them.

'We can leave the minister out,' the managing editor said. 'The story will still have impact.'

'But it's not the whole truth.' Rosie heard her voice go up an octave.

Silence. She took a deep breath. She needed to get out of here now, before she said any more. Maybe they were right, maybe she would see sense in the morning.

She looked each one of them squarely in the eye.

'Okay. Do what you like. I'll phone in copy with a few paragraphs about Houdini in the zipped-up hold-all. You guys can just sit here and try to find each other's balls. I'm out of here.'

She strode off and downstairs, out of the revolving door, her eyes filled with tears. When she got home and closed the door of her flat, she poured herself a glass of wine, lit a cigarette then went out onto the balcony and stood staring across the city. Then she dialled the copy-takers at the *Post* and began relaying the story off the top of her head about Ryegate in the hold-all. It would be the new nose to the front page – whatever the watered-down story that followed it would be.

She stood for a while until the evening chill forced her off the balcony, then sat staring at the television for the best part of an hour, her mind racing through all the events of the last forty-eight hours. She drained her glass and was about to pour a refill when her mobile rang. It was McGuire.

'Gilmour. Where are you?'

'Well, I'm not in the pokey. Not yet anyway.'

'Where are you?'

'In my flat. I've sent the copy over. What's the problem?' She was deadpan.

'Right. Listen. Get yourself out of there tonight and booked into a hotel, and in the morning make yourself scarce for a couple of days.'

'Why?

'Because all sorts of shit is about to hit the fan when the story comes out tomorrow. The *full* story. Not the abridged pish they were trying to sell me in my office an hour ago.'

'Christ, Mick!' Rosie felt her face smiling. 'You're really using everything?'

'It's my shout. I'm the editor. Fuck Westminster and

these bastards who think they can call the shots if it gets too hot for them.'

'I do love you, Mick. You know that.'

'Aye. Fine. There goes my fucking knighthood, and maybe even my job.'

'That won't happen, Mick. You'll get huge kudos from it. Everyone will follow our story.'

'Listen, Rosie. You'll be getting lifted by the cops in the morning, so get the fuck out of there until we come to some kind of agreement with them about what they're going to do.'

'Okay. Will do.'

Rosie put down the glass, phoned a taxi and was out of the flat in five minutes.

CHAPTER FORTY

Rosie stood in the shower, the cold water taking her breath away. It had been a restless night. Her fevered dreams were a collection of everything that had happened – from the beatings in the warehouse, to the body flying through the air and crashing on to the concrete at Olenca's flat. She woke up unable to breathe, panicking that she was suffocating inside a zipped-up hold-all. Jesus! That brought a new dimension to her nightmares. Her mobile rang as she came out of the bathroom and she saw Ruby's number. She'd told her last night that she was leaving early and wanted to say goodbye. Rosie asked her to come to the car park of One Devonshire Gardens, the discreet boutique hotel where she was holed up in case the cops came to her flat to arrest her.

She saw Ruby standing by the car as she came out of the hotel door into the morning sunshine. Rosie peered into the car. Roddy Thompson sat in the driver's seat. He nodded to her. Judy was in the back and Rosie waved to her, but she didn't really register her, just stared out of the side window.

'Hello, Ruby.' Rosie came forward and hugged her. 'Great to see you. All set?'

'Yep.' Even in her casual tracksuit bottoms and a baggy sweatshirt, Ruby still looked stunning – apart from a few bruises. 'Can't wait to get out of here. Christ knows when or if I'll ever come back. New life for me now, Rosie.'

'How's Judy?'

'She's good. She might look like she's miles away, and she still is a lot of the time, but we're working on it. I've got a really good therapist lined up in France. I'm gradually getting her back. I always knew she was in there. Maybe I won't get the same person back, but Christ – I'm not the same person. Judy didn't even get a chance to grow up. We have a lot of years to make up.'

'I'm so glad for you. It's taken a lot, Ruby, for you to get this far.'

'Yeah.' She sighed. 'I saw your story this morning. Blew me away. Nearly choked on my coffee.'

Rosie smiled.

'There's a warrant out for my arrest. They want me to give up Adrian. But I can't do that.'

'Good on you. They're all fucking gangsters – cops, politicians . . . all of them. It's only the likes of us who gets shat upon from a great height. No wonder so many kids turn out the way they do. Angry and hitting back.'

Rosie nodded.

'So what will you do now?'

'Just live my life in France. I've made enough money. I've siphoned off plenty from those thieving, robbing bastards who did my mother in. I made them pay, all right, and I'll be fine. I gave my statement to the cops about what I saw that night, so Tam Dunn will get jailed for life. Fuck him.'

They stood in silence for a long moment, then Rosie looked Ruby in the eye.

'Did the cops question you about the fire in the house in Spain and in Ayrshire at Malky Cameron's house?'

'Of course they did. They're not that thick.'

'And what did you tell them?'

'I told them not to be so stupid. That I wasn't daft enough to even think about bumping them off.' She turned to the car. 'Listen, I need to get moving.'

Rosie couldn't resist it.

'But you did, Ruby. You did kill those two bastards.'

Ruby gave her a long, hard look, then shrugged her shoulders.

'And your point is?'

She turned and walked towards the car. Rosie stood watching as she got in, turned to Judy and said something that made Judy wave a hand. Then they were off, and Rosie watched as they drove out of the car park and onto the road.

Rosie's phone rang. It was McGuire.

'I hope you're out of the way, Gilmour.'

'Yeah. I was in One Devonshire last night, and I'm going down to Loch Lomond today. Stay somewhere smart.'

'Well, don't mind my fucking expenses.'

'Don't worry, Mick, I won't.'

'And Rosie.'

'Yeah?'

'Great paper today. We stuffed every bastard. But there's a shitload of trouble coming our way. The cops are looking for you.'

'Tell them I've gone AWOL. I've had a breakdown or something.'

She hung up, a satisfied smile spread across her face as she walked back into the hotel.

Therapy at Glasgow University, for his advice on the effects of childhood emotional trauma. Thanks also to Dr Iain Campbell, Clinical Psychologist.

And thanks to the great friends who have stayed the course. Here are a few of them who have been with me through the best and worst of times.

Eileen O'Rourke, Liz Dorman, Anne Sharpe, Annmarie Newall, Helen and Irene Timmons, Sarah Hendrie and Alice Cowan.

All the Motherwell Smiths – and the Timmonses and the McGoldricks.

Mags, Annie, Mary, Phil, Helen, Barbara, Donna, Jan, Louise, Si, Lynn, Annie, Maureen, Keith, Mark, and Thomas.

In Dingle, thanks to Mary, Paud, Siobhan, Martin, Cristin, and Sean Brendain.

On the Costa del Sol, thanks to Lisa, Lillias, Nat, Mara, Yvonne, Wendy, Sally G, Sarah, Fran, Sally, Jean and Dave, Billy and Davina.

And I'm very grateful to all my Facebook friends and random readers who get in touch. All of this encourages and enriches me as a writer, and always surprises me.

A huge thanks to Jane Wood, my publisher at Quercus who inspires me every time we meet, and to my brilliant editor Katie Gordon for all her hard work, Lauren Woosey in publicity, and all the Quercus team.

And also my agent Euan Thorneycroft, and hopefully a great future.

ACKNOWLEDGEMENTS

It's a strange old life being a writer – euphoric and lonely in equal measure – and always rewarding.

I count my blessings every day. Especially having so many people around me – family and true friends who are always there in some form. So this is a chance to say thanks to them.

To my sister Sadie, my rock, and without her I'm not sure how I'd function; my brothers Des, Hugh and Arthur, and all their children and grandchildren, who spell out the bright future.

Thanks to my niece Kat Campbell – my PR guru – and Matthew Costello along with Paul Smith for the website wizardry and great banter. And Christopher Costello who makes me laugh.

A Cold Killing involved a bit of research into the Eastern Europe of old, and for that I thank Eve Rosenhaft, Professor of German Historical Studies at the University of Liverpool.

Thanks also to Andrew Gumley, Professor of Psychological